The HAWTHORNE *Inheritance*

KATE DIKE BLAIR

MILFORD HOUSE

an imprint of Sunbury Press, Inc.
Mechanicsburg, PA USA

MILFORD HOUSE

an imprint of Sunbury Press, Inc.
Mechanicsburg, PA USA

For information about special discounts for bulk purchases, please contact Sunbury Press Orders Dept. at (855) 338-8359 or orders@sunburypress.com.

To request one of our authors for speaking engagements or book signings, please contact Sunbury Press Publicity Dept. at publicity@sunburypress.com.

FIRST MILFORD HOUSE PRESS EDITION: August 2021

Set in Adobe Garamond | Interior design by Crystal Devine | Cover by Victoria Mitchell | Edited by Lawrence Knorr.

Publisher's Cataloging-in-Publication Data
Names: Dike Blair, Kate, author.
Title: The Hawthorne inheritance / Kate Dike Blair.
Description: First trade paperback edition. | Mechanicsburg, PA : Milford House Press, 2021.
Summary: Author Nathaniel Hawthorne's sister Louisa drowns in an 1852 steamship accident. Cousin John Stephens Dike suspects foul play. Reading family documents bequeathed to him by cousin Elizabeth will prove his theory of a tragic love triangle, but first he must conquer his own demons. Will he and Pittsburgh lawyer Tom Blair assure justice is served?
Identifiers: ISBN : 978-1-62006-552-5 (softcover).
Subjects: FICTION / Biographical | FICTION / Historical / Civil War Era | FICTION / General.

Product of the United States of America
0 1 1 2 3 5 8 13 21 34 55

Continue the Enlightenment!

To my father and genial proprietor of the Vermont Book Shop,
Robert Dike Blair, who inspired me to write a book about
our Blair, Dike, and Hawthorne ancestors.

ACKNOWLEDGMENTS

From its conception as a combination modern day/nineteenth century murder mystery, to its maturation as an entirely historical novel, *The Hawthorne Inheritance* has taken ten years to birth. I have many people to thank for this successful delivery: Scott Anderson for his first reading and advice on tackling historical research; Anne Ketchen for her first reading and thoughtful suggestions about character development; Dianne Plantamura, Marcia Chertok, Cathie Regan and Marlene Mandel for their optimism; Diane Statkus for her careful notes; The SAG-AFTRA Screen Writers Group for their continuing inspiration and guidance; Duncan Putney for his expertise in publishing and publicity; Beth Aarons for her legal counsel; editor Sulay Hernandez of Unveiled Ink for her astute and good-humored consultation; editor Mary McVicker for her confidence in my historical prose; editor Lawrence Knorr and his entire Sunbury Press team for their kind expertise; Ann Collette for her understanding of the publishing world; my Blair and Bearg family members for their enthusiastic encouragement; Nat Bearg for his patient tech support; Susan Blair Johnson for her cogent ideas and stalwart faith in the project; and my dear husband David, who suffered along with me all the trials and tribulations of a first time novelist: Thank you for your patience and understanding.

The docents in the Old Manse and the Orchard House dipped into their deep, juicy vats of gossip concerning their museums' former owners. Much gratitude to them and to Lis Adams at the Orchard House for casting me as Anna Alcott Pratt and Rose Hawthorne during two festively educational Christmas Open Houses, and to Jayne Gordon and the Friends of Sleepy Hollow Cemetery for filling in the gaps in information concerning Hawthorne's funeral. Kudos to the research librarians at The Concord Free Public Library for their technical expertise, and to the library itself for having such a wealth of information about the Hawthorne, Thoreau and Alcott families. I spent many productive research hours in the stacks, with a wide choice of books for further study at home. Please see the bibliography at the end of this novel for specifics.

Finally, I wish to thank the spirits who reside at Authors' Ridge in Sleepy Hollow Cemetery. My monthly pilgrimages down the curving paved path, up the cupped stone steps guarded by the twisted metal hand rail, to their unassuming graves, to lay offerings of pens and promises that their stories would be told respectfully, seem to have convinced them to bless this enterprise. I only hope that I have met their expectations.

A NOTE TO THE READER

The Manning, Hawthorne, and Dike families were prolific letter writers, and much of the dialogue and plot in this story is derived from those missives. For clarification, asterisks (*) bracket the passages or letters that are quoted directly. The following Family Lineages detail the connections between the characters. For further historical information, please see the Author's Note at the end of the book. But beware: Plot points may be revealed.

THE FAMILIES FEATURED

Principal characters are in bold.
Arranged here in family groups.

THE DIKE/STEPHENS FAMILY

John Dike, Sr. married **Abigail Stephens** c. 1770. Their progeny:
>   **John Dike (Jr)** (b. 1783)
>   **Nathaniel Dike** (b. 1792)
>   (among other offspring)

THE DIKE/WOOD FAMILY

John Dike married **Mercy Wood** in 1805. Their progeny:
>   **Mary Wood Dike** (b. 1805)
>   **John Stephens Dike** (b. 1807)

THE DIKE/MANNING FAMILY

John Dike married **Priscilla Manning** in 1817. No progeny.

THE DIKE/WOODS FAMILY

Nathaniel Dike married **Anna Woods** in 1825. Their progeny:
>   **Virginia Dike** (b. 1830)
>   (among other offspring)

THE DIKE/WOODS FAMILY

John Stephens Dike married **Margaretta Woods** in 1834. No progeny.

THE BLAIR/DIKE FAMILY

Thomas S. Blair (b. 1825) married **Virginia Dike** in 1847. Their progeny:
>   **George Dike Blair, Sr.** (b. 1850)
>   (among other offspring)

THE BLAIR/HENDERSON FAMILY

George Dike Blair, Sr. married **Katherine Henderson** in 1880.
Their progeny:
>   **George Dike Blair, Jr.** (b. 1887)
>   (among other offspring)

THE BLAIR/SLINGLUFF FAMILY
George Dike Blair, Jr. married Hazel Slingluff. Their progeny:
Robert Dike Blair (b. 1919)
(among other offspring)

THE BLAIR/BLIZZARD FAMILY
Robert Dike Blair married Reba Blizzard in 1940. Their progeny:
Kate Dike Blair
(among other offspring)

THE MANNING/LORD FAMILY
Richard Manning, Jr. (b. 1755) married **Miriam Lord** (b. 1748) c. 1770.
Their progeny:
William Manning (b. 1778)
Elizabeth (Betsey) Manning (b. 1780)
Robert Manning (b. 1784)
Priscilla Manning (b. 1790)
(among other offspring)

THE HA(W)THORNE/MANNING FAMILY
Captain Nathaniel Hathorne married **Betsey Manning** in 1802.
Their progeny:
Elizabeth (Ebe) Ha(w)thorne (b. 1802)
Nathaniel (Nath) Ha(w)thorne (b. 1804)
(Maria) Louisa (Louze) Ha(w)thorne (b. 1808)

THE HAWTHORNE/PEABODY FAMILY
Nathaniel Hawthorne married **Sophia Peabody** (b.1809) in 1842.
Their progeny:
Una Hawthorne (b. 1844)
Julian Hawthorne (b. 1846)
Rose Hawthorne (b. 1851)

THE FAMILIES FEATURED

Principal characters are in bold.
Arranged here chronologically.

THE MANNING/LORD FAMILY

Richard Manning, Jr. (b. 1755) married **Miriam Lord** (b. 1748) c. 1770.
Their progeny:
  William Manning (b. 1778)
  Elizabeth (Betsey) Manning (b. 1780)
  Robert Manning (b. 1784)
  Priscilla Manning (b. 1790)
  (among other offspring)

THE DIKE/STEPHENS FAMILY

John Dike, Sr. married **Abigail Stephens** c. 1770. Their progeny:
  John Dike (Jr.) (b. 1783)
  Nathaniel Dike (b. 1792)
  (among other offspring)

THE HA(W)THORNE/MANNING FAMILY

Captain Nathaniel Hathorne married **Betsey Manning** in 1802.
Their progeny:
  Elizabeth (Ebe) Ha(w)thorne (b. 1802)
  Nathaniel (Nath) Ha(w)thorne (b. 1804)
  (Maria) Louisa (Louze) Ha(w)thorne (b. 1808)

THE DIKE/WOOD FAMILY

John Dike married **Mercy Wood** in 1805. Their progeny:
  Mary Wood Dike (b. 1805)
  John Stephens Dike (b. 1807)

THE DIKE/MANNING FAMILY

John Dike married **Priscilla Manning** in 1817. No progeny.

THE DIKE/WOODS FAMILY
Nathaniel Dike married **Anna Woods** in 1825. Their progeny:
  Virginia Dike (b. 1830)
  (among other offspring)

THE DIKE/WOODS FAMILY
John Stephens Dike married Margaretta Woods in 1834. No progeny.

THE HAWTHORNE/PEABODY FAMILY
Nathaniel Hawthorne married **Sophia Peabody** (b.1809) in 1842.
Their progeny:
  Una Hawthorne (b. 1844)
  Julian Hawthorne (b. 1846)
  Rose Hawthorne (b. 1851)

THE BLAIR/DIKE FAMILY
Thomas S. Blair (b. 1825) married **Virginia Dike** in 1847. Their progeny:
  George Dike Blair, Sr. (b. 1850)
  (among other offspring)

THE BLAIR/HENDERSON FAMILY
George Dike Blair, Sr. married Katherine Henderson in 1880. Their progeny:
  George Dike Blair, Jr. (b. 1887)
  (among other offspring)

THE BLAIR/SLINGLUFF FAMILY
George Dike Blair, Jr. married Hazel Slingluff in 1913. Their progeny:
  Robert Dike Blair (b. 1919)
  (among other offspring)

THE BLAIR/BLIZZARD FAMILY
Robert Dike Blair married Reba Blizzard in 1940. Their progeny:
  Kate Dike Blair
  (among other offspring)

Salem, September 1st, 1830

Dear John Stephens,
   . . . I heard your father's voice downstairs . . . He is very well himself, and your (step)mother enjoys as good health as usual, but they are both very apprehensive about you. It is two or three months since they have heard from you, and they think that nothing but sickness, or something worse, could induce you to delay writing so long . . .
   Your affectionate Cousin,
   Nath. Hawthorne.*

---

* Excerpt from a letter written in 1830 by Nathaniel Hawthorne, residing in Salem, Massachusetts, to his cousin John Stephens Dike, residing in Steubenville, Ohio.

"You have a message, Mr. Dike."

Master Jimmie Ross, my newest employee, wiped his perspiring palms on the bib of his soiled apron before offering me a crumpled envelope. He was accustomed to stocking shelves, not hobnobbing with the proprietor in the back office, and his nervous twitching reminded me of myself at my greenest, trying to impress and succeeding only in amusing.

I kept my voice low so as not to panic him further. "Thank you, son. I will attend to it straight away. Meanwhile, there is inventory to be shelved in the grain aisle." I nodded toward the door and his salvation. "But change your apron first. A Dike's Emporium employee must always look his best."

"Yes, sir, thank you, sir."

He scampered away, a hare escaping a hound, unaware that this old dog was loathe to bite, even if provoked. I shook my head, remembering my own difficult early days here and my uncle showing me, a wounded pup from an unhappy home, only kindness. I strived to emulate his managerial style with every employee I hired.

But the message required my attention. I uncrumpled the envelope and drew out a sheet of cream stationery upon which my wife had written in her rounded script, "John Stephens, please come home at once. There has been a delivery."

This was odd. Margaretta, an excellent housewife, was usually quite capable of responding to whatever surprises the season might offer, from partridges to pear trees. But my damsel apparently needed rescuing, and so I creaked to a stand, wishing that the winter cold had delayed its arrival until at least New Years for my old joints' sake. The store's big pot-bellied stove could not heat the back reaches of the brick building, and my Franklin had succumbed to the drafts gusting in through my shuttered window. Time to warm myself with a walk through the store. A little customer service did wonders for the constitution.

But a Dike's Emporium employee must always look his best. I ran a comb through my silver hair, still thick even at seventy-six, as had been my uncle's and father's, but unlike those two clean-shaven gents, I wore a mustache in honor of the tragic Prince Albert, patron saint of every business owner at this time of the year. Coat brushed, and vest settled over a bourgeois paunch, I deemed myself ready to meet the public. My uncle smiled approvingly from his oil portrait above the safe, and I nodded a salute to him before entering the retail fray.

A steady buzz of conversation punctuated by the rings of the register and a few modest laughs indicated a happy clientele. I made my way through the crowd, shaking hands here and patting children's heads there, straightening boxes and bags, and finally bowing to Mrs. Wells, who was exploring the root vegetables in their bins across from the shelves of breads and pastries. "How may we help, Madam?"

"Oh, Mr. Dike, how nice to see you out here on the floor. Master Ross has already assisted me in choosing some fresh rye. You always hire such nice young people. And it feels quite festive in here, despite the chill in the air." She smiled as she gestured to the mistletoe hanging from the rafters before she returned to squeezing the potatoes. A faint whiff of mold undercut the pleasant scents of pine and polish, and I made a note to ask Ross to throw away any soft vegetables before they infected the rest of the inventory.

The store's Christmas tree, decorated with colorful seed packages and yarn bows, stood sentry by the register at the entrance. I signaled to the manager that he had the store, pulled my top coat from the hook by the door, and stepped carefully out onto the snowy stairs, grateful for the banister installed last year ostensibly to assist elderly customers. At some point, I supposed, I must retire, but the idea of taking it easy seemed anathema when working gave me such joy.

Falling snow muffled the sounds and sights of Market Street but couldn't dim the twinkling gas lights or completely shroud the wreaths and swags festooning store and restaurant fronts. Shoppers gossiped, carriage horses shook the snow from beribboned manes, and workers escaping the nearby factories trudged purposefully through the drifts toward home. Smoke plumed above the chimneys of the booming steel and textile mills lining the river, signaling Santa, and a tiny tug boat merrily tooted its horn at a huge barge. On a snowy December afternoon, Steubenville lived up to its nickname, La Belle, and I felt a certain possessive pride in the success of my adopted city. In a childlike celebration of the season, I tipped my face up to the heavens and caught a snowflake on my tongue.

And plummeted into darkness as a clap of thunder reverberated inside my skull. Steubenville disappeared, and I was a little boy in Salem again, plunged into a frigid family circumstance, my father unavailable, my stepmother unconscionable, Steubenville unimaginable and rescue impossible. Gasping, my hands fisted in terrible tension, I huddled beneath an overhang to catch my breath.

Tears mingled with snow. No matter how many years I had lived away from my noxious birthplace, a smell, a touch, a sound could hurtle me back. Though I might now be the genial proprietor of a successful emporium, I was also that scared, unhappy little pup, searching for love and finding only a viper's nest. As if it were a magic talisman, I pulled from my pocket Margaretta's knitted hat, jammed it upon my head, and hobbled as fast as my old knees would allow up Market Street toward the safety of home.

Unlike the clapboard construction of Massachusetts, Steubenville was built of brick. 100 Market Street, once a modest dwelling and now a two-storied manor, lounged comfortably on the corner, its two wings beckoning visitors toward its trellised front entrance, over which evergreen swags draped. I stumbled up the steps and into Margaretta's welcoming arms

"John Stephens, where have you been?" She waited till my trembling had abated before holding me at arms' length for a better look. "Is everything all right?" Her kindly blue eyes sought my own anxious amber and then narrowed at the trails of tears streaking my wind-chapped cheeks. She wiped them gently with her handkerchief before guessing, "Another spell?"

I shrugged, too overwhelmed to answer, and instead doffed the hat, which shot my hair up into a static corona, and we both giggled despite ourselves. I sought to reassure her. "The wind chilled me, but I am fine. Just a slight headache." She took my coat, her feathers still ruffled, and it wasn't until she had tucked me up under a blanket in one of the parlor chairs and stirred the fire that she felt comfortable enough to launch into one of her domestic interrogations.

"I sent that note over at noon! No doubt you allowed some customer to waylay you," she tutted, protecting her roost. "Mrs. Wells, perhaps? You were needed at home." Judging by her aggrieved tone, Margaretta's pert nose was seriously out of joint. Emily Wells, a similarly aged matron, threatened no competition whatsoever other than her large purse, so there must be more to my wife's overreaction than misplaced envy, most probably the mysterious delivery.

Indeed, she fetched a thick envelope from the side table and handed it to me. "I did not open it, as it is addressed to you, but I recognized the return address as your family's lawyer and feared it might be unfortunate news." She stood back, hands folded primly over her comfortable middle, concerned but respectful of my privacy.

I opened the unwieldy envelope and withdrew a black-bordered letter. We bowed our heads reflexively, and Margaretta murmured a prayer before I read aloud,

George Hillard, Jr., Esq.
14 West Street
Boston, Massachusetts

December 1st, 1883
Dear Mr. Dike,

Please accept my deepest sympathies upon the death of your cousin, Miss Elizabeth Hawthorne. Miss Hawthorne has named you as the heir to her estate. Most of her belongings must go through probate and will be shipped later, but these documents were deemed personal and without worth.

I shall notify you when the estate has been settled, but please do not hesitate to contact me if you have any questions. Again, my sympathies.

Sincerely,
George Hillard, Jr.

"Poor Elizabeth. Do you suppose she died alone?" Margaretta poured us each a sherry from the sideboard and stood to warm herself before the fire.

I nodded, saddened. "She was unmarried. Both of her siblings are long gone, Louisa in the steamship accident, and Nathaniel of a stomach ailment. You might remember that the last time I heard from Elizabeth was twelve years ago. A few weeks after the reading of my father's will, she wrote to ask if she could examine more closely the treatise he had bequeathed to me. I sent it to her in the next post and never heard from her again, despite my several requests for its return." I leafed through the sheaf of mismatched papers still in the envelope. "But it is here, along with some other documents."

"May I see?" Margaretta perched on the desk chair and set the stack of documents on the rolltop's mahogany surface. She pointed to the top sheet with its very formal but quavering writing. "I recognize your father's first page." She drew from below his initial chapter a crumpled paper. "But who's is this?" she asked of what looked like a child's uneven penmanship and cross-outs.

I smiled at a distant but fond memory. "My cousin Louisa's." Margaretta nodded and flipped to the next grouping of heavy stationery, and we both read the letterhead.

My vision tunneled, and I put my head between my knees. Was my spell this afternoon a premonition? Would I be forced to remember my childhood's darkest hours? What if my courage failed? I shook my head, unable to dislodge the terrible images the letterhead exhumed and instead worsening the left-sided ache that had already blossomed.

Margaretta came at once to my side, offering the sherry, and when I had sipped enough to make the spinning stop, she reassured me, "We shall read the new documents together. Remember, they are only words. Your stepmother cannot hurt you now."

But of this, I was not so sure.

John Dike
4 Andover Street
Salem, Massachusetts

September 2, 1871

George Hillard, Esquire
14 West Street
Boston, Massachusetts

Dear Mr. Hillard,

My apologies for the intrigue, but a Gorgon shares my bed, and nothing is safe. If my maid alone delivered this sealed packet to your office, you may assume that she acted in accordance with my post-mortem instructions.

Your legal services over the years have been exemplary, and now I must beg from you one last favor. The Hillard firm holds secure my last will and testament, along with several personal articles. I wish to make an addendum to that legacy. Please assure that only my son, John Stephens Dike, inherits the enclosed documents, along with the afore-mentioned items.

Sincerely,
John Dike

John Dike
4 Andover Street
Salem, Massachusetts

September 2, 1871

Mr. John Stephens Dike
100 Market Street
Steubenville, Ohio

My Dear John Stephens,

My sincere hope is that this letter finds you and Margaretta well. Please know that your family has always been in my thoughts and prayers. However, I must take this opportunity now, as my health deteriorates, to impart important information. This may evoke memories that cause you grief, and for this, I am truly sorry.

If I might quote your beloved cousin, Nathaniel Hawthorne, "Once in every half-century, at longest, a family should be merged into the great obscure mass of humanity and forget all about its ancestors." As you know, Nathaniel sought to distance himself from an infamous ancestor by adding a 'w' to his surname. I would just as gladly forget certain members of our ancestry, but I must resurrect their voices herein to prove to you the value of this bequest.

I shall therefore begin this treatise with the date that I purchased the vessel that bore me toward my successful merchandising career and the infamous family to whom I owe much gratitude and regret.

〜〜〜

"Your surname?" asked the clerk, quill poised under the ledger date of April 14, 1812.

"Dike." I pronounced my family's name with quiet pride.

"Christian name?"

"John," I announced with finality, but along with a hard nudge to my ribs, my father added, "Junior." I suppressed a rude rejoinder and swore to myself that, when gone from my parents' house, I would drop the "junior" and become my own man.

The magistrate swiped his dripping nose with his sleeve, dipped the quill into the ink well at his elbow, and recorded my name with meticulous care. The motley queue behind my father and me groaned in unison at this delay.

"All right, Master John Dike, *Junior*," announced the magistrate. "On this fourteenth day of April 1812, I declare you to be the owner and sole master of the brig, the *Lion*. If you keep her dry and safe, she'll make your fortune."

"He's a Dike, ain't he? He knows how to plug a hole." The custom-house erupted with bawdy laughter. My father's patrician features hardened. He turned and gave the men a withering look, then clapped me on the shoulder and shouted, "Congratulations to my son! If any other man of twenty-nine can boast of owning a brig, let him come forward to be feted as well."

The crowd gave me a good-natured cheer. Most knew me from the docks and would not begrudge me their well wishes, as my family had always treated them fairly in our merchandizing business. We exited the gloom of the hall and strode out into the bright sunshine glinting off the water in Salem harbor and to the wharf where the *Lion*, and my future, awaited.

That evening, while helping my children to bed in my parents' crowded home in Beverly, I discussed with them our circumstances.

"We shall be staying here with Gramma and Grampa for a bit longer, so try to be on your best behavior." I unrolled the sleeping pallets on the wide pine boards and plumped two pillows.

"Would Mama have liked the *Lion*?" asked five-year-old John Stephens. He missed his mother sorely, so much so that he sometimes suffered headaches, and I could hear even now the grief in his voice. I drew his nightshirt over his frowsy hair and assured him, "She would have liked her because I liked her. Your mother had great faith in my judgment where brigs were concerned."

"Do you think Mama is watching over us from Heaven, Papa?" His older sister Mary Wood, whose health had also been fragile, was more concerned with the spiritual side.

"Each and every day." I tucked in their quilts and kissed each little fair head in turn, then climbed down from the sleeping loft and sought out my parents in their snug parlor. My brothers and sisters had retired for the evening, and my mother and father were enjoying a rare moment of tranquility.

"Are they down?" My mother's dimpled but tight-lipped smile proved the adage that a woman lost a tooth for each child she bore. Mama had birthed nine and retained several pounds with each. Mary Wood and John Stephens assumed that Jack Spratt and his wife were based upon their beloved grandparents.

"Yes, finally." I roamed the room, gathering a cornhusk doll, a lead soldier, a woolen jacket, and my thoughts before I addressed my parents.

"I am grateful to you both for your support while I grieve, but I do not wish to depend on your generosity for any longer than is necessary."

My father put down his paper and regarded me with kindly but practical eyes. "Junior, you and your family are not a burden." He picked up his pipe and tobacco while he considered his next remarks.

"You know that I thought you and Mercy married too young. But Mercy gave us two wonderful grandchildren, and, I am proud to say, you proved to have a good head for business." He dropped his gaze and tamped his pipe. "But then Mercy succumbed to pneumonia, and we watched you fall into a deep melancholy. It is no wonder that your enterprises failed."

He glanced at my mother. "Abigail, do you wish to add anything?"

My mother nodded. "Having your little ones in the house is a blessing. And loaning you the funds for the brig is our pleasure. We know you are anxious to be on your own, but you are welcome to stay here for as long as you need."

"Thank you both. I promise I will pay back every penny with the money I make merchandising along the coast on the *Lion*."

My father, a respected deacon in his church, steepled his boney fingers and sermonized, "I should hope so. Sailing is part of the Dike family history."

I interrupted my chores to say, "I know well the family history, Father."

His eyes narrowed at my exasperated expression, but he would not be deterred. "Our ancestor, Captain Anthony Dike, was Master of the *Blessing of the Bay*, the first sea-going vessel built in Massachusetts." He took a breath, but I interrupted him before he could launch his own voyage into our family's tale.

"And it is my intention to continue in that tradition."

Disappointed that his excursion had been berthed, my father nodded in reluctant approval, and my mother dimpled again at her family's accord. I finished my tasks, wished them both a good evening, and retreated to the loft to strategize.

It took me another year to gather my wits and my wallet, but in 1813, the children and I moved from my parents' house to live with my brother Nathaniel in Salem. Because of the war, Salem presented many opportunities for merchandising, and Nathaniel, with his dignified personage and trustworthy demeanor, gleaned no doubt from his alma mater Yale, had been enjoying a brisk business down on the docks. It was there that I met my future in-laws.

"Allow me to introduce you to the Manning brothers," said Nathaniel as we strolled along the breezy wharf on a sunny Salem summer day in 1815. "Robert and William own the Manning Stage Lines, which they inherited from their father Richard, and they are in need of partners with ties to the docks."

Soon the brothers Manning and Dike were assisting each other in their respective businesses. I placed ads in the *Salem Gazette* for goods our ships had brought to port, and the Mannings then delivered the wares inland on their stages. This partnership proved worthy, and I was once again a man of means, purchasing a handsome three-story brick dwelling on affluent Pickman Street and hiring a fifteen-year-old, freckle-faced Irish girl named Bridget O'Malley to mind the children and the house.

The Mannings were generous not only with their business acumen but with their social contacts as well.

"John, would you care to join us at home for supper one night? My sisters would be very content to have you take supper with us. Especially Priscilla." Gregarious but diminutive William nudged his sedate and spindly older brother Robert and winked at me.

"I am much obliged. Thank you for such a kind invitation." I wondered about this sister whose time and efforts they had so magnanimously volunteered.

At home, I tried to explain the situation but was met with arguments and tears. "Why cannot we come too?" Ten-year-old Mary Wood stuck out a petulant lower lip.

"They invited only me. But once they have heard me brag about my angelic children, they will welcome you with open arms. Now give me kisses. Bridget, make sure they are in bed by eight."

Dressed in my best surtout and cravat, I walked with determination and not a little anxiety across Salem Common to a large, worn, three-story wooden frame house on congested Herbert Street. A knock upon the door resulted in an almost immediate opening, with three eager children's faces gazing up at me. These must be the fatherless nephew and nieces that I had heard so much about.

"How do you do?" I said, bowing with mock formality. The boy, who looked to be about eleven, bowed in return. "Very well, thank you." He turned and shouted, "Grandmama! The gentleman is here for Aunt Priscilla!" There was a ruckus behind him, and a stern-faced elderly woman in widow's black serge pulled him away from the door, shooed away the girls, and put out her hands in greeting.

"I am so sorry for all the commotion. Please come in, Mr. Dike. I am Mrs. Manning. It is a pleasure to meet the man who helped my sons to make their fortunes."

She led me into the sparsely furnished but pleasant parlor where the family had gathered. I shook hands with the Manning brothers, and then Mrs. Manning introduced me around.

"My daughter, Mrs. Betsey Hathorne. She lives here as her husband, Captain Hathorne, died at sea some years ago." Mrs. Hathorne, perhaps in youth a black-haired beauty but now a faded flower, rose with reluctance from her chair, her eyes down-cast. She curtseyed and, once I had greeted her, retreated to her seat.

"And I believe you have already met her children, but they must be properly introduced so that they may practice their manners."

The boy stood, shook his shock of curly dark hair out of his bright blue eyes, and offered his hand. "My name is Nathaniel, but you may call me Nath."

I gave his hand a firm shake. "Nathaniel is also my brother's name, so I am pleased to have a special name by which to address you."

His older sister, a potential future beauty with her mother's black hair and gray eyes, took her time marking her place in her book before standing to address me. "Elizabeth, but I suppose you may call me Ebe." She bobbed a cursory curtsey and then flounced back to her reading.

The third child, a redhead, hid behind her mother's chair and would not be coaxed out, and so she was introduced to me in *absentia* as Louisa.

"And, of course, you must meet my younger daughter, Miss Priscilla Manning." Mrs. Manning gestured to a stately personage in serviceable gray wool, who rose from behind a large crescent desk and extended a steady hand.

"Welcome. My brothers have told us so much about you. We thank the Lord for guiding you to our family to help with the business." She possessed the familial auburn hair shared by Robert and William, but her slender form and elegant carriage were all her own. My lips barely brushed her fingers before she broke contact to motion me towards the hearth.

"Will you not sit down and enjoy some of our brothers' wares?" Miss Manning offered me a tray displaying a cup of tea and a plate of bread and cheese and settled me in a wing chair before the fire, where I savored the brie which I had inventoried a week ago. She sat behind the desk again and took up her knitting. The stench of camphor oil emanated from the wool, and I remembered that Robert had ordered the sachets for her, explaining that she used them to keep the moths away. I marveled that she could tolerate the scent.

"My brothers tell me that you and they have a reciprocal arrangement. I look forward to hearing more about the business." She dipped her head in answer to my quizzical look. "The Lord has blessed me with an affinity for numbers. Perhaps I could be of assistance in your counting-house. I am already the accountant here at home." Her hazel eyes flicked up from beneath their thick, black lashes, seeking my approval.

A woman in the counting-house. I had never considered such a thing, but the Manning family certainly had proven their business acumen, and I was not averse to the idea. My brother Nathaniel and I were very fortunate to have allied ourselves with the Mannings, and I had every intention of continuing the association. And before me sat their sister, possessed of an interesting mind and a pleasing figure. My children were in need of a mother and I a companion. Mercy's spirit retreated as I participated in a lively conversation with Mrs. Manning and her daughter.

"We ladies of Salem are not a retiring lot," remarked Mrs. Manning, taking note of my surprised expression. "While our men are out at sea, we must rise to the many occasions which might usually require the more masculine talents. Our neighbor is the proprietress of the local tavern, my cousin manages her husband's business, and my daughters have been schooled by several well-read women, including myself, in math and science as well as in the literary arts. Therefore, a woman in the counting-house in Salem is more a norm than a surprise." Miss Manning chuckled quietly into her knitting even as I gulped a bit at her mother's litany.

Perhaps to soothe my male sympathies, Mrs. Manning sought to change the subject. "But please, tell us a little about your family, Mr. Dike. My sons relate that your parents and several of your sisters still reside in Beverly. Has your family always lived here on the north shore?"

"No. According to family legend, my ancestor Captain Anthony Dike sailed in 1623 on the *Ann* to Plymouth Plantation. He was a particular, not a Pilgrim." I glanced at Miss Manning to gauge her reaction to this bit of news about my religious background. She kept her gaze on her knitting, but her lips tightened.

"I see." Mrs. Manning poured me a second cup of tea, but I could see in her eyes a frustrated curiosity about my pedigree. I took pity upon her and fed her another morsel of information.

"Anthony Dike was an adventurer of the first order, defying the pirate Dixie Bull, and befriending Roger Williams." Miss Manning looked up from her knitting. Apparently, heroes, even of two centuries past, still appealed to the ladies. The Manning brothers, however, merely exchanged bemused glances. Men were not as easily swayed by the swagger of earlier generations.

"And business runs in the Dike blood. Anthony and his partner Roger Conant traded fur with the Maine Indians."

"Goodness! Whatever happened to him?" asked Miss Manning, a bit breathless.

"Unfortunately, he succumbed when his vessel was wrecked in a blizzard off Cape Cod in 1638. But his descendants continue to thrive as sailors and merchants to this very day," I finished proudly and looked to Robert for confirmation. He rewarded me with a thin smile.

"And what of your female ancestors? I suspect they did not lie dormant whilst their menfolk traded with Indians and conquered the high seas?" Mrs. Manning's eyes twinkled at me behind her spectacles. I could feel my face flush even as I sought my memory for some family fable featuring a Dike heroine.

Mrs. Manning came to my rescue. "No matter. We are fortunate to live in a time and a place where the sexes are more similar in their expectations than perhaps in other eras. And we are grateful for your generosity in sharing your family's talents with us." She raised her tea cup and addressed the room. Robert, William, Mrs. Hathorne, and Miss Manning raised theirs as well.

"My thanks to the partnership of the Dike and Manning families. May they find continued success."

"Cheers!" William and Robert clicked cups and then smirked at me over the teacup rims.

I raised my cup and saluted them all. "Thank you for welcoming me into your family and your business. My brother's introduction was truly a blessing."

"Mr. Dike, please allow me to refresh your plate." Miss Manning skirted the desk to fetch the tray but startled when Louisa, the younger Hathorne daughter, approached me and, without ceremony, deposited a small tortoise-shell cat in my lap, then stood back to observe my reaction. The cat dug its claws into my leg, and I flinched.

"Louisa. Please do not bother Mr. Dike." Miss Manning glared at her niece, so to protect the girl from a scolding, I sought to reassure them both. "Why, thank you, Miss Louisa. How did you know that I am fond of pets?" I stroked the dappled fur with a practiced hand and was rewarded with a purr.

"What is her name?" I asked, hoping to draw the child out.

"Molly," Louisa answered in a soft voice, and she crept forward, her shyness overcome, to join me. Her little hand found mine, and I gave it a gentle squeeze of reassurance. She leaned against me, and together we petted the cat. Miss Manning retreated to the desk and took up her knitting again, allowing her niece a little paternal attention.

The older Hathorne daughter, taking notice of the commotion, crossed her arms and gave me a predatory stare. Over Louisa's head, I returned her gaze and, with my most self-effacing smile, said, "Miss Ebe, your uncles tell me that you are a great reader. What have you studied lately that I might recognize?"

"I am partial to Shakespeare, especially the sonnets. Do you have a favorite?"

"Shall I compare thee to a summer's day?" I recited with wry obedience. She frowned, turned her back, and retreated to her book. Obviously, my plebian taste was not to her liking.

Her brother spoke up. "Please do not take offense at my sister's manners, Mr. Dike. She is thirteen and can be very trying at times. I write poetry and publish it in a magazine which I call *The Spectator*. Would you care to see a copy?" He limped over and held out a smudged sheet of pen and ink scrawls.

I felt some concern for his awkward gait, yet I saw intelligence in those vivid blue eyes. "Thank you. I shall take it home and read it and query you next time."

Mrs. Manning sent the children to the kitchen for their suppers, and the rest of us sat down in the dining room to enjoy a wholesome meal. Although Mrs. Manning and her daughters kept a rather formal home with high expectations for the children, I thought Mary Wood, John Stephens, and I could be comfortable with this family.

So, as the months passed, and my businesses grew, I courted Miss Manning, first coming to her house on the pretext of discussing business with her brothers, then bringing John Stephens and Mary Wood to visit the Hathorne children, and finally escorting Miss Manning to view the ships in the harbor at sunset. She was shy and demure at first, but her interest in the business and my children gave us much to discuss.

"I am a God-fearing woman, Mr. Dike. I believe it is my duty to care for my family, community, and Christian principles. My sister chose unwisely and was left destitute with three children for whose catechism I take responsibility. Have you raised dear Mary Wood and John Stephens to believe in Jesus Christ as their Savior?" Her face shone with fervor. "And," she dropped her eyes, "should we be blessed with a child of our own, I would insist that he or she be brought up in the grace of the Lord."

To raise another child was more than I could ever have hoped. I put an arm about her waist and murmured into her ear, "I can think of nothing that would please me more." We both blushed, but then she stiffened and withdrew from my embrace.

I sought to sustain the affectionate mood. "Please come to Sunday dinner after church, and you may quiz my children on their Bible studies to your heart's content." She nodded, and my pulse quickened. Perhaps her cool demeanor was nothing more than reserve.

I walked her back to her home, took her worn, strong hand in mine, and kissed her fingers, but she pulled her hand back and said, "Mr. Dike, we must be patient." She opened the front door and stepped in but turned back and graced me with a secretive smile before closing the door, and I strolled back to Pickman Street with my head in the clouds, dreaming of the day when I might bring her home.

I waited to propose until my businesses were truly flourishing, and in June of 1817, with Robert Manning's approval, I asked Miss Manning to sup with me.

"Papa, your eyes look very well with your deep brown surtout," said Mary Wood as she dusted off my shoulders. "And Bridget has just washed your linens." She adjusted my neck cloth. "Remember to be charming and dashing. That is what a woman wants." My daughter, at twelve, was an avid reader of torrid tales in the papers, as her chronic cough prevented her from more physical outdoor activities. She gave me a last critical appraisal and turned me toward the mirror. A tall, lean, brown-haired man of thirty-four with amber eyes and a self-conscious, crooked smile stared back.

"Papa, your eyes are the same color as Skipper's," said John Stephens, offering our puppy for comparison. I held a squirming Skipper up to the mirror, and we laughed at my son's observation, but I hoped that my eyes would be as captivating to Miss Manning as they had been to Mercy.

"Wish me luck." I kissed Mary Wood and John Stephens goodbye, caught up a walking stick, and set off to greet my future bride. My children waved from the doorway, and I read in their enthusiasm the hope for a kind new mother.

After claiming Miss Manning on Herbert Street, I chaperoned her around the wharves, showing off my fleet, calling out greetings to the sailors, and ignoring their crude comments. Some of the women plying their trade on the docks winked at me, but I knew better than to wink back while walking with my intended. Miss Manning gripped my arm a little tighter.

"Mr. Dike, I hope you do not know any of those women."

"Miss Manning, I have worked these docks since I was a youth of fifteen. I am on a first-name basis with most of them." She flinched away from me until I assured her, "But they know I am only interested in them as congenial acquaintances." She relaxed against my arm again, even eying their attire.

"Perhaps I can bring them to Jesus," she said. I swallowed a chuckle and steered her towards home.

The sea air had whetted our appetites, and we walked purposefully to Pickman Street. Bridget curtseyed to Miss Manning, hung up her shawl, and seated her in the head chair at the table. Mary Wood and John Stephens had eaten their suppers earlier, as instructed, but I wagered they were hiding, observant, on the stairs.

Cook demonstrated her abilities to her possible new mistress by serving tender chops of veal, braised vegetables, scalloped potatoes, and to end the meal, peach cobbler. Bridget cleared the table, and on our pre-arranged sign, she and Cook stood by as witnesses.

I knelt on one knee and opened a tiny box I had hidden in my waist-coat pocket. The emerald ring that my brother and I had purchased in Boston two weeks before nestled within. Miss Manning gasped, and I heard answering giggles from the secret audience on the stairs. I willed them to be patient.

"Miss Manning, would you do me the honor of consenting to be my wife?"

Her hazel eyes glistened. She nodded and proffered her left hand to receive the ring. I slipped it on one slender finger, kissed her cheek, and turned to acknowledge the clapping from the staff and the stairs.

Mary Wood and John Stephens ran into the room, an excited Skipper at their heels, but stopped when they saw the angry expression on their new mother's face.

Miss Manning drew herself up to her full height and addressed my children in a sterner tone than I would ever care to use. "Why are you not in bed? You should be fast asleep at this hour. I am ashamed of your behavior. Go upstairs at once." She pointed one indignant index finger toward the stairs.

John Stephens, chin quivering, ran to me. Mary Wood, white-faced, walked close behind him, and I looked to Miss Manning for forgiveness.

"This is my fault, Miss Manning. I thought they would enjoy witnessing the start of their new lives. But you are quite right. They should be asleep."

"Indeed." Her expression chilled even my blood. "I would like to go home now. Bridget must put these two scofflaws in their beds, and no peach cobbler tomorrow as punishment."

My children clung to me, one on each side. I knew I had to make this right.

"Bridget, would you walk Miss Manning to Herbert Street, please? I shall put the rascals to bed myself." I stood to take my betrothed's hand. "Thank you for accepting my offer."

"You are welcome." Her expression softened. She gave my children a rueful smile. "Well. I did not mean to upset everyone." She straightened her shoulders. "But we have rules which must be obeyed." Her eyes narrowed as they met mine. "You and I have much to discuss." She brushed my cheek with her lips, accepted her shawl from Bridget, and the two walked out into the balmy evening.

I bent down and drew the children close. John Stephens had calmed, but his fists were clenched, and I worried that all this tension might precipitate one of his sick headaches. Mary Wood was pale, too, and her cough had tightened. I certainly did not want them to go to bed ill, and so I took the blame upon myself.

"My dears, it was not fair of me to surprise Miss Manning. I am sure that tomorrow she will forgive us, and all will be forgotten. We will celebrate another time, but for now, you must go to sleep. Who wants to hear the next chapter of *Pilgrim's Progress?*"

With John Stephens slung like a cloak upon my back and Mary Wood and Skipper tight at my side, we climbed the stairs to their bedroom. Both were asleep, with Skipper between them, before the pilgrims progressed to page three. I, on the other hand, slept not a whit, thinking about this new chapter in our lives.

Comely Miss Manning was possessed of a clever mind and a zealous soul, but could we claim her heart? I hoped that my love could soften her rigidity and persuade her in my little family's favor, but I wondered if I had inadvertently invited a snake into our tranquil garden.

September 20, 1817

Nath has always advised me to keep a journal as he has filled many volumes with observations and bits of stories. Nath and Ebe are the writers in the family, but Mother says my letters are very entertaining and that I have a flare for fiction, so I shall endeavor to write my entries as chapters in a book like some of the works of Jane Austen.

Ebe says with a sneer, "You are comparing yourself to the author of *Sense and Sensibility*?" But I think our lives could rival the English countryside for interest and intrigue, although some of my descriptions may not flatter certain members of my family, and so I must hide this volume from prying eyes.

My story begins with the wonderful news concerning our Aunt Priscilla and Mr. Dike:

"Aunt Priscilla is to be married!"

I burst into the bed-sitting room I share with Ebe and twirl with joy.

"Mr. Dike gave her a beautiful ring, and she said yes." I fall back onto the bed and stare up at the ceiling. "What will she wear?" I close my eyes and imagine the silk gown our cousin wore to the last dance in our town hall.

Ebe throws a pillow at me from the chaise longue upon which she has draped herself.

"Maria Louisa Hathorne, Aunt Priscilla does not care for those sorts of concerns. She thinks it is not good for the soul to be too comfortable. She wants to suffer in the eyes of her lord." Elizabeth has been called Ebe by the family ever since Nath was a baby and tried to pronounce her name, but I am usually Louze, never Maria, because that was my aunt who passed on, so when Ebe uses my formal name, I know I am in trouble as no one in my family calls me Maria Louisa Hathorne unless they wish my full attention.

"She is to marry a widower with two children, so I think something dignified and matronly would be best. She is too Puritanical to care, anyway," Ebe says with a haughty sniff.

Ebe is all of fifteen and very bossy, but she should not be so sure of what is or is not best for anyone other than herself, I have told her this many times when she has tried to tell me what to do, older sisters are put upon this earth to try us of this I am certain, but Ebe is the genius and the beauty of the family, and so she can do no wrong.

Uncle Robert brags to his friends, "My niece Ebe could read Shakespeare when she was just a girl of six. She can compose a letter that rivals any popular fiction. She devours books from the library and requests the latest novel for her birthday."

My cousin Rebecca says, "Ebe reminds me of a wood nymph because she is so tiny and prefers walking alone in the forests." And indeed, when we go visiting in Salem, she causes quite a stir with her dark eyes and tresses, and I, with my auburn hair, pale eyes, and gangly height, feel like an ugly duckling whenever I accompany her.

"I think Aunt Priscilla will wish to look pretty. It is every bride's right," I say and run out to the landing and peer downstairs, hoping to catch a glimpse of an adult who might know the answers to all these extremely important questions, but no one is about, the house is quiet except for our cousin Hannah who my grandmother took in out of the goodness of her heart, she does our washing and is out in the back, mopping her merry face with one hand while stirring the steaming laundry cauldron with the other and gossiping with the neighbor's maid.

Our Aunt Priscilla is twenty-seven, which means she is younger than our mother by twelve years, and Mr. Dike, her betrothed, is older than she is and a merchant in town doing business with our uncles. He is funny and kind, always ready to sit and play, tease, or be teased. I quite like his children, John Stephens, a year older than I am, is quiet and obviously still misses his mother, but he is good company when he forgets himself a bit, and his sister Mary Wood is a year younger than Nath and is much to his liking as she seems to have one fragile foot in another world even as she lives in this one.

But I, being nine years old and quite wise for my years, think that these two children will be very happy to have a new mother who comes into their lives with such relations. Imagine the celebrations and presents these two will now have, which has been Ebe's, Nath's, and my experience, and although we get a little weary sometimes of all the attention, the Mannings have been very kind to us since our father died at sea.

Nath says, "I remember when our father died. Mother called Ebe and me into the sitting room in our old house. You were just a baby in the cradle. Mother said, 'Your father is dead,' and we moved here with Grandmama and Grandpapa. But I have very few memories of him, except that he was never home for long."

Our mother tells us, "Your father loved books and elegant things and his family, but he loved sailing most of all." When she is feeling melancholy, she unpacks a beautiful blue china tea service that he brought home for her, and she sits and polishes it with a soft cloth all the while humming a sad little tune, and if we wish to hear bed-time stories about our father she lets us play with his gold watch while she tells his tales of sailing the seven seas and she always makes him the hero, so I fall asleep with visions of my father as larger than life, captain of the world, with a quick mind and a sharp sword.

I, of course, never knew him as he died three months after I was born, but I look for traces of him in every uncle, cousin, or new friend that I meet.

"Your house seems like a tavern, with all these people coming and going," says Rebecca as we sit at luncheon one day, and indeed it is certainly a large family living in our three-story wooden house on Herbert Street. My handsome Uncle Robert comes home from his stagecoach business and tells us stories of his day, Aunt Priscilla always has a Bible lesson to share and disciplines us if we are naughty, Uncle William, by his own admission, is the plain-faced runt of the family and is not very agile in business but always has a scheme, and Grandmama gives us gentle reminders to save our pennies and be good citizens of Salem. Only our mother is quiet and shy, she does not go about the town visiting but sits in the parlor and listens to Nath declaim his lessons and takes her meals in her room, and often she is not feeling well and hardly ever goes out of the house.

But I am allowed to explore the town of Salem from Herbert Street as long as I go with my aunt or one of my uncles, who let me run out to the docks to see the ships come in and go out of the harbor. Sometimes we visit Mr. Dike, who has a shop on the wharf and sells the lumber he buys from Uncle Robert's mill in Maine. He says he has money in some of the boats in the harbor, and he and Uncle Robert joke with Aunt Priscilla that it is kept in the hold.

"It matters not, so long as it is dry enough when I need to buy something," says Aunt Priscilla with a frosty smile. "Mr. Dike owns a fine dwelling on Pickman Street with nine rooms and even an indoor bathing chamber, but we must pray that his businesses continue to improve. I do not wish ever to return to Mother's house."

When we go to Mr. Dike's shop, he always offers me a stick of candy and some paper and pencils with which to draw, and Aunt Priscilla allows me to accept the candy and then directs me to sketch quietly by the window, and I listen while Mr. Dike and Aunt Priscilla discuss plans for his children.

"John Stephens could attend school with Nath," says Aunt Priscilla. "Having a friend might cure him of his shyness and those self-indulgent headaches. I can teach both the children their catechisms."

Sometimes Uncle Robert and Uncle William come into the shop to talk business, and Aunt Priscilla joins their conversation while I look out the window at the boats in their slips and the sailors come home from the sea.

Salem seems to me to be a bustling port, but Uncle Robert corrects me, "Before the war with England, Salem owned over two hundred vessels, and now, she owns only a few. That is why your Uncle William's import business failed to thrive, and I had to give him aid, and even Mr. Dike lost his business a few years ago."

Ebe rarely accompanies me to town. She smooths her skirts and says, "I am now a young lady and want nothing to do with you silly children. Besides, if I cannot walk in the woods or on the beach, I prefer to read in my room." When I disturb her, she declares, "One day, I shall live all by myself and not have to see any of you, especially Aunt Priscilla, I do not need to be saved."

In August, Mr. Dike invites Aunt Priscilla, Uncle William, Nath, Ebe, and me to accompany him, John Stephens and Mary Wood, on an outing to Nahant, and we are very excited to swim at a real beach, not where we usually do which is an outlet near the harbor where the water is brackish and smelly. Mr. Dike's brother Nathaniel is also invited, and in the stage, he and Mr. Dike tease each other about who is the major Mr. Dike and who is the minor Mr. Dike, because Ebe, Nath, and I must call them both Mr. Dike, and it is very confusing.

"I have an idea." Mr. Nathaniel Dike says. "Why cannot the Hathorne children call us Mr. Nathaniel and Mr. John when we are together?" Aunt Priscilla nods, as this seems a good compromise, and we continue to travel in a state of high excitement till we cross the causeway and the scents of salt and fried food tell us that we have at least arrived at the seashore.

The beach at Nahant has little wooden houses for changing into our bathing costumes and a boardwalk to enjoy concessions and entertainments, but Aunt Priscilla leads us away from these temptations to an open space on the sand where we spread our blankets and hampers and unpack.

Mr. Nathaniel is very silly and funny and makes us all laugh with his antics in the water and on the sand, and he and Mr. John splash each other and try to dunk each other in the waves while Aunt Priscilla sits on the sand and fusses with her bonnet and the picnic food, Uncle William roams the beach looking for washed-up treasure, and Ebe and Mary Wood read the latest novellas. Even John Stephens forgets that he is still in mourning for his mama and allows his father to gently draw him into the shallows, and Nath, who yearns for a father almost as much as I, looks upon this with envy, but soon he and Mr. John and Mr. Nathaniel and John Stephens are tossing a ball in the wet sand, and then Mr. Nathaniel tosses the ball to me as well, he and Mr. John come from a large family, and they are happy with a crowd of children, girls as well as boys.

Nath and I are proud to show off our swimming skills to our new family. "Watch!" I cry to anyone who will listen, and although Aunt

Priscilla shakes her head at me to remind me that pride goest before a fall, I still dive into a wave and stand up with my back to the ocean to bow to my audience, only to be dunked by a following wave and dashed onto the sand, and Mr. John hauls me up, pats my back as I cough, and ensures that I have my breath before delivering me to Aunt Priscilla for a lecture and a sip of tea.

Then Aunt Priscilla calls everyone over for our picnic, and we are very hungry from all the play and games and stuff ourselves with bread and butter, but before they eat, Mr. John and Mr. Nathaniel excuse themselves and push their way past the breakers, and we watch them swimming in the current, their two heads visible just above the water, stroking together in perfect rhythm. Uncle William returns, disappointed from his walk, stares out at the swimming Dike brothers, and runs into the water, dives into the waves and meets them as they fight the current back, and finally, they all emerge from the ocean cold and tired, ready to eat and warm up before the long stage ride home.

⌘

At last, the wedding date has arrived: September 14, 1817, it is a lucky day with bright sunshine and a brilliant blue autumn sky. Grandmama, Uncle Robert, Uncle William, Ebe, Nath, and I attend the Evangelical Tabernacle Church and sit on the bride's side while Mr. Dike's parents, his children, and Mr. Nathaniel, sit in the front row on the opposite side of the aisle. Mrs. Dike Senior snuggles her two grandchildren to her pillowy sides and pays close attention to their whispered confidences. Ebe sneers that Mrs. Dike Senior is too well-upholstered, not slim like the Mannings, but I appreciate her soft embrace when she includes me in their family outings, Mr. Dike Senior is more dignified, and his kindly smile reminds me of his son.

The Reverend Thomas Carlisle, our cousin Eleanor's husband, squints at us from his exalted place behind the pulpit and admonishes us to renounce the sins of greed and pride. Then Aunt Priscilla, in her Sunday best wool gown, takes her place at the altar, her hazel eyes shining greener than her emerald ring, and Mr. Dike beams at her his crooked smile, his copper eyes moist, and after leading them through their vows to love, to cherish, and to obey, till death do them part, the Reverend pronounces Aunt Priscilla and Mr. Dike man and wife.

After the ceremony, we all go to Mr. and Mrs. Dike's house for a reception. That is the first time I have said it, "Mrs. Dike," and she smiles at me as she hands me a plate of cakes for the table.

"Louze, truly this is the happiest day of my life." She surely looks it, and when Mr. Dike comes and puts his arm about her waist, she blushes.

So, I am surprised when I hear the front door of our home flung in with an angry bang the next morning, I am helping Hannah scrub the kitchen table, but I come out into the hall and see Grandmama start out of her day room.

"What is it, daughter? Is John ill?" She peers down the corridor and gestures for me to go back into the kitchen.

"Mother." There is a tone in Aunt Priscilla's voice that I have never heard before, and I peek around the kitchen doorway to catch a glimpse of her before she goes into Grandmama's day room. My aunt has such a pinched, angry, sad expression that I cannot imagine what could be wrong, and she slams the day room door, and Hannah and I are left to eye each other, shrug our shoulders and go back to our business.

That evening after supper, I listen outside the dining room door as my uncles, mother, and grandmother discuss Aunt Priscilla's morning appearance in our house.

Uncle Robert says, "Priscilla was repulsed by the wedding night. Mother asked her if John were gentle. He is a widower, after all, and should be aware of how to treat a woman. Priscilla would only say that she did not appreciate the physicality of the act. I do not know what she expected. Surely, she realizes how babies are made. She helped to midwife Betsey."

Grandmother says, "Yes, but I do not believe Prissy ever forgave Betsey for birthing Ebe seven months after her wedding, thus proving her premarital sins. Prissy has always been more comfortable with immortal souls than with earthly forms, while the rest of us are quite accepting of our sensualities. I am certain she thought God would make procreation less distasteful for one of his favorite acolytes. She has been praying and praying for guidance, but nothing can make the first time anything but a chore. I have reminded her that it becomes less abhorrent. I know John to be a gentle, kind man. He will have all the patience in the world, but it will be up to her to be open to him, especially if she desires children."

"Who knows," Mama says softly, "she might even come to enjoy it."

Uncle William's voice is somber, not like his usual cheery tone when he says, "Prissy will need some time to accept her wifely duties. They may induce," he pauses, "uncomfortable memories." He closes the dining room door with a firm hand, and I cannot hear further discussion.

I creep back up the stairs to our second-floor bedroom. Ebe is triumphant at my report. "I knew she could never be happy with a man. No one that saintly could ever 'revel in the flesh'," she says and goes back to her reading.

I snuggle into the covers next to my bad-tempered older sister, who puts an arm around me and asks, "Would you like me to read to you?" I nod and hand her *Mother Goose Tales*, which Mr. Dike gave to me on one of our visits to his shop.

"Which story? They are all so insipid and stupid."

"My favorite is *Cinderella or the Little Glass Slipper*."

Ebe snorts but settles into her reading after the first paragraph, and at the end, she slams the book shut. "See? Even back in the seventeenth century, Charles Perrault knew romance was impossible. The Prince only loved Cinderella because she wore beautiful clothes and went to court, not because she was good and kind." She drifts off to sleep, but I stay wide awake because I cannot believe that marriage is that much of a trial, and I pray that someday I will have a husband as handsome as the Prince, as brave as my father, and Dear Journal, despite what Ebe says, I do think that it is possible to find True Love.

Priscilla Manning Dike
20 Pickman Street
Salem, Massachusetts

July 20, 1818

The Reverend Thomas Carlisle
The Evangelical Tabernacle Church
Salem, Massachusetts

My Dear Reverend Carlisle,

Thank you for your offer to be my spiritual shepherd. My young cousin Eleanor is certainly blessed to have found such a devoted husband as yourself. When first she introduced us, I was struck by your courteous manner and graceful demeanor. I know I shall feel safe in your reverential arms.

At last, I understand the Papists' preference for the confessional. However, I prefer to communicate my sins on paper rather than in an insecure public setting. And I shall attempt to hold my head in the light even as I write of subjects more appropriate to the gutter.

As we have discussed, I aspire to the holy aspect of motherhood. But I view the marriage bed as an unhappy penance toward that end. It is my hope that you, with your vast experience in counseling your female congregants, can offer me some advice on this conflict.

I had assumed to be a childless spinster. My brothers first broached the subject of a possible marriage when they met Mr. Dike through their business. And indeed, when they introduced us, I thanked God for presenting me with such a handsome, worthy, intelligent partner. I was so grateful to be given the chance to marry and raise a family. I was eager to do God's bidding and conceive as the Bible commanded.

But I was not expecting my own revulsion.

On my wedding night, I wanted nothing more than to feel the grace of God so that I might bring a new soul into the world. Instead, I was forced to ask, "Lord, why hast thou forsaken me?"

For, to my horror, my new husband's presence reminded me of a long-ago suppressed memory. Even now, I can barely recount it without nausea.

Upon the occasion of my thirteenth birthday, my uncle, always with a peppermint in his pocket or a silly joke to tell, lured me into the study to present his gift to me privately. "You are a young lady now, with grown-up responsibilities." He sat me down upon his knee and held a wrapped package before me. But as I reached for it, he dropped the gift. He pushed my hand away and gripped me hard about the waist. "First, my payment," he murmured into my ear. He unhooked the front of my bodice. Had not my brother William blundered into the room, forcing my uncle to release me, my virtue might have been lost.

My uncle swore William and me to secrecy after the promise of a treat. But any trust I enjoyed in men purporting to love me withered that day. And now John is the unwitting new victim of our familial perversions.

John was gentle and patient but passionate. I tried to match his feelings. But my disgust at the sins of the flesh overcame me. And I could not confess to him my childhood trauma.

His concern for my comfort outweighed his own pleasure. He begged me for suggestions and guidance. He tried everything imaginable to help me relax. But nothing helped. So, I accepted my uncomfortable fate with the hope of bearing a child.

Ten moons from my wedding night waxed and waned. Time enough for a child to have been conceived and born. John learned that I would only agree to his advances in the middle of the month. Otherwise, I found some excuse to hide in the spare bedroom.

"I have a terrible headache. I must be up early to go to the counting-house. You do understand?" He nodded, kissed my cheek with great tenderness, and made no more reference to conjugal visits. He followed my lead on those rare occasions when I felt the effort might lead to success. Otherwise, he sat in the parlor late into the evening, reading his newspapers. His disappointment in our failure to procreate was obvious in the defeated set of his shoulders.

But there might be surcease. Robert, William, Betsey, and the children relocated for the season to the family's new country house in Raymond,

Maine. July seemed a ripe time for me to join them. At breakfast, I hoped to ask permission from John before he left for the office. But when I entered the dining room, I found his little Irish maid Bridget standing before him. Her fingers nervously pleated her smudged apron. Her eyes beseeched his.

"Thank you, Sir, for your attention. My brother is so grateful that you were able to find him work on the docks. Now we beg you to send for my parents so that we might all be reunited."

"Please do not trouble yourself, Bridget. I know several of the captains who sail to Ireland. I am sure we can find your parents' passage." John's voice was businesslike but compassionate. She nodded and bobbed me a curtsey. She carried the empty tea pot to the kitchen with a jig in her step.

"You must not be making promises you cannot keep," I said. "The Irish are overrunning the town as it is."

"I intend to help as many of my countrymen as possible." John's voice remained calm in contrast to my shrillness. "My ancestor immigrated in 1623. Why does that make me any better than Bridget and her family? They deserve the same chance."

I tried a new tactic. "I would like to visit my family in Maine. Can the counting-house do without me for a few weeks? Your children can play with Ebe, Nath, and Louze there."

A shadow passed over John's kindly face. I thought I detected a hint of mistrust in my mothering abilities.

"If you wish. Bridget will pack them each a small bag. I shall miss you all, but I understand the desire to visit the country, and the fresh air will do everyone good." He gave me one of his mischievous crooked little smiles. I acknowledged it with a brief nod. It was mutually understood that the country atmosphere might boost my fecundity.

But what a relief to know that I could escape my wifely duties for a spell. I packed my bags with my usual plain dresses and collars. I eschewed Bridget's suggestions for dancing gowns or visiting frocks. I stood at the roadside, one stiff arm around each of the children. We were ready when Robert drove the carriage over to fetch us from our handsome prison on Pickman Street.

"Goodbye, my dears, and God speed," said John. He shook Robert's hand. He knelt to hug his children each in turn. He gave me a polite peck on the cheek. Robert pretended not to notice the lack of passion.

"Is everything all right with you and your husband?" Robert asked me in the stage. I ignored the question. I reprimanded the children when they fidgeted. I ordered them to be quiet in the flea-bitten tavern in which we spent the night. I stared with jaded eyes at the moving scenery. In the two-day journey, it changed gradually from a large seaside community to a rural lakeside village.

The Mannings' house in Maine was a perfect refuge, large and spacious, with a commodious kitchen, several bedrooms, and clean outbuildings. I settled John Stephens in Nath's room and Mary Wood in the spare room. I found an apron and set to work in the vegetable garden. It had been neglected and needed cultivation.

Mary Wood and John Stephens joined their cousins in play. After a bit, they all grew bored. They offered to help me. I gave them each a stick. They weeded around the tomatoes. I reminded them all to keep their clothes as clean as possible. Suddenly Mary Wood gave a little shriek and pointed to a sunny rock wall.

She threw down her stick and shouted, "Snakes!" Two garter snakes basked in the sun. All the children were curious about the creatures and crept towards them. The snakes uncoiled themselves and reared up. They stuck out their little forked tongues and slithered toward the children.

Serpents are creatures of Satan. I took up my hoe and advanced toward the snakes. I raised my hoe above my head. One of the serpents, sensing a change in motion and shadow, darted its head out. It struck Mary Wood in the leg just above her boot.

I brought my weapon down upon the vipers like the Grim Reaper and his scythe of death. I severed both snakes in two. The halves wriggled briefly in the dirt before succumbing.

Nath limped over. "I shall write of your noble conquest in letters to the family and articles in the *Spectator*." He, Ebe, and Louze conferred over the manner of corpse disposal.

But John Stephens was more concerned for his sister. Mary Wood lay on the path, her bleeding leg outstretched. As was her wont in stressful situations, her tight little cough overpowered her. Her brother dabbed at the wound with his handkerchief while instructing her to breathe deeply. John's children always overreacted to life's little challenges. They had never recovered from their mother's death. John Stephens, in particular, embodied an anxious orphan.

I pulled Mary Wood to her feet and escorted her into the kitchen. John Stephens followed close behind. I ordered her to lie down with a warm compress on her chest while I made a poultice for her leg. She was a very sensitive child. I felt some measure of guilt that she had to endure an injury. However, I suspected that her histrionics were a ploy to gain sympathy from her brother and cousins. I forced her to eat supper with the rest of the children, though she complained of pain and limped to the table.

We lit candles to see our way to bed. I escorted each child to his or her room. John Stephens insisted on sleeping in his sister's room. Mary Wood asked me to sit with them until she fell asleep. She was perhaps still trying to make sense of the day's events. I fetched my knitting and sat in the bedroom chair.

"Mrs. Dike, why did you kill those poor snakes?" Her voice was hoarse from coughing. "They are God's creatures. They were simply protecting themselves."

"They are creatures of Satan. The Bible warns us of serpents' forked tongues and declares that they cannot be trusted. They advanced on you children and attacked you with their fangs." I purled a row, formulating my defense. "I was protecting you."

"No, they were simply scenting us. That's how they do. I read about it in one of Mr. Manning's books about the creatures of Maine."

"I am charged with keeping you children safe. How do you think your father would react if he knew you were injured under my watch?" I changed stitches and tactics. "You know that Satan took on the form of a serpent in the Garden of Eden, do you not? It seemed like the righteous thing to do." I jerked hard at the skein of yarn. I felt as though I were on trial here and certainly did not appreciate the implications.

"Thank you for protecting me, but please do not hurt another creature on my account." Mary Wood relaxed against her raised pillow, and with a final cough, relinquished herself to sleep. John Stephens snuggled protectively at her back, closed his eyes as well. I finished my row, packed up my knitting basket, and retreated from their room.

Why I wondered, did Mary Wood and I always seem to be on opposite sides of any argument? She was not a spoilt or angry child. Indeed, she was a child no longer. She had just turned thirteen.

I nearly dropped my basket.

My repressed memory surfaced again in all its horror. I closed my eyes to keep the vision at bay. Instead, Mary Wood's budding physique and angelic appearance materialized. They inspired in me a dread that I dared not name. Male relatives could not be trusted with nubile females. Though surely my husband, with his paternal sensibilities, would never succumb.

Yet jealousy arose, a serpent suckling at my breast. I resolved to discipline my stepdaughter more rigorously. She could never be allowed to flower while under my tutelage. My affect would remain cold, diffident to keep her budding heat in check. Other women might think me heartless. But the males of the family must never be tempted.

The house breathed around me. Robert and William had ridden into town to meet business acquaintances. Betsey was hiding in her room. My stepchildren and I would have to journey back to Salem in a fortnight so that John and I might try again to conceive. I sat in the dim circle of light cast by the globe lamp and purled a row, the black yarn a symbol of mourning for yet another barren month.

Reverend Carlisle, I trust that you will keep our counsel strictly confidential. Your wife, as my cousin, may be curious. But I believe there is a sacred pact between a reverend and his congregant. Please accept the enclosed offering as a token of my appreciation for your reticence. I hope that the amount is satisfactory.

Your Daughter in Christ,
PMD

October 15, 1820

It seems that I have filled my White Journal and must now begin anew. Please forgive the White Journal's breathless accountings of the foibles of my family members. I shall endeavor to be more generous in this latest volume.

But a bit of gossip is always welcome.

"I am to keep Nath company while he goes to dancing school," I explain to Ebe as we walk along the lake shore. I am very excited to return to Salem, Maine is beautiful if one likes the wilderness, but I prefer a more civilized society. Ebe is happy here, as she is shy, and the wilds of Maine suit her. She has grown into a beautiful young woman of eighteen, but as society does not interest her, she sits in her room in Maine and reads, just as she did in Salem. She and Nath have imparted in me a respect for books and all things intellectual, but dancing school sounds like a great deal more fun.

"Perhaps I shall go to a ball!" I race past Ebe and leap over the pebbles that line the highwater mark, raising my skirts gracefully. Ebe smiles at my antics but does not copy them, as she is far too stately these days, a gazelle, she proclaims, among hyenas.

Uncle Robert stands waiting at the head of the shoreline. "Girls, hurry along. It is time for supper and to pack for tomorrow's journey back to Salem," he calls.

Early the next morning, Uncle Robert and I board the coach and discover that we are two of four passengers, the others being a couple from Raymond going to Boston to visit relatives.

"Gee up!" calls the driver, and we are off. I wave goodbye to Mother, Uncle William, and Ebe and then settle in my seat as comfortably as I might, with my valise in my lap and my elbows close to my sides. Even in this tight little coach, I am happy to be leaving Raymond and going on this overnight adventure. Uncle Robert and I gaze out the window, watching the trees change from scrub to pine to oak and maple, and breathing in the new scent of salt instead of pine sap. After a very long day's journey down the coast, we arrive at an inn and tavern in Portsmouth, and I am asleep before Uncle Robert has doused the lamp in our tiny room, and in the morning, after a hasty breakfast, we board the coach again. Country becomes town becomes city, and we are in Salem at last, just in time for a late supper with Nath and Grandmama.

I am readying myself for bed when Nath slinks into my room. "I am so glad you have come to relieve me of this terrible boredom," he says as he flops onto my chaise longue. "I have invented a new club for us: The Pin Society. You can be the second pin counter, after me. And you can help me edit the *Spectator*."

"What will I write about?" I ask, sitting at my mirrored dressing table and brushing my hair the required one-hundred strokes.

"Whatever you like. I write stories. You could write poems . . ." He trails off, watching me. "You are growing up," he says with grudging admiration.

"I am almost thirteen. Of course, I am growing up." I give my hair its twentieth stroke.

"When you come to Turner's Dancing School, all the boys will wish to dance with you." Nath sounds disquieted by this, as it does not fall into his intellectual vision of his little sister, and I laugh.

"I promise to be careful. Now I wish to go to bed, it was terribly noisy at the inn last night, and Uncle Robert is a fidgety sleeper."

Nath shrugs and retreats to his own upstairs attic room, and I go to bed and dream of boisterous boys dancing in wild Maine waves.

The next day, Nath brings me to my first class at Turner's Dancing School, on the second floor of an old warehouse. Mr. Turner brandishes a stick that he thumps on the floor to help us keep track of the rhythm, while Mrs. Turner plays jigs and reels on the old piano. The giggly girls, sweaty hands encased in white gloves, stand on one side, while the fidgety boys, fingering the linty candies in their pockets, line up on the other. Nath's mysterious limp has vanished, and he shows a natural rhythm, as do I, for we are like our mother in this respect, although her frolicsome days are over, of course. But some of the other boys and girls taking class are not as graceful, and so out of kindness, we cross the wide pine floor to invite them to dance.

By the end of the day, I have learned many of the figures to several English country dances, as well as the waltz, which I find romantic, though none of the boys meet my intellectual criteria for interest, as they cannot keep my gaze but must glance about the hall even as we spin.

"Remember, ladies and gentlemen, the recital will be this coming Saturday. Please tell your parents and families. They, and other guests, are all invited." Mr. Turner makes this announcement just as we scamper down the stairs.

"Nath, whom shall we invite? Our family is so large, and they might all wish to come." I fear that our uncles, aunts, and cousins will fill the hall and leave no room for dancing.

"Grandmama, of course, but Mother, Ebe, and the uncles are all up in Maine. Perhaps Aunt Rachel and the Dikes?"

My head feels light at the idea of Mr. Dike watching me dance, he cut a very dashing figure in his dark brown surtout at his wedding, and although Aunt Priscilla looks unhappy much of the time, he is unfailingly affectionate and solicitous towards her and very kind to his children, nephews, and nieces, allowing us all to visit him at home and at his business. In June, Mr. Dike presented me with another book, *The Little Family*, "for the amusement and instruction of young persons." I was thrilled that he singled me out for this honor, although Ebe just scoffed, she dislikes him and says that he and Aunt Priscilla are common, and she would sooner stay in isolation in Raymond, but I would much rather live at the Dikes' grand residence in town and see him every day.

Nath and I think about whom to invite and how. Nath hides himself away in his little attic bedroom, which he has christened 'The Owl's Nest,' and scribbles several articles about the recital which we publish in a new edition of the *Spectator*, and while I submit a melancholy little five-line poem called "Address to the Sun," Nath writes of me, "Louisa seems to be quite full of her dancing acquirements. She is continually putting on very stately airs and making curtsies." We also send out laboriously hand-copied invitations to our relatives, and we are rewarded with several affirmative replies.

Our elderly Aunt Rachel Forrester visits to personally accept the invitation. Due to my mother's ever-failing health, Aunt Rachel has taken upon her stout shoulders the task of schooling her nieces in the arts and ways of womanhood, and she shares her late husband's wealth with her female relatives as best as she is able. To that end, her maid, Amy, follows her into our house, bearing the most beautiful dress I have ever seen. Cousin Rebecca wore it to her first ball, so Aunt Rachel thought I might use it as well. It is a pale gray-blue, which flatters my eyes, with white satin ribbon at the empire waist and hem, and the neckline is scooped into the shoulders and edged with the same satin ribbon tied in a front bow. I run to the hall mirror, hold the dress against my breast, and Amy sweeps my hair up to show the full effect. I cannot believe how grown-up I look.

"It is perfect. I do thank you." I curtsey to Aunt Rachel with due dignity, and she smiles at me, her eyes merry beneath her lacy cap.

"Here is a pin to dress it up a little." She opens her gloved hand to reveal a small silver bar brooch with a tiny garnet set in the middle. On the back has been engraved, "Rachel Forrester," so that I might always remember her kindness. I am speechless. I have a new dress and a new piece of jewelry all at once.

The day of the dance proves clear and fine, with no thunderclouds on the horizon. We students are to be at the hall by five in the afternoon to help set up the tables and chairs and refreshments. Nath and I, in our excitement, walk over early, and Mr. Turner orders us about, banging his stick up and down to keep us lively. Finally, at seven, the guests arrive: Kitty Foote's mother is wearing false hair-pieces in front of her ears, but she has placed them incorrectly, and the combs show, Mrs. Palmer's gown has grown shabby with a stain upon the skirt that no amount of pleating can obscure, and *some of the other women look as if they had dropped from the Moon ready dressed for the occasion and had got a little tumbled by the fall,* and I look forward to describing it all to Mother in a letter.

So, it is with pride that I escort my quite properly dressed relatives to their seats and then join my fellow students in our two lines. I blot my damp fingers with my handkerchief and try not to fidget until I hear Mr. Turner command Mrs. Turner to strike up a chord.

Mr. Turner bangs his stick upon the floor, and we prance through various country dance figures. We finish facing our audience, which erupts into applause, and we bow shyly, then with more confidence as the applause continues, and finally, Mr. Turner raises his arms to garner attention, and the audience settles down.

"Thank you to our students. We would like to invite our guests to participate in our final dance of the evening, a contra dance in honor of a great patriot. Please take a partner for *Hull's Victory.*"

There is confusion as everyone hurries to find a preferred partner for this very popular dance. John Stephens squirms his way past several would-be suitors to ask me to join him and leads me to a line of dancers facing the front of the hall. Nath chooses Mary Wood and gently escorts her to a slower set near the fireplace since her health has been even more delicate of late, and she clutches a stained handkerchief in a skeletal hand. Mr. Dike and Aunt Priscilla have joined our line, and we stand ready to move as soon as Mrs. Turner starts the reel.

John Stephens and I are at the head of the set. We follow the calls and come back up the hall to cast off with our neighbors. Aunt Priscilla, stiff in her best green dress and lace collar, spins me with a rigid arm while Mr. Dike swings his son twice around just for fun. She frowns at this break in decorum and refuses to take her husband's hand as they ready themselves to twirl the next couple. John Stephens and I turn to take our neighbors' hands, and I peer up the line at my aunt and uncle again. They are not staring fondly into each other's eyes as so many couples do, for she is looking down in discomfort, while his eyes search her face as if for any sign of affection.

Mr. Turner gestures to his wife to bring the dance to a close, bangs his stick, and announces, "We will end the evening with a waltz. Please find a partner."

Although John Stephens holds on to my hand after our bow, probably hoping that I will waltz with him, I shake my head no because we students have been instructed to fan out and choose another audience member with whom to waltz, and it is my hope that I shall dance with

Mr. Dike, so handsome this evening in his chestnut surtout and snowy stock.

As I approach him, he honors me with a courtly bow, then looks to Aunt Priscilla for permission to leave her side. She gives him a glacial nod and observes us with icy stoicism as he takes me in his arms, and we whirl away.

"You dance very nicely, Louze." He gazes down at me, his eyes warm, and I am suddenly turned to stone. A bead of perspiration runs down my back, and my gloves are damp, and I am reminded of my cousin Rebecca, who once told me that she had her first crush when she was about my age, on my Uncle William, of all people.

"You dance very well too!" I stammer, absolutely smitten and wondering at these new overwhelming emotions.

"How have you been enjoying the books I gave you?" His voice is jolly but bemused. Perhaps he, too, is aware of the moist glove in his hand, the glow in his partner's eyes.

"Very much, thank you. I especially like *Cinderella*." I am horrified at the tremor in my own voice.

"Ah, I hope you find your handsome prince someday." He winks at me, and I almost swoon. He continues, unaware of, or perhaps choosing to ignore my discomfort, "Frankly, I could use a fairy godmother with the economy as it is. Well, here we are."

He flashes his crooked little grin and spins me around to a seat next to Aunt Priscilla, then offers her his hand. She gives him a tight smile and allows herself to be pulled to her feet. They twirl away into the crowd, and I am left swinging my legs in my chair, my new dress suddenly too hot and snug. Aunt Rachel's brooch twinkles in the candlelight, and I touch it for luck, hoping that Mr. Dike, my new prince charming, has noticed how grown-up I look this evening.

I feel the need for company and go in search of John Stephens and discover him sitting out on in the stairwell, resting his head on one fisted hand. He often has sick headaches, so I fetch him a biscuit and lemonade, as eating sometimes helps him feel better.

I nibble a biscuit too and say, "Your parents seem to dance very well together," hoping he will add some juicy gossip, but instead, he says in a tight little voice, "Mrs. Dike is very unhappy. My father has tried everything, but we must listen to her complaints almost every night." He takes a gulp of lemonade and adds, "She forced us to give Skipper away. She said he was the cause of Mary Wood's cough, but I know that is not true. And now Papa is spending more and more time at his shop, even late into the evenings sometimes." He swipes at his nose. "Mrs. Dike is not a kind mother. Mary Wood fares the worst. She can scarcely eat for the anxiety." His eyes well, and he gestures for me to return to the dance hall so that he might have his privacy.

My own head spins. I have been focused so much on my own obsessions that I have not noticed that my cousins are miserable. I have noted the tension between the elder Dikes, but I had no idea that it was so dire, and Nath and I will have to discuss this and plan some entertaining adventure for the cousins to take their minds off their predicament. Or perhaps Mr. Dike alone will join us, and my heart beats faster at the thought.

"Louisa, have you seen John Stephens? We must take our leave as Mary Wood is not feeling well." The object of my dreams suddenly stands before me, and I am too flummoxed to do anything more than point. He disappears into the stairwell, and I hear raised voices before John Stephens, his shoulders hunched, his face pale, slouches out to unhook his cloak and join his family as they say their farewells and thanks.

The recital ends, and Mr. Turner expects his students to stay and clean the hall, so Nath and I join our compatriots with brooms and cloths to scrub the refreshment table and sweep the dance floor before we run, flushed and proud, down the stairs and out into the clear, cool autumnal night to the waiting carriage. My thoughts turn to Cinderella's coach and her handsome prince, and the trip home becomes a magic carpet ride of impossible girlish fantasies.

December 28, 1820

My Dear Reverend Carlisle:

Thank you for your continued support. I trust you will find an appropriate use for the enclosed donation.

My parenting techniques reflect the Bible's view on sparing the rod. However, after reading the following confession and plea for forgiveness, you may require additional sums. Perhaps for the purchase of new altar candlesticks? I shall call upon you in several days to submit to your decision.

Like the Concord grapes my brother Robert tried unsuccessfully to cultivate, my seeds failed to germinate, and my marriage to John withered on the vine. Conversely, John's businesses prospered, consuming him and requiring his undivided attention.

The childcare responsibilities, therefore, fell upon my shoulders. Mary Wood and John Stephens, so quiet and polite, awoke in me the benevolent despot. I took great pride in my heightened expectations. I demanded superior scholarship. I commanded obedience. I gave away the dog and other earthly bonds. And at bedtime, I waved off affections without a whisper of a kiss or the semblance of an embrace.

I then retreated to my own room and wrapped myself in an unbecoming muslin nightdress. I blew out the candle and stared into the blackness. I prayed that I would be asleep before John tiptoed up the stairs. If I remained awake when I heard the door open, I feigned slumber so that I could avoid my wifely duties. I believe John knew my feelings. He had not deigned to awaken me in months but crept into the spare room to sleep alone.

October teased us with several warm, sunny days. November lashed us with bitter winds and icy storms. John, miserable with a nasty cold caught most likely on the docks, stayed at work later and later so as not to spread it to the family. He was especially concerned about Mary Wood, whose chronic cough refused to abate. John Stephens continued to attend school but never stayed out past four to avoid walking home in the frigid dark.

Mary Wood, trapped inside for too many days, suffered from cabin fever. She became fractious and irritable. In an attempt to break her spirit, I withheld meals and sent her to her room hungry. Sometimes I succumbed to the temptation of a raised hand. I certainly did not spare the rod. By the end of November, I could barely stand the sight of her. So, on that fateful sunny Saturday in early December, when the breeze blew unseasonably warm, I pushed Mary Wood and John Stephens out the door to walk to the shops on the pretext of finding their father a birthday gift.

"Gramma says this is the kind of weather that can lead to pneumonia," whined John Stephens, ever the anxious little brother. He tried to press upon Mary Wood an extra scarf.

"Your grandmother is overprotective. Mary Wood will be fine," I said and waved my stepdaughter out the door. John Stephens shrugged his shoulders and followed her, his own scarf wrapped snuggly about his neck.

I stood at the window and watched as they hurried down the road toward town, their faces turned up to bask in the sunshine. The breeze whipped color into their cheeks. Cook and Bridget were also persuaded to take the day off. They soon departed for town.

Such joy to be alone. No sulky young woman sniveling about her menses, while mine came with such hateful regularity. No prying young woman reading personal letters. No spiteful young woman comparing me to her dead mother. No cunning young woman flirting with her father.

Instead, a sickly young woman venturing foolishly out into the fickle wind, without a scarf to protect her throat. I will not name the fantasies those circumstances engendered.

John Stephens and Mary Wood returned just before dark. John Stephens, hungry from the exertion, flung himself down at the table. He bolted his left-over mutton and peas with enthusiasm. Mary Wood, however, had scarcely the strength to shrug off her coat. She sat toying with her food. She answered my interrogations about town news and what they had bought for their father in monosyllables. And she tried unsuccessfully to hide a tightened cough.

"You should have listened to your brother." I banged a mug of hot tea and honey down on the table. She sipped at it without seeming to find comfort and headed up early to bed. Her cheeks were pink and her eyes glassy. I reassured myself that it was merely from the day of exercise, nothing more. I was asleep when John shook me awake later that night.

"Something is amiss with Mary Wood," he whispered. I followed him into her room. I immediately recognized the barks of croup as she struggled to breathe.

"You must take her outside into the cold air," I said. He helped her up, and half carried her outside. She held her head at an odd angle, trying in vain to catch a breath. Her chest heaved with each attempted cough. Her panicked eyes rolled.

"Help her hold her chin upright," I said. She had a mind of her own and struggled against his efforts. But once he showed her the position, she seemed to breathe a little easier. She relaxed a bit. The barks diminished.

We stayed outside for a quarter-hour in the biting cold. Mary Wood's head finally came to rest upon her father's shoulder. Her breathing sounded easier. Still, John planned to fetch the doctor in the morning. He helped her to bed. I busied myself in the kitchen, making more chamomile tea and honey. He spooned it into her mouth. She swallowed a few sips and then collapsed into her covers. He tiptoed out and left the door ajar to listen for another bout of croup.

John sat moping on our bed's edge. He rubbed his hands through his dark hair. "How could this happen?" He sounded more worried than accusatory. I placed a tentative hand on his shoulder. He covered it with his own warm palm. "They wished to buy you a birthday gift." It was a lie of omission. I neglected to tell him that I had insisted his fragile daughter go out into the wind.

He shook his head. "This is pneumonia weather," he said. I could not resist a little fib. "That is what *I* said," and he smiled too. "They can be very stubborn," he admitted with a glum shrug.

For the first time in many months, I felt close to John. I almost wished to be physically intimate. But he was too worried about his daughter. He turned his back to me, listening for any little sound from next door. He prayed aloud that God would make her breathing easier.

She awoke the next morning with bright red cheeks, a higher fever, and a different, deeper cough. Bridget set out to fetch the doctor. John stayed home to hear the diagnosis.

"I am not sure what I can do for your daughter at this point." Doctor Peabody washed his hands in the basin I provided. He led John into the parlor.

"After listening to her chest, I suspect she has pneumonia complicated by an already weakened constitution. All we can do now is make her comfortable, keep the fever down, and hope that she is strong enough to overcome the disease." He gave John a sympathetic pat on the shoulder before continuing his rounds.

John stayed in Mary Wood's room throughout the day. He fed her what little supper her appetite allowed, read to her, and emerged only when she drifted off to sleep.

"I have brewed some soothing tea. And you must pray," I said and guided him toward his chair. Only then did I notice John Stephens standing on the landing. His hands were clenched with worry. I readied myself for a defense should John Stephens point an accusatory finger at me. Instead, his own guilt overwhelmed him.

"I just wanted to go outside. I did not mean to make her sick."

John crossed to his son and locked eyes. He laid gentle hands on the boy's shoulders. He spoke measured words to reassure him.

"This is not your fault. The weather and Mary Wood's own body are to blame. Please do not make yourself ill with guilt." He escorted the boy to bed and laid a cold compress across his forehead to ease the ache. Then he sat with me in the parlor. He prayed for his girl to be made whole again. I prayed that my culpability might never be revealed.

She lingered for nine days. Cough and fever wracked her body. John tried everything, cold baths, willow bark tea, homeopathy. Nothing eased her.

With no thought for his own health, John stayed by his daughter's side. He tried to lower her fever with ice rubs and spooned sips of water into her slack mouth. The stench of the sickroom overpowered me. John took it with grace. He emptied the chamber pots himself, mopped up the bloody phlegm, and changed Mary Wood's night dress. But even he could see that his ministrations had no effect.

"Mercy's death haunts me still," he said, "and now Mary Wood suffers as her mother did. And John Stephens may never forgive himself for that one selfish walk." John cradled his head in his hands and wept for his family.

My conscience roiled just as my soul rejoiced. I could not admit to my husband that my disdain for his daughter was the true power behind her illness. Nor could I admit my joy at the prospect of my rival's demise.

One the tenth day, Mary Wood succumbed. Her father and brother stayed by her side to help her into the next world. John's parents came to support their son. His mother would not allow me into the death room. She never warmed to me. No doubt her grandchildren tattled tales of their evil stepmother. Therefore, Abigail and Bridget prepared Mary Wood's wasted body for burial. The rest of the family kept vigil with John and John Stephens in the parlor, trying to ease their grief with remembrances.

I aided Cook in the kitchen.

Your officiation of the service was much appreciated. The Senior Dikes kept a worried watch over their son. John had eyes only for the coffin. At the grave, he stayed on his knees in the snow and wept as the shovels of dirt slowly covered the lid. His parents pleaded with him to leave the grave. He would not be persuaded.

And when at last he came home, he sat before the fire, head bowed, speaking only when necessary. As the days wore on, Cook tempted him with his favorite foods. But he had no appetite. John Stephens flaunted his sick headaches. John gave him only cursory sympathy. He withdrew into his business. He no longer prayed with me. He refused to attend church on Sunday. His hair turned from chestnut to silver. His merry amber eyes lost their twinkle. We rarely spoke over dinner. He retreated to his study in the evenings. And he did not approach me in my bed.

My satisfaction revealed itself in my knitting. With each stitch, I created an impenetrable mantle of triumph. I chose red as the secret symbol of my joy.

Reverent Carlisle, your understanding of my true nature is my balm. My trust in your confidence is secure. I anticipate our next meeting with great joy and an additional donation.

Your Daughter in Christ,

PMD

Steubenville, Ohio
January 15, 1884

"How can I help you, John Stephens?"

Tom Blair, my nephew and a Harvard-educated attorney with the firm Shoenberger, Blair, and Company, had offered to give me some advice when he learned that I had inherited several potentially incriminating documents. He rode the train from Pittsburgh to meet me for luncheon at the best table in one of Steubenville's oldest establishments, the Black Horse Tavern. My retailer's soul appreciated the feel of the fine table linen and thin crystal, and Tom and I were good friends as well as relatives, but still, my belly felt exposed, and I ordered a whiskey from the formally attired waiter before handing Tom the pertinent pages.

"This letter from my stepmother Priscilla seems to me to be a confession to the murder of my sister, Mary Wood. I want to know if there is any way we can prosecute Priscilla *in absentia*." I drained my glass to smooth my hackles. Tom lifted a concerned eyebrow before donning his spectacles and turning to the documents.

When he had finished, he sat back in his chair but would not meet my eyes as he spoke. "I am afraid that this would never hold up in court." I cupped my ear to hear his hushed tone over the clatter of cutlery and the chatter of other patrons. "The cause of death is too vague. Yes, your stepmother writes, 'I could not admit to my husband that my disdain for his daughter was the true power behind her illness,' and certainly, Priscilla was guilty of cruelty, but pneumonia is a complicated diagnosis, and Mary Wood's body has been too long interred to be of any forensic use. There is also the issue of the statute of limitations since the crime occurred sixty-four years ago, and the corroborating witness, meaning your father, has died." He smoothed back his receding mane of salt and pepper hair, perhaps to give me time to lick my wounds, and then said dryly, "John Stephens, you cannot hang a corpse. I realize you want justice for your sister, but you will have to be content with your evil stepmother burning in Hell." Though he had never met Priscilla, my horror stories had influenced his opinion over the more than fifty years that we had known each other, and he granted her no leeway.

But then he eyed my untouched soup, and his tone softened. "And how are you faring? These documents must be dredging up some very painful memories."

"I can only read them a few at a time. I am familiar with my father's treatise, of course, but Louze's voice comes through so poignantly. I miss her more with each diary entry I read. As for my stepmother's letters, I can only read a bit at a time before I must lie down with a cold compress on my head . . ." I shivered, and Tom signaled a waiter to bring me another whiskey. "Her corruption is almost too much for me to bear. Margaretta says we should just burn them all and be done with it, but I cannot do that, for Ebe's sake. She somehow collected the diary entries and letters and made a tremendous effort to organize them all chronologically. The least I can do is to follow her lead to the end."

"The end being Louze's death on the *Henry Clay*? If you have any new information about that, I would be very interested to read it." Tom's dark eyes shone with a new, fervent light. Although the infamous steamboat disaster had been litigated thirty years ago, a revelation could be career-changing.

"As you may remember, my father's treatise proved to be nothing but hearsay. And the one piece of evidence in my father's possession was destroyed. I have gleaned nothing new." I drained my second glass and stared at the bottom, depressed that again I had failed my sister and my cousins due to my own weakness.

Tom sipped at his whiskey before broaching another difficult subject. "I was saddened to hear about Captain. He was such a loyal, patient, happy dog. Have you and Margaretta considered adopting another puppy?"

I shook my head and closed my eyes against the tears that threatened. "We are too old to train a puppy, and now I must read documents that remind me of a former painful canine loss. It would be too much."

Tom twirled the liquid in his glass before changing from one troubling topic to another. "Virginia and I fear that you might be obsessed by the past tragedies in your family. Sometimes, when one does not have immediate obligations to distract, the past can become present. I know when we lost Johnny to diphtheria, it took many years for Virginia to stop grieving, and she had George to dote on."

"How is young Georgy doing? Margaretta will be as mad as a wet hen if I do not come home with news about her grand-nephew." Talking about Tom's family slightly lifted the pall from my own.

"At thirty-three, he is not so young anymore. But thank you for asking. He is doing very well as manager of the Huntington Furnace Company, and he and Catherine are spoiling their little cub George Jr. rotten. Virginia and I visit them as often as we can, given our commitments to work and charities. The Blair name is as influential in Pittsburgh as it is in Blair County."

I must have looked haunted because Tom flushed at his own boasting and took another sip of whiskey to give us both time to recover before apologizing for his insensitivities.

"Please forgive me, John Stephens. My pride stood in the way of my sympathies. You and Margaretta had tragic luck, and I hope this inheritance will not resurrect your grief."

The conversation had now ventured too far into dangerous territory for my current fragile state. Reading about my stepmother's evils and my sister's death was painful enough. Being reminded of my own failure to continue the family line pushed my guilty conscience to another level. I gestured to the waiter to bring the bill, tossed my napkin on the tablecloth, and stood, swaying slightly. "I must return to the Emporium," I slurred before scrawling my signature and struggling, with Tom's help, into my coat.

Tom took my arm to steady me on our way to the door and said, "And I must board the train to Pittsburgh this evening, but first I will see you safely to the Emporium. Or better yet," his hand tightened as I stumbled down the steps toward the carriage, "home."

He handed me up into a hansom cab and directed the driver to Market Street before springing into the cabin. I needed to concentrate on keeping down my gorge as the horse trotted over dips and rises in the brick street, making the carriage lurch and dive, and so rather than converse with my nephew, I put my head out the window to steady my stomach.

We were in the middle of a January thaw, and all of Steubenville seemed to be enjoying the wan sun. Ebullient birds sang over the din of the bridle and wheels, gleeful boys and their playful pups jumped over slumped snow drifts, and cheerful nannies pushed prams through the puddles towards the shops. I wished that I, too, could revel in the thaw, but it only served to remind me of another fateful warm winter day when the world as I knew it collapsed.

At last, we arrived at our own welcoming corner of Market Street, and I gratefully descended, with Tom's help, onto my home's walkway without any embarrassing incidents. Still, I must convince Margaretta that all was well, and so as I wove into the vestibule, I tossed my bowler at the hat rack. And missed.

Tom picked up the hat, dusted it, hung it on the rack, doffed his own bowler at my wife, and with a wry smile, said, "Margaretta, Virginia sends her best. We will have to find a time when all four of us can dine. Perhaps it will bring John Stephens to heel."

Margaretta bobbed her head to Tom. "Thank you for returning my wayward husband." She noticed my wavering stability, quickly looped her arm in mine, and continued, "We have had another delivery, and I think John Stephens may well need us both to help with the unpacking." My hackles rose at this ominous-sounding news, but she had me firmly by the arm, and there was no escape.

Tom made a little mock bow. "I'd be happy to help. I have plenty of time to catch the evening train."

Margaretta led us through the back hallway to the service entrance. None of her cheery nesting had penetrated this part of the house. Dark paneling loomed over frayed carpets, shuttered windows discouraged sunlight as well as thievery, and a musty odor replaced the usual homey cooking smells. My sense of doom increased with each muffled step until we entered the back vestibule, and Margaretta again squeezed my arm in encouragement.

In the center of the black and white checkered marble floor, four large wooden crates squatted, daring an exhumation.

"I kept these closed for you. They are the final items from Ebe's inheritance, and I thought there might be something . . . personal . . .

in them." Margaretta did not challenge me with her gaze. Instead, she continued, her voice gentle, "I know why you are not yourself this afternoon. Your sister's ghost has been disinterred. Perhaps with Tom's help, you will be able to resurrect whatever else may lie in these boxes without becoming so overwhelmed."

I sank into one of the wooden chairs lining the hallway and leaned against the wall, readying myself for whatever might yet be revealed. My head had cleared, but my heart beat hard against my chest, and my hands clenched the seat of my chair. I took a deep breath before nodding to Margaretta to continue.

She handed a crowbar to Tom. "Tom, as you are almost twenty years younger and much stronger than John Stephens, perhaps you might do the honors."

Tom draped his folded jacket over a side table, rolled up his sleeves, and tucked his tie into his vest before wielding the crowbar on the thick slats at the top of the first crate. They gave way with a harsh squeal, and all three of us gasped at the release of an overpowering stench.

"Camphor," muttered Tom, waving a hand in front of his face to dissipate the odor. "Virginia uses it to keep the mice away when the cat refuses to do his job."

But Margaretta knew too well what else that odor might mean. She came at once to my side, but I had already heard the inward thunderous clang and sat with my head between my knees, gagging and wishing I had emptied my stomach onto the Steubenville roadway instead of here on Margaretta's gleaming marble floor.

"John Stephens, what can I do to help?" She held her cool palm against the back of my hot neck until my breath had steadied and then asked Tom, "What is in the crate?"

He peered over the wooden rim. "A large, crescent-shaped desk. Does that sound familiar?"

My cousins' desk. It had resided at the Manning and Hawthorne home, storing all crucial business and social information. As the last surviving Hawthorne cousin, Ebe would have inherited it. I nodded through my blinding headache, and Margaretta interpreted, "Yes."

Tom looked up, and his eyes widened at my pale and perspiring face. He padded at once to my other side and murmured, "John Stephens, this anxiety you are experiencing is not good for anyone, let alone a man of your age. Let me help you upstairs to bed. The groom and his apprentice can open these crates and haul whatever lurks inside to the attic for storage until you are strong enough to confront it." I nodded, too overcome to speak.

"That reminds me," Tom added, fishing in his vest pocket. "Virginia knows of a doctor who might be able to help you conquer these sick headaches. He is originally from Germany, but he now has a practice in Pittsburgh. He is rather infamous in certain circles." He passed the card to Margaretta, and then the two of them hauled me up by my arms and bundled me upstairs, where Margaretta tucked me into bed with a cold compress and a kiss and then saw Tom off in a cab to the train station.

I spent the morning after in what I assumed to be a hangover fog. Nothing at the Emporium piqued more than my perfunctory attention. Customers in whom I usually took delight stayed away. Even our new inventory lacked luster. The only bright spot in an otherwise dreary day was the doctor's card, about which Margaretta reminded me when I, at last, limped home in the evening. Together we planned an excursion to Pittsburgh, I to see the doctor, she to visit with our niece and nephew, and both of us hoping that with the doctor's help, I could eventually conquer my headaches and read the rest of the dreaded familial documents.

May 15, 1825

"Sisters! Your brother is returned from college at last," Nath calls from downstairs, and then he runs up the stairs two at a time, and he is in my room before I can look up from the chaise where I am stitching a dress seam or Ebe can put down the manuscript she is editing at my desk.

Without moving the hand-me-down gowns scattered on the bed in preparation for tailoring, he flops upon the mattress and crosses his hands behind his head in his usual pose of expectant boredom, as if we had nothing else to do but to entertain him.

With a cursory knock, Grandmama enters our room and observes his position.

"Nath, you are a college graduate now. Leave your sisters be, come downstairs and make yourself useful with your mother in the parlor."

He rolls off the bed and ducks his way out the door, turning to wink at us as he rounds the corner. He is so tall now that he cannot stand upright in his upstairs Owl's Nest, and indeed he takes up so much more room in general that the whole house feels unquestionably smaller. Ebe and I exchange frustrated eye rolls as we return to our tasks, dreaming of being anywhere but here where we must share the space with a college-educated scarecrow.

We siblings strategize the next morning over breakfast. "I cannot wait to move to our cousin's house in Beverly," Ebe says as she nibbles her toast, "and have a little privacy."

"I should like to stay here and write. But John Stephens and I may have come up with a solution for Louze. There is an empty room in the Dike's house, and John Stephens would enjoy some younger company since Mary Wood passed on." Nath eyes me over his tea cup. "You might suggest to the Dikes that you could fill that room with yourself and your myriad remodeled dresses."

I frown at the tease, but I am obliged to agree. "I would like to board at the Dikes'," I say, "I think it would please Mr. Dike. He chooses to be at work day and night because Mary Wood's spirit hangs over that house like a shroud. Yet if I go there for supper, he and John Stephens and Aunt Priscilla seem much more content. It would do them all good to have a lighthearted young woman under their roof."

"I am forever grateful to him for aiding Uncle Robert with my college tuition," Nath says. *"Mr. Dike always thinks the best of me,* so I would ensure his happiness in any way that I can, but why that would involve your company is beyond me." I stick my tongue out at him in response, and he tosses a piece of toast in my direction.

"Personally, I would rather administer an orphan asylum than manage him." Ebe's voice takes on that disdainful tone she reserves for those she deems unworthy. "But if you wish to live with the Dikes, best to petition them first, and then Grandmama. I shall stay here and write to the cousins."

As it is a bright, sunny spring day, Nath and I decide to walk along the docks and visit Aunt Priscilla in the counting-house and Mr. Dike at his shop. "I shall go on ahead and speak with Aunt Priscilla," Nath calls to me from the cloakroom. "You go to see Mr. Dike, as you like to favor him with your company." He spreads a hand upon his chest, rolls his eyes skyward, and intones wistfully, "I can just imagine how quiet and comfortable the house will be when you both are gone away," and then with a sly wink, he strolls out the door.

I take my time buttoning my fashionable empire-waisted coat and drawing on my kid gloves. I set my feathered hat at a flirtatious angle and tie it at the side with a wide bow. The blue ribbon sets off my gray eyes. Pleased that my appearance might persuade Mr. Dike in my favor, I set off down the street toward the wharves.

Mr. Dike's shop on Derby Street is the center of the Manning and Dike enterprises. He and Uncle Robert order their wares from here, walk down to the docks to accept them when they are delivered, and send them on to warehouses in the district. He is speaking with several business associates when I enter, but he stops his conversation and motions me over to join them.

"May I present my niece, Miss Louisa Hathorne. Miss Hathorne, this is Captain Goodman from my schooner The *Adventure*, and his first mate Mr. Jackson." I curtsey, they bow, and we make pleasantries until Mr. Dike signals his intentions, and they all group together at the desk for more negotiating while I stroll about the shop taking note of the engravings on the walls of all the schooners of which Mr. Dike has acquired partial ownership these last few years. He really is doing very well.

Hanging upon another wall are framed certificates and letters from organizations that Mr. Dike supports. One is titled *"The Salem Society for the Moral and Religious Instruction of the Poor." There is a letter of thanks from *The East India Marine Society* for a sizable donation. A third certificate includes an insignia from "The Salem and Danvers Association for the Detection of Thieves and Robbers."* My uncle is very active in both business and politics, and I wonder that my Aunt Priscilla does not show more pride in her husband.

The captain and first mate soon depart to oversee the unloading of their cargo, and Mr. Dike, at last, turns his attention to me. "What brings you here on such a fine morning dressed in such a comely fashion?" I startle at his mention of my attire, and he blushes when he perhaps realizes that he might be overstepping his uncle bounds.

"I do apologize for being so forward." He takes his time choosing a walking stick, avoiding my eyes.

"Nonsense!" I gesture toward the shore. "Let us stroll about the docks. I have something I wish to discuss."

His smile fades. "Ah, of course, you are just buttering your old uncle up for something." He closes and locks the door, and we make our way towards the water.

As we walk, he greets customers and business associates with his cordial crooked smile and a tip of his silk hat. He cuts a very handsome figure, and many of the ladies cast a curious eye toward me. One fashionably dressed, heavyset woman stops and holds out her hand for him to take.

He cups it warmly in both of his and introduces me. "Mrs. Felt, how nice to see you. May I present my niece Miss Louisa Hathorne? Miss Hathorne, Mrs. Felt's husband, Jonathan, is on the high seas presently, as captain of one of my brigs." Mr. Dike pauses and gives her hand a squeeze. "I'm certain he is faring well. Whatever storms he meets at this season are light, and the ship is quite sea worthy."

"Thank you, Mr. Dike. *You always take the time to reassure me about my husband's safety." She turns to me. "Your uncle is very tender-hearted.* I do hope you appreciate him. Well, it was lovely to see you both. I must be on my way home to the children. I will see you at meeting, Mr. Dike."

She sails on her way, and we continue along the boardwalk. It is apparent to me that my uncle has a very good standing among the citizens of Salem.

"Aunt Priscilla seems so sad of late," I say, beginning my own negotiations. "Would she not like some company? You are at the office most days and into the evenings. I believe Mary Wood's room is unoccupied, and I would be content to stay there without ever being in your way. I could assist with cooking and cleaning if necessary, keep John Stephens entertained, and read to you and Aunt Priscilla in the evenings. Now that Nath has come home, he needs his privacy to write, so there is little room for me on Herbert Street." I clasp my hands as if in prayer and raise my eyes to entreat him. "Oh, please say yes!"

His gaze shifts to the shore in thought, and I hope that he is wavering. If Nath has convinced Aunt Priscilla to allow me access, I might have a new dwelling by suppertime.

"I would enjoy your company very much," he says at last. "But we must ask your aunt. What about Nath? Will he not miss you?"

"He says he has much writing to do, and I irritate him with my need for conversation. He tolerates Ebe because as you know, she is a woman of few words." I smile and wink at him, and he answers with his usual crooked little grin.

"Then if your Aunt Priscilla agrees, it is settled," he says. "And I am certain that John Stephens will welcome you as well. Perhaps your presence will stave off his headache spells. We will send Bridget over to help you move your things."

We turn back toward the office. Mr. Dike has a lightness in his step that I had not noticed when first we left, and I feel the fluttering in my chest that I have come to recognize as my usual reaction to his kind and loving presence. A tiny serpent of guilt raises its ugly head, but I beat it back, telling myself that I need a fairy godfather but knowing in my heart that I am really on a quest for a handsome prince.

May 29, 1827

Aunt Priscilla knocks briskly upon my door to awaken me for a long-anticipated journey to the prosperous town of Newburyport. Mr. Dike must travel there to oversee the building of a clipper ship that he has commissioned, and as John Stephens is to accompany him, Mr. Dike thought I might enjoy the experience as well. Of course, I said yes as I seize any opportunity to be in his presence.

"Louisa. Do not be a trial to Mr. Dike." Aunt Priscilla's voice is strident as she brushes past me in the hall on her way into her office. "Remember, he is there on business, not to show you and your cousin the sights. You are nineteen now and able to entertain yourself. As for John Stephens," she sniffs and makes a little grimace of disgust, "even at twenty, he is still a child. Give a care for him as well."

"And would you not enjoy the trip, too, Aunty?" I truly hope that she says no, but it is only polite to ask.

"I have more important things to do here. Someone must keep an eye on the accounts." She sits down at the old crescent desk with the carved feet that remind me of griffin claws and rifles through a drawer, ignoring me and John Stephens, who has come to say farewell and turns away disappointed but not surprised at the snub.

Mr. Dike, John Stephens, and I escape into the bright sunshine and brackish sea air and walk to our uncles' Manning Stage Lines, where, as relatives of the owners, we are not required to pay our fares and may take the preferred window seats and watch the world go by. Mr. Dike is transfixed by his accounting books and pays us no mind, but John Stephens looks quite happy as he chats about his Uncle Nathaniel, Mr. Dike's brother, who has moved to Ohio to open a business.

"Uncle Nathaniel has written me about his grocer's store in Steuben-ville. His new wife, Aunt Anna, has the last name Woods. Isn't that odd that she should have such a similar name to Mary?" His eyes cloud for a moment with grief but then brighten at a new thought. "Mary Wood was named for Mama's family, just as my middle name is Gramma's maiden name. Would it not be funny if we were all related?" Without the stern presence of his stepmother, he is another person altogether, without even a hint of the headache spells that often plague him, and I decide that I could enjoy this chatty cousin to whom I have just been introduced.

Mr. Dike hands me down from the stage at the station in Newburyport, and we gaze about at another world, so similar and so different from our grimy city of Salem. Mr. Dike explains that the town was split in two so that one part could concentrate on seafaring and the other on husbandry. The smaller seafaring side concerns us today, but John Stephens and I vow to see all of it before we must travel back to Salem.

"You may see as much as you wish once business is concluded," agrees Mr. Dike, his voice affable but his brow creased with worry. I put my hand on his arm to take some of the burden away. He has been very worried of late because Uncle William's business acumen has been a disappointment to the family, but this new clipper, with its ties to Newburyport and the rum trade, may help to shore up the sagging accounts.

"Uncle Nathaniel has asked me to take note of a particular general store on the hill above the harbor," John Stephens informs us. Mr. Dike nods and, with an arm through mine, guides me towards the docks where his clipper awaits while his son heads in the opposite direction. Although I am enjoying my cousin, being alone with his father is really my ulterior motive on this trip, and my pulse quickens at his touch.

The dockyard reminds me of Salem, teeming with sailors and stevedores, but the ringing of hammers and the buzzing of saws are unfamiliar, and the novel scent of fresh sawdust mingles with the usual odor of brine. Mr. Dike gazes skyward at the enormous wooden skeleton of his new clipper, his eyes narrowed in appraisal, his hand gripping my arm a bit more firmly than would be necessary to assure my safety around all the strange men and tools. We are interrupted by a stout, tanned gentleman in salt-stained attire.

"Mr. Dike, welcome. And young lady, you have me at a disadvantage. I am Captain Chamberlain, but we have not yet been introduced."

Captain Chamberlain doffs his hat to me even as his eyes roam my fitted jacket. Mr. Dike draws me closer. "May I present my niece, Miss Louisa Hathorne. Miss Hathorne, Captain Chamberlain, who will be sailing my new clipper *The Hope* to the West Indies for molasses."

"Let us retreat from the noise of construction into my office," suggests Captain Chamberlain, and he guides us back up the dockyard to a small brick building reminiscent of Mr. Dike's shop in Salem. While the captain and Mr. Dike sort out their differences concerning the clipper, I sit watching the beehive of activity that is Newburyport harbor.

Business concluded, Mr. Chamberlain shakes Mr. Dike's hand and ushers us out the door to sightsee. We turn away from the harbor and down a tree-lined street and stroll past the handsome merchant houses illustrative of the very lucrative rum trade. He squeezes my arm affectionately as we commiserate on the dubious taste of some of the more garish decorations, and I decide that I must take advantage of this situation. I recognize in his warmth an answering need, and it gives me the confidence to pursue my desires.

"John," I begin. He starts and withdraws his hand from my arm. He shades his eyes, already in shadow from his hat brim, and stares at me until I blush and drop my gaze.

"Louisa." His voice is sober. "What must I make of this?"

"You and Mrs. Dike seem so unhappy," I begin lamely, not sure that I can voice my feelings now that I have brought them to bear.

"Indeed, but that is not your concern," he says, his voice a bit gruff in his confusion.

"But I feel that I can make you happy." My tears betray me and spill down my cheeks so that he is forced to fumble for his handkerchief and gently staunch them before I have a chance to explain myself. It is in this uncomfortable duet that John Stephens discovers us. He looks confused and embarrassed but also, oddly, happy to see us so enmeshed.

"Excuse the interruption," he says as John steps back and stuffs the handkerchief into his breast pocket. "Papa, you will want to see this supply business. They have so many different wares, displayed so invitingly. We really must report back to Uncle Nathaniel about some of the unusual devices."

"Of course. Perhaps you could bring us there now." John looks at me for confirmation, and I nod, but he refrains from taking my arm as we turn the corner toward the hill, and I hate that we are now at odds.

The general store is indeed elaborate and quite unusual, as there are fruits and vegetables displayed outside, with the accustomed bags of grains and spices stored in unique stackable metal bins within. Instead of the familiar odors of mold and rancid oil, the air is sweet with spices and fresh herbs. John Stephens takes a little notebook from his pocket and records the advice of the very gregarious store owner, and I know that Mr. Nathaniel will have more than enough information from his eager nephew.

This is just the cover I need to continue a subversive conversation, and I beckon to John to join me in an unpopulated aisle of mops and brooms.

"Why will you not consider my happiness if you will not consider your own?" My eyes threaten to well again, and I stiffen my back and hold my head up. At nineteen, I have reached my full height and can meet his eyes.

"Louisa, you know very well that this conversation is inappropriate and that what you are proposing is impossible. You must forget this infatuation and set your sights on one of the eligible suitors I know have come to your door." Even with this denial, his face is flushed, and encouraged by this subtle sign, I argue my point as I would with Ebe or Nath.

"Aunt Priscilla makes everyone unhappy. She is cruel to John Stephens and to me." John drops his eyes. "And to you." He nods, his face to the floor, his shoulders slumped. "What will you do with the rest of your days? Are you willing to be so miserable when life is such a short tenure?"

When he brings his head upright, his amber eyes are alight with a fire that I have not seen since the early days of his marriage. But again, we are interrupted.

"Papa, shall we bring a sample of these stacking metal bins for Uncle Nathaniel?" John Stephens blusters towards us through the maze of aisles, calling as he comes, and his father and I separate with no more said. But as John heads over to the counter to buy the bins, John Stephens catches my arm and pulls me around to face him. His expression is friendly, but his voice is sober.

"My father deserves some happiness. I would not be averse to him finding it elsewhere than in his marriage. But be careful. Danger lurks in the most mundane of settings." And with this warning, he turns and hurries down the aisle to join John at the counter.

The tour of the grocery store has lasted the afternoon, and so we must hurry to catch the evening stage. Conversation on the bumpy ride to Salem consists of discussions of wares and clipper ships, and we arrive home late for supper. Aunt Priscilla is annoyed and refuses to come downstairs to join us, and so we dine on Cook's leftovers and compare ideas for grocery displays until we all droop from exhaustion.

When I return to my room, I shrug off my jacket and contemplate John Stephens' comments and his father's reluctance. We all know that what I am proposing is antithetical to church, moral, and societal teachings, but Ebe and Nath have schooled me in the art of debate as well as in the more sophisticated ways of the world, and I know I can win John over if only he would recognize the dangers in his current situation. But aside from that, my once girlish crush has become a womanly desire, and I can only dare to dream that his princely passions will ultimately prevail.

April 9, 1829

On a rainy Monday, an errand boy delivers to me an alarming letter from my brother: *"Louze, I must speak with you concerning our cousin. Please come at once to Herbert Street.*
Your brother, Nath. Hathorne."

He is not specific about which cousin, and so I am left to speculate as I don my bonnet and cloak and make my way from Pickman Street, across the Common, to Herbert Street. My imagination runs away with my sensibility as I maneuver between puddles and horse manure.

Several of our female cousins have found themselves widowed early. Others, like Eleanor Carlisle, are in need of funds despite their marriages. Still more seem destined to choose the wrong suitor or have chosen wisely but have been unable to bear children. I wonder who the unfortunate cousin might be. My present single state seems a blessing.

I arrive at Herbert Street only a trifle mud-spattered but none the worse for wear. Nath greets me without a smile, pulls my cloak from my shoulders, and tosses it and my bonnet upon the table with no more ceremony than a stable hand in a barn, grasps my arm, and leads me upstairs to the Owl's Nest.

I wait for a lecture about some unfortunate cousin or other to commence, but instead, he aims his attack at me.

"Tell me any news you have concerning John Stephens." His eyes are a dark sapphire with concern, and I am immediately on alert.

"John Stephens? Why? Do you think something is amiss?"

Nath and John Stephens have become very companionable, especially so since Mary Wood died. Indeed, I would say that their friendship is the closest that Nath has enjoyed other than with his siblings. The two are often seen together at taverns and salons. John has remarked on several occasions of his gratitude that his son has found a peer to lean on in his grief since his sister's death, and therefore I am surprised that Nath seems so disturbed.

"Did you know that John Stephens intends to follow his uncle, Mr. Nathaniel Dike, to Ohio?" Nath paces about his small room as he interrogates me. He is too tall to stand straight in the dormers and alternately stoops and straightens from end to end.

"I had not heard, no." I wonder that John did not mention this tremendous change in his household, but perhaps he is not yet privy to the information.

"Apparently, Mr. Nathaniel has married and is offering John Stephens a place in his home and a position at the general store he now owns in Steubenville."

"I am not entirely surprised by this news. John has not said anything to me, but if I were John Stephens, I would perhaps be looking for a friendlier atmosphere than what he endures on Pickman Street. Aunt Priscilla seems determined to treat him as just another unwelcome mouth to feed. No matter that John Stephens is now an adult of twenty-one, he is made to feel like a naughty little boy. I must hold my tongue at dinner when she reprimands him for some tiny fault of manners. John tries to diffuse the situation, but it usually ends with John Stephens abruptly standing up from the table and retreating. At some point, I suspect he will simply eat from a tray in his room, just as our mother has done for all these years."

Nath's eyebrows have risen at my cavalier use of our uncle's Christian name, but the shock is not enough to disturb his train of thought.

"John Stephens has told me of some of this. He tried to make light of Aunt Priscilla's cruelties, but when she forced him to give away his dog, it was a final straw. His headache spells are worse than ever, though sometimes a visit to the tavern can avert them. I even suggested that he board here. We could swap cousins, as it were. But he has made his decision. A stage goes to Steubenville every week, and he plans to travel with only a day or so's notice to his family. He fears that Mr. Dike may try to dissuade him or will be so distraught at the idea of his only surviving child leaving that John Stephens will be forced to stay out of guilt."

I imagine John grieving at this latest loss, and I am grateful that I can be there to help him survive it. But a journey such as this is dangerous, and I am not naïve enough to think that my presence will be enough to assuage his father's worry. John will be unable to rest until he has received a letter proving his son's safe arrival.

"What do you plan to do? Will you advise John Stephens to keep to this scheme?"

"As his friend, it is my only choice. I cannot stand by and watch him slowly disintegrate in our aunt's venomous atmosphere. But I shall miss him. It has been a joy to have such a loyal friend and confidant."

"Ebe and I do not count in that assessment?" I know full well that our relationships are far too complicated to be so steadying, but I cannot help teasing him just a little.

Nath does not rise to the bait of my mockery, as the subject is too serious to be made light. "I value you both beyond measure, but John Stephens has fulfilled that boyhood dream of a close companion and compatriot, which sisterly affections cannot meet. Now I must put aside my own needs to help him escape an unhappy situation. Please aid him in any way that you can. Keep the secret, and then help his father when the deed is done."

"I shall. John and I have found a great affinity."

Nath raises an eyebrow again at this. I shrug my shoulders in defense and continue.

"Surely you and John Stephens have discussed my crush? It has only intensified, but Aunt Priscilla keeps one jealous eye on me even as she denigrates her stepson. But I was raised by her. I know she would do me no real harm. At least, I hope that is true." I chuckle, but Nath does not join in. He keeps his eyes fixed to the far wall as if to anchor himself and says, "Do not underestimate a woman who would be so cold-hearted as to allow her stepson to shoulder the burden of his own sister's death."

I am brought up short by this accusation. I seize his arm and force him to face me.

"What do you mean? Mary Wood died of pneumonia brought on by the wind."

Nath takes a deep breath. What he is about to say will prove to be a burden for us both.

"Aunt Priscilla pointed her finger at John Stephens, saying it was he who forced his sister into the weather. But John Stephens confided to me that it was Aunt Priscilla who sent them out simply because she was angry at Mary Wood. And then she told Mr. Dike that John Stephens was to blame."

This overwhelms me. I take breakfast every morning with this woman, listen as she prays with the Reverend Carlisle, sit and chat with her while she knits in the evenings. Despite her cold demeanor, I cannot fathom that she might wish anyone real harm, least of all the children with whose care she has been entrusted. And beyond that, the thought that she, so seemingly pious, would not admit her guilt in the situation seems ludicrous. I shake my head.

"John Stephens is exaggerating because of his own damaged feelings. I will not harbor these thoughts without proof."

"Louze, you have just described to me how cruelly she treats her stepson. Why do you defend her?" I blink at his voice, raised in anger and, perhaps, fear. Maybe I have been naïve regarding my aunt. And does John know about his wife's role in his daughter's death?

Nath continues, more calmly, "We shall see what happens when John Stephens escapes her wrath. I suspect that he will thrive. I understand that his uncle has married well and that his wife is looking forward to having a young man to mother. John Stephens will no doubt send me very detailed letters." Nath resumes pacing as if in concert with John Stephens' escape.

In my own defense, I say sarcastically, "While I anticipate with pleasure your description of John Stephens' happy times, I am not looking forward to helping John through his grieving process. Thank you for telling me this secret, and I shall feign surprise when John Stephens announces his departure."

"You are welcome," says Nath, equally dry. "And Louze," Nath stops his pacing, stands before me, lifts my chin with one finger, and fixes me with a grim eye. "Be careful in Aunt Priscilla's domain. If threatened, she may well strike, even at a once-beloved niece."

"I understand. Thank you for the warning." I attempt to change the subject to a happier note. "I wish you well with your scribbling. What are you writing these days?"

"Short stories, mostly, some of which I have sold to magazines, although I have saved several outlines in my notebooks for future novels. It is no mystery that my work lately has been centered on sin and moral hypocrisy."

I shrug my shoulders as it to discount his implication that I am the only Hathorne who might have sinned.

He aims an accusatory frown at me. "You are flirting not only with an uncle—I know, I know, he is not a blood relation—but with danger in the guise of his fanatical wife. I cannot give you my blessing on either account. Your foibles are inspiration for my literary efforts, but I do not wish to encourage you to foster my own persuasions. You must take care. If John Stephens is so frightened of our aunt that he must travel hundreds of miles to escape her, what of those he abandons at home?"

I nod. "I will take my chances, thank you." I lean in to plead my case. "John is the father I never knew, the best friend I never made, the lover I may finally embrace. If Priscilla were to know our true feelings, she might grant a divorce, especially with the aid of her reverend, and John and I would be free. Without Priscilla, we are just a man and a woman, related only by passion. And now I can use the truth about Mary Wood's death as ammunition should Priscilla not be persuaded. But I must wait until John's business takes a turn for the better so that he might buy Priscilla's acquiescence more easily."

Nath nods. "The economy has certainly taken a downward turn. Mr. Dike's demeanor has been circumspect of late. Uncle Robert and Uncle William discuss their business behind closed doors. I wish my stories could contribute more heartily to the family coffers. But at least I do not have to listen to your endless fashion commentary while I attempt to write. Yet strangely enough, every once in a while, I miss you."

He winks, walks me back down the stairs, helps me into my cloak, and hands me my bonnet to tie. We embrace, and then I am back on the wet road, my heart heavy at the thought of Priscilla's villainy, my cousin's misery, John's coming loss, and the timing of my next move.

Priscilla Manning Dike
10 Herbert Street
Salem, Massachusetts

May 20, 1830

My Dear Reverend Carlisle,

I am Job. My husband ignores me. My stepson has deserted me. My stepdaughter is dead. And yesterday, I lost at auction my magnificent house and all my beloved possessions. Every busybody in town whom I ever slighted was in attendance. And my husband's malpractice is to blame.

John came to me at last year's end, business ledger in hand. "Priscilla, have you noticed that our income has sunk into the negative numbers?"

I peered up at him, protected by the curve of my desk, now overloaded with John's neat paperwork and the detritus of William's endeavors. "Of course. I record the debts every Friday. One has only to look at the invoices and cheques to see that you are paying out more than you are receiving." I shuffled a few documents to give myself something on which to focus. I would not allow myself to be accused of mismanagement.

John continued his attack. "I am sorry to tell you that most of this is William's doing. Surely you have noticed that his schemes often end with us paying one off his so-called friends for a business arrangement which even a novice merchant would have recognized as shady."

I shook my head. "It is your fault for hiring Captain Felt. He turned back in last winter's hurricane, and that cost us dearly for all the undelivered merchandise."

"Would you rather that he and those goods were at the bottom of the sea? He chose the less dangerous option, and I am glad of it, as I am certain is his wife."

"Margaret Felt will take full advantage of our failure, of that you can be sure. Her husband would rather work for a successful man. You have too soft a heart. Now leave me be so that I can attend to the business at hand." I bent and surveyed the bottom drawer of files to avoid his worried eyes.

And indeed, it was John's soft heart that led us into this mess. He lost his original business after his wife died, and he fell into an exaggerated mourning. I attempted to toughen him when I took over the counting-house. But he was too kind. He worried about his captains, his crews, his brothers-in-law. His son moved away to live with the more successful uncle. His niece paid him too many compliments. So, I was forced to play the villain. I reminded him every day of his responsibilities, even as I counted our losses.

Ebe and Nath helped sort and pack my beloved household to ready it for the auction block. Nath took care in wrapping the wine goblets and then hid them away for his own use. Louisa and Ebe crated the books, which Ebe then commandeered. I doubt they would have brought much of a profit. However, I did not appreciate my nephew and nieces' pilfering.

John wrote the advertisement in the *Salem Gazette*: *The estate pleas-antly situated on Pickman Street in Salem, recently owned and occupied by Mr. John Dike, is offered for sale, fee of any encumbrances. It consists of a large three-story dwelling house, well built, with six rooms and two store closets on the first floor and nine chambers, finished throughout, and in most excellent order; good yards, and wood-houses, bathing room, etc. under cover; pump in the pantry, aqueducts in the kitchen and in the cellars, which are planked and perfectly dry—also, the land belonging to the same, being in front about 180 feet, extending back about 75 feet affording a garden at each end of the house, containing a variety of choice fruit trees.*

Those fruit trees, planted for us so many years ago by Robert, were the setting for the auctioneer's tent. His workers trampled my early flow-ering bulbs and tracked mud into the kitchen when they came in for their dinners. But it would no longer be my concern if the lawn were brown or the trees barren. Herbert Street had a garden which I planned to cultivate. I grieved mostly for the bathing room. I was not looking forward to sharing my sister's primitive accommodations.

The dreaded auction day arrived. Neighbors, cousins, acquaintances joined the jeering throng under the tent. I peered out at them from the kitchen window. I had no intention of thrusting myself into such an unwelcome and judgmental crowd, inviting taunts, or the supposed sup-port of my purported friends. But John stood stoutly by the auctioneer as each bedstead, each vase, each candle stick, were displayed for all of Salem to see.

I hid my face behind the curtains but sneaked a glance at the buyers. Margaret Felt acquired at a very good price my favorite Oriental rug. Other Salem cousins who once called me friend stole prized paintings, silver flatware, and crystal decanters. My heart ached with each object's loss. My impoverished soul cried out for mercy. The auctioneer showed none. Not a single chamber pot survived by day's end.

Later that week, John busied himself in the Boston courthouse. The lawyers and judges decided how much debt we would be obliged to pay. I feared that the monies we made from the auction would not be enough. And after our creditors were paid, we were indeed bankrupt.

"You have only yourself to blame for this," I said to John, my voice shrill with frustration and grief. "I am grateful that our parents are dead and cannot see our humiliation." He hunched his shoulders against my attack but launched his own.

"William must be better schooled in the ways of business. And please do not speak of my parents in such a caustic tone. They were nothing but supportive of any of my endeavors. I am grateful that John Stephens is in Steubenville. Perhaps he will learn from my brother how to survive in business despite the 'aid' of one's relatives."

John and I moved our clothes and a few remaining family heirlooms into one side of the Herbert Street house. After much negotiation, Bridget agreed to accompany us. She and Hannah would split the chores and the kitchen. Bridget would delay her fees but eat her meals with Hannah.

Betsey, Louisa, and William share the other side. We will probably see them rarely, except for Louisa. I vow to keep a sharp eye on my niece. She has an unwelcome affinity for my husband's company.

Reverend Carlisle, I am well aware of our reciprocal arrangement. You hear my confession. In exchange for your forgiveness, I donate to whatever cause you deem worthy. It is my hope that we might delay the donations for a month or so, just until John raises a few funds with his newest partners on the docks. I appreciate your understanding.

Your Daughter in Christ,

PMD

John Dike
4 Andover Street
Salem, Massachusetts

(September 7, 1871)

The shame I felt when my business failed in 1830 was overwhelming. To lose one's business is to lose one's identity. Accustomed as I was to being introduced as "Mr. Dike, an esteemed leader of our merchant community," it was torturous to be ostracized by that same group. And yet, I understood. Failure has an odor, a slime trail. Success avoids contact, lest it rub off.

Margaret Felt, for instance, crossed the road rather than be forced to speak with me. Her husband signed on with one of our competitors, and I wished him well. But she refused to acknowledge that other establishments were not as concerned for their employees' well-being as was I.

Nath, on the other hand, made a great point of doffing his hat to me in front of the courthouse. *"Mr. Dike, you look positively younger than ever!"* he said. I doubt he truly believed it.

"Have you had any news from John Stephens?" I was too embarrassed by my failure to write to my son, as he would surely tell my brother.

"I wrote to him of your troubles but said that you were handling the changes with aplomb. I am sure he will respond soon." Nath plopped his hat back onto his head and went on his way, leaving his old uncle to the torture of bankruptcy.

Several Salem social organizations to which I still held memberships sent representatives to gently dissuade me from attending their meetings until my status in the merchandizing community had changed. A young man with a failed business has nowhere to go but up. An old man must watch his reputation plummet along with his bank account.

My wife would not permit me to forget my failings. "Had I known you to have a soft heart and a softer head, I would have turned you out on your ear when you came to dinner all those years ago. I would sooner have been a spinster than a laughing stock."

Reverend Carlisle came to call at Herbert Street after our move, ostensibly to offer assistance, but really, I suspect, to gauge our predicament. He and Priscilla disappeared into the closet that now served as an office, and their raised voices indicated that perhaps whatever arrangement they had made early in their relationship was no longer appropriate. The donations to Reverend Carlisle that liberally sprinkled the accounting books put an additional strain on our already sinking ship. If that ship sank altogether, the reverend would have to set sail upon another sinful soul.

Eventually, Priscilla opened the office door and ushered an even more unctuous than usual reverend toward the foyer. "Please do not hesitate to call upon me if you need compassion," he said to her, his short-sighted eyes soft behind his spectacles. On his black-clad pigeon chest sparkled a gold cross that I believe had once belonged to Miriam Manning.

My wife reached out a gentle hand and carefully turned the cross over to reveal the crucified Christ, then laid that hand briefly on the reverend's bosom before withdrawing. He bowed his way out. Priscilla would have her redemption at whatever the cost.

"If that is a man of God, then I am the king of England," I said.

"Suit yourself," said Priscilla with a haughty toss of her head. "He gives me comfort in my times of need. Surely you would not begrudge me some small happiness." Her cold eyes met mine briefly before she retreated to the parlor to knit.

My strength lived only in Louisa. She met me at the door when I dragged myself home dejected from court, handed me a hot cup of tea, and told me a silly story about the cat to cheer me. She stoked the fire and sat by my side while I described the indignation I was forced to suffer at each judge's or creditor's office. She knew when to surround me with a supportive silence. Her years with an unhappy mother and a needy brother had schooled her in the healing arts.

Admittedly I knew there was more to her interest than that of a devoted niece, and I was ashamed to encourage it. Yet I felt crushed, and her warmth, her laughter, her kind touch, brought me slowly out of my melancholy until I could see my way clear to start again. We might be living here on Herbert Street for the foreseeable future, but I had pulled myself out of quagmires before.

This time I was dealing not with a widower's grief but merely the foibles of an unfortunate business partner. If William's instincts could be sharpened, then perhaps the Dike and Manning venture would rise again, phoenix-like, from the ashes.

October 1, 1831

Glimpsed from a distance, it would seem a tranquil domestic scene: A silver tea service gleams on a table before a fire blazing in the grate, while Aunt Priscilla, in white cap and dark gown, sits in her favorite high-backed chair, knits, and listens to silver-haired Mr. Dike read a letter from his loving son John Stephens. He speaks with animation and great feeling, and she nods and smiles.

But upon closer examination, the fire burns in a simple sitting room, not a sumptuous parlor, Aunt Priscilla's knitting needles clack in annoyance, not contentment, she nods with impatience, not pleasure, and grimaces rather than smiles at some little joke in the text. John holds the letter with hands trembling in anxiety and frustration, and I embroider a handkerchief and enjoy the newsy letter but shrink from the tension that fogs the air.

"*My Dear Papa*," reads Mr. Dike, his voice deep with feeling. "*I am writing to you in my newly appointed role as happy husband. My bride Margaretta and I were married yesterday at the Steubenville home of Uncle Nathaniel and Aunt Anna. As you may remember, Margaretta and Anna are sisters, so she is not only my bride but my aunt.*"

"It sounds vaguely incestuous," says prudish Aunt Priscilla, pulling at a strand of yarn from the skein in her basket near her chair. Her needles clack with indignation.

"*I have enjoyed being a guest in their well-appointed home here in Ohio, but Uncle Nathaniel and Aunt Anna have plans to buy us a modest nest nearby. Uncle Nathaniel's general store continues to be successful, and he has offered me a partnership, which I believe I will accept. His associates all call him "doctor," as he cures them with his business acumen. Margaretta and I look forward to a family of our own, and I hope to learn from your brother how to assure them a comfortable future.*

I am disappointed that you could not be here to see me wed, but I under-stand that an arduous ten-day stage journey could not be undertaken at this time. There is talk of train service to our area, but Uncle Nathaniel does not expect it for several more years. Perhaps you and Mrs. Dike will be able to join us then." John looks up at Aunt Priscilla, hope for her acquiescence shining in his eyes.

Aunt Priscilla glares back at him. "It would seem that I married the wrong brother. *Doctor* Dike must be doing rather well to host a wedding and then to buy the happy couple a house. His wife was not forced to bivouac on one side of her family home because her husband's businesses failed." She gathers her knitting into her basket and stands. "I have heard enough, John. I do not have time to entertain fantasies about train trips and weddings. The day has been long and tiring. Please do not wake me when you come to bed." She starts out of the room but stops at the threshold and turns to me.

"Louisa, I expect that you will wish to retire as well. Good night."

We listen to her heavy steps retreating down the hall and climbing the stairs to her bedroom, and both of us exhale in a release of tension when we hear the door close. I stand and move to the stool at his feet.

"Please read more, John, if you don't mind. I miss John Stephens and am glad to hear of his newfound happiness."

I settle my skirts around the little stool, lean against his thigh, and gaze up at him with rapt attention. While it is true that I wish to hear more about John Stephens, my ulterior motive is to be close to his father.

Living in the same house with John has been both a dream and a nightmare. John has told me that he suspected my fond emotions when first I went to live with them but insisted on treating me as he would any beloved niece. However, chinks developed in his armor when I made less subtle overtures, and then his business failed, and he and Aunt Priscilla were forced to sell their lovely house on Pickman Street. I returned to my family's home, and soon John and Aunt Priscilla came to live on Herbert Street as well. The embarrassment of failure and Aunt Priscilla's cruel criticism added to the grief over his daughter's death and the longing for his son, lowered his guard, and our mutual affections have blossomed into something more.

But Aunt Priscilla suspects my true nature and keeps a sharp eye upon me even as she allows me limited contact with her husband. She retained their maid Bridget and the rest of their staff, so she and John are independent of my mother, Nath, and myself. Ebe still resides in Beverly, and my mother continues her reclusive ways, so as our affair developed, I learned to be serene in any public appearances but stealthy in my secret movements about the house so as to quell Aunt Priscilla's suspicions.

John continues to read, "*The wedding was held in the garden, with a flutist and violinist to play us up and down the lawn. Several of the elder Dikes' friends braved the trip, including widow Mrs. Florinda Cust Blair from Pittsburgh and her young son Tom. He and my little niece Virginia made a pretty pair. Apparently, the two families had been close before Mr. Blair died, and Florinda and Tom relocated to Pittsburgh. Everyone teased that the children would be the next couple to wed, although they are but three and six years of age. Florinda seemed amused that we held the wedding ceremony out of doors, as she and her husband were married by the famous Bishop White in a grand cathedral in Pittsburgh, but I believe our simple wedding was exactly what the doctor ordered if you understand my meaning. Margaretta sends her regards, and I look forward to the day I can introduce the two of you in propria persona. Until then, Dear Papa, I remain your loving son, John Stephens.*"

John folds the letter with tender care, tucks it into his waistcoat pocket, removes his spectacles, and wipes his eyes. "Do you suppose we will ever see him again?" His eyes are red, and it is not just from the rubbing. When Mary Wood died, he paid all his attentions to his son and grieves now that John Stephens is so far away in Ohio. I pat his knee in sympathy.

"Perhaps, as he says, there will be train service there, and we can visit him, but meanwhile, you have Nath and me to spoil." He strokes my hair, and my heart quickens, but when I reach up to clasp his hand, he withdraws it and stands to feed the fire, then leans on the mantel, his back to me.

"Louisa." His voice is hoarse with controlled emotion. "I invited you to stay in our former house to keep my wife and son company and to aid your brother's writing endeavors. Now your family has repaid that kindness by allowing Mrs. Dike and me to reside in a portion of your home. She is unhappy with my business failure and with her childless fate, and I am lonely, but it has never been my intention to seduce you." His head is bowed with the weight of guilt as he utters this.

His pain is too much for me to bear, and I stand, go to him, and caress his shoulder, not as a niece, not as a friend, but as a lover. His back stiffens beneath my touch and then relaxes, and he turns to me and takes my hands in both of his.

We have stolen kisses, fumbled embraces in similar private moments before, but both of us are hungry for more. I answer him with a passion born of loss and forged in deprivation.

"John, I have loved you from that very first moment that you appeared on my family's doorstep. There is nothing you could do or say that would change my heart. I know I cannot confess this without bearing some guilt, for your wife is my aunt." We both drop our gaze at this complication, yet my feelings will not be so easily subverted. I search his eyes again and continue, "But you are my fairy godfather, my knight in shining armor, my charming prince, and I adore you."

He pulls me close. His kiss is urgent but sweet, his hands strong circling my waist, and I melt into this unexpected pleasure till I feel his mood shift, and we reluctantly break apart.

His voice is gruff with frustration as he admits, "And I am desperate for you. But I am torn between that desire and my obeyance to my marriage vows."

"But your wife does not deserve such unbridled respect." I sound more strident than I intend, and I realize, too late, that I have inadvertently crossed the line from lover to prosecutor, and I curse my siblings for my schooling in didactics.

He startles and gives me a quizzical look. I sigh but continue, as it is now too late to relent, despite the unfortunate timing.

"Have you not wondered why John Stephens traveled so far from you, joining in his uncle's business instead of his father's? Are you not aware of a certain coldness between your son and your wife?" John stares at me, daring me to name a serpent coiled just beneath the surface of his marriage.

I explain, "John Stephens confessed to Nath that it was Priscilla, not he, who forced Mary Wood to take that fateful walk into town. It was Priscilla who wanted the day to herself and cared not that her fragile stepdaughter might take a chill. When she allowed John Stephens to take the blame, when she refused to name her own responsibility for her selfish desires, he made a promise to himself that he would find another motherly soul in whom he could trust. I suspect that person was Anna Woods. Is it any wonder that he has married her sister?"

A play of shadows crosses John's face, his eyes well, and then his mouth works into a grim line of fortitude. I feel the last barrier between us crumble, and he again takes me into his arms, and our hearts beat together for only a few seconds before we hear Bridget in the hall, and we must separate. He turns to the fire and adds another log, and I busy myself with the tea service. Bridget draws the drapes and dims the lamps. If she is aware of our discomfort, she does not show it but bobs a curtsey and departs to her bed.

John turns to me, his amber eyes glittering with desire, and I am seized with a sudden inspiration. I motion for him to follow, pluck one of Aunt Priscilla's myriad knitted shawls from a chair, and we tiptoe down the hall, turn the front door latch quietly so as not to wake the house, and escape into a cool early autumn evening, the moon just coming full, the scent of brine lifted on the sea breeze. John drapes the shawl about my shoulders and pulls me to his side to warm me, and we walk with brisk steps toward the beach. It is but a short distance to the shore where we can see for a mile in either direction whether we are alone.

"John." I lean into him and pull the shawl closer against the gritty breeze. "I think our carriage has reverted to a pumpkin. Perhaps this is not the best venue for our first tryst."

He raises one wry eyebrow and says, "Well, given the choices, it will have to make do. Is that shawl available?" He pulls me down onto the sand and drapes the shawl over us so that our privacy is complete.

The shawl becomes our bower, the beach our bed, and the randy waves our romantic ballad. All my senses are on fire, and I open like a flower to his touch. I am grateful for his first wife's tutelage, for soon I am gasping in pleasure, and with his gentle but ardent encouragement, we end the evening in mutual satisfaction.

Sleep is impossible, and in the glimmer of dawn, I arrange my garments and search for a missing boot while I plan our reentry into reality after our night of enchantment. A prophylactic herbal remedy that I had secretly researched is heavy on my mind even as I endeavor to construct a cover tale.

"I must hurry home and drink a secret elixir." I wink at him, and he blushes and nods, aware suddenly of the possible real consequences of our magical evening.

I continue, "But the servants will be about making breakfast, and Aunt Priscilla rises early to pray. I shall go in and say that I was out for a walk. And you," I cup his dear face in my hand, "have been at the shop all night." I kiss him deeply, gather up the shawl, recover the boot, and steal off towards Herbert Street, brushing the sand from my skirts and wishing I could preserve this night in amber.

My heart is light, my steps quick, but as I turn the corner onto the boardwalk, I glance back at the silhouette of my beloved, bowed perhaps in prayer, perhaps in sorrow, or perhaps in guilt, dark against the glow of the horizon.

Pittsburgh, or the Smoky City, loomed hazily through the railcar window. Huge smokestacks belched blasts of ash, speckling the city's red brick buildings black and gray. I imagined sweating workmen shoveling coal into the bellies of the steel mills' boilers, then heating and beating that glowing steel into the shining rails upon which we rode.

Despite the fear of more spells and headaches, I had continued to read some of Ebe's documents. Louisa's diary entries were often warm and funny, and while I was grateful for the concern which both she and Nath expressed for me, her descriptions of the adulterous affair with my own father made me squirm. I was, of course, cognizant of their desires at the time and tacitly approved, but reading the details was overwhelming, and my mood was often disquieted after a session with her writings. And I could stomach only small portions at a time of Priscilla's disgustingly smarmy letters to her reverend, so Margaretta had taken to prereading them while I was at work and then showing me certain passages. We were both on the alert for revelations, but so far, there were only suspicions, complaints, and gossip.

This trip to Pittsburgh was a welcome respite from the inheritance, and due to serendipitous timing, it promised the added reward of witnessing our niece Virginia being honored for her voluminous charity work, as a new city hospital owed much of its funding to her efforts.

Margaretta could not keep the excitement from her voice as she leaned forward in her seat to sight-see, her nose almost pressed against the railcar window. "Virginia says Pittsburgh stores receive the Paris couture a whole year ahead of the Emporium. I feel like such an ugly duckling." She tugged her suddenly dowdy jacket over her pigeon-breasted corset and arranged her horsehair bustle behind her, and I thought, not for the first time, that women's clothing was not made for comfort. Even someone Margaretta's age must keep up appearances, to the detriment of her health.

"I shall think of you with envy as you tour Virginia's charity ward. Maybe afterward you could convince her to take you to one of those couture houses to order a gown and perhaps purchase a new accessory for tonight's event since the Emporium has disappointed you so." Although I attempted to disguise the anxiety in my own voice with a bit of humor, I could not fool my wife, who immediately abandoned her fashion fantasies to cluck over me.

"John Stephens, you have nothing to worry about. The neurologist you are seeing today is highly recommended by all the physicians with whom Virginia works. I should think you will be in good hands." She patted my arm and then leaned again to the window, dreaming of a worthwhile day of philanthropy rewarded by a shopping spree, leaving me to my dour thoughts of lunatic asylums and blood-letting. When at last we rolled into the Pittsburgh Station, I settled my vest over my paunch, donned my bowler, handed Margaretta onto the platform, and prepared myself for adventures unknown.

Virginia, whom I would always think of as my baby niece, was, in reality, an elegant, intelligent woman in her fifties. She met us at the railway station entrance, dressed stylishly in a tailored day skirt and jacket, her gray-blonde hair perfectly coiffed under the feathered hat perched rakishly above her graceful neck. As the wife of a prestigious Pittsburgh attorney as well as a board member of a prominent city charity, she knew how to navigate the different areas of Pittsburgh and gathered her wide-eyed cygnets for the carriage ride to the east end neighborhood where the doctor had his practice.

The driver fought his way through the downtown's congested streets and byways, competing with food carts, delivery wagons, hansom cabs, and pedestrians distracted by the soft asphalt and horse manure underfoot. In advance of the installation of copper telephone wires, tall wooden poles, like denuded trees, lined the streets of apartment buildings and shops. The scent of bubbling tomato sauce with a subtle undertone of sewer perfumed the air. But hanging laundry and Italian restaurants gradually gave way to German signage and finally to English as we reached the east side and our destination in one of the imposing three-story brick buildings lining Forbes Avenue.

"All will be well, John Stephens. I do look forward to hearing about it." Margaretta squeezed both my hands and bobbed a kiss, and with the driver's help, I descended onto the pavement, climbed the building's narrow stone steps, and rang the bell, wondering if my head would be as tightly secured in two hours' time as it appeared to be at present.

A nurse in a crisp blue dress, white apron, and cap ushered me through a cavernous vestibule, down a narrow marble-floored hallway into the doctor's office, and seated me in a chair across from an imposing desk behind which sat a wiry man in a vested herringbone suit. She introduced us and left me to my fate.

"Welcome. Mr. Dike. Please, tell me about your headaches," began Dr. Edmund Voight. Between my hearing loss and his Germanic accent, I had to cup my ear to understand him. He sat with his elbows balanced on the desk, the slender fingers of each hand lightly touching the other's, and peered at me over their steeple, his thick spectacles magnifying ice blue eyes. Diplomas from Leipzig University and other German institutions decorated the office walls. A plaster head, as bald as the doctor's own but with strange symbols marking the skull, overlooked the mantle, and a syringe and basin sat at the ready on a side table. The fire burned brightly in the grate, but still, I squirmed in my armchair, chilled at the clinical atmosphere, used as I was to doctors visiting my home, and not vice versa.

"My spells, as I call them, started when I was very young. They come on when I have been given unfortunate news or when I am otherwise agitated. Sometimes there is a smell or a sensation that provokes them. There is a loud bang, like a clap of thunder, in my head. Often, I feel nauseated. Sometimes I vomit. I feel faint and must lower my head. My hands clench. Visions come mostly from my childhood, and I am overcome with a feeling of dread. It all lasts about fifteen minutes, and then I start to come around. I am often left with a terrible left-sided headache. If I am able, I lie down in a darkened room with a cold compress over my eyes. However, I do not always have that luxury." I stopped, surprised at how easily I was able to describe my symptoms. Somehow, I had not noticed that the spells all started and ended much the same way. Perhaps they were more medically oriented than emotional, and I was not, as I had feared, simply going mad.

"Fevers, chills, sweats?" Dr. Voight recorded my answers on a sheet of paper, then stood, came to my side, removed his pocket watch from his vest, and counted my pulse. His hand was cool and dry, but not cold, and I felt strangely at ease.

"When was your last 'spell'?" He returned to his desk to record my answer.

"Two weeks ago. That is when Thomas Blair gave me your name. I was overcome by a particular odor, and he was concerned."

"Yes, so his wife told me. She also said that you had been drinking. Do you often imbibe?" His pen was poised to record this answer as well, but he did not look up.

"No. We had met for luncheon and discussed some difficult . . . issues. I felt the need for extra sustenance."

"Mr. Dike." Dr. Voight sat back in his chair and regarded me with those icy eyes. "I cannot help you if you withhold information. I suspect your problem is medically based, complicated by your emotions, but you will have to be honest about both. Do you understand?"

I nodded, my tail between my legs, and he continued his exam. He listened with his stethoscope to my chest; peered into my eyes with a magnifying lens; checked my ears with the same lens; looked in my mouth and noted the diminished number of teeth; counted the pulses in my feet. He then asked me to stick out my tongue; stand on one foot and then the other with my eyes open and then shut, the latter of which I found to be very difficult; touch my finger to my nose multiple times, which made me laugh despite the circumstances; sniff and identify several noxious odors, which made me gag; read letters from a chart on the wall; and finally walk up and down the corridor outside his office, on my toes and then my heels, which particularly bothered my knees.

He recorded the results of each test and finally laid down his pen and steepled his fingers again. "Mr. Dike, your exam is almost entirely normal for an elderly man. Your eyes show some changes which might point towards a certain diagnosis and for which there are some very effective therapies. But I could not know for certain unless I witnessed one of your spells myself." He smiled slightly at that possibility and then continued, "Are you willing to continue treatment?"

"Of course."

"Excellent. We will also be discussing your emotional turmoil. Patients who talk about their problems seem to heal more quickly. Shall we say next week?" His pen hovered over his appointment book, and when I did not immediately reply, he assured me, "Mr. Dike, although I am a proponent of psycho-therapeia, I heal the body as well as the mind. Please trust that I can help you."

I nodded, accepted the business card upon which he had written the date and time of our next appointment, and waited in the vestibule for the carriage ride through the various neighborhoods of Pittsburgh to Virginia's palatial home on Shadyside Avenue.

"What did the doctor have to say?" Margaretta and I were given privacy to dress in the east wing of the house while Virginia and Tom readied themselves for the evening's event in their own apartments. Margaretta, in her old lavender satin and lace gown, looped a new string of pearls about her plump neck as she listened to my recounting of what had been a difficult afternoon.

"He thought I was in very good health for an elderly man. But he wishes to see me again next week. I suspect that session to be more revealing. But perhaps after several appointments, I shall be strong enough to examine all the documents and the contents of the attic."

"Very well, but now I think it is time for you to put on your evening wear. We do not wish to be known as Virginia's poor relations." Margaretta helped me out of my day jacket and into the bath, and all thoughts of my inheritance were replaced with preening for the evening's festivities.

(September 12, 1871)

The new Dike-Manning venture took longer to succeed than anticipated, and Priscilla and I remained in the Herbert Street house until 1832. Although very much aware that Louisa had developed a crush on me over her young life, I was unprepared for an equally romantic impulse on my own part when she reached maturity. I endeavored to quell my feelings, but her proximity and her clumsy attempts at seduction made her difficult to ignore. When my wife's already frosty demeanor chilled to zero at my business failure, Louisa stepped in to warm me. Finally, her revelations of Priscilla's complicity in Mary Wood's death and John Stephens' subsequent defection allowed me to accept and act upon my desires.

When at last we consummated our love, Louisa's cerebral attitude seemed at first to moderate her passion. Admittedly, I was out of practice because of the coldness in my second marriage, yet I felt melancholic gratitude to Mercy for her teachings on the ways to pleasure a woman. Apparently, I remembered enough to satisfy Louisa, for she blossomed beneath my caresses, and we ended the evening equally sated.

But at daybreak, Louisa left me. I watched her scamper along the beach toward home, so youthful, so carefree, yet responsible enough to consider the possible consequences, while my own black heart filled with remorse even as my body reveled in that contented exhaustion that only a passionate embrace can bring.

I brushed the sand from my clothing and hurried to Herbert Street. My fury at my wife and her role in my daughter's death and my son's flight fueled my resolve to accept Louisa's affection, but first, I must confront Priscilla about her egregious behavior toward my beloved children.

She was just returned from sunrise services. The ever-solicitous Reverend Carlisle had escorted her and now stood smiling obsequiously in our sitting room, awaiting his weekly donation.

"Thank you for your chivalry, but Mrs. Dike and I must speak privately," I said and pressed a dollar into his waiting hand. Priscilla moved to block the door.

"Whatever you must say to me, you may say in front of my cousin. We have no secrets," she said and directed a sly smile to him.

I wondered at the extent of Reverend Carlisle's knowledge.

"Very well," I agreed. "Since you are a member of Mrs. Dike's family, I cannot deny you access. In fact, we may need your advice concerning the fate of our marriage." Priscilla dropped her gaze, moved to a chair, and reached automatically for her knitting.

I sat across from Priscilla and attempted to catch her eye. "Nath has been corresponding with John Stephens." She kept her head down and counted stitches, apparently unconcerned at this starting volley. I continued my attack.

"What exactly did you say to my daughter on that unseasonable December day to send her out into the warm wind? And in what manner had you been treating my children? It appears that John Stephens chose to leave his home and seek solace elsewhere rather than to suffer your cruelty."

Priscilla's eyes stayed on her knitting, but her hands trembled as she changed needles.

"I do not know what you are talking about. John Stephens insisted on taking his sister out into the warm weather. As for my mothering, I always treated your children as I would my own." She finally met my gaze. "And where were *you* last night?"

I felt my face flush. "Please do not attempt to change the subject. Are you willing to swear to me that you did not mistreat my children? John Stephens told Nath otherwise."

"Oh, Nath. Always one to exaggerate. What would he know of mothering? Betsey barely took notice of her children. Now, if you are finished with your accusations, I must return to the counting-house. We are slowly paying up our deepest debts, no small thanks to my nimble figuring." She stowed her knitting, rose to stand over me, and delivered an answering accusation.

"Know that I am aware of Louisa's habits. And I can tell by the ledgers when you have been comporting business. We are neither of us without sin." Her hazel eyes glittered emerald-cold in the morning sunlight.

I had nothing left to lose. I stood to meet her head-on. "Then you should be willing to grant me a divorce. I am loath to live with the abuser of my children. You are unhappy with my business circumstances, and our marriage bed has grown cold. You would no longer be the heir to my future fortunes, but you would be free."

Greed darkened her eyes again. The fear of losing her husband's income would prove more compelling than freedom from his disloyalty. She lifted her chin in defiance and replied, "You cannot confirm child abuse when that child is dead. But I could accuse you of adultery, and all of Salem would know of your disgusting dalliances with your own niece."

"A niece by marriage only," I snapped, weary of this argument.

Reverend Carlisle sensed a dangerous turn in the conversation and stepped between us. He retrieved a lacy handkerchief from his breast pocket and wiped the sheen of perspiration from his upper lip while he cleared his throat to intervene. Most likely, the prospect of losing his weekly donations gave him the strength to speak.

"The Tabernacle looks very unfavorably upon adultery. A divorce trial would advertise your indiscretions, and your reputations would be ruined. I must advise you to stay together, if for no other reason than to combine your complementary business acumens. Perhaps you would both prefer to confess to me your sins privately in my office? I am there every evening."

"Thank you, cousin," said Priscilla. She stepped toward the door and gathered her bonnet and cloak. "I shall walk you back to church before I go to the counting-house." Without another glance at me, she left the house arm in arm with her cousin and conspirator.

He would never again see me in his congregation. Greed was his god, but though I valued my business, my soul cried more for redemption. I grieved my children's wounds and my failure as a father to protect them.

For my wife was correct. Except for John Stephen's admissions to Nath, I had no proof that Priscilla had wronged Mary Wood. John

Stephens answered my subsequent letters asking for confirmation of his sister's fate with obfuscation. Perhaps he did not wish me to feel responsible, but more likely, he harbored resentment that I had not protected him and his sister from their stepmother's wrath. Indeed, I did not deserve his, or God's, forgiveness.

And yet, I might be saved. Considerable religious excitement pervaded Salem in 1831, owing to the great number of revival conversions held by the Calvinists, Baptists, and Methodists. The Dikes had always been devout. My dear deceased father served as a deacon in his church. My older sister married a minister. If I attended one of these revivals, were converted, and repented my transgressions against my children, perhaps I could be forgiven by my God, my daughter, and my son.

"I shall prostrate myself in the revival tent, repent my sins, and go to the marvelous light," I told Priscilla, quoting the phrases cited on every leaflet posted through town. "If you will not grant me a divorce, I shall wash myself clean of our combined sins."

She folded her arms. "I refuse to take responsibility for sins for which I bear no guilt. Besides, the Reverend Carlisle is my confessor. I have no need of another." Her defiant green eyes met mine. "Perhaps the preacher will wash you clean of adulterous thoughts, as well."

⌒⌒⌒

"Renounce your sins! Come up and accept the light of God!"

A stalwart, bald acolyte in white robes, led me by the sleeve toward the platform in the center of the tent. Other pilgrims struggled up the aisles on either side of us. We were sinners all, marching towards Bethlehem to be saved.

"Come to the marvelous light! God knows your sins, and he loves you still. Allow Jesus into your soul. Let Jesus be your personal savior!" The preacher's voice reverberated off the tent walls, his face streaming sweat, his eyes gleaming rapture, his pure righteousness washing over me until I wanted nothing more than to be saved.

I trembled with so many sentiments that I felt nearly overwhelmed. The biggest emotion, of course, was guilt, for how could I have allowed my children to suffer? I must repent so that I might look my daughter in the eye when at last we met in Heaven.

"Please bring me to Jesus!" I pleaded, on my knees before my God and my daughter.

Pastor Michael took my head in both his beefy hands and looked deep into my soul with eyes so bloodshot that a tiny part of me wondered why Jesus had not yet cured him of obvious sin. He saw me lose focus and brought me back to attention by bending me backward, clamping my nose, and dunking my head in a horse trough. The water filled my eyes, my ears, my throat. I was drowning, drifting, floating toward a warm, glistening, golden sun.

Through the shimmering haze, a voice called, "Jesus loves you! Renounce your demons and come home!"

The pastor pulled me upright. Water coursed down my body, and I felt cleansed, healed, sanctified. I leaned back, coughing and howling, "Thank you, Jesus! I have seen the marvelous light! I am whole again!"

The acolyte helped me to stand, and, with his arm around my shoulders, I limped back down the aisle to the waiting crowd, some of whom clapped me on the back and congratulated me now that I had seen the light, renounced Satan, and accepted Jesus, amen.

My helpmate pushed me down into a chair in the back of the tent, wiped my face with a handkerchief, and fetched a ladle of water to refresh me.

"Are you well enough to stand, sir?" The acolyte peered into my eyes. "And do you realize that you are newly baptized?"

I did. And I felt a peace that I had not experienced since before my daughter's death. God had washed me clean of my sins, Mary Wood would forgive me my inadequacies, and I might still win the absolution of my son, in Jesus's name, amen.

Disciples continued to aid initiates in their journey to the platform, but my session was over. The acolyte helped me to the tent flap. But as we moved along the periphery, a beloved face in the crowd gazed back at me with worried eyes. Louisa. I turned away and focused on my newly baptized soul.

My memory does not serve me well enough to know how I traveled home or who put me to bed. Upon awakening, my head felt light, as though I had imbibed too much alcohol. But I was gratified to realize that the reason was redemption. I was saved, my sins washed away. From this day forward, I would endeavor to be the father my son deserved, in Jesus's name, amen.

In the coming weeks, I walked around Salem in a daze. Nath greeted me on the street with his usual smile and tip of the hat, but all I could muster was a brief nod. "Why so serious, Mr. Dike?" His brow crinkled in concern. "Are you and Mrs. Dike well?"

"We are fine," I assured him, although I knew that this was not true. Priscilla and I lived an uneasy truce, and as the glow from my conversion faded, I focused instead on her guilt. A baptism could not replace my darling Mary Wood, nor my trust in my wife.

And in trying for a redemptive life, I had relinquished Louisa. By the defeated slump of her shoulders when we passed in the hallway and by her refusal to meet my eyes, I knew she mourned the loss of our relationship and yet respected my intentions to cleanse my soul. Instead of seeking me out, she avoided my side of Herbert Street and my Derby Street office and instead spent time with Nath.

Although Betsey refused visitors, Nath and Louisa welcomed them, and the Hathorne parlor often rang with laughter and conviviality. Priscilla and I were given cursory invitations to these gatherings, but Priscilla declined for both of us. Instead, I relied on Bridget's tendency to gossip.

"A Miss Mary Silsbee called last night to play Whist with Mr. Nathaniel and Miss Louisa," Bridge informed us as she served breakfast one morning.

Priscilla stirred her tea a bit too violently, and some slopped over the rim and into the saucer. "That Silsbee girl is hoping for a proposal. I have heard that she has been paying her attentions on Nath at those ridiculous gatherings at Susan Burley's." I raised an inquiring eyebrow. "Oh, you know, those 'Hurley-Burleys,' as she insists on calling them. They are simply gossip-fests disguised as political salons. But I wonder that Mary is not embarrassed to be so obvious in her intentions. And why he should be such bait is beyond me. The boy doesn't even have employment. All those silly stories he is writing have come to nothing, as I always said they would." She stood, patted crumbs from her mouth, and threw down her napkin. "Bridget, I wish to go to the counting-house soon. Please call the carriage."

I was also informed by a couple of the sailors in my employ that Nath frequented some of the taverns thereabouts and that my niece quite often walked out to the shore at night. It took much effort to remember that I was a man of God now and that my energies must be saved for prayer, not for adulterous longings, in Jesus's name, amen.

Nine months passed. Priscilla and I remained estranged. She continued her denial of her role in Mary Wood's death, and my anger and remorse intensified.

Although she professed a disliking for Salem, Ebe occasionally visited Herbert Street. She was living in Beverly in a tiny room she rented from her cousin, Mr. Elliot, and though we heard that she was content there, she arrived in Salem in style, wearing her dark cloak, the hood emphasizing her unusually large eyes, which she refused to obscure with the appropriate spectacles.

She condescended to take tea in our little parlor. For appearance's sake, Priscilla and I greeted her together. We were not her favorite people, but at least we did not hide in our rooms like her mother.

"How are the Elliots?" inquired Priscilla, serving Ebe a muffin.

"They are well, although they are a bit boring since they cannot read or write. I have offered to teach their children, but they prefer to keep them ignorant." Ebe pinched the muffin between thumb and finger, peered at it, took a nibble, grimaced, and dropped it on her plate. "I spend my time editing manuscripts sent to me from publishers in Boston."

"Is there a library in town?" I asked, knowing that libraries were among Ebe's favorite places.

She shook her head. "That is why I have come down to Salem. I need to borrow some books to keep from dying of boredom." She gave Priscilla an impertinent little glance. "Of course, I know, Aunt Priscilla, that you do not approve of books because they may contain something irreverent, but Louze, Nath, and I shall all go to the library tomorrow if

Mother can do without Louze for the morning. Please excuse me while I discuss such plans with my siblings." She stood without ceremony and headed for the stairs, an uncharacteristic smile upon her lips. Priscilla just shook her head at her niece's rude behavior and rang for Bridget to clear the tea service.

The clock chimed midnight. I sat before our parlor fire going over some paperwork, Priscilla abed and asleep upstairs. At such a late hour, the house should be silent, so I was surprised to hear voices coming from Louisa's room. Ebe and Louisa must be chatting, I thought and felt a pang of loneliness, made more so when I heard Nath's tenor voice join in. Although fully aware that my longing for my niece was inappropriate, I told myself that my feelings would be diluted by the presence of her siblings. I lit a candle and tiptoed down the hall to the other side of the house. Louisa's bedroom was just up the stairs.

Soft conversation emanated from that small room, and I knocked gently before opening the door and announcing myself.

Three appraising sets of eyes, one sapphire and welcoming, one gray and critical, and one gray and red-rimmed, stared back at me from the chaise, desk, and bed.

Nath rose, bowed, and said, "Please join us. Perhaps you can elucidate your own defense."

Ebe squinted at me over an edited manuscript and quipped, "Louisa, your *uncle* has come courting."

Louisa just patted the side of her mattress and sniffled.

I closed the door with a careful hand and sat as bidden to face my judge, jury, and executioner. It was obvious that Louisa's and my relationship was not a surprise, or even a shock, to her siblings. The question was more whom they blamed for her current distress.

"Mrs. Dike is asleep?" Nath nodded toward the hallway, concerned that our conversation might be overheard.

"Indeed. But perhaps I have interrupted something about which I too should remain ignorant?"

"Too late." Ebe snorted a short laugh and pushed the manuscript aside. "I am certain you can guess what we were discussing." She gestured toward Louisa. "She tells us that you have had a conversion and feel you must honor your wedding vows."

Louisa shuddered with another sob. I resisted the urge to comfort her and instead stood up and faced my accusers as though in the prisoner's dock, willing to bear witness for my sins.

"I am guilty of loving your sister. I am also guilty of adultery. Your aunt has refused a divorce, and my God says that I must honor my wedding vows. Unless there is other evidence to tip the scales, I am in limbo."

Ebe leaned forward in her desk chair as she made her point. "One has only to count the months between my parents' marriage and my birth to know that wedded bliss is not a prerequisite for love. Apparently, it is the Hathorne and Manning way."

"But if that is not enough to persuade you, perhaps you would be interested in some even more ancient family history," suggested Nath. "Go to the first floor of the courthouse and ask for the ledgers registering the last two hundred years of court documents. Look for the pages relating to March 29, 1681. They will explain everything. It is in our blood."

Louisa looked from one sibling to the other as if for strength and then turned to face me. "If you love me, please go and do your research. I will await your decision."

Nath opened the door and waved me through without further decorum. I crept back to my room, eased myself into bed beside Priscilla, and stared at the ceiling, trying to imagine what the court documents might reveal about the Manning and Hathorne families.

"Where are you off to so early?" Priscilla asked in the dawn light. I had not been able to sleep, and so I was up and ready to go to the courthouse as soon as it opened. "Early meeting at the docks," I replied. Only she and I and Bridget were awake. Nath, Ebe, and Louisa were late risers, and Betsey never came downstairs to eat.

Priscilla nodded and fixed me with a stern eye. "I hope it is a successful one." I knew she did not want to be in this house any longer than necessary. It was obviously demoralizing to be back in her childhood home again when she had been a wealthy merchant's wife with a large house and holdings.

"I shall be home for supper." I found my hat and stick and escaped the premises.

The courthouse was but a short distance. I hoped not to run into anyone we knew, as Priscilla might hear of my whereabouts and wonder what I was doing away from the wharves. I climbed the steps of the handsome building and stopped at the clerk's office on the first floor.

"May I please see the ledgers for the last two hundred years?" He slammed a huge bound collection of documents upon the counter and held out a grimy hand for the penny fee. I lugged the dusty book over to one of the high desks that lined the room, sat upon the accompanying stool, and leafed through the heavy pages. Hathorne, or Manning, I wondered. The parchments were in chronological order, and I hurried forward in time till I approached March of 1681.

A peculiarity caught my eye. An old piece of rag was pasted in the middle of page 69. It was in fair condition, and the ink was legible. The names rang in my head: *"Anstis Manning and Margaret Manning, now Polfery being brought before the court at Salem in November 1680 for incestuous carriage with their brother Nicholas Manning who is fled or out of the way."* My head felt light. I sat back on the stool and wiped my face with my handkerchief, the Bible passage "the sins of the father . . ." ringing in my head.

The next paragraph was testimony from a servant: *"testifieth that sum time the last winter at night there was a quarreling and disturbance between my master Nicholas Manning and his wife whereupon his wife went away out of the house and lodged at another place . . ."*

There was more, but I could not bear to read it. All the present-day Mannings and Hathornes must be cognizant of this history, but Robert, William, Betsey, and Priscilla had attempted to keep the matter hidden.

Even so, I had fallen into the thick of a family with incestuous and adulterous secrets. Louisa and I were simply following her natural tendencies. I flung the ledger back at the surprised clerk, skipped down the courthouse stairs, and turned onto the road to the wharves to rebuild my business, recoup my losses, and pursue Louisa, encouraged by the idea that familial love might in fact for us be preordained.

November 18, 1837

"Louze, I am told that the comely Mary Silsbee will be in attendance this evening," Ebe gossips as she helps me dress. Ebe has left her aerie in Beverly to join us in Salem for one of Susan Burley's 'Hurley-Burley's.' These parties are very popular with the more intellectual segment of Salem society.

"We shall have to keep an eye on Nath, in that case," I gasp out as Ebe pulls roughly at my stays.

"She has a very peculiar hold over him," agrees Ebe, grunting a bit herself with the exertion. "Have you noticed how he attends to her every little murmur, stooping and cupping his ear as though diamonds might drip from her lips? He was quite ready to fight a duel with that idiot editor of the *United States Magazine* simply because of some slight the man caused her. Our brother is too quick to avenge a damsel in distress."

I escape from Ebe's grasp and reach for my dark gray silk overskirt, but she grabs it from my hand, gathers it from the bottom, stands on her tip-toes, and slips it over my head. She hoists my arms through the waist, pulls the skirt down over my hoop petticoat and underskirt, and arranges the ruffles so that none are hung up on the wire, and the gap in the overskirt displays the dove gray underskirt properly. She spins me around, ties the back strings a bit too tightly for my comfort, and while I straighten the front pleats, she shakes out the matching bodice and holds it by the dropped shoulders so that I might slip my arms into the tapered sleeves. Dressing our hair and wardrobe for this evening's entertainment has taken us more than an hour, and we have yet to begin Nath's costume.

"Even as a little girl Miss Silsbee was overly dramatic," continues Ebe as she spins me around again and pulls the bodice tight across my stomacher. "It was our father who died at sea and her father who merely hired him, yet it was she who mourned the tragedy as if it were her own."

Ebe fastens the last of the many bodice hooks and arranges the organza shoulder pieces at a becoming angle before pinning my favorite silver and garnet brooch at my bosom.

I nod. "I have heard that she loves to be admired, and you know how susceptible Nath is to feminine wiles. But perhaps there will be someone else with whom he can flirt, and Mary will have to pay her attentions elsewhere. For instance, Elizabeth Peabody is rumored to attend, and I know she has set her cap at Nath."

I hold Ebe's blue silk skirt over her head, slide it down past her outstretched arms and over her hoop, and tie the back strings. She reaches for her own bodice and hooks it efficiently, then arranges the dropped collar over her pale shoulders and ties a black velvet ribbon around her throat.

She nods thoughtfully as she checks her fore and aft reflections in the dressing table mirror.

"Elizabeth would be a convenient sister-in-law because I would be sure of employment. She has commissioned me several times to contribute to her little magazine, *The Dial*, which I am happy to do, if only for the money. I certainly do not espouse any of that Transcendentalist nonsense." She picks up her gloves and reticule. "Sophia may also make an appearance tonight. You know that she has been very ill?"

I nod. Their father, Dr. Peabody, had been our family physician, and Elizabeth and Sophia our childhood friends. But their family moved to Boston when we reached our late teens, and so we have not seen Sophia in many years. She was always a bit sickly and stayed at home while Elizabeth and we enjoyed out-of-door activities.

Ebe draws on her gloves. "I never much cared for her, with all her attempts at sympathy for what seemed to me to be hypochondria. However, she is just returned from a restorative tour of Cuba. Meeting with her is one of the reasons that I have decided to accompany you and Nath to this gathering tonight. I would like to facilitate a lucrative literary partnership between Nath and Sophia."

Nath appears at the door, his cravat askew. He fumbles at an attempt to knot it, but Ebe bats his hands away and deftly ties a bow, then pulls the collar tips up to frame his face.

"You must look your most handsome this evening," she instructs him as she flicks away a bit of ginger cat fur from his black coat. "I believe I have found you an illustrator for *Twice-Told Tales.*"

"Would you care to elaborate?" asks Nath, pulling down his cuffs and checking his reflection in our mirror.

"You will see. Come." And she leads us downstairs to the front door where we don our cloaks and hoods and slip out into the blustery night.

The Burley's house is ablaze with hurricane lanterns lining the front walkway. Nath steps from the carriage, offers his hands for Ebe and me to hold as we alight, and tips the driver. We approach the house, hoods drawn against the cold wind, Ebe gripping Nath's right arm, I his left, and we climb the steps three abreast. Nath knocks.

But instead of Susan Burley's cheerful personage greeting us, a slight, pale waif, dressed all in white, drags open the heavy door. She stares at us without a word or a gesture of welcome.

"May we enter?" Ebe's voice is gruff in reaction to the bitter breeze but also to this seeming rift in decorum. The waif stammers, "I do apologize. *You were all so swallowed up in your cloaks, like three spirits, that I was startled.* Yes, please come in." She struggles to pull the door wider, and Nath extricates himself from our grips and springs up the stairs to help. Ebe and I exchange bemused glances and follow our chivalrous brother into the candle-lit, noisy gathering.

The Burleys' grand house, decorated with expensive elegance reflecting Mr. Burley's success in business, mocks John's recent troubles. His daughter Susan, intellectual and politically astute, loves to entertain. It is she who dubbed her infamous salons 'Hurley-Burleys.' She pushes her way through the crowd, her handsome face florid from the warmth of the many fireplaces, busses our cheeks, and hangs our cloaks.

"Did you see Sophia?" she asks as she leads us toward the parlor.

"Indeed. I believe she has spirited Nath away," says Ebe in an aggrieved tone. She surveys the gathered horde in an attempt to spy our already smitten brother and his prey.

"She told me that she has fallen in love with his book and would be thrilled to illustrate it if that is still your plan," says Susan to Ebe. Ebe looks a bit taken aback. Although this was indeed her idea, I imagine she thought it to be in her control, and things are moving a bit too fast for her liking.

"Of course. By the way, is Mary Silsbee in attendance this evening?" Ebe is obviously thinking that Mary will take Nath's interest away from Sophia, whom Ebe obviously still dislikes.

"Yes, Mary is in the library. Would you care to visit her there? I believe she already has an audience in attendance. You know she has her admirers." We all exchange wry smiles. "If you will excuse me, I must greet our next guest." Susan hurries out to the foyer where the slight-figured Margaret Fuller, her spectacles fogging in the sudden warmth, is just relinquishing her cloak to the maid.

Ebe snorts in derision at this new addition to the attendance list and takes my elbow. "Now the conversation is sure to turn lofty. Let us seek out the dessert table before we are called upon to defend all of womankind."

We fill our plates with tea cakes and preserved fruit, settle into a worn but comfortable couch beside the fire in the main parlor, and watch and listen as Salem's most prominent philosophers and pundits parade before us. However, gossip is not beneath them. I keep my ears open for tales about my own family and am grateful that John's business seems an unpopular subject, and no one mentions John Stephens' defection to Ohio. However, the personal bankruptcy of my cousin Eleanor's husband, the Reverend Thomas Carlisle, is fodder. I wonder that he can still retain his post at the Tabernacle, and I resolve to call upon that household in the coming holiday season to offer Eleanor my support.

Elizabeth Peabody, in a billowy gown that does little to flatter her portly figure, perches carefully on a spindly chair across from our couch.

"Ebe, it is a surprise to see you here in Salem. Did you have a chance to meet with Sophia? I believe she and Nath are already discussing her ideas for illustrating his book, and when I have published it, I plan to serve as his biographer in light of his subsequent and deserved fame. Perhaps when all of you attend one of our conversation salons in Boston, we can speak about it further."

Ebe deposits her plate upon the end table and dabs at her mouth before responding. Her voice can barely contain her condescension. "I assumed that I would be the negotiating party. However, she seems to have taken the responsibility upon herself, although she hardly looks capable of standing up to a stiff breeze. I fear Nath will be captivated by her fragility, and his desire to be her white knight will be his undoing, for if she cannot keep her promises of work, he will be forced to delay his publisher."

Elizabeth laughs a bit unkindly. "Ebe, just because you are happy to live the hermitress's life, and compose, somewhat haphazardly, in a garret, does not mean everyone must follow suit. I am grateful that you have written pieces for *The Dial*, but do not let my generosity in giving you work go to your head. Sophia is still my sister, and I must come to her defense. Her art is really quite spectacular. Nath is lucky to have piqued her interest. He has no genius for negotiations with booksellers, and her illustrations will make his *Twice-Told Tales* much more marketable."

Ebe's retort is interrupted by raised voices emanating from the library. The conversation in the parlor quiets so that we might all to attend this new entertainment.

"Nath, why must you abandon our plans just because this," there is a pause as the shrill speaker attempts to find an appropriate jibe, "*stray* wishes to entrap you with her promises? Have you seen her artistic attempts? I doubt her illustrations would meet even your lowest standards."

There is a baritone mumble, and then a different soprano voice pipes up. "I am not attempting to entrap him in any way. My sister suggested that I contact him about a possible illustrating opportunity, and we met here. Now then, please excuse me, for all this passion has given me a headache." The crowd in front of the staircase parts, and Sophia, her head bowed, her arms crossed before her breasts, runs out of the library and up the stairs. A door at the top of the steps bangs shut.

Elizabeth rises ponderously from her chair to go to her sister's rescue. Ebe just shakes her head and turns her attention back to her plate. My sympathies, however, side with the wounded artist, and I put out a hand to Elizabeth as she lumbers by.

"Perhaps I might be of assistance?"

"Go and see if Cook has any ice in the kitchen. Put some in a cloth and meet me upstairs."

I make my way through the throng to the kitchen, where Cook very generously allows me access to the pantry. I wrap a bit of ice from the stone sink in a towel and steal upstairs so as not to invite too much attention.

Susan's bedroom, where Sophia has taken refuge, is a hodgepodge of dressing gowns, discarded corsets, and hair curling implements, but Elizabeth has made a nest for Sophia on the bed and is singing her little sister into a fitful rest. She stops her crooning enough to take the ice, with which she slowly and methodically massages Sophia's temples.

"Is there anything else I can do for you?" I murmur.

Sophia starts at my voice, and then holds out a cold, quivering hand. I take it and rub it gently to warm it. She nods.

"Please tell your brother I am truly sorry to make trouble for him with Mary Silsbee. It was certainly not my intention."

"I will tell him, but I think he may be ready to drop his allegiance with her at any rate."

"Would you care to see the illustrations I created for *Twice-Told Tales?*"

Elizabeth stops her ministrations and asks, "Sophia, are you well enough to discuss this?"

As if in answer, Sophia arises from the bed, phantom-like in her white gown, and drifts to the dressing table where several drawings have been displayed. I follow and peer over her shoulder as she discusses them in her breathy soprano.

"Do you see how I have introduced the characters in each piece? The colors are reminiscent of the mood. Do you not agree?"

And I do indeed agree. The sketches are beautiful: very detailed and delicate, with a watercolor wash that enhances the art as well as the literature. I am impressed.

"Which is the illustration for *Peter Goldthwaite's Treasure?*" I ask. Sophia points to a study of the story's two protagonists confronting one another over a treasure chest. On the right is a handsome, well-dressed individual with a kindly face. Opposite him is a slovenly character wearing a patched surtout and a nasty grimace.

"What is your interest in this particular story?" asks Sophia shyly, turning around to stare up at me.

"My brother based these two men on our two uncles," I explain. "John Brown is a perfect match for our successful uncle John Dike." I quote the story, "Naturally a good sort of man and kind and pitiful."

Sophia nods. "And your other uncle?"

"William. I am very fond of him, but he makes bad business decisions, and, like Peter Goldthwaite, he always thinks that his fortune is just around the corner."

"Well, I hope that your brother agrees that I have captured his characters' souls in these illustrations."

"He will love them," I say with sincerity. "As will Ebe, if we allow her to think that she is the instigator in the partnership."

Sophia nods, shivers, and crawls back onto the bed, where Elizabeth resumes her temple massage.

"I shall go downstairs now, but it truly was a pleasure to see you, Miss Peabody," I say, as softly as I can so as not to rekindle the headache.

"Please call me Sophia," she murmurs. Elizabeth peers up at me with a grateful smile.

"Thank you for helping," she whispers. "I hope to see you and Nath at one of our salons in Boston. Ebe can hide in her garret." We both smile in mutual acceptance of my sister's difficult personality, and then I tiptoe out of the room and down the stairs.

Nath greets me at the bottom.

"Is she quite well?" He looks both guilty and enticed.

"She will be. I look forward to your reaction to her art. It is really quite special."

He nods and, shoulders hunched, returns to the library.

I wind my way through the crowd, back to the couch. Ebe is in conversation with the tiny but intense Margaret Fuller. In accordance with her philosophy, she has dressed casually for this formal occasion, with a plain brown shawl drawn tightly about her shoulders.

"Do you not consider yourself to be your brother's equal in all things intellectual, physical, and artistic?" Margaret squints through her spectacles at Ebe, daring my sister to quarrel with this woman-centric tract.

"Actually," says Ebe, "I consider myself to be his superior."

There are hoots of laughter from all sides at this quip. Margaret colors, then giggles and raises her teacup to my aggrandizing sister.

"Indeed!" says Margaret, "I shall have to address this with him when next we converse. He is one of my favorite sparring partners."

Ebe takes a breath to retort when a ripple of excitement moves through the crowd. Mary Silsbee, still in the library, raises her voice to make the most of all this delicious attention. "Nathaniel Hathorne, you may never call upon me again. Consider our relationship done." There is the resounding smack of a slap upon flesh and a subsequent grunt of pain.

Nath strides from the library and shoulders his way through the crowd to our couch. Upon the left side of his face glows a red palm print. He pulls Ebe and me up from the sofa and, holding our hands, barrels toward the door. I struggle from his grasp and turn to mouth our thanks to Susan. She nods, and from the gleam in her eye I know very well that we shall now be the objects of gossip for months to come.

Pittsburgh, Pennsylvania
May 14, 1884

"Mrs. Virginia Dike Blair is the embodiment of all that is charitable and giving in the Pittsburgh medical community."

Dr. McClelland stood before a crowd of elite contributors in his mansion's vast dining room and led a round of applause for my cousin Virginia, the guest of honor at Shadyside Hospital's fundraising campaign celebration. I sat at the head table with a very proud Tom on one side and a flustered Margaretta on the other, both she and I feeling out of place in a roomful of dignitaries slurping oysters and sipping champagne. I tugged at my wing collar and tried to loosen my cravat, but Margaretta brushed away my hand, so I gave up and paid my full attention to the speaker.

"Without Mrs. Blair's help and support, Shadyside Hospital would still be an overworked doctor's daydream, but with her organizational skills, hard work, and perseverance, the people of Pittsburgh will enjoy a modern hospital, utilizing Mr. Bell's newest invention, for the best in patient care. We break ground in the fall and plan to open in the spring of 1886. In thanks and in celebration, we give Mrs. Blair this certificate of appreciation." He unrolled the scroll for all to see. "And now we would like to hear from the lady herself."

Virginia, graceful and dignified in a white silk jacket and draped skirt, stood and bowed to more applause, then glided to the front of the room to shake the doctor's hand and accept the certificate before turning to address the audience.

"Thank you, Dr. McClelland, for all your good works, both in the Shadyside community and in the city at large. We are extremely fortunate to have a continentally-educated doctor serve in our humble little clinic. My small efforts have been magnified by your reputation and expertise, and I am forever grateful that our mutual dream of a community hospital has come to fruition."

He smiled and started his closing remarks, but to his obvious surprise, she raised a delicate hand and interrupted. "But I must also take a moment to thank my late parents, Nathaniel and Anna Dike, for teaching me from a young age about the charitable spirit. My father always set aside a portion of his very successful business proceeds for the needy, and now my uncle John Stephens is following his lead." She gestured toward our table, and I flushed and nodded my thanks to enthusiastic applause.

She continued, "And I am very proud to say that in 1830, my mother Anna and her sister Margaretta both signed the infamous Ladies of Steubenville petition sent to President Jackson, appealing to him to allow the Indians to stay on their lands. Aunt Margaretta has continued these charitable efforts in her city, volunteering at the Steubenville Female Seminary." In her turn, Margaretta blushed and waved shyly to the applauding crowd.

Virginia concluded, "But it was the . . ." she took a breath before using a clinical term in front of this pompous assembly, "reproductive difficulties of my mother, my aunt, and myself, that inspired me to create an accessible women's clinic. With Dr. McClelland's help, the ladies of Pittsburgh will now have a safe and welcoming hospital to see to all their medical needs."

She sat down to slightly diminished applause, whether due to the unsettling subject matter or the oncoming refreshments, I could not say. Tom leaned over to congratulate his wife, but I turned to Margaretta for mutual support. Neither of us knew that Virginia would use our very personal tragedy for her very public speech, and I wanted to make sure that Margaretta was not similarly disturbed.

But Margaretta's seat was empty. I stood and looked over the crowd, hoping to spot her lavender gown among the many colorful evening ensembles and formal coats, but instead, I recognized another guest, who had turned his gaze to me, one brow raised in greeting. Naturally, he would be here to fete Virginia. Still, his presence fueled my anxiety. I nodded to Dr. Voight before continuing my search for Margaretta.

I limped to the hallway, thinking she might have visited one of the two water-closets boasted by our host's mansion, but they were both open while the guests took advantage of the food. The only other option was the outdoor courtyard, and indeed, when I stepped outside, I heard muffled sobs behind the fountain.

"Margaretta?" She flung herself into my arms, and I held her gently through several minutes of trembling gasps until finally she relaxed into my embrace. We stood silently while she gathered herself, and then she stepped back and brushed at my chest as if to downplay her very understandable grief.

"I am sorry I ruined your shirtfront, John Stephens." I shrugged and handed her my handkerchief to wipe her eyes and then my shirt. We sat on a bench facing a garden bed of early blooming pansies, and after a bit, she explained, "Of course, I was very grateful that Virginia mentioned you and Anna and Nathaniel and your giving natures. But I was not prepared to remember . . ." Her eyes sought mine, and I nodded, overwhelmed, too, at the memories that flooded us both.

I agreed, "I also was surprised, but we should be proud that our troubles have led to solace for a city full of women and their offspring." She nodded, her sorrow abated somewhat by the prospect of philanthropy.

But then her sunny nature prevailed, and she said, "We must go back and congratulate Virginia. She has truly made the family proud. I just wish her mother could have been here to enjoy the moment." She sought my eyes again for agreement but instead recognized a concerning sign. "John Stephens, are you quite well? You look pale."

I shook my head to clear the tension that had been building since Virginia's speech. "It is nothing that a little dinner will not cure. Let us seek out Tom and Virginia."

We joined Tom at the head table, where the meal had just been served. The scent of lamb and potatoes, ordinarily pleasurable, now disgusted me, and I picked at the food, trying to ignore the faint unease in both my stomach and my head.

"How is the lamb? Dr. McClelland employed a new cook for the occasion, and I hear she has an excellent hand." Serenely content from the congratulations paid to her by her illustrious friends and colleagues, Virginia rejoined us and raised her fork to test the rumor. In deference to the warmth in the room, she had removed her jacket to reveal a fashionable off-the-shoulder gown. But in doing so, she had also uncovered a familiar silver and garnet bar brooch pinned below her graceful throat.

The gaslights in the room flared and dimmed. I stretched out my clenched hands and wiped my perspiring forehead with my sleeve, but the dreaded lopsided headache continued to bloom.

"John Stephens, is the lamb not to your liking?" Tom clapped me on the back. His proud comportment was made more so by the delight he took in his wife. I turned to Margaretta, hoping that she would notice my discomfort, and indeed, she understood only too well. She whispered, "John Stephens, I am so sorry. I gave Louze's brooch to Virginia ten years ago to remove it from the house. I had no idea she would wear it this evening."

The tragic significance of the brooch, coupled with the memory of our other loss, finally overwhelmed me. My only hope was to escape the room before the clap of thunder sounded in my head, and I lost all control. I stood and searched over the crowd for the best route to the door, but it was too late. I staggered a moment and then felt my legs give way. Tom caught me as I slipped to the floor, the reverberations still pounding in my temples.

Through the pain, I heard Virginia call out for help in a room full of doctors, and the resulting stampede of dress shoes competed with my internal cacophony. All I could do was curl into a ball on the floor and try to keep down my gorge.

"Mr. Dike." A soothing, Germanic voice cut through all the noise. "Take a deep breath. You are in a safe space." Cool fingers sought my pulse, and a damp cloth soothed my forehead.

"I am so sorry," I whispered to Tom, who knelt at my other side, loosening my collar and cravat while growling at the crowd to stay back.

He flashed me a wry grin. "Well, at least you weren't sick on this no doubt priceless Oriental carpet." I tried to smile in turn but closed my eyes instead and let the pain overtake me, trusting that my friends and the doctor would keep me safe. As one of the larger butlers lifted me to a couch, the doctor whispered in my ear, "We shall talk about this next week, Mr. Dike. Until then, rest." And I drifted into oblivion.

June 17, 1840

My Dear Thomas,

I must thank you once again. Your efforts to support my ongoing attempts to rebuild the Dike-Manning enterprises have been rewarded. Had it not been for your firm and potent guidance, I might still be living a life of desperation in my family's house.

Instead, I find myself once again the mistress of a commanding residence. As you know, Number 4 Andover Street is a spacious Georgian, painted my favorite pale yellow, with an inside bathing chamber. Never again will I share an outbuilding with my sister.

My bedroom is located on the second floor, next to John's. I intend to keep eyes and ears on his whereabouts. It is a disappointment that Bridget chose to move with us. She is obviously loyal to her master. But I suppose it is easier to keep a servant with bad habits than to train a new one. Hannah, more my confidant, remained at Herbert Street. Those two women will miss each other's company. However, the gossip they hear while marketing or visiting will prove important as you and I continue our investigation.

To that end, I planned to question my nephew and niece for information about their sister and my duplicitous husband. On the pretense of showing off my new home, I invited Nath to tea a Saturday ago. His appetite for sweets was always voracious. Apparently, his new lodgings do not offer enough sustenance. His black frock coat hung on his lanky frame. He sat with alacrity and helped himself to a full plate.

"Thank you for the invitation, Mrs. Dike," he said after hastily swallowing a mouthful of cake. "Did you know that I accepted a position at the Boston Custom House?"

I nodded. Of course, I had heard from Betsey that her spoilt little boy was no longer living at home.

"I am renting a room from Mr. Hillard rather than take the daily stage from Salem. But I return to Salem occasionally to pick up shirts which Hannah launders especially for me." He brushed crumbs from his breast as if a phantom Hannah were reprimanding him with a shaken finger. "And Ebe comes down to Salem on Saturdays, too. Louze, Ebe, and I must attend Susan Burley's parties, of course."

I began my interrogation. "But what of Miss Peabody? Do you not meet with her at these gatherings as well?"

"I suppose you have been speaking with my mother." Nath wiped his mouth fastidiously to play for time. "Unfortunately, not. Ebe and Sophia do not admire each other, and so I must see Sophia at her home in Boston, without my sisters in attendance. Dr. and Mrs. Peabody have been very gracious hosts."

"And what are you writing these days?" I really had no interest, but Nath's scribblings often foretold the mood of his family.

His voice sank to a mournful baritone. "I cannot write while I work. I am trying to resume my pen. Whenever I sit alone or walk alone, I find myself dreaming about stories, as of old, but those forenoons in the Custom House undo all that the afternoons and evenings have done. I should be happier if I could write." He gazed into his teacup as if the leaves foretold the future of his inertia.

I nodded in pretend sympathy as I strategized my next move. My need for information must not appear too desperate.

"Have you had any word from John Stephens? Will you be welcoming any new little cousins into the world?" I asked as I refreshed his tea.

Nath stuffed half a cucumber sandwich into his mouth, chewed thoughtfully, and swallowed before replying.

"John Stephens has always been a very private person, as you know. I do not think that I would be his confidant in this matter, being neither married nor a father. I should think Mr. Dike would be more likely to have heard. However, I imagine that there are good doctors in Steubenville so that if there were any," his face pinked, "physical issues, they would be addressed."

I nodded. "Perhaps his sick headaches are to blame. He was always so sensitive."

Nath kept his eyes on his teacup while answering, "Actually, he reports that he has not had a spell in months. I suppose he has the Ohio climate to thank."

I refused to rise to that bait, nor did I offer any other information. If John Stephens had written of his attempts at fatherhood to John, I had not heard of it. I changed tactics again.

"And what of Ebe? Has she any suitors?"

"A Captain Briggs proposed a few years ago, but Ebe quickly quashed that idea." Nath smiled into his teacup. I could not quite discern the source of his amusement.

"What does she do for money, up there in the Beverly wilderness?"

"I send her an occasional cheque. Now that I have steady employment, I can contribute funds to the family. And Elizabeth Peabody gives her editorial work. Have you heard of *The Dial*? It is a paper devoted to the Transcendentalist movement. Ebe sometimes writes articles for it as well."

"It sounds transient at best. She is fortunate to have a brother who will support her."

He nodded and sipped his tea.

I took a breath and asked the question that simmered beneath all of this preamble.

"And Louze?"

"Has she any suitors, do you mean?" Nath gazed at me in wide-eyed innocence. An actor he was not. My marriage was obviously fodder for sibling gossip.

"Yes," I wheedled. "Surely a comely, intelligent young woman, from a good family, would have attracted attention."

"Louze is more interested in caring for our mother than in finding a husband. It is too much to ask Hannah to cook, clean, and nurse an invalid as well."

"I hardly think Betsey an invalid," I said with some asperity. "She fares well in Raymond."

"Yes, but in Raymond, she is not called upon to play the society matron and go visiting or hold teas." Nath eyed the French damask curtains, silk cushions, and plush Oriental carpets in my formal dining room. I had abandoned all the shabby family pieces back on Herbert Street. "She does not have your eye for décor or the space for entertaining. She finds it all too demanding, and then her cough returns."

"Perhaps you will meet a nice young man in Boston to whom you might introduce your sister," I suggested. He shrugged.

"I have tried that from time to time. College friends, peers from other communities. Louze would have none of it. As far as I can tell, she is content with things as they are." He placed his crumpled napkin by his plate and stood. "Thank you for tea, Mrs. Dike. I shall return to Boston well-nourished. Please give my best to Mr. Dike." I escorted him to the door. He tipped his hat and turned toward home to retrieve his shirts. Unfortunately, his visit did not reveal to me any more significant soiled laundry.

Subsequently, I invited Ebe to travel down from Beverly. Rather than allow her to sully my new house with her caustic wit, I chose to be the first to attack instead of playing my usual defense.

"Ebe, dear, whatever happened with that nice Captain Briggs? I heard from Nath that you had a proposal from him. Did you decide to disappoint the unfortunate man?" I sipped my tea and endeavored to look neutral.

She stared into her teacup. I was surprised to see her eyes moisten. But then her inappropriate confidence won out. "He has gone abroad to lick his wounds," she said, holding her head high, "and I would not be surprised if he returns with a dowager on his arm. I was too poor for him, apparently. Not that I cared about his money."

"A captain's salary would be an improvement over the few pennies you earn with your pen," I pointed out. "You cannot rely on your brother's generosity forever."

She shrugged her shoulders. "I prefer to be a hermitress. My meager earnings are just enough to keep me in my one room and allow me rambles along the shore. If I need luxury, I shall come here." She turned over her wafer-thin porcelain saucer and squinted at the mark. I was rebuilding my china collection, but her short sight could not appreciate the fine quality. If I wanted to rile her, I would need to try another tack.

"Have you visited much with Sophia? I hear that Nath is positively smitten."

She banged the saucer down with such velocity that I feared for its integrity.

"She is one of the few human beings that I truly dislike."

"Why, pray tell?" My conversation with Nath had not prepared me for this much vitriol.

"Her hypochondria, her meager diet, even her choice of wardrobe, strike me as being manipulative. And Nath has fallen for all of it." Ebe's voice was tinged with disgust and just a hint of grudging admiration.

"What are your plans if he decides to marry?" I asked, curious at her negative reaction to her brother's joy. I pondered the cerebral ties that bound the Hathorne siblings. Ebe's sisterly envy seemed highly disproportionate. The unfortunate Miss Peabody might be romancing a hellish Cerberus instead of a single mate.

"I shall stay in Beverly. Or perhaps I shall live with Louze and Mother on Herbert Street. Nath and his 'dove' hold no interest for me."

"So, Louze has no beaus and no plans other than to care for your mother?" I could not keep the irony from coloring my voice. Ebe squinted at me. I could see the wheels turning.

"Does that concern you?" she asked.

"It is my wish that she be happy, of course." I rang the bell to summon Bridget. Ebe and I shared a brief handshake before she left to catch her stage. Neither of us said another word about her sister. I could not afford to pique Ebe's curiosity. If the siblings knew about John's adultery but not of my similar comprehension, I did not wish to tip my hand.

I must continue to be vigilant in my investigation into the truth. Thank you, Cousin, for your assistance. It is a great comfort to me that you are available day or night for consultation. Enclosed, please find a small token of my appreciation.

Your Sister in Christ,

PMD

August 8, 1842

> *My Dear Louze,*
>   *The stage for Concord leaves Earle's Coffee House, Hanover-
> street, every day at four o'clock. I know you will be delighted with
> our home and the neighboring scenery; and I have confident hope
> that you will be delighted with ourselves likewise.*
>   *Also, commend me to the voluntary nun, the lady Elizabeth,
> and tell her I wish her to let us know what time she will come. Tell
> her that nobody walks in Concord but us so that she can have all
> the hills, vales, woods, and plains to herself and will need no one,
> and she shall sail in the boat and do everything she pleases.*
>   *Sophia informs me that she has written you a newsy letter
> about my humble exploits. Please know that everything said in my
> praise and glory in the fore-going letter is no more than the simple
> truth.*
>   *Your brother,*
>   *Nath**

Nath posted this just a few days ago. His teasing aside, I am anxious
to be away from Salem and my Aunt Priscilla's venomous glare, to visit
my newly-wedded brother and his bride Sophia in Concord.

Ebe declined Nath's invitation to join her siblings in a ramble around
the Concord countryside, and so at a little before four o'clock, only John
and I disembark the Salem stage at Hanover Street in Boston. John enters
the coffee house to pay my fare and rejoins me in the street to wait for
my connecting stage to Concord. He tucks my hand in his arm, takes his
handkerchief from his coat sleeve and mops his forehead, then dips his
head to peer under my bonnet rim, his crooked smile encouraging, but
his amber eyes mournful at our separation.

"Why can you not join me?" I ask, feeling wistful. His loving presence is making it difficult to tear myself away. "Sophia and Nath would be very happy to host you, as they are anxious to show off their cozy new home."

"As I explained to Nath, I have business here in Boston. With my brother gone off to Ohio, and William aiding Robert in Maine, it is all on my shoulders." His shoulders stoop in anticipation of those responsibilities, and I long to embrace him in sympathy, but we are on a public thoroughfare so that all I can do is to squeeze his arm with my gloved hand.

The street is noisy with wooden wheels on gravel, the clack of horses' hooves, hawkers, and criers, but still, I lower my voice. "Since you moved out of Herbert Street and into your grand new house on Andover Street, my days and nights are lonely. Aunt Priscilla guards your door as though the Garden of Eden were within." My eyes well, and I blink back the tears, not wishing to weep in public, but I must tell him my feelings before we part. "I miss you. Herbert Street is cold since Grandmama passed, and it is just Hannah and Mother for company. Hannah is busy with her chores, and I try to help like a good little cinder wench, but sometimes I do not see Mother for days. I leave her a dinner tray at her bedroom door and then go out at midnight to walk the beach, and it is all I can do not to throw myself into the waves."

I sniff and try to smile at him for reassurance, but I see the answering pain in his eyes. His arm tenses as he contemplates what he can do and say here in public. "There is nothing I would like better than to whisk you away in a pumpkin coach to Nath and Sophia's. But I cannot risk the business failing again, nor give Priscilla ammunition for a deeper mistrust. We must keep our distance for now." His voice is quiet and somber, and anyone watching us would have thought we had just suffered a death in the family.

The stage looms around the corner, the horses whinnying and shying at the street commotion, and with reluctance, I release John's arm. He strides over to the stage master's side of the bench when the carriage has finally jolted to a stop.

"You have precious cargo," he says to the driver as he gives him my chit, then hands me in behind the other passengers and tips his hat as he slams the door. We share one last look of longing before he taps the stage lightly with his stick, and we are off.

Wedged in between a retired seafarer who tells me he is visiting Concord in search of millwork and a younger man admitting that he is summonsed to the county courthouse, and with my valise balanced on my lap, I peer out the window in eager anticipation as we leave the urban, seaside city of Boston and wend our way on gravel and dirt highways, past forests, fields, and farms, to the bucolic village of Concord. The trip is just long enough to make my backside uncomfortable, and for once, I am grateful for the many layers of clothing between myself and the seat. We arrive at around eight in the evening, as the sun is setting. After discharging most of his passengers in the town center, the stage master stops at my brother's rented property, helps me to alight, and tips his hat in farewell as he hastens to his supper.

I peer down a long tree-lined avenue and wave to Sophia and Nath, who stand between two tall gateposts of roughhewn stone, their arms entwined about each other, but they disentangle themselves and come out to meet me as I make my way along the path from the road.

"Louze!" Nath lopes over and embraces me, and I smile at the old familial name. Sophia looks on, a pleasant expression on her face, and I cannot tell if she is truly happy to see me or is simply playing hostess for my brother's sake, but she links her arm in mine while Nath relieves me of my valise.

"Come see our darling house," she invites, and soon we are touring the place.

"When it is light, we will walk down the path to view Mr. Emerson's 'rude bridge,'" says Nath. I shake my head in confusion. "I am sure you remember Mr. Emerson's verse about 'the shot heard round the world.'" I nod, dredging up Grandmama's long-forgotten history lessons. "We shall have to reacquaint you with the poem." Nath's voice has taken on that stern, older brother tone which usually foretells a lecture. I redirect him.

"May I see what you've done with your new home?"

Their rented house, an old parsonage, is a gray, three-story Georgian with a dormer window on the third floor facing the main road. "And a view of the Concord River out the back," says Nath. We enter through the cool of the woodshed and buttery and enter a commodious kitchen.

"This is quite modern for a rental property." I admire the stove and sink.

Nath gives a harsh little laugh. "You should have seen the original stove. It was so primitive the maid could barely cook on it. Our first dinner took her three hours to make, and even then, she burned it, so the next day, I installed this one. There is the hole I drilled." He points proudly to a ragged gap around a pipe.

I look about the room. "What a hideous wall decoration."

"We know," agree Sophia and Nath in unison.

"It is called Colonial Chevron, and it gives me a headache," says Nath, "but we are renters and under strict orders not to repaint the walls."

Down another passageway and up the curtain-pattern-papered stairway is a little room with a more agreeable golden-tinted wallpaper and several cheerful prints upon the walls. Books stand in order all about, while three windows make the small room feel light-filled and cozy simultaneously. "I have chosen this as my new Owl's Nest. The views shall be my inspiration. Although," Nath's eyes twinkle, "it is awful to reflect how many sermons may have been written here. Who knows what ghostly hand may command my pen while I stare out upon this familiar landscape? So, I have asked my friend Henry to construct a sober writing space." He pulls a little folding wall desk down, draws up a chair, and sits as if to demonstrate his work ethic.

"Has the ghostly hand inspired any new stories?"

"Several. But I am always searching for more earthy ideas." He raises an eyebrow at me as if to invite salubrious gossip, and I back out of the room, intent on keeping my privacy.

"You may sleep in here," murmurs Sophia, escorting me down the hall and opening the door to a charming floral-papered chamber across from their bedroom. As she swings the door fully open to reveal the space, she gives a little scream as if she has been startled by a mouse. Peering in with some trepidation, I see a large stuffed owl on a wooden stand balanced precariously on the bed. I raise an inquiring eyebrow at Sophia, who just shrugs in embarrassment. "Your brother likes to startle me with this ugly thing and hides it about the house. He calls it Longfellow."

"Named after his friend Henry Longfellow, no doubt. There is a passing resemblance," I joke, giving the gleaming feathers a stroke with my index finger. She picks up the offending taxidermy, her arms extended as if the thing smells offensive. I offer to take it from her, but she declines. "I know just where to put it," she murmurs and tucks it into a hall closet.

"The maid sleeps on the third floor." Sophia points to a set of stairs at the end of the hall. We retrieve Nath from his study and descend to the first-floor hall.

"What will the other room on the second floor be?" I ask. Nath and Sophia exchange glances.

"A nursery," says Nath, and Sophia smiles and blushes.

We end in the kitchen, where Sophia pours cool milk from a stone jug in the buttery and slices chicken and bread. Concord grapes round out a meal perfect for a warm August evening. A small orange cat slinks in and winds herself around Nath's legs.

"Pigwiggen, meet Louze. Louze, this is the best little mouser in Concord."

I shake my finger in the adorable little furry face. "Just you wait, Miss Kitty. This gentleman has been known to poke at cats and toss them over fences." Sophia gasps in horror, but Nath just looks serene and tugs at the cat's tail.

"Come." Sophia beckons to me. "Time for bed. Breakfast is at seven. I know you are not given to waking early, but if you expect to be fed, that is when Sarah, our Irish girl, serves us. And we are to have another guest tomorrow. You may remember her. Margaret Fuller?"

Indeed, I do, although I have not seen her since the night at Susan Burley's when Nath and Mary Silsbee had their final argument. But Margaret and Nath have developed an interesting relationship, to say the least. Nath told me of a conversation he and Margaret shared while walking home from Sleepy Hollow Cemetery one evening in which he seemed to have been entirely bewitched and indeed almost missed tea with Sophia in his entrancement. And apparently, Margaret interrupted Nath and Sophia in what sounded like a compromising position one afternoon at home. Yet Sophia seems charmed, speaking of Margaret in affectionate terms, as though such a triad were acceptable. I wonder if I might therefore take Margaret into my own confidence as she seems a woman of flexible mores.

The fresh air and rural quiet lull me to sleep much earlier than is customary for me. I dream of John in a coachman's uniform, whisking me away to a ball, but I awaken in time for breakfast at seven when the scent of toasting bread wafts up the stairs. Sarah's accent and complexion remind me of John's maid Bridget, and I feel right at home. I ask for toast and tea.

"Good morning," says Nath, so proud of his new house and wife. "How did you sleep in my 'Old Manse,' as I have decided to christen it?"

I grunt my congratulatory answer around a mouthful of toast. I may be a tiny bit envious of this new chapter in his life, but perhaps there is a place for me here as well.

At nine, we hear a voice calling, "Hello, the house!" It is Margaret, come for the promised visit. Nath and Sophia invite her in, stow her shawl and book, and serve her a reviving tea after her walk from "Bush," the Emerson's house. She looks her usual self, not unattractive in a rather owlish way, in a lightweight little brown frock and snowy collar. She is very near-sighted, but her eyes are merry behind her spectacles, and she laughs a good deal when she tells her stories. I have been told that her warmth and personality have won over even the most severe critics.

"Margaret, you know my sister Louisa," says Nath with a languid wave in my direction.

Margaret comes toward me, arms outstretched, her smile warm with friendship and perhaps some mischief.

"Louisa. How nice to see you again. Tell me, do you now spell Hawthorne with a 'w' like your famous brother, or have you kept the modest familial spelling?"

Nath cuts in, his voice strident. "I changed it many years ago to distance myself from my horrid ancestor, Judge John Hathorne, who believed in witchcraft and sent innocent women to the scaffold. Now that I have a chance at fame, I can erase some of the family's scandal." Sophia lays a calming hand upon Nath's arm, and he takes a ragged breath. I offer another explanation to lighten the mood.

"My mother, Ebe, and I have changed our names to match Nath's, as it seemed the easier thing to do, now that he is a well-known author. *Twice-Told Tales* and other stories published in our local magazines have become inexplicably popular. Indeed, our cousin John Stephens wrote that Nath has a stellar reputation even in Ohio." I aim an affectionate little slap at Nath's elbow to prove that I am merely teasing, as I am quite proud of his literary achievements.

My brother's face turns ruddy, and he seeks to take the attention away from himself.

"How are the Emersons faring?" he asks Margaret. "I hear that Lidian is still quite devastated."

"Indeed. The death of a child must be the worst pain a human being can ever endure. Waldo was only five and a precious little boy." Margaret's eyes well. I know she played aunt to the Emerson children, and this must have been a bitter blow.

"And Mr. Emerson?" I ask. I have only met him once but am in awe of his intellect. His description of his son's death and the family's subsequent suffering was loquacious, but Transcendentalist philosophy, no matter how profound, cannot completely protect the heart.

"He mourns, but he finds diversion in his writings. Transcendentalism is a complicated mistress. He travels and gives lectures, which takes his mind off of his troubles. Lidian does not have that luxury. And now she is suffering from a tooth extraction. I think I may cut my visit short so as not to be in their way."

"How wonderful that you can spend some time with us, then," says Nath. "Let us go for a ramble."

I feel the need to bathe, so we decide to make our way to Walden Pond. It is more than two miles from the house, but all of us are happy to walk at least some of the way. "Don't worry about your clothes," Sophia says to Margaret and me. "Everyone bathes in the nude, the women on one side, the men on the other." I raise an eyebrow at her, but she just shrugs her shoulders. "Mr. Emerson says we are all God's creatures!"

Nath hitches the horse to the chaise, we wedge ourselves in along with a picnic basket and a blanket, and he tickles the horse with the reins to wake him up.

The Hawthornes have a standing invitation to leave their rig at "Bush" while they bathe at Walden. I suppose it is an example of writers supporting each other, and certainly, the author of the essay *Nature* would approve of our adventure. We alight at the side entrance of the grand home, quarter the horse with the groom, walk a bit down the road, and take a turn onto a path and into the woods.

The day has grown hot quickly. Perspiration collects under my bonnet, and I wish I had thought to leave a petticoat or two back in my room. Pine trees and honeysuckle perfume the air, and bees bumble about in the bushes. Trees shade us here and there, but we must heave ourselves over rock walls and swerve to avoid mud patches, and I feel myself straining against my stays. My boots are old and comfortable, though, and hitching my skirt up protects it from catching on brambles. Nath is carrying the basket, walking with his usual sober dignity, and he and Margaret are lost in quiet conversation, while Sophia, clutching the blanket, brings up the rear. She is a bit out of breath, and as I remember that she has some health problems, I drop back to relieve her of the blanket and to keep her company.

"What do you think of Margaret?" she says, her voice low. "Must I worry about my husband having affectionate feelings for another woman?" She laughs a little, but I can tell she is serious beneath the merriment.

"Nath loves you with all his heart and soul," I say to reassure her. "Anyone can see that. Margaret just likes to talk to whoever will listen, and Nath has a good ear." She nods, and though her pace quickens as her mood lifts, I realize that my assumption of her acceptance of Nath's affection for Margaret was not entirely accurate. Not everyone ascribes to our family's peccadillos.

But we have fallen behind our companions and must hurry to catch up. The path through the trees here is smooth, and the air has thickened with humidity, and through the trees, we see an expanse of blue water. We have found Walden Pond. The path dips, and we must step carefully so as not to tumble down the embankment.

When we reach the high shoreline, Nath waxes eloquent of his new discovery. "Is it not a piece of blue firmament, earth encircled? She has a sister pond a few miles west that Henry Thoreau likes to call 'the gem of the woods' because the water is crystal clear and the sand there is so white and fine. His father uses it to make pencils in their factory. But I am partial to Walden."

Speak of the devil: Henry has come to the pond to swim, too. His trousers and shirt are spread out on the sand, and we can see his sleek, dark head, like an otter's, breaking the surface a few yards out. Nath calls to him, and Henry turns and strokes back towards us. Sophia waves to him to stop coming ashore before Nath can bring him his britches, but Henry just laughs and strides up the beach, his curly beard streaming water, his drawers clinging to his thighs. Sophia and Margaret drop their eyes, but I am not shy around a male figure and raise my gaze in greeting.

"Mr. Thoreau. How nice it is to see you again." He and I met when he came to Salem to visit. He is nine years younger than I, but I think Nath was playing Cupid still. Despite his kindly face and hale physique, Henry is too rough for me, but his attitude toward the natural world is fascinating, and I could listen to him tell his tales of flora and fauna all day.

However, we must relent to the rules of society, and so the men and women separate.

Sophia leads Margaret and me to a more secluded cove on the north side of the pond. There we strip down to our chemises, carefully folding our dresses and underthings on the grass. I dip my toe in the clear, cool water and then take the plunge. Margaret is more circumspect, but she joins me after consideration of the temperature. Sophia only goes in up to her waist before she gasps and turns around to sit and watch us from the grassy bank. Margaret and I paddle around in the shallows for a bit before I strike out for deeper parts, and she returns to shore.

Thanks to my childhood of swimming in Salem, Nahant, and Maine, I am at ease in the water. I shimmy out of my chemise and fling it back to Sophia, who spreads it out on the bank to dry. She and Margaret sit in the grass, and I can hear their voices murmuring, joining with the bird song and insect chirps. I float on my back, savoring the feeling of weightlessness, the sensation of cold on my overheated skin, and enjoy the blue sky, white clouds, and treetops. My mind drifts, and I am swept away into sensual pleasures—what a delightful way to pass an afternoon.

I stroke back to shore when Sophia calls me in for our picnic. Margaret meets me at the low water mark with my chemise held up to shield me from the prying eyes of the menfolk, and I draw it down over myself neatly and then don the drawers, the petticoats, the bodice and skirt, and the socks and boots onshore. The clothing feels like an encumbrance when one has been free of it all afternoon. I wring out my hair and pin it up as best I can, but as Margaret takes my arm to follow Sophia, I pull her back and motion toward a mossy sitting area.

"Louisa, are you quite well?" Margaret peers up at me, checking for some sort of imagined swimmer's exhaustion, and I wave away her concern.

"It is nothing. It is simply that water reminds me of my father, and I need a bit of time to collect myself before I can continue my social obligations." I hope to elicit her empathy before making my less than sympathetic case for elicit love.

"Ah yes." Her voice is gentle. "Your father died at sea when you were very young, as I recall. Do you pine for what might have been?"

I nod, my vulnerabilities exposed. Margaret plumps herself down on the moss cushion and pats the padded bank beside her. When I have drawn together my skirts and joined her, she says, "Is there something you wish to discuss? Anything with which I might be of service?"

Many of Margaret's writings and speeches are about the sexual equality of women and men, and our past discussions have been frank, and so I decide to forge ahead, social mores be damned.

"You may have heard that I had been living with my Aunt Priscilla and her husband, John Dike. He is my uncle only by marriage."

"Indeed." She squints at me, confused by the change in topic. "Your point?"

"The Dikes allowed me to live with them when Nath requested privacy for his writing." Margaret nods. "But then, Mr. Dike's business failed, and we all moved back into Herbert Street." She tilts her head, a bit befuddled by the history. I try to simplify. "Well. Something happened during their stay. Between John and me. We . . ."

Margaret goes very still. "Louisa. Are you saying that you are having an," she swallows and continues with measured words, "affectionate relationship with your uncle?"

I nod.

She stares off into the woods, her face impassive. "Does your Aunt Priscilla know?"

"I do not believe so. They have grown far apart over the years, and she is extremely cold to him. When his daughter from his first marriage died, Priscilla neglected to tell him that she was in part responsible, and they never had children of their own, perhaps because she did not enjoy the act of love." Margaret coughs briefly but recovers and continues to listen without comment. "But from the first day that I met him when I was only seven, and he was kind to me, I have adored him, and finally, about ten years ago, in mutual agreement, we consummated our relationship." Margaret brings her hand to her mouth, but she remains silent. "Then a Revival meeting came to town which he attended to make amends with God and his daughter, and some family history came to light which assuaged John's guilt in other ways." Margaret's eyebrows rise and her lips purse.

"Recently," I continue, "when John's business improved, and they moved to their new house, Priscilla demanded that I remain in my family's home and cease my visitations. She keeps a cold hand on John, and it seems to me that the only sinner in this situation is Priscilla, who is dishonest with her husband and does not take delight in him." I am out of breath from trying to win my argument.

Margaret contemplates the tranquil pond for what seems like an eternity, her eyes narrowed in thought, her head tipped to one side, and then she nods as if deciding something. "I think that you yearn for the father whom you never knew, and Mr. Dike is fulfilling that need, as well as your hunger for a soul mate. *Male and female represent the two sides of the great radical dualism, but they are perpetually passing into one another, fluid hardening to solid, solid rushing to fluid.* Such are the forces affecting you and John. Together you will find a future good. And we women must embrace our female strength, our *feminisme*, as the French say. I contend that you are espousing yours, while Priscilla chooses to subvert her own. We are lucky to be living in an age when such urges can be understood as natural and necessary for both sexes. If it is of any import, I give you my blessing to seek your happiness."

I squeeze her hand in gratitude, but further discussion is interrupted by Sophia's entreaties to come and join the others. We enjoy leftover chicken and bread and the delightful company of old and new friends till it is time to find our way home before darkness comes.

In the twilight, the pairings have changed, and now Margaret and Sophia commune, while Nath and Henry converse about the local farmers, and I, in a pensive mood, bring up the rear. We say good night to Margaret and Henry at the Emersons', hitch up the horse, and ride home from our adventure. Sarah has set out upon the sideboard a cold but satisfying meal of cheese, bread, squash, corn, and milk. We fill our plates and bring them to the table, where Nath entertains us with more ghost tales about the house until I can no longer stifle my yawns.

"Good night, you two. See you in the morning." I embrace the happy couple and climb to my solitary chamber, undress in the warm dark, and fall asleep to the sound of crickets in the breeze, feeling secure in the knowledge that, with wise woman Margaret Fuller's blessing, I can return to Salem to pursue my happiness with John.

January 17, 1843

My Dear Thomas,

You are a genius. Such a diabolical plan formulated by a man of God must mean that it is doubly blessed.

I had heard that private investigators were available in Europe. However, I was unaware of their existence here in the United States. I am uncomfortable with your idea of a former prisoner being employed to watch my niece. Perhaps there might be a laborer from the docks who would welcome additional funds. My brother William could be a source for such a candidate.

Louisa often visits my nephew and his wife in Concord. The employee would be required to follow her wherever she might travel. Expenses for meals and lodging would be paid anonymously.

She is not a foolish woman. She would recognize someone if he were a constant presence. I trust that appropriate training would be undertaken to ensure success. Perhaps several employees might be hired for variety.

Nothing must be traced back to me. Should there be any questions, I will deny any knowledge of this enterprise. You have my eternal gratitude.

Your Sister in Christ,
PMD

March 10, 1844

Sophia writes to me in January to request help from Mother, Ebe, and myself with the birth of her first child, due in March. As she miscarried a child the year before, she is understandably nervous and desires the reassurance of family attendance.

Yet my mother refuses. "Louisa, you know very well that I cannot leave this house. I have neither the clothes nor the funds to undertake such a journey, and my cough has returned. I realize that Sophia's feelings are hurt because I have not yet seen this rental home of hers, but I am sure Nath understands. Ask Ebe to accompany you."

Ebe replies with tart sarcasm to my letter. "I can't stand that little wisp of a thing Nath calls his 'dove,' and you know Mother will never leave Herbert Street, so you alone must play the nursemaid."

Sophia has also asked her own mother for help, which makes more sense to me. Although I have helped with various cousins' births, it is an extremely personal experience, and a close family member would seem to be the best choice. However, Mrs. Peabody is otherwise engaged with an ailing cousin. Concord's physician, Doctor Bartlett, is on call, so Dr. Peabody would be superfluous, and I expect that Nath will be of no use whatsoever, so another pair of experienced hands would no doubt be appreciated.

As neither my mother nor my sister will rise to the occasion, I decide to ask John for help as well. Having had two children of his own and nursed family members through illnesses, I know he will not quail at the sight of blood, and he enjoys playing fairy godfather to the Hawthorne family. Sophia judges Aunt Priscilla to be too hard and cold and would not want her in the birthing room, but Sophia might think John could be a calming presence. I write to Sophia and suggest that John join me, at the least to keep Nath company, and at the most to be of help if need be, and she agrees.

Following my conversation with Margaret Fuller in 1842, I returned to Salem, persuaded that my relationship with John was indeed valid. Margaret's assertion that the sensual urges of both men and women could be legitimate and natural reiterated my own belief that we live in an era of sexual awakening. However, though philosophers such as Susan Burley and Elizabeth Peabody also espouse that reasoning, not all of Salem may be ready to embrace this new enlightenment. Its women might toil alongside its men, but societal mores are still a hindrance to true equality.

Yet my family has positioned itself in the forefront of this dawning revolution. The ancient Manning parchment documented a familial love even at a time of Puritanical repression. Ebe's early birth proved that our own parents embraced such sensual liberties. And now, with Margaret's measured analysis of Aunt Priscilla's transgressions and my familial needs, my shame has abated, and I am grateful to live in this time and in this place, as imperfect as they still may be, to reap the benefit of change.

And John's discoveries of the truth behind his daughter's death and my family's proclivities have assuaged much of his terrible guilt as well. We do not deny our love to certain close friends and family, but we keep it a strict secret from our enemies. John takes great pains to keep his wife ignorant, and so the shore, my room, his office, all have been clandestine settings for our physical pleasure.

But traveling to Concord means that we will be in the open, so it is best to be transparent. I venture a visit to Aunt Priscilla in her serpent's lair and suggest that she come with me to help Sophia in her lying in, knowing full well that she will never acquiesce.

"I cannot abandon my responsibilities at the church, Louisa. Besides, Sophia has made it perfectly clear that she does not welcome my company." Aunt Priscilla's knitting needles drum an angry percussion to her complaints. "She and Nath have secluded themselves in Concord. God forbid they should come back to his hometown."

"My mother has declined, and Ebe as well," I reply, "But Sophia is determined to have several people there in case something goes awry. Do you think you could spare Mr. Dike for a few days? If he can leave the business, that is."

Aunt Priscilla narrows her eyes at me. "What would a man do? Is there not already a doctor on call?"

"Indeed. But I think Sophia is concerned that Nath might need some looking after."

Aunt Priscilla gives a little grunt of dismissal. "That boy always was too sensitive for his own good. He made up that boyhood limp, you know, because someone was bullying him at school. He just wanted to say home with his mother and read." She jerks at the skein of yarn, and her knitting needles click rapidly as she considers my proposal.

Finally, she agrees, "Business is slow at this time of year. I will check on the books at the office myself. If Mr. Dike wishes to go, then I give him my blessing. Send word when the child has arrived, and I will expect my husband home forthwith." She nods her dismissal of me, but there is an odd little smile playing at the corners of her mouth that makes me wonder at some possible alternative motive.

I shrug and let myself out the front door with a lightness in my step and in my heart. I am surprised but joyful that my aunt is so amenable. John and I will have Concord and its environs in which to enjoy each other, with discretion, of course. Nath and Sophia are now both aware of our love, but we do not want to offend anyone else or put ourselves in jeopardy with the local constabulary.

"She said yes." I find John checking invoices in his office. His assistant is in the adjoining room, and we are careful not to hand him any fodder for gossip, so we keep our distance, but John's grin reveals his excitement. In a few days, we will be on a stage traveling away from Salem to Concord.

I write to Sophia and Nath of our plans. "I shall stay in my usual room at the Old Manse, but although Mr. Dike is grateful for your kind invitation, he will board at the tavern in the center of Concord." I do not add that propriety will thereby be served, but if an opportunity is afforded us, John and I have a venue in which to enjoy each other's company.

Sophia writes back, "Understood. Dr. Bartlett has given me about a week before my lying in, so you and Mr. Dike should make your arrangements and come to Concord as soon as possible."

We meet, well wrapped against the cold February morning, at the Salem stage junction. John goes inside to pay our fares while I stamp my feet to keep them from freezing.

"I am so happy to travel to Concord with you. I cannot wait to introduce you to Nath and Sophia's Old Manse and Henry's Walden," I say to John after we seat ourselves in the crowded stage.

"I hope we will not be bathing in the pond in this weather." John blows on his hands. "Could they not have arranged for their baby to be born in the summer? Nath wrote me that the house has given them chilblains and that the maid's hair froze one morning in the steam over the washbasin. I am looking forward to splitting and stacking their wood and spending the rest of my visit in front of the fire. With you," he finishes in a whisper, with a furtive glance at our coach-mates, but they are all too intent on keeping warm to pay us any mind.

After an uneventful but chilly journey to Boston and then to Concord, John hands me down into the trodden snow at the entrance to the Old Manse, tips the driver, and retrieves our valises while I pick up my skirts and hurry down the drive and into the comparative warmth of the buttery. Sarah fusses over our blue hands and faces before hanging up our cloaks and leading us into the kitchen where we enjoy tea and scones.

"Louze, Mr. Dike, thank you so much for helping us in our time of need." Nath saunters in from his study, kisses my cheek, shakes John's hand, takes a scone and a cup of tea and a chair, and invites Pigwiggin to jump into his lap and settle down.

"Nath, please do me the honor of calling me John. We are all adults now, and I will feel particularly ancient if you and Sophia insist on such formality."

"Of course, John." Nath strokes the cat while aiming a conspiratorial wink at me. "Thank you for the invitation. Though I doubt I could address Mrs. Dike by only her first name without a bit of venom hissed my way." John smiles wryly at this in-joke told at his ophidian wife's expense.

"Have you received any word from John Stephens?" John attempts to disguise the worry and envy in his voice with false jocularity, but Nath is not fooled at this deception.

He keeps his attention on Pigwiggen as he answers, "John Stephens wrote a month or so ago with congratulations at our happy baby news. I shall write him again once the deed is done." Nath takes a breath to gauge his audience and ventures more. "I am sorry that he and Margaretta have not enjoyed the same sort of luck. I know you were looking forward to grandchildren, so you will just have to be content with spoiling little Hawthornes instead of Dikes."

John smiles, but Nath and I recognize the sorrow, both at the lack of communication with his son and the barren marriage, hidden in that crooked little grin, and we all take sips of tea to cover our discomfort.

After we have given John a chance to collect himself, Nath lifts the cat to the floor and stands.

"Louze, you will be staying in your usual aerie. Let me help you with your valise." Nath swings my little case onto his shoulder like a stevedore, and John and I follow him up the stairs.

John pauses at Nath's study door and points to the window, where ghostly words are engraved upon the glass.

"Nath, what is that writing? Has someone been scratching to come in?"

Nath sets my valise down in the hall. "Let me read it to you."

John listens, rapt, as Nath intones the words. *"*Man's accidents are God's purposes. Sophia Hawthorne, 1843. Nath Hawthorne. This is his study. The smallest twig leans clear against the sky. Composed by my wife and written with her diamond. Inscribed by my husband at sunset in the Gold Light. SAH.'"*

"That is beautiful," John says, his voice hushed.

"A writer's income is never certain. We engraved it indelibly with Sophia's diamond ring so that, should we be forced to leave, our love will remain. And it inspires me as I attempt to write," says Nath.

"Are you working on anything in particular?" asks John.

"Short stories. I shall name the collection after this house, as its ministerial ghost has inspired much of its lofty language, but I must decide on a name. *Tales from an Old Manse* is too reminiscent of *Twice-Told Tales*." He sinks into his writing chair, his eyes searching the horizon for a title. We leave him to his reverie, deliver my bag to my room, and return to the steamy kitchen.

"Where is Sophia? Does she not need a little sustenance?" I ask, and Sarah nods and prepares a tray. I go back upstairs and knock on Sophia's door. There is a muted cough, and then a weak voice calls, "Please come in, but do not let the cat through the door. She insists on lying on my chest."

Sophia is sitting up in bed, but I am alarmed by her pale skin and dark-circled eyes. I am not a healer, but I know enough to recognize anemia. Sophia has never eaten well, and pregnancy can bring on scurvy and other imbalances, so I decide to buy some meat and prepare a broth that might soothe her while also nourishing the child.

I smooth Sophia's hair back from her forehead and watch to make sure she eats her scone and drinks the tea, and when she is finished, I bring the tray downstairs to the kitchen and gather information. "Nath, where does one buy provisions in this town?" Sarah looks up from the sink where she is scrubbing a pot and says in her brogue, "I can take you, Miss. We servants know the best places to buy the meat and potatoes."

"John, you and Nath stay here and keep Sophia company. Sarah and I are going marketing." We are home in plenty of time to put the beef, bought at the aptly named Mr. Blood's Butchery, in the oven along with some root vegetables from the cellar.

Sophia eats some of the beef and carrots, and the next day her color is better, and she has the energy to come downstairs to discuss the plans for her lying in. "Dr. Bartlett is on call," she tells us. "Please do not try to bring Nath into the room. He cannot even watch the cat have her kittens. I am afraid he would be a distraction." Nath colors, and we all have a little chuckle at his expense, but I know from experience that my brother is not one to help in an emergency, as he tends to stand back, observe, and then write about it later.

Supper that evening is hash made from the left-over roast. Sarah is quite a competent cook, and both John and I compliment her as we help her clear the table. We are all laughing at each other's accents when Nath shouts from Sophia's room, "Fetch Dr. Bartlett! It has begun!"

John hitches the horse to the chaise and races down the drive while Sarah and I rush to boil water and gather towels. Sophia's hair is damp, and her lips are slack with exhaustion when I check in on her. I sponge her forehead and speak soothing words, but a pain grips her, and she moans and clenches my hand. From my experiences helping at my cousins' births, I know that we are in for a long night.

In half an hour, I hear a bridle jingling. Thank goodness Concord is a small town where people live in each other's pockets. Dr. Bartlett, freshly shaven and smelling of clean laundry, comes into the birthing room with a cheerful greeting and washes his hands in the bowl I have readied. Sophia is resting between contractions, so he instructs me in how to position her and checks her progress.

"Another few hours, I should think." His tone is soothing as he washes his hands again. "Miss Hawthorne, could you help me roll Mrs. Hawthorne over so you can massage her back? I think that would ease her pains just a little." We try the maneuver, and after a few minutes of massage, Sophia starts the next contraction but seems to be in somewhat less pain.

"Miss Hawthorne, a midwife, taught me another technique. Try instructing her to blow out strong, short breaths while she is feeling the pains. Breathing in such a way seems to relieve the pressure."

We try it, and Sophia is grateful that she can focus on something other than the pain. We practice the breathing and panting method for several cycles of contractions. Then, many hours in, her pain level seems to increase, and the breathing techniques are no longer as successful. When she has a chance to rest again, Dr. Bartlett checks her progress. "You may start pushing now, Mrs. Hawthorne. It won't be long until you have a babe in your arms."

Sophia grunts and pushes with all her might, and it all ends in a great gush of blood and fluid as a tiny baby with a mop of red hair slides into Dr. Bartlett's capable hands.

I open the chamber door to see John standing at the ready in case he is needed. His eyes gleam with unshed tears, and I suspect that he grieves for opportunities missed in his second marriage. I smile at him with sympathy, for I, too, feel envious, but I look past him in search of Nath, who has apparently retreated to his study, ostensibly to write, but more likely to hide from his wife's discomfort.

Dr. Bartlett holds the baby up by the feet and gives it a good smack on the behind which results in a wail from the child. *"She's a girl! And by George, she looks just like me!"* he exclaims. John chuckles at this old obstetrical jest, but Sophia is not in the mood for humor and frowns into the next contraction. Dr. Bartlett cuts the cord and hands the baby to me to swaddle while Sophia pushes out the afterbirth, and Dr. Bartlett examines it for any irregularities.

When he is certain that all is well with Sophia and the baby, he says, "Mr. Dike, could you please help Mrs. Hawthorne to sit up?" John stoops over Sophia and, with gentle hands, raises her on the pillow so that I may place the baby in her arms. "What will you call her?" asks Dr. Bartlett.

"Una," Sophia croons and adds, "so she will always be true." Dr. Bartlett, John, and I exchange bemused glances. Expectations will be high for a little girl named for the character personifying Truth in *The Faerie Queene*. The doctor washes his hands one last time, gives me instructions for Sophia's care, packs up his medical bag and shrugs on his coat. I accompany him into the hall and see by the light in the window that the sun is rising. "Thank you, Doctor Bartlett. This birth seemed less painful than others I have attended."

"It is due entirely to the midwife's techniques. I cannot take the credit. Please pass them along to other women if you have the chance."

John has the horse and chaise ready and drives the doctor home to his well-deserved rest, and I go back upstairs to see if I can help with the nursing process. But when I open the door, I see mother and baby sleeping in peace, so I close the door quietly so as not to disturb them and go to my own room for a welcome rest.

But sleep does not immediately come. John's grief has awakened in me a longing that I immediately recognize. Though I have been successfully diligent with the prophylactic potions and douches, I have never lost sight of the fact that I may never birth a child, may never experience what is a woman's greatest achievement. My tears drop onto Sophia's embroidered pillowcase even as I squeeze my eyes shut to keep out the morning ray's interruptions. But the night's exertions take their toll, and soon my sadness dissolves into anxious dreams concerning boiling diapers and nourishing diets.

When I awaken, I run across the hall to check on the new little family and see that Una is nursing with enthusiasm while her mother watches, entranced. Nath is nowhere to be seen, but upon a further search, he is found in his study, writing. I wave to him and go to the kitchen, thinking that Sarah might need help with the evening meal, but she has bought a plump chicken and is in the process of stuffing it with onions and carrots in preparation for roasting. I realize that now might be an excellent time for me to visit John at the tavern.

It is a glorious early spring afternoon, sunny and not too cold, so I decide to walk as I need the exercise, and the less attention I attract, the better. As I recall, it is about a mile to the town center, and Wright's tavern is situated upon the green. I pick my way through the snow and mud, open the heavy front door, and greet the serving girl who approaches me to offer help. "Mr. Dike, please?"

"Ah, yes, he is on the second floor, the door on the right. I will have a boy run up for you."

"Oh, no need, thank you. I am only delivering a meal." I display a basket I have slung over one arm, hoping to quell suspicion. It seems to work, as the girl answers, "Of course, Miss. The stairs are through that door and on your right." She returns to her duties, which I hope will distract her. I survey the room and see only a laborer nodding over his cider. He will take no note of a delivery woman.

Even so, I scurry up the steps, grateful that the stairway and landing are deserted. I arrive at John's door breathless with exertion and anticipation.

"It is about time," he murmurs and draws me into his room. His cravat and surtout are draped over the armchair by the window, and his shirt is half unbuttoned as if he were just about to bathe. "What did you bring me for luncheon?"

We spend the next hour enjoying each other's company. My basket is overturned in the festivities, but it contained only apples, which have rolled onto the floor and under the bed, and we retrieve them and trade bites while helping each other dress again.

"I should be walking back to the house. It's getting late." I peer out the window at the sun setting over the common.

"I shall wait a minute or two and then meet you at the church steps across the way." John stands behind me, nestles me against his chest, and points it out.

The serving girl is helping the laborer to another glass of cider and does not notice me as I pad down the stairs, open the front door, step out onto the snowy path, and pause to relish the atmosphere. Concord Center in twilight is so very different from Salem. Without gas street lamps, stars are visible. Supper odors do not compete with brackish air. And instead of the roar of a crowded street, there is only silence. The coming railroad will change some of that, but Concord will remain a small, rural town with ties to the big city.

John finds me on the church's steps, and we wind our way past Concord common, along frosty paths to the ice-crusted road, but when we turn the corner into the drive to the Old Manse, we are surprised to see an unfamiliar carriage. Children's voices raised in excitement emanate from the house, and a kind but firm motherly voice answers in good nature. We open the buttery door to hear, "Louisa May, give me back my bonnet! You know very well you are not allowed to borrow my things!" A lanky girl of about twelve, her long, auburn hair flying behind her and the stolen bonnet in hand, runs out the door with an older, buxom blonde, more cognizant of her skirts, chasing behind. I am familiar with sisterly arguments and suspect that there is some mischief in all of this, and indeed, when we go into the kitchen, a plump, dark-haired woman, her shawl wrapped snugly about her broad shoulders, enters, extends her hand, and says, "Good evening. I am Abba Alcott, and those silly girls who so rudely rushed by you are my daughters, Lou and Anna."

We hang up our outer wraps and join Nath and Abba in the parlor. Sophia and Una are ensconced in bed, but the two younger Alcott girls, Lizzie and May, tiptoe down the stairs from their visit with the baby. To mimic mother and child, Lizzie retrieves May's doll and helps her cradle it in her arms. May reminds me of a bisque doll with her perfect blonde ringlets and pink cheeks, but Lizzie's beauty lies in her calm and kind expression as she plays quietly with her little sister.

Lou and Anna burst into the room, their cheeks rosy with exercise and excitement. "Marmee, Lou has ruined my bonnet, just as I knew she would. She dropped it in the mud." Anna swats her sister with a glove and then throws herself into a chair in a fit of pique. Her histrionics highlight her round blue eyes and pouty mouth. Surely, she is the other beauty in the family.

Lou's handsome face brightens, and she exclaims, "Let us use the bonnet in a play. Come on, Anna, you can be the poor maiden who has no nice clothes to wear to the ball because your evil step sister ruined them, and I shall be Rodrigo, who falls in love with you anyway."

Anna swings her feet back and forth under her chair, considering this suggestion. "Can I borrow your nice lace collar? And will you wear a cape and be gallant?"

Lou nods. "And Lizzie and May can be the ball guests. And all these friends will be our audience. Please? Please, Marmee?"

"After supper, girls. Why don't you go gather your costumes and write something quickly, and we'll call you in time to eat."

"They can use my room to plan their adventures," I offer, enjoying this family. The mother, jolly and warm, is the exact opposite of mine, and the children seem to bask in their loving mother's attention as they would the sun. I must admit to feeling a little envious.

The girls run up to my room while the grownups sit and talk. "Abba, how did you escape Utopia?" Nath cocks an eyebrow at his tranquil guest. John looks confused, so Nath explains a bit about Brook Farm, the experiment in Transcendentalist communal living to which Mr. Alcott subscribes. Nath himself had lived in the community for a year but found the monk-like atmosphere and menu too demanding.

Abba shrugs her shoulders and looks resigned. "You know how Mr. Alcott is. I told him the children were hungry, and he told me that they should look inside themselves for sustenance. Well, of course, my temper got the better of me. I argued that my children need more than philosophy to stay alive, so we came back to Concord for a little rest and resuscitation."

"Your children seem to have a great deal of energy despite their meager diet," I observe. "I am looking forward to their play."

"Oh, Louisa will put on a good show. That girl has such a wonderful imagination. Someday she will be a great writer, of this, I have no doubt. That is if her sister does not kill her first." Abba chuckles and sips her tea. "But my girls have good hearts. They are more concerned with others than with themselves. Their father calls them his little women because they take such responsibility for their friends and neighbors. We are very proud of them."

Sarah comes to the doorway to announce supper. She has outdone herself, as the roast chicken is tender, the carrots sweet, the bread warm from the oven, and for dessert, she proudly presents a brown and crispy apple pie spiced with cinnamon and nutmeg.

I put together a tray for Sophia as she is still upstairs with the baby, and John and I climb up to her room. We watch to make sure she eats and drinks plenty as Dr. Bartlett instructed. Her color looks better, but she still seems groggy, and her head droops while she watches the baby at her breast.

John's brow furrows. He has told me that he remembers the births of his two children well and gives me a pointed look when Sophia flags after nursing. "Would you allow me to take Una down to enjoy the revelries? I think you could use a little break," he asks her, his voice thick with longing, and I can tell that he yearns to hold the baby.

Sophia gives a great yawn and snuggles down into the covers. "Just don't let the children breathe on her," she murmurs and closes her eyes. Pigwiggin leaps up, and I make sure that the cat nestles into the foot of the quilt.

We come downstairs holding the babe aloft, much to the delight of the other supper guests. The girls have set up a stage area in the larger parlor, with chairs arranged for the audience, and we troop in obediently and are greeted by a prince dressed in Nath's gardening boots, cape, and cap, with a coal-drawn mustache decorating his upper lip. He bows and declares, "I am noble Rodrigo, here to rescue the damsel in distress, who is sad because she cannot go to the ball." The damsel enters wearing the soiled bonnet and an equally dirty dress (I suspect it is Lou's from this afternoon's brawl). She puts a hand to her forehead and declares, "Oh woe is me, I cannot go to the ball, for I have nothing to wear!" Two ball-goers, dressed rather elegantly in Sophia's shoes and jackets, call out rudely and toss little pieces of kindling at the poor girl, who falls to her knees in histrionics.

Rodrigo strides over to her, flings back his cape, takes her hand, and lifts her up with great ceremony. "Come, my lovely. We shall away to yonder shore where clothes are nothing but a nuisance." He tucks her hand into his arm and leads her off stage to wild applause from the enchanted audience.

John must be careful not to clap with Una asleep in his arms, so I applaud hard for both of us. He catches my eye and winks but then gazes down at Una, and I see a dark cloud of grief pass over his face. Aunt Priscilla has given him no children. He was a caring father to John Stephens, but now they live so far apart, and John Stephens has ceased almost all communications. John must be yearning to have children once again in his life, and perhaps Una and her possible future siblings will be able to fulfill some of that longing. My heart breaks that I cannot give him what he desires.

Abba rises and calls to her girls. "We need to be back at Lovejoy Farm so that the housekeeper does not sound out an alarm." She turns to John and caresses the tiny baby in his arms. "I am so glad that this birth was uneventful. We were all a little concerned after the miscarriage, and Sophia seems so delicate. It was lovely to meet you both, and I look forward to seeing you during other visits." She shakes my hand with her large, warm one, pats John's elbow, and rounds up her children, who are all starting to look a little sleepy. John returns a hungry Una to her waiting mother.

"Good night, Nath. Please give Sophia my love." Nath and I help Abba to gather up her belongings and escort her and the girls to the waiting carriage while John tacks the horse and hitches her to the rig. Lou climbs up to sit with her mother on the seat, and Anna, Lizzie, and May clamor into the cabin. Abba takes the reins, gives the horse a little tap, and they are off, waving madly from seat and window, and I find myself wishing I could be a part of this boisterous, loving family.

Nath climbs the stairs to tuck Sophia and Una in, leaving John and me relaxing before the fire. John seems reluctant to go back to the tavern.

Sarah has long since retired to bed in her third-floor room, so as it is just the two of us, he reaches for my hand.

"Do you ever dream that we might have a child together?" His voice is soft with longing.

"Always. But it would be divorce ammunition for your wife and the ruin of the both of us. Better to spoil Una and hope that John Stephens and Margaretta might have better luck." I bring his hand to my lips, close my eyes against the tears that threaten to spill, and we stay entwined until the fire has burned to embers.

After seeing him off on his walk to the tavern, I climb to my lonely room. The girls have left their borrowed costume pieces all in a jumble on my bed, so I hang them up on the wall hooks and find my nightdress. Sleep comes easily after our thoughtful conversation, and I dream of John dressed as Rodrigo, carrying me off to a faraway shore where clothes are but a nuisance.

The next morning, I awaken to the smell of frying bacon and steeping tea. I check in on Sophia to take her breakfast order.

"Louisa," she says, "I am so grateful to you and John for being here to help Nath and Una. But please feel free to leave whenever you need to. Sarah is here, and my mother is due tomorrow."

"Thank you for the information. John and I will probably take the stage back to Boston and then on to Salem today. We do not wish to overburden you with too many house guests." I want to avoid Mrs. Peabody if possible, as she is convinced that her daughter is a sickly soul, and I do not enjoy watching their interactions.

When John arrives an hour later, I explain the situation. He is disappointed but resigned, and though we are both grateful that we still have opportunities in Salem to enjoy each other, I suspect that Concord will be our refuge as time passes. We take our leave of the little family, making promises to visit again in the very near future, then wait by the gate for the stage back to Boston and our own responsibilities.

Pittsburgh, Pennsylvania
May 21, 1884

Springtime in the Smoky City featured trees blooming in a fog of soot. It was difficult to differentiate between the pink of the cherry trees and the white of the magnolias in their many variations of gray. Ash lay thick on the steps of Dr. Voight's building, and I wiped my feet carefully before following the nurse to the now-familiar office.

"I trust you have recovered from our encounter last week. I really must thank you for complying with my request to witness one of your spells." Doctor Voight's delivery was dry, but I was not in the mood to appreciate the humor.

Although I often felt dog-tired after a spell, I could usually shake off the effects in a day or two. But despite Margaretta's best efforts to nourish and groom me, I had to lay low for several days, missing work and overstaying our welcome at Tom and Virginia's. And when at last I returned to the Emporium, my belly felt too exposed to handle more than a modicum of management.

At home, the documents languished, as Margaretta sought to protect me from certain diary entries and letters, not wishing to delay my recovery. Yet when I encountered her in the study weeping over a page, I could not let her suffer alone, and so we relived some of our darkest heartaches, sometimes inducing a spell, though none as severe as what I experienced at the fete.

Dr. Voight saw my concentration wane and brought me back to the present. "I understand that you have been unwell. We shall endeavor to find the source of your spells so that you may eventually heal. Do you have any idea why you might have reacted as you did last week?"

I cleared my gummy throat and tried to focus on the question and not the memory. "I believe so. My cousin Virginia mentioned certain tragic events in my married life."

"I see. And how long are you married?" asked Dr. Voight, pen poised above the perennial sheet of paper, eyes cast down, his accent making the questions seem more of an interrogation than possibly intended.

"Fifty-two years," I said, not without some pride. "Margaretta and I enjoy a happy marriage. Many of our friends could not say the same."

He nodded, keeping his eyes to the page, seemingly unimpressed. "And how many children?" When he did not hear an immediate answer, he raised his eyes to find me looking even more troubled. He sat back and waved a hand to encourage elucidation.

I shrugged. "I never know how to answer that question." My voice sounded defensive, even to me, and I could not rid myself of the fear that discussing this subject might bring on another spell.

He blinked owlishly behind his spectacles. "Ah. Should I ask then, how many living children?" He steepled his fingers again, but instead of meeting my eyes, he stared out the window, allowing me my privacy.

"None." To my embarrassment, tears threatened. The tragedy was fifty years ago, yet somehow talking about it in this office, to this man, made it painfully fresh.

"I am sorry. Perhaps you would elucidate? Sometimes talking about a disturbing subject can make it easier to bear."

Could I talk about it? Margaretta and I had buried this subject, both literally and figuratively, until Virginia's speech resurrected it. But if talking about our experiences would help me conquer my spells, even if it brought one on, I was willing to try.

I took a deep breath and began, "My wife Margaretta is the sister of my Aunt Anna, my Uncle Nathaniel's wife. Technically, then, she is not only my wife but also my aunt." Dr. Voight raised an eyebrow but otherwise made no reaction. "We met when I moved at twenty-one to Steubenville to work for Uncle Nathaniel. Aunt Anna was an extremely motherly woman and took me under her wing. Margaretta had the same loving nature, and we fell in love and married in 1831 and immediately set up a nest in a small house that my uncle and aunt purchased for us nearby. I walked to the Emporium each day and returned home to a delicious dinner and a loving wife. We had every expectation of expecting, but as Margaretta counted the months, and then a year, since the honeymoon, panic overcame the bedroom, and my homecoming every night became a marathon of exacting specifications, each determined to be more promising than the last."

I hunched my shoulders at the last admission and peered at the doctor, but he was still gazing impassively out the window, so I continued.

"When a year and a half had gone by with no success, Uncle Nathaniel suggested I see his physician. Aunt Anna had a similar conversation with Margaretta, resulting in the two of us spending a tense afternoon at my uncle's home meeting with his doctor and being subjected to several uncomfortable and embarrassing conversations. Margaretta was led away to the bedroom for testing and reappeared in tears. The doctor seemed genuinely sorrowful when he gave us the unfortunate diagnosis of a tilted womb."

Dr. Voight interjected a clinical question. "What year was this?"

"1833." He nodded, lips pursed, and I continued, "We took solace in each other's arms, and six weeks later, Margaretta met me at the door not with dinner but with a much bigger reward. Apparently, at least according to Aunt Anna and all the other ladies in their sewing circle, there was nothing better for conceiving children than being told one can never have them. Aunt Anna had herself suffered two stillborn sons, and then, miraculously, her daughter Virginia, whom you know, was born. Perhaps it ran in the family."

Dr. Voight shook his head at this, whether at my ridiculous suggestion or disgust at the medical knowledge of the time, I could not tell.

I continued, "Margaretta spent her first few months knitting baby clothes, grateful for feeling well with none of the morning sickness about which she had been warned and dreaming of the day when she could walk to the park with a pram. My pride grew with her expanding girth, and we spent our evenings planning for our new lives as a family of three.

"When Margaretta reached the milestone of five months, Aunt Anna and Uncle Nathaniel invited us in for a celebratory dinner. Margaretta, whose appetite had always been hearty and had now become legion, that evening picked at her food, complaining that it was too salty, despite Aunt Anna's insistence that the cook had adhered strictly to her usual recipe. We left early as Margaretta complained of headache, but it was not until we arrived home that she admitted to me that she had noticed something amiss when she used the privy. I insisted that we send for the doctor, but she demurred, trying to convince herself and me that it was nothing. We attempted to take our minds off this new worry by reading quietly in the parlor until she cried out, stood, and collapsed onto the carpet.

"I shouted for the housemaid to fetch the doctor, then carried my stricken wife to our bedroom where I tried to staunch the red river that soaked her skirts, the blankets, the sheets, the mattress until the doctor and Aunt Anna arrived and forced me from the room. I waited in the parlor, and there the doctor found me at first light. He told me that although Margaretta had lived, she would never bear another child. And . . . the baby did not survive. I could not help but blame myself for not coming sooner to their rescue."

That last confession echoed with my sobs in the otherwise silent room. Dr. Voight said nothing, but I felt a handkerchief being stuffed into my clenched hand and heard a sigh and a squeak as he sat back down in his chair.

His pen scratched for a bit, and then he said, "Mr. Dike, you and your wife experienced a great loss. But it was not your fault that she miscarried, nor was it something you could control. Forgive yourself. You are not to blame." He paused until I had blown my nose and collected myself. "I think we have done enough for today. You are making great progress, even if it does not yet feel so. We will find the root of your spells; of this, I am certain. Until next week."

He escorted me to a hansom cab, and I rode in a daze of sorrow back to the train station, onto the train to Steubenville, home, and into Margaretta's comforting arms. I recounted to her my transformative session with Dr. Voight, and we grieved together, finding solace at last in revealing to each other our true feelings.

And although Margaretta attempted to filter the documents, it became obvious that I must vanquish my spells and read them all if I wished to discover the truth behind my family's tragedies and find justice for my sister and cousin. Therefore, I looked forward, with some trepidation, to my next healing session with Dr. Voight.

Priscilla Manning Dike
4 Andover Street
Salem, Massachusetts

August 10, 1849

My Dear Thomas,

From my dying sister's lips, I heard our vindication. She verified our employees' reports of my husband's transgressions and my niece's disloyalty. We may now increase our surveillance, secure in the knowledge that we are virtuous in our cause. Truly I am a fortunate woman. It is a blessing indeed that a man of God should aid me in this righteous crusade.

～⌒～

In Betsey's sickroom, her obsequious daughters tiptoed about, turning her to prevent bedsores, moistening her lips with water, rearranging the covers. I knelt in the corner and begged Jesus to forgive my egocentric sister for her transgressions against her family and her God.

Betsey had sequestered herself away for so many years that I no longer quite knew her. When her husband died in Suriname, she retreated from life. She chose old-fashioned widow's weeds and refused the company of her children, her sister, her brothers, her friends. Even the clergy were rebuffed. It had become my duty to bring God to her whenever I had the chance.

"Aunt Priscilla, she is asking for you," Louisa whispered. I knelt by the bedside. Louisa hovered nearby, but I waved her away. Whatever my sister desired to impart to me might be private. Our family had far too many unnatural secrets.

"Prissy, come closer," Betsey murmured. I bent my head to her mouth, thinking that I would be privy to her dying confession. As the family acolyte, it was my duty to grant her absolution for the sexual sins she committed so long ago. I composed myself, nun-like. With steely reserve, I took her hand. "Speak, sister, empty your soul."

But I was not prepared for an attack. "Prissy, you are a woman of faith. You must pray harder to forget your troubled past and accept the present. John has a sensitive soul. He suffers at your harsh words and his empty bed. If you are not careful, you could see it filled with another. Louisa has always yearned for male affection. She may well seize the day."

I reared back at this verbal slap. Light motes danced before my eyes. My legs gave way as I tried to stand. I swayed, perhaps to swoon. Louisa ran to me. Had she not caught me, my head might have met the floor.

"Aunty, are you well? Do you need a sip of water?" She placed a firm arm about my waist. She seated me in a chair in the corner and curled my fingers around a cup. My emotions roiled. I hung my head over my knees. Louisa put her hand on my back. I begged God to dampen my disgust at her touch. I took a deep breath. I sat up. And I calmed myself till I was but a seated stone statue.

Sophia knocked and, without waiting for acknowledgment, minced in. At the sight of me so white-faced and still, she turned to Louisa for guidance. Louisa just shrugged her shoulders and gestured for her sister-in-law to speak.

"Una and Julian are asking how their grandmother is faring," Sophia whispered.

Louisa shook her head and murmured, "It won't be long now. You had best bring them in to say their goodbyes."

Sophia left briefly and returned with the children. They tiptoed to the death bed and knelt on the side benches. Una, always an unnatural child, seemed fascinated with her grandmother's frail appearance. She stared for a long time, her face inches from her grandmother's. Julian tugged on her sleeve to pull her back from the bed.

They turned and only then noticed me. I had not moved. Nor could I weep. I must have seemed heartless, a stone statue in my chair. They did not understand. I could not acknowledge the sister who had betrayed me.

Sophia ushered the children out and returned to the sickroom. Then Nath stalked in. His relationship with his mother had been difficult at best. He was not one to interrupt his writing for sentimental reasons. I was shocked that he sat by her bedside as Louisa directed him. He took Betsey's hand in his. She said a few indistinct words to him. He smiled. My gorge rose. She spoke of love to him and had only hurtful words for me.

My presence here was perfunctory. I must take myself away. Without a word to anyone, I rose and left the chamber. Sophia shut the door behind me with a firm hand.

I found myself at my own front door without recollection of the walk. John stood in the dim hall candlelight. His face was a mask of concern. "Priscilla, you are too pale. Come sit down and tell me what happened." He moved to take my hand. I avoided him. Undeterred, he followed me to the parlor.

"Did she pass on?" he asked. I shrugged. He wrapped a shawl about my shivering shoulders. I shrank from his touch and sat stiff-backed in my chair. I automatically took up my knitting. The familiar scent of camphor calmed me.

"Did she have any last words for you?"

I took a deep breath to harden my resolve. "She told me to be kinder to you." My voice was as hard as steel. "She seemed to think that I do not nurture you and our love. She believes that I am too much of God and not enough woman for you."

John looked startled. Then he nodded in acquiescence. He knew full well that people suspected something unnatural about our relationship.

Indeed, just a week ago, that busybody Margaret Felt visited me and made suggestive remarks. She practically salivated at the prospect of ingratiating herself with John while her husband was off at sea.

"Priscilla," she said in that simpering tone that so aggrieved me, "I have noticed Mr. Dike looking sad and lonely at meeting. Perhaps you ought to come down from the pulpit before someone else fills his pew."

"How dare you say such a thing," I said to her, scandalized. "You know my husband is a man of principle. He is quite content in whatever form our marriage takes."

She left wearing a sly smile. I wondered if John and I were the talk of the town. But Salem's randy inhabitants had no more gentility than did the flotsam and jetsam that washed up upon its ragged shores. It was none of their business. The Mannings always rose above it all.

But now our front door opened. John moved quickly down the corridor and whispered to someone. The door closed, and he returned to me. "Louisa wanted you to know that Betsey passed on a few minutes ago. Louisa regrets that you are feeling troubled and hopes that her mother's words did not somehow wound you. Betsey has been even more of a mystery than usual lately, but you know that she loved you."

He bent to kiss the top of my head. I ducked away from his lips. He took a quick breath. "Would you rather be alone?" he asked, ever solicitous.

I took my vengeful feelings out upon my knitting. I pulled the yarn from the skein too fiercely and created a great tangle. I paused to unravel it. I took a calming breath and struck for the jugular. "Yes, please. We might as well prove my sister right. From now on, our marriage will be only of convenience. We must respect the words of the dead."

He nodded. His face flushed in embarrassment. He bent to pick up his spectacles and book from the table and moved toward the door.

"One more thing, John," He turned slowly and peered at me, wary of my harsh tone. "I forbid you to see Louisa without an escort. If you go to Herbert Street, you must ensure that William is at home. And she may only visit here when I am present. My sister has decreed it."

He stilled, a thief caught with the goods. There was no denial, no pleading. The guilt was obvious in his rigid stance and his stoic silence. Then he nodded again and walked through the archway and up the stairs. There was no backward glance.

The fourth finger on my left hand ached with the weight of the gaudy emerald ring encircling it. I pulled off the offending bauble and dropped it into my knitting basket. The yarn obliterated its light, just as my anger destroyed any affection I might once have felt for my philandering husband.

Thomas, you and I have every reason now to continue our surveillance. My sister, my nieces, my nephew, and my husband may all be in collusion. But I am so very grateful that I have your torrid righteousness on my side.

Your Sister in Christ.

PMD

March 25, 1850

Ebe and I are bursting with pride. Our brother, Mr. Nathaniel Hawthorne, has written a best-selling romance! *The Scarlet Letter*, as he has
christened it, was published in a new and exciting mode called mass
producing so that thousands of Nath's fans will be able to read it instead
of merely hundreds. John Stephens wrote to Nath that the Steubenville
bookshops are bursting with copies, but the pokey bookstalls here in
Salem boast only two books apiece, and so Ebe and I plan a trip to Boston to gloat over the stacks that we imagine are displayed in our friend
Elizabeth Peabody's West Street Bookstore.

However, when I visit John in his office to tell him of our plans, he
is less than pleased. "Boston is overrun with the Irish escaping the potato
famine. My heart aches for these families, living in squalor fourteen to a
room down by the docks. But I cannot recommend you traveling now.
The streets are rife with beggars and pickpockets, many of them children.
Our Salem charities are sending aid." He removes his spectacles to clean
them as a ruse to wipe his eyes. "Cannot you convince the booksellers here
in town to hold an author's signing so that more copies might be ordered?"

"Ebe has tried, but the merchants are angry that Nath has painted
Salem in a less than positive light. His introductory essay concerning
the Custom House is not complimentary to our community as you well
know, and so they are loath to display a book that might do damage to
their reputations."

"Then, if you must go, take Nath with you. I am sure he would relish
the sight of his little book in the company of Dickens and Austen, and
his height alone will be enough of a deterrence to anyone seeking you
harm."

"Nath is unavailable. Sophia insists he help her pack the house for
their move to the Berkshires at the end of the month."

"Then I shall play the escort. Priscilla is consumed with her reverend's church renovations, so she will scarcely notice my absence, and I could never forgive myself if something were to happen to you." He checks that his secretary has abandoned his desk before caressing my waist.

"What about Ebe?" I ask with a wink. He smiles and shrugs his shoulders. He must protect the foe as well as the friend.

Ebe travels in from Beverly, and we all meet at the Salem stagecoach station at four o'clock for our journey into Boston. Although I am grateful for the many fashionable layers of cloth that protect me from the early spring chill, my skirts are a burden as I must manipulate the modern hoop into an oblong to navigate the steps and then find room for its circumference at my feet. Ebe, of course, eschews all form of new dress and gathers her soft skirts neatly under her seat.

John keeps his eyes on his business ledger, and Ebe draws a book from her bag, but I enjoy watching the scenery and our fellow passengers, who range from a tradesman in a dusty overcoat to a gentleman in tails and top hat. Ebe and I are the only women, due partly, no doubt, to the difficulties our fashions force upon us. When one is weighted down with forty pounds of skirts and corsets, traveling away from the house becomes an ordeal. I think of my friend Margaret, now working in Rome, and her feminist notions of fashion, which reminds me of the philosophical gatherings she attended, and I dare to interrupt my traveling companions.

"Elizabeth Peabody informs me that Bronson Alcott now hosts Conversations in his office above her shop," I mention as the stage lumbers along.

"Abba's husband?" asks John, his brow furrowing as he tries to remember what little he learned about Mr. Alcott when Una was born.

"Indeed. But instead of a gossip fest, which is what Susan's Hurley-Burleys have become, his gatherings are more celestial. I believe Nath has participated in one or two. Perhaps we shall have the luck to encounter a session."

"If it is that Transcendentalist garbage, I have no interest." Ebe's words are partly obscured by her book, which she holds just below the tip of her nose, but the asperity of her tone is quite clear.

"What if it were Nath, escaped from Sophia's clutches, pontificating on the meaning of the 'A' carved upon Dimsdale's chest? Surely you would like to hear him explain it all to an adoring audience?" The book dips enough for me to see her eyes roll, but she shrugs and says, "I shall attend as long as you are willing to depart should anyone wax too philosophical."

"I have never heard Mr. Alcott speak, so I vote in the affirmative," says John, his eyes twinkling behind his spectacles. Sisterly fights continue to amuse him. I nudge him affectionately, and I believe he reciprocates, although the boning in my corset obscures only the sharpest of jabs.

The stage lurches into the grimy Boston station, redolent of sewer, grease, and unwashed bodies, and after another fight with my hoop, we make our way through the throng onto the cobblestones and the city of immigrants that has become Boston.

On Tremont Street, my wardrobe becomes another sort of liability. Tiny mud-stained hands reach out to touch, to grab, to wrest. It is all I can do to walk a straight line as I am pushed and pulled by desperate beggars. John and Ebe flank me, and the three of us stride down the center of the road, dodging carriages and food stalls, trash, and horse dung, avoiding hundreds of hungry eyes and the human tragedy they represent. My heart feels as torn as my clothes.

West Street is somewhat of a haven, as book buyers are generally richer in thought than in cash, and beggars have chosen other venues. John takes out his handkerchief and wipes his brow, for, despite the chill, our gallop through the streets of Boston has left us all a little damp.

"Ebe! Louze! How nice to see you out and about and not stuck in your little Salem nest." Elizabeth emerges from behind a display of books and greets us, meaty arms outstretched, spectacles pushed up upon her graying hair. John doffs his hat and bows, and Elizabeth blushes and returns a curtsy. "And Mr. Dike. It really is a pleasure to see you as well. How is Mrs. Dike?"

"She is fine, thank you, but could not wrest herself away from her church obligations." John's voice trails off as he turns in a dazed circle to observe the lantern-lit, dusty store. I understand his vertigo, for every surface is covered with multicolored books. Some lean in imitation of the infamous Italian tower, others overflow their boxes, a few display their covers faced out, many more stand at attention on high shelves and low. In contrast, several thin ones have toppled over like drunkards, but all are enticing and enthralling in their glorious multitude. It is a bibliophile's paradise.

And on the center table, its title reflected in its bright red letters preens my older brother's creation: *The Scarlet Letter*.

"One copy?" Ebe is horrified.

"Have you not heard?" Elizabeth's voice is triumphant. "It is sold out!"

John gives a whoop, and the four of us shake congratulatory hands all around.

"But where is Nath?" asks Elizabeth. "We were hoping he would join us tonight during Mr. Alcott's Conversation. He was to explain his book to us, and it is almost seven."

"We were not privy to his schedule, but we imagine that Sophia holds a tight rein." Ebe sounds peeved, as well she might. Nath could have joined us and saved John an unnecessary trip, although I, of course, am grateful for his company.

The frosted glass door bangs open, and what appear to be two of the street beggars from Tremont Street barge in. John makes a move to intercept them, but at Elizabeth's calming gesture, he relaxes. The female of the pair carries herself like a young adult, though her age is hard to judge by her boyish frame. She is dressed in clothing one wearing away from the rag bin, yet there is a charming wildness to her loose auburn hair and intelligent eyes. The older gent, white hair flying in all directions, stained cravat askew, eyes bulging, strides toward Elizabeth.

"Are we late?" He gropes for the cracked pocket watch tied with a length of twine to a fraying belt loop, but Elizabeth puts out a gentling hand to stop him.

"No, Mr. Alcott, you are right on time. And thank you, Louisa, for escorting your father. Have you met Mr. Hawthorne's sisters, Ebe and Louisa Hawthorne, and their uncle, Mr. Dike?"

I am agog. The last time I met Louisa Alcott, she was a rosy-cheeked adolescent, intent on nothing more than torturing her older sister and writing a good play. Now I am confronted by a hollow-cheeked ragamuffin, who looks for all the world as though she has just stepped out of a food line.

"Mr. Alcott, I am so pleased to meet you. My nephew has told me of your philosophies, and I am looking forward to hearing you speak." John pumps Mr. Alcott's hand, and the poor man has so little mass that his entire body shakes. John takes a cue from Elizabeth, halts his enthusiastic greeting, and steers Mr. Alcott gently toward a chair.

Ebe, for once in her life, shows better manners than I. "Hello, Miss Alcott, I am Elizabeth, but please call me Ebe." She proffers a hand, and it is obvious that the young woman appreciates the warmth by the length of time that her fingers linger in Ebe's.

"Louisa, how nice to see you again," I say when at last Ebe has stepped aside. "Since I am also Louisa, perhaps everyone should call me Louze to avoid confusion." Elizabeth and Ebe laugh to dispel some of the tension emanating from the pair. Mr. Alcott seems exhilarated, but Louisa simply looks starved.

John, too, has noticed Louisa's emaciation, and his paternal instincts rise. "I shall run to a food stall and buy us all supper." We exchange concerned glances, I nod, and he slings on his topcoat to go in search of some badly needed sustenance.

Ebe escorts Louisa to a chair near her father and murmurs something comforting as if calming a skittish colt. I have never seen my sister this interested in another human being, and I wonder what it is about this young woman that has attracted her so.

John returns with several greasy parcels of meat pies, and Elizabeth removes a stack of leather-bound books from the side table to make room for the food. Louisa takes a wrapped pie, returns to her chair, and concentrates entirely on her meal, ignoring her father's frenzied instructions, which are given between gargantuan bites of food, to Elizabeth regarding this evening's talk.

"Well, shall we all repair to the salon?" Mr. Alcott wipes his mouth with his threadbare handkerchief, breaks towards the stairs, takes them two at a time, and we hear the scrape of furniture and his footsteps thundering overhead as he rearranges the room. But his daughter leans back in her chair and motions for us to gather around.

"Thank you all for your kindnesses. The meal was most welcome. I am embarrassed to say that my family is in dire straits, as my father has no permanent employment, and my mother is working for pennies at an employment agency. My younger sister Lizzie is minding the house as she is too shy to seek a job, but now that I am eighteen, I can teach in the neighborhood school. Still, my mother and I do not earn enough money to cover both rent and food."

"What of Anna? Has she not gone out into service?" Elizabeth seems to know the Alcotts well, whereas I must rely on my memory of that single encounter six years ago.

"Anna was employed by a family in Lenox, but she was so homesick that they let her go. She left her wages on the dresser in protest."

"Protests are not made of meat." John offers Louisa the last pie as illustration, and she accepts it willingly.

I think back to the entertainment she and her sisters produced. "As I recall, you are rather a gifted writer. Have none of your efforts been rewarded?"

"My scribblings have met with some paltry success. Five dollars here and there. Poems, mostly written, of course, under a pseudonym. Women are rarely considered salable authors."

Elizabeth makes a little scoffing noise. "Well, if that is true, present company is a big exception. Perhaps it is your choice of composition that has been the source of your failure. Have you considered writing articles for the *Dial*? As you know, I am the editor, and Ebe is a frequent contributor." Ebe nods her encouragement.

Louisa shakes her head. "I leave the philosophy to my father. My interests lie more in human interactions than in the divine. But perhaps you would care to read my novel, *The Inheritance*, and honor me with a critique?" She peers under her lashes at Elizabeth in shy hopefulness.

Elizabeth is suddenly preoccupied with her receipt book, but Ebe raises her hand. "Please, I would very much like to read your work. I shall give you my address in Beverly. And if you require a respite from this mad city existence, you may hand-deliver the parcel so that I might acquaint you with our little seaside town and its gorgeous shore."

"But what of your husband? Will he not mind a surprise house guest?" Unlike most girls her age, Louisa has not noticed that neither Ebe nor I wear wedding rings. We are, according to the societal norms, spinsters, though I, with my secret relationship, do not fit the usual mold. Ebe, still very single at forty-eight, is the perfect example, although she refuses to accept the role as tragic.

"I am lucky enough to be unencumbered. It will just be you and me and the great outdoors." Ebe's voice, usually an alto growl, has risen to a lyric soprano, and her complexion is rosy beneath her bonnet. I wonder if Louisa will be Ebe's new plaything. If so, I cannot think of a better mentor-pupil relationship for both parties.

We have been so engaged in our conversation that Mr. Alcott's motley followers have slipped by us unnoticed. Elizabeth makes her excuses to us and runs up to assist Mr. Alcott with the crowd.

But Louisa seems content to stay among the books. "Please do not allow me to distract you from my father's speech," she says, stretching luxuriously and wiping her fingers. "But he will talk to his admirers far into the night, and as I must be up and out first thing in the morning, I shall be on my way." She stands, pulls her frayed shawl tight about her shoulders, and tucks the remaining pie into her reticule.

"We can walk you there," offers John, reaching for his hat and cane.

"Of course," agrees Ebe with more enthusiasm than I can remember her ever expressing about a walk in Boston.

"Ordinarily, I would dissuade you, but the streets are not safe at night. Though most of the unfortunate recognize me as one of their own, still I possess more warm layers than do they. I do not blame them, but neither do I wish to be a victim. An escort would be most welcome."

We follow Louisa down gas-lit, cheerful West Street, past store windows displaying their latest wares, and mannikins delighting in their own hoop skirts, to less well-traveled and lit brick and mortared residential streets, and finally to the rat and beggar-infested wharves.

John has taken the lead and surveys his decaying surroundings with some confusion, as he cannot believe that the Alcott family has truly sunk this low into poverty. But indeed, Louisa pulls at his coat sleeve and nods at a run-down tenement building flanked by an overflowing privy and a bait shop.

"Thank you for the escort and for the meal." Louisa curtsies to John and then turns to Ebe. "I would very much like to show you my little book."

"Miss Peabody has my address. Write to me, and we can plan a visit." Ebe takes Louisa's hands in both of hers, and the two share a little smile before Louisa turns to me. "You were kind to my sisters and me in Concord all those years ago. I hope we shall have yet another chance to meet."

"I look forward to it. And now, please go in. The night is chilly, and there is mischief about." We wave her inside, then return without incident to Elizabeth's in time for cake and punch and a round of questions and answers with one of the great philosophers of our time.

BLUE JOURNAL
Louisa Hawthorne
Entry 1

August 12, 1850

Watery graves haunt me. My father died at sea; a self-drowned young woman walked the Old Manse; and now my dear friend Margaret, with her tiny babe in arms and her revolutionary husband by her side, has met Death on a sand bar off the stormy coast of Fire Island.

The newspapers' florid descriptions of the wreck of the *Elizabeth* were gruesome indeed. Survivors were interviewed, and their stories published. Apparently, the captain outlived the accident by jumping overboard instead of going down with his ship as any decent captain ought. This may have been because he was originally the first mate, the captain having expired from smallpox during the voyage. Thus, this inexperienced new captain ran aground on the sand bar during the height of a storm and urged his passengers, including Margaret and her husband, to jump with him. Crew members related that Margaret refused for reasons that are unclear to everyone.

Residents of the town came to the beach with carts to gather any cargo that might have come in on the tide, but no one attempted a rescue, even though the wreck was but fifty feet offshore. Bodies washed up onto the beach and were identified by crew members.

Margaret's baby boy was found on the cold sand, all alone. His mother and father were kept captive by the greedy waves.

Nath wrote me recently from Lenox where he and his family are living to report that Mr. Emerson, mired in grief and horror at the death of the woman he called 'his little friend,' commissioned Henry Thoreau to travel to Fire Island to search for any remains. Henry was unsuccessful, and Mr. Emerson was left to mourn a woman he revered for her intellect, her humor, and her resolve.

I, too, weep at the bitter end of such a warm, energetic presence. Margaret's empty arms will be filled again when she meets her babe in

Heaven, but we will not be privy to their loving reunion here on Earth. Instead, we must wonder at her decision to stay aboard rather than to take her chances in the sea. Had she some premonition that this was her time to die? Was she afraid that she would be unable to swim to shore? I remember our day at Walden Pond. She swam only in the shallows. I thought nothing of it at the time, but now I wonder if she could not swim very well. And of course, our women's skirts make swimming that much more difficult. What a pity that Margaret's feminist ideals could not have changed our fashions as well as our minds in time to ensure her survival.

Her death comes at a difficult time for me. My dear mother passed away only a year ago. My siblings and I were cast adrift, orphans in the sea of Salem, with no parental deck, however infirm, upon which to stand. Ebe, Sophia, Margaret, and my female cousins and friends stepped in to fill the void, but now I am bereft yet again. I resolve to read all of Margaret's writings and to gather strength from her philosophies so that I might continue my journey with John. Death is a reminder that we must cherish those we love and hold them close. Only God knows when we might someday be torn apart, never to see our dear ones alive again.

~∞∾∾∾∾∾∾∾∾∾∾∾∾∾∾∾∾∾∾∾∾∾∾∾∾∾∾∾

John Dike
4 Andover Street
Salem, Massachusetts

(September 20, 1871)

It is with embarrassment and guilt that I record these next chapters of my life. I am not proud of my endeavors to manipulate my wife, but certain circumstances conspired to influence decisions which would change our lives forever.

The spring of 1852 proved miserable for Louisa. Still reeling from her mother's and Margaret Fuller's deaths, she was conscripted to nurse a cousin back to health while Ebe enjoyed seclusion in Beverly and Nath and Sophia and their children moved to their new house in Concord. I wished nothing more than to rescue Louisa from this servile situation, but a ruse would be necessary to convince my suspicious wife to relax her restrictions on Louisa's and my relationship instigated after Betsey's death.

Louisa and I had been forced to find imaginative seclusions due to my wife's strict directives, but I had a plan. Limping into the parlor one evening at the end of June, I complained to Priscilla, "My knee has been terribly painful of late." She would not care, had not cared for decades, but I needed her to agree to my next proposal.

"No doubt you have heard of the healing waters at Saratoga Springs," I continued. "Allow me to read you a paragraph from one of their guide-books." In sepulchral tones, I recited: ***The most prominent and per-ceptible effects of these waters when taken into the stomach are Cathartick, Diuretick, and Tonick. They are much used in a great variety of complaints; but the diseases in which they are most efficacious are, Jaundice and billious affections generally, Rheumatism, some species of gout, Amenorrhea, Dys-menorrhea, . . .* "Priscilla's lips pursed in disgust at the mention of female bodily functions. "*Cutaneous eruptions, scorbutic ulcers . . .*"*

"Stop!" She shuddered and almost dropped her knitting. Beads of perspiration ringed the rim of her white cap. "John, I have heard enough. Please do not read any more of these alarming diseases."

"Of course, my dear. It was not my intent to distress you." Waiting a beat to allow her discomfort to ripen, I asked, "Do you wish to accompany me to take the waters? Perhaps they might give you some surcease from the ache in your wrists. And I am sure that those with the more contagious afflictions are in quarantine, although I hear that the most egregiously affected congregate at the fountains in the mornings."

My heart turned summersaults while I awaited her response, as my plan for a holiday with Louisa would be thwarted if Priscilla agreed to accompany me.

She peered at me through her spectacles. "I have heard nothing but distressing news about Saratoga Springs. Gambling, gaming, and otherwise ungodly behavior is enjoyed there by a lower class of people than I would care to encounter. Whatever cures the waters might contain would hardly make such a disastrous trip worthwhile." She sniffed and gathered her stitches onto a needle. "However, if you think the water might help heal your knee, I will not stand in your way." Her voice changed from condescension to a disinterested, almost overly-casual tone. "But could you manage by yourself? What if something were to happen? If the train were to break down, you were robbed, or you became ill along the way? We are neither of us spry anymore."

After taking a deep breath and commanding my heart to slow, I replied in an equally casual tone, "I agree that it would be wise to bring someone younger as a help-mate." I paused to give her time to consider this and continued, "According to Nath, John Stephens is ensconced in his managerial position at the Emporium, and Margaretta is busy with her charity work. What would you say to Louisa accompanying me? She would enjoy the fashion and festivities, and she has become quite adept at caring for ailing relatives. You know how much her cousin appreciated Louisa's recent aid. And we would be in the public eye." I willed myself to appear nonchalant, my eyes innocent, my body relaxed in its posture upon the chair.

Priscilla concentrated on her knitting, purling one entire row. She had ceased wearing her engagement ring sometime earlier, and I missed the familiar green glint of the jewel flickering with the movement of her fingers.

It seemed an eternity before she lifted her eyes. They were narrowed as if in irritation, suspicion, and oddly, scheming.

"What an interesting suggestion." Her casual tone continued, "I am certain Louisa would be of help. Perhaps Nath and Sophia could suggest an appropriate venue for the two of you. I know Nath has given lectures at a hotel there. I do not understand the popularity of his grotesque romances, but I have heard his speeches are very well attended."

"Oh? Which hotel was that?" I asked, seeming to be distracted by my paper. This was important information. Louisa and I would not want to stay where we might be recognized.

"I believe it was the United States Hotel. Write to him of your plans. Perhaps he can tell you which hotel is better suited to healing and which to pleasure." She gave me a cool smile, but suspicion still lurked in her eyes. And did I detect a touch of duplicity? I would have to tread carefully.

"Thank you, Priscilla. I shall write to him tomorrow and gather information about the area." I reached to touch her arm, and she flinched away. Our marriage was a duel. One thrust and the other parried. Thankfully, neither of us had caused any real damage in quite some time, but it was serendipitous that I would be leaving soon. A separation would be welcome.

The next morning, I was not greeted by the usual sight of my wife hunched in her chair spooning up her coddled eggs while studying her Bible verses.

"Mrs. Dike has gone to the counting-house, sir," Bridget told me as she served me my toast. "She and Mr. Manning were to meet there." This was good news, as I could now go to Herbert Street to see Louisa with no fear of encountering William. Although he inherited the Manning house when Betsey passed away two years ago, he allowed Louisa to live in her old room and welcome her friends and relations.

Hannah greeted me at the front door. "Miss Louisa is in the parlor, Mr. Dike."

Louisa sat at her desk reading a letter. Her hair in its simple bun gleamed in the sunlight, but strands of white now accented the auburn. She stood when I entered, her wide gray eyes seeking mine for confirmation of her hopes.

"And what, pray tell, did my dear aunt say?" she asked, one eyebrow cocked. Only the slight tremor in her voice belayed her anxiety. I knew she longed to go to Saratoga Springs with its balls and entertainments but had not allowed herself to become too excited about the prospect, thinking that Priscilla could quash the entire enterprise.

"She says God speed." I clasped her hands, and then with a guilty glance at the door, let them go. We knew we could not indulge our passions here with others in the house, but I wanted to share the good news. Her mother's death and her cousin's illness had been difficult for Louisa. Her happiness would be my reward for my machinations, as troubled as I might feel about our conspiracies.

She paced about the room, her hands clasped at her waist as if to contain her joy. "I had not dared to hope that you would succeed, and so I was making other plans. Nath and Sophia have been begging me to visit." She stopped at her desk, retrieved the letter, and read it aloud. "He says, *'We wish you very much to come immediately, as we fear something may intervene to prevent your coming this summer,'* so I must agree to stay with them afterward. I long to see their children, and they are all anxious to introduce me to The Wayside, their new house. But," she paused and faced me, her brows furrowed, "How are we to travel safely? Where will we stay? And what shall I wear?" This last sentence was uttered in a tone of desperation.

"These are questions that as yet have no answers. But I shall pick you up in a pumpkin coach and bring you to the train depot on the fifteenth, and you shall have the holiday you deserve. I look forward to seeing what accouterments you may bring with you, for," I lifted her chin with a tender hand and gazed at her with much affection, "Cinderella must go to the ball. Until then, I bid you good day." Her eyes shone with excitement as she waved me out the door, and I wondered how many cousins would be called upon to lend gowns for this occasion.

I spent that evening at the office, planning our itinerary. In Saratoga, I hoped that we would stay at the commodious Columbian Hotel, which boasted the best water for my condition. And although it sat on Broadway, the main street, it was not the most socially desirable hotel, which would mean less chance of discovery by any of our friends or family. We would keep our distance from the United States Hotel, where Nath had lectured to a probably adoring audience. Louisa and I, on the other hand, would be traveling incognito, enjoying an opportunity for happiness at last.

June 26, 1852

In April, Aunt Priscilla spent an inordinate amount of time at home instead of at the counting-house, forcing John and me to find distant comforts, and we spent several joyous evenings on the beach where his passionate attentions almost assuaged the grief of my mother's passing. Then in May, cousin Rebecca took ill, and I scarcely had time to think about anything save her sick room and what delicacies might tempt her appetite. I assumed the queasiness I experienced while preparing her meals to be in sympathy with her own, and it was not until mid-June when Hannah asked me where I had stored by soiled muslin strips that I took notice of the change in my monthly rhythms.

At forty-four, I thought that I was safe from pregnancy. I had ceased using any prophylactic douches and herbal draughts when I turned forty, thinking them unnecessary expenses as well as bleak reminders that I must forswear a desired child. But now I can feel a difference in my shape, in my appetite, in my mood, Hannah can no longer cinch my corset at its tightest hook, and sometimes in the morning, I do not make it to the privy in time but must vomit into my chamber pot.

My heart bursts even as my stomach clenches. This is not how I foretold my waning years, but it is a delightful surprise. I waffle from elation: John and I have created a new being! Finally, I will experience womankind's greatest achievement! To depression: I have witnessed in similarly aged cousins the tendency to miscarry. To reality: If I should have the great good fortune to carry John's child to term, what would be our fates? The whole city of Salem would presumably turn its hypocritical back, or I could be banished to Concord to live out a lie, a spinster who somehow adopted a foundling.

And how and when should I tell John? I am joyful and know he will be as well, as he has always wished for us to have a child of our own, but he might use the pregnancy as the final fuel to explode his marriage, potentially landing us all in the poorhouse.

Perhaps, as we are about to undertake an arduous train trip to Saratoga Springs, I shall keep the news to myself until we arrive at our destination. By then, the issue may be moot.

I ride the stage, seemingly a safer mode of transport, to Beverly and call upon Ebe, but, as usual. she holds no sympathy.

"Did you not keep track of your monthlies? What of the herbs and the douches? Really, you are nearly as unfortunate as one of Nath's protagonists. I shall be forced to rename you Hester. And if a train ride were all it took to rid oneself of a child, the stations would be rife with women wearing scarlet letters. There is nothing to be done now unless you wish to risk your life with one of the doxies who ply their trade at the docks. I hear John is friendly with them." She sniffs and pulls at her knitting, reminding me uncomfortably of Aunt Priscilla.

"I assumed that at forty-four, I was beyond my fertile years, but obviously, I was wrong. And I would never rid myself of someone who is partly of my beloved," I counter. "Had our mother made a similar decision, you and I would not be having this conversation." Ebe snorts in derision. "My plan is to wait and give him the happy news when we have arrived in Saratoga so that he may express his joy in the absence of his wife. We will have a chance there to celebrate and plan. For instance, perhaps I could live with Nath and Sophia during my lying in. They were very grateful for my help during Una's birth, and now I have a chance to ask for reciprocity."

"We shall see whether Sophia can practice the feminist philosophies that she so smugly preaches," says Ebe with some rancor. "Can she support a child born not only out of wedlock but to an uncle and his niece?"

"Related only through marriage, I will remind you. "

"Whom else have you told?"

"Just Hannah. She became suspicious when my monthly laundry diminished. She wondered if I had begun the menopause, and I hadn't the wit to lie."

Ebe concentrates on purling a row and keeps her voice even, but I can sense she is disturbed. "Are you not concerned that she will gossip with Bridget? I see them with their heads together at market or at meeting. They are both getting on in years, and the household stories are their favorite entertainment. It would take only a thoughtless remark within Uncle William's or Aunt Priscilla's earshot to make your private news public."

"At the moment, there is nothing to tell. At my advanced age, I will probably miscarry. But I wish to accompany John on a celebratory journey and give him one more chance at happiness. He longs for another child and who can foretell what will happen. Perhaps Aunt Priscilla will divorce him, or I will live in Concord with Nath and Sophia, and he will visit when he can. All I know is that this child is a great gift to an older spinster and an eternally paternal man, and it will be loved."

I stand and offer my hand. "Will you not wish me well in this endeavor?" Ebe rises and embraces me, then holds me at arms' length, looks up into my eyes, and shivers. Her voice takes on a softer tone. "Someone just walked across our graves. Please be careful on this journey of yours. Remember, you are carrying my nephew or niece."

Upon my return home, I greet Uncle William, who sits in the dining room perusing the *Salem Gazette* for employment opportunities. He stares at the print and does not acknowledge me. I hear convivial voices in the kitchen and hurry in to discuss supper with Hannah, who rises from her worn chair and turns to me, but my attention is paid to Bridget, who moves as quickly from the table to the door as her rheumatism will allow as if to avoid contact with me.

"Good evening, Bridget," I say, wondering at this break in her decorum.

"Good evening, Miss Louisa. I am on my way back to your aunt's house. Are there any messages?" She refuses to meet my eyes. I glance at Hannah and see a worried crease between her brows. Perhaps Ebe was correct, and my circumstances will be well-known by the time I return from Saratoga. But by then, the only person whose opinion I care to honor will have had his chance to speak his piece.

Priscilla Manning Dike
4 Andover Street
Salem, Massachusetts

June 27, 1852

Thomas:

All I ever asked of Him was a child. I devoted my life to Him. Worshiped Him. Adored Him. In return, He granted me an abusive uncle, a mad sister, a philandering husband, ungrateful stepchildren, and a devious niece. Is it any wonder that I instead chose to accept the Serpent as my Lord and Master?

William came to me last night like a gossiping crone in the marketplace.

"Have you heard that Louisa is with child?" he asked me gleefully, so eager was he to wound me in his hatred for my prosperous husband.

My knitting needles shook in my fingers. I dropped several stitches before I could quiet my hands and my mind.

"How on earth could you know this?"

His face flushed in his embarrassment at speaking of women's functions. "I overheard Bridget and Hannah talking in the kitchen. Apparently, Louisa has been sick of late, and Hannah noticed some, uh, changes in her laundry." He ducked his head and thrust his hands into his pockets.

"Is there supposition as to the father?" My voice wavered, but I sat as rigid and upright as possible to present an unfeeling façade.

"You are as aware as I of our family's predilection for incestuous dalliances. And you informed me of Betsey's deathbed admonition." He refused to meet my eyes.

"Indeed. Leave me now and let me think upon this new information."

William turned. Before he could exit, I added, "I may have a new task for one of our employees for which I would pay handsomely. Do you have a business acquaintance whom you trust implicitly?"

He nodded, smirking, and took a breath to speak. I held up a hand to silence him.

"I shall send to him alone my instructions. You will be paid as the middleman. Speak of this to no one but him." William retreated to contact his associate. The Serpent and I composed our missive.

The die was cast. I set into motion a chain of events which would grant me peace at last. And no one, not my brother, nor my husband, nor my niece, nor my God, could argue that my actions were anything but warranted. I washed my hands of them all.

PMD

(September 20, 1871)

July 15, 1852, dawned warm and humid. Priscilla and I breakfasted together. "When shall you and Louisa return?" she asked without emotion as she lopped off the shell of her coddled egg and spooned up the congealed yolk.

"I believe we shall take the train back on July 30th, and barring any unforeseen calamities, we would arrive in Salem on August 1st." I stood up with some difficulty, as my knee was truly sore this morning, and motioned for Bridget to bring my valise from upstairs. "Will you see us off?"

Priscilla dabbed at her mouth and stood. "Of course. And William will meet us there to say God speed." This was a surprise. William spent his days on the docks and in the taverns attempting to shore up his failing businesses. Surely, he had better things to do than to come to the train station.

We loaded the carriage with my small valise and proceeded to Herbert Street. Louisa, dressed in modest attire to not alarm Priscilla, sat with her aunt in the cabin while I tied her bulging bag to the back railing and then climbed in to join them. William met us at the depot, and our little party made its way to the ticket agent.

After leaving our luggage with a porter, we gathered on the platform for farewells. I turned to Priscilla. "Goodbye, my dear. Thank you for seeing us off." I bowed and kissed her on the cheek. She startled at even this brief contact. Louisa lowered her eyes and stared at the rails.

"William, take care of your sister for me," I said, but he had disappeared. "Now, where did William run off to?" I scanned the platform for my errant brother-in-law.

"He is searching for a newspaper hawker. I am sure he will return soon." Priscilla flushed and gazed about the station, seeming to search as well.

"Ah, there he is. It is just like him to make us wait," I said, a bit annoyed. William had always been the black sheep of the family. He could not be relied upon, even in social situations. Now he stood by a distant vendor, ignoring the time, talking with someone out of our sight. He must have felt our gazes upon him, for he broke contact with his associate and hurried toward us just as the whistle sounded.

I shook his hand, somewhat disquieted when he refused to meet my gaze even as he attempted a humorous farewell. "John, I am sure you will comport yourself like a gentleman. I do not want to hear any rumors about you attending to any of the ladies on Promenade." Priscilla looked horrified at her brother's jest. A chill ran down my spine at the thought that he might suspect something.

The train whistle sounded again. I tipped my hat one last time to Priscilla, handed Louisa up the car steps, and together we turned to wave goodbye to Salem. With the train's thunderous clack and chug ringing in our ears, we steamed out of the station. Priscilla and William disappeared, and Louisa sagged against me in what I presumed was relief and triumph. We had succeeded in our escape.

We passed the time pleasantly enough, traveling the rails from Salem to Boston to Schenectady to Saratoga, changing trains with ease, and strolling about on the platforms to stretch our legs and find sustenance. Louisa's appetite seemed diminished, but I assumed it was due to a bit of motion sickness. "Did you write to Nath and Sophia to give them your itinerary?" I asked.

"Indeed, but I had other news for my brother. Did I tell you that I saw two of his college friends at the Boston train depot a month ago? David Roberts had the audacity to suggest that if Pierce won the presidency due to Nath's campaign biography, Nath could be named Minister of Russia or some such nonsense. I made it clear that I thought Nath should continue with his usual novels and leave such propaganda to some other hack. I think they thought me quite ridiculous."

While I listened to the trials and tribulations of my nephew and his possible attempt to write a political biography for his famous college chum, I noticed that every once in a little while, a tall man in a cloth cap pulled down low over his brow would make an appearance nearby. He was there in a train car aisle, but when I looked again, he had disappeared. He walked by us on a platform before he ducked into a vendor stall. I tried to hail him, but he always melted away. I decided against informing Louisa as it would only worry her. I wished this to be her special treat after so many months of work and worry. Rest and relaxation away from her family obligations left no time for concern about a phantom shadow.

Saratoga Springs, with its healing waters, resort hotels, gambling houses, and racecourses, was our destination. The tree-lined Broadway Street was reported to offer upscale hotels, mansions, restaurants, and pavilions where one could take the waters in style. As we pulled into the train depot, a bell in the cupola of the barnlike building announced our arrival. Porters with signs designating their hotels lined up to wait for potential customers as they disembarked. Louisa and I scanned the many placards till we recognized the Columbian and waved to one of the appropriate porters to take our luggage to the waiting cart.

On our way to the hotel, we were delighted by the sights and sounds of what Priscilla would call Sodom. Handsomely dressed women, their parasols cocked to block out the sun, strolled arm in arm with their dapper chaperones. Gaily painted carriages hitched to horses in bridle plumes and tail weaves, stood waiting to take patrons to the various springs. Criers hawked their betting houses, billiard rooms, and bowling alleys. Our appetites were whetted by the promise of all manner of amusements as we climbed with impatience off the cart at our stop.

But at the Columbian Hotel's imposing door, Louisa grasped my arm. "John, you may accuse me of hysteria, but I am convinced that there is a man following us. Do you see him?" She pointed to a figure in a cap disappearing into the Grand Union Hotel opposite us.

I shivered at the realization that the stalker was no phantom. This was the same man whom I had seen several times on our journey. "It must be a coincidence," I said, keeping my voice steady to reassure her. But her observation gave me pause, and I resolved to confront this fellow the next time that I saw him.

We were dwarfed by the towering brick facades all around us on Broadway, but when we entered the ornate door of the Columbian, we were swept up into an even more extravagant world. The hotel was designed in a U shape, with an interior public space surrounded on three sides by three tiers of rooms, salons, piazzas, and ballrooms. Exterior gardens, visible through the tall windows, overflowed with flowering trees and shrubs. An orchestra situated on one of the upper balconies had struck up a waltz. The scents of baking bread and roasting meat permeated the atmosphere. In the center of the room, aromatic fizzing water gushed from a pink marble fountain. This, I supposed, was the healing water that I had come so far to sample.

"We would like two rooms on the American plan," I said to the room clerk when at last we had reached the front of the line.

"Of course, sir. Two rooms for two weeks on the American plan will be $24.00. Mr. Shaughnessy, please show these good people to their rooms." A pomaded young man carted our luggage and gestured to us to follow him. Louisa and I paraded arm-in-arm through the lobby and up the stairs to the second floor, but our energy soon flagged as we marched down a seemingly endless carpet. My limp returned with a vengeance, and my walking stick supported more of my weight than usual.

"Take your time. We have half a mile of hall to go," Shaughnessy joked with a wink. At last, he put keys to locks and opened two adjacent doors to tiny twin rooms with bedsteads, bureaus, and small mirrors, washbowls, and pitchers, tables, and chairs. They did not echo the luxury of the lobby but were adequate for our meager needs.

"If you wish to bathe, there are several public bathhouses from which to choose, twenty-five cents each, but they will give you soap and a towel. Do not forget to pick up a candle on your way up from tea this evening." I flipped the boy a dime, ushered him out, and returned to Louisa, who was gazing raptly out the window onto Broadway.

"So, my dear, what is your pleasure? Shall we go take the waters now, or have a little breakfast first?"

"John, there is something I must tell you." She drew me down to the single bedstead and placed my hand upon her breast. "Do you feel anything different here?"

"I have noticed that you have become slightly rounder in appearance overall." I kept my voice neutral, not wishing to offend. "Are you saying that you will not be partaking of all the proffered sweet-meats?"

She shook her head. "Have you also noticed that I have been a bit more tired than usual, a trifle bilious?"

"I thought you were still grieving your mother."

"It is something much, much more joyous." She paused and searched my eyes for support. "John, I believe I am with child. Your child."

I do not remember exactly what transpired then. Perhaps I lost consciousness for a split second.

"John, are you quite well?" Louisa helped me to lie down on the quilt and poured a tumbler of water from the pitcher.

"*Our* child," I affirmed.

She wept. I wept. We stayed on that bed for what seemed like hours, laughing, crying, talking, and planning.

I babbled a bit. "John Stephens will have another sibling! Perhaps it will assuage some of his remorse. But what of our lives in Salem? Our reputations would for certain be ruined. And then there is Priscilla. Should I beg her for a divorce? The courts would rule in her favor, and I would lose my business once again. But it would all be worth it for a child of our own."

She countered, "Or, as the pregnancy progressed, I could stay with Nath and Sophia. They owe me a favor, and you could visit whenever you had the chance. No one really knows us in Concord. The baby could be explained as the child of a maid or a charity case. Priscilla might never be the wiser."

"Whom else have you told?"

"Hannah guessed because of my laundry. And of course, I told Ebe, who is concerned that Hannah might tell Bridget. Otherwise, it is a secret."

"And so it shall remain. But meanwhile, you must be careful. We shall eat only the healthiest options, and you may take a water cure as well. Was the train a problem, do you think?"

"As Ebe said, if pregnancies were that fragile, the trains would be full of hapless young ladies on day trips with their angry mothers."

"I suppose that is true for any form of exercise or exertion. Well. Shall we go downstairs and quaff a tumbler together or explore the town?"

She voted for a third option. The bedstead proved just large enough to accommodate our joyful celebration.

Afterward, Louisa insisted we change into appropriate attire before making an appearance downstairs. We trudged back along the endless carpet to the piazza, Louisa panting in her too-tight corset, and joined other boarders in lounging or strolling in the gardens enjoying the fresh air while waiting for dinner at noon. A musician sang in the garden, and while Louisa sat in a rocking chair to listen, I stole into the lobby to quaff a tumbler of the Columbian spring water, hoping that it would make the return walk to the room a bit easier on my knee. The bard's voice, a high tenor with a wide vibrato, filled the lobby:

> *Of all the gay places the world can afford,*
> *By gentle and simple for pastime adored,*
> *Fine balls and fine singing, fine building and springs,*
> *Fine rides and fine views, and a thousand fine things,*
> *(Not to mention the sweet situation and air)*
> *What place with these Springs can ever compare?*
> *First in manners, in dress, and in fashion to shine,*
> *Saratoga, the glory must ever be thine!**

But as I returned the tumbler to the waiter, a familiar figure in a cap darted by the dining room. I turned to follow, but Louisa had come to join me and suggested we go in for dinner.

Dining was a luxurious rite. We were met at the dining room doorway by wait staff, who escorted us to our table. After all the diners were seated, the head waiter sounded a gong, and the waiters, in a sort of dance, brought the dishes to the tables, starting with soup and including fish, vegetables, meat, and many sorts of desserts, puddings, and fruit.

The thought of the long walk to the rooms after eating was too much for me, so I spent the hour after dinner on one of the rocking chairs in the piazza while Louisa retired to her room to rest. But she soon descended the stairs, ready for our next adventure, and I linked my arm in hers to escort her to her first Promenade.

The guidebook's description of The Saratoga Promenade did not do the ceremony justice. Nothing could have prepared us for the pomp and pageantry of this ritual tour through the streets of the city. Every hotel disgorged its boarders to join the line of ladies and gentlemen, hawkers and criers, gamblers and thieves, all there to see and be seen. Louisa held tight my arm, and together we made the circuit, finishing where we had started with a mutual promise to never participate again.

"I no longer have the energy for such a long walk. How is your poor knee?" Louisa's brow was creased in sympathy.

"I believe I shall take another tumbler of water. Please feel free to enjoy whatever entertainer is performing in the piazza. I shall bring you a restoring cup of tea."

And that was how we spent our days, she enjoying the myriad jugglers, singers, puppeteers, ventriloquists, and other entertainers who frequented the lobby and piazza, I partaking of the waters and surveying the crowd. The waters seemed to have a positive effect upon my knee, and I relied less and less on the support of my walking stick. We played many hands of Whist, with Louisa always victorious, and I ate far too much of the rich and delicious food. Louisa ate carefully, and I wondered how she fared in the mornings.

And in the evenings, after tea, there were the balls. Louisa had packed several refashioned gowns from her many cousins and aunts. After scouring the crowds for any familiar faces, we danced as enthusiastically as my knee and her energy would allow. I watched Louisa emerge from her drab Salem cocoon and take flight as a Saratoga butterfly. My heart swelled as she held my hand, and we whirled away on the strains of the latest Strauss waltz.

She whispered in my ear, "Thank you for granting my wishes. Are you my fairy godfather or my handsome prince?"

"A little of both, I hope," I answered with modesty. "I am simply content to make your dreams a reality." We gazed into each other's eyes, entranced by the magic of the moment.

But of course, all dreams must end.

"Mr. Dike, what a surprise!" We stopped cold mid-step, and I turned amid the whirling dancers, my face flushing, my hand automatically outstretched to greet whoever had caught us in this compromising position.

It was the captain's wife. She knew me well, and there was nothing I could do but answer her. "Mrs. Felt, how do you do! You remember my niece Miss Hawthorne?" Louisa took Mrs. Felt's hand in turn and guided her to the edge of the dance floor.

"How is your husband faring on the high seas?" Louisa asked, trying to hide her embarrassment with good manners. She was hoping, as was I, that small talk would deflect the situation. But Mrs. Felt was not so easily distracted. She eyed Louisa's gown and my tails. "How nice to see that you are well enough to enjoy the dance floor. Mrs. Dike led me to believe that you were coming to Saratoga for the cure."

"Indeed, the waters have been quite invigorating," I said. "I shall be on my way back to Salem and the business quite soon."

Louisa, pale with suppressed anxiety, asked Mrs. Felt, "What brings you to Saratoga?"

"My son and daughter-in-law live here. I am visiting them while taking a little holiday myself and enjoying the hotel. But I shall be returning by train to Salem on Thursday. Mr. Dike, I look forward to seeing you at meeting." She gave us each an arch smile and set off at full steam toward the door. I could tell by the set of her shoulders that she had a very big story to tell when at last, she returned to Salem.

"She is a terrible gossip," Louisa whispered. "Our story will be all over town by the time we arrive home."

"Agreed. I'm afraid I have lost my taste for dancing. Let us go back to our rooms." She nodded in grim acceptance, and we walked those endless halls as somberly as if they led us to the gallows.

"Mrs. Felt is scheduled to go home by train on Thursday, but we are not to leave till Friday. She will have time to visit Aunt Priscilla and fill her ear with poison." Louisa paced back and forth in my room, a tigress in a cage barred with social mores.

"Perhaps this would be a good time for your extended visit with Nath and Sophia," I said. "Concord is an easy trip for me to make. I promise to come and visit you there. We could plead our case for secret asylum."

She stopped to stroke my shoulder, but her eyes were narrowed in speculation.

"We might think about alternative plans. Is there an earlier train so that you could arrive ahead of Mrs. Felt to quell any gossip or speculation?"

"That is an excellent suggestion. I do not wish to wound Priscilla. She may have committed her own sins, and my anger at her abuse of my children has not abated, but my case in divorce court will not be strengthened by gossip. If I could return to Salem alone and ahead of Mrs. Felt, I might be able to save all of our reputations. And, if there were not an earlier train, perhaps we could shorten our trip with a boat voyage down the Hudson to New York City. Steamboats have excellent reputations for fast travel. We could take a train from Saratoga to the Albany docks, ride a steamboat down the Hudson to New York City, board trains to Boston, Salem and Concord, and easily outrun Mrs. Felt."

She nodded, and we spent the night together in muted embrace.

Early the next morning, I hastened down to see the hotel clerk.

"Do you have the train schedule for Schenectady and the schedule of steamboats leaving Albany for New York?" I asked.

"Indeed, sir. Let's see. The next train leaving Saratoga for Schenectady is on Thursday. But the *Armenia* and the *Henry Clay* are both scheduled to depart from the Albany docks at seven o'clock tomorrow morning."

"Which boat do you recommend?"

He removed his spectacles with a flourish and leaned across the counter to look me in the eye. "Well, sir, the *Henry Clay* is the newer, faster boat. They race sometimes, you know, and lately, she's taken the wins. However, the word is that the owners have agreed to cease their racing, so you should be quite safe."

"Excellent. Could you please send a wire to Priscilla Dike in Salem for me? I shall write out the message."

I found Louisa in her room, composing a letter to Nath. "I am just telling him that I will see him soon at the Wayside. Will I be taking a train to Concord?"

I kissed the top of her head. "Indeed. We shall take a steamboat to New York City, and from there, it is a quick train journey to Boston and Concord. It will be an interesting adventure, I assure you."

We spent the day packing and keeping out of sight. When I slipped down to the lobby to finalize the bill, I spied a familiar figure at the desk. His cap still sat low on his forehead, and his dress seemed far too casual for this opulent setting. He and the desk clerk were discussing something.

Mr. Cap slid a coin toward the clerk, who pocketed it furtively. I hailed our mysterious shadow and hurried toward him as fast as my knee would allow, but he fled out the door, and I knew I would not be able to catch up with him in my current condition. The clerk pulled at his collar while he wrote up my bill.

Louisa and I bid each other good night early in preparation for the journey from Saratoga to Albany. Louisa was anxious about the trip, but what concerned her more was the vision of Mrs. Felt in Priscilla's parlor. I felt confident that we could outrun Mrs. Felt. What worried me was Mr. Cap.

John Dike
4 Andover Street
Salem, Massachusetts

(September 24, 1871)

The wicked and reckless events of July 28, 1852, when the *Henry Clay* steamship illegally raced another boat, then exploded and burned, drowning and killing over eighty passengers and crew, have been described, reviewed, and analyzed by many panels of experts. Several judges have ruled on the criminality of those who, unmindful of a sacred trust, brought mourning and desolation to so many.

However, in addition to the criminal actions of the steamship owners and crew, there was a more personal affront. I believe the statute of limitations has taken effect, but please accept this document as both an admission of guilt and an accusation of murder.

The sights and sounds of July 28, 1852, haunt me still. I shall never forgive myself for gambling on our lives simply because of a possible threat to our reputations. Reputations can be resurrected. Lives cannot. If I could live that one day over, I would gladly have booked return tickets on the train and accepted the social ramifications of whatever gossip Mrs. Felt deemed worthy of spreading. Instead, I put Louisa, and our child, in double jeopardy.

The steamship the *Henry Clay* loomed above us, its graceful lines, impressive paddle wheel, and tall smoke pipe silhouetted against the pink and gold of the early morning sky. In the next berth sat her rival, the *Armenia*, an equally regal, though shorter and smaller, ship. Puffs of smoke from the stacks hung in the humid air, and the cries of ticket sellers mingled with the shouts of the two crews flinging valises and trunks up to waiting stewards on the decks above.

There seemed to be some tension between the crews. My days on the docks had sensitized me to the moods of ship-mates, and I could read a certain anxiety among the sailors as they moved with alacrity about their tasks and glared at their rivals. These boats had raced before, but the desk clerk had given me every reason to believe that we had bought passage on nothing more than a leisurely cruise down the Hudson. Still, I alerted myself to the nautical atmosphere and tone.

Several industrial magnates, their top hats tipped back in the heat, engaged each other in conversation, barely noticing whether their valises accompanied them up the gangway. Prosperous-looking men and women milled about the dock, bidding fond farewells and gathering belongings for their journeys. Louisa paused to eye a particularly well-dressed young woman, her parasol raised to protect her lovely skin, her fashionably ruffled gown draped wide over its hoop.

"Well, at least we are going to our executions in style," Louisa said with a tight smile as we stood in line to board.

"I shall arrive in Salem well before Mrs. Felt, and whatever gossip she might monger, I can disprove. And you will have time to beg for help from Nath and Sophia. Your reputation may yet remain unsullied."

Sad as I was to return to Salem, I trusted that I had made the correct travel decision to ensure a swift and sure passage home. So why did I feel a sense of impending doom as Louisa ascended the gangway, gripping the railing to assure her footing and eying the stewards as they transported our luggage to our cabins? I limped along behind, leaning heavily on my stick, favoring my knee. We had booked separate accommodations, Louisa in the aft of the boat, I in the fore, to decrease any new unsavory speculations, yet the thought of separation seemed overly distressing. My instincts were on guard. I slipped my arm through Louisa's to protect my little family when I, at last, caught up with her on the deck.

"I wish I could wave a wand and send us all home," I murmured, gazing out at the roiling blue-green water.

"I am afraid your godfather magic has run out." Louisa gave me a wistful smile. "But here we are on this handsome boat, on a balmy day, with hundreds of people to spy upon, so we might as well take advantage of our circumstances. You are familiar with all things shipping. Would you care to take me on a tour?"

Putting one hand behind my back in my best professorial demeanor, I gestured with the other as I bowed her along the railing. "I have read that the *Henry Clay* measures one hundred and ninety-eight feet in length." We swung by the wheelhouse. "Good morning, sir!" I tipped my hat to the pilot and then guided Louisa along the boat's length on the promenade deck, under the awning, past the paddle wheel, to the aft of the ship, where we viewed the walking beam and hurricane deck. "She is advertised as 'the new and swift steamer', and I have heard that she lives up to her promise. We shall see."

The crew members, anxious to be away, pulled up the lines and cast off. We strolled forward again along the railing, enjoying vast vistas of countryside, handsome villas, the Catskill Mountains, and other vessels sailing the waters. I rejoiced in the caress of the wind and the scent of the water and shore. It had been much too long since I had sailed a vessel.

The *Armenia* rushed past, much to the consternation of our crew. "Put your back into it, men!" called a sailor. The *Henry Clay* heaved to, and we could feel the strain of the engines through the railing as the paddles revolved. We pulled into several ports, but the crew was impatient at each dock to herd the passengers on board.

"John, why are they in such a hurry? We are on time, are we not?" asked Louisa as passengers stumbled up the gangway. I, too, was concerned at the frantic behavior. When we steamed past one port, a passenger held his ticket aloft and shouted to a steward, "Why did you not let me off at Bristol Landing?" The steward simply shrugged his shoulders and disappeared into the engine room.

"I shall sue the company for making me miss my stop!" The exasperated passenger shook his fist at the engine room door. It was then that I understood that we were indeed participating unwillingly in a competition and that I might have placed my family in a dangerous situation. As I steered us toward the safer aft section of the boat, we noticed that the other steamer, the *Armenia*, was gaining on us again. The two boats raced. First, we pulled ahead, and then the *Armenia* took the lead. As we approached another landing, a crewman threw a fender overboard to protect the hull. I feared that we might collide and drew Louisa back toward the lounge area.

We clapped our hands over our ears at the devastating crunch of boat on boat as the *Henry Clay* turned into and struck the *Armenia*. We were thrown briefly off balance and clung to each other and the deck chairs for purchase. Crew members ordered, "Move to the larboard side!" before checking that the fender held and that the ships were uncoupled. Once we had recovered our equilibrium, Louisa, calm even in such a frightening situation, herded a governess, her charge, and several other families into one of the women's lounges while I joined a group of male passengers to storm the pilothouse, shouting our displeasure at his treacherous behavior.

The self-proclaimed owner of the ship, Thomas Collyer, emerged from his stateroom and tried to dispel our fears. "You are quite safe on my ship! Please, return to your lounges!" he shouted, but we were not convinced. I made my way through the milling crowds to the women's lounge, instructed Louisa and the others to stay inside, and joined the men pacing up and down the railing, watching for the *Armenia*, berating myself for choosing to bring Louisa and our child on such a perilous voyage.

We continued to steam down the river at an alarming rate, stopping only at sporadic landings along the way, taking on more and more passengers until the decks were full. The crew had apparently disengaged with the *Armenia*, and some male passengers relaxed a bit, enjoying drinks at the bar. But even after escorting Louisa from the lounge so that she might enjoy the view, I kept a close eye on the sailors. The crew spelled one another with breaks on the deck to survive the heat of the engine room as they stoked the fire with wood and tar to increase our speed. I wondered if the added fuel would have a deleterious effect on the ability of the boiler to maintain equilibrium on such an already warm day. Yet the pilot continued his duties seemingly unconcerned, and at last, I relaxed and enjoyed the scenery.

The dinner-gong rang, and while Louisa and I took our seats in the sumptuous dining room, neither of us had much of an appetite as we contemplated our imminent separation. Louisa, with sudden inspiration, yawned behind her handkerchief and remarked to one of our table mates, "Please excuse me, I think the excitement of the morning has been too much." She retreated below deck. I waited a discrete minute and then excused myself as well, ostensibly to find a deck chair.

I strolled to her cabin, checked in both directions to ensure I was not observed, and knocked on her door with my stick. She opened it with a cautious hand, and we both peered about the passageway.

"Your prince wishes to ensure that you arrived safely home from the ball," I whispered when we had determined that we were unobserved.

"Perhaps I could try on that glass slipper?" She pulled me by my cravat into the tiny room.

"I shall never forgive myself for bringing you and our child on this treacherous journey." She hushed me gently with one finger upon my lips and then pointed to her collar. My fingers fumbled to unclasp the little garnet and silver brooch pinned there, and we said our sad goodbyes while the ship heaved and strained beneath us.

At last, she collapsed next to me, snuggled her head into my shoulder, and sighed in satisfaction and sorrow. I would have stayed in that cabin with her forever, but propriety would not allow it.

"I cannot bear that our enchanted time together must end," she whispered.

"I shall visit Concord soon, I promise. Where is your handkerchief?" She pointed to her skirt pocket. I retrieved it from the floor and blotted her tears.

"It is time that I made my way back to the deck, or tongues will wag."

Louisa nodded and stood to gather together the parts of her traveling costume that had been tossed aside.

"I shall stay here and read *Pilgrim's Progress* to cleanse my soul, although, as you know," she shrugged into her bodice and drew the collar together, "I am beyond redemption." I kissed one last glistening tear from her wry smile and helped her with the clasp of her pin. Then, before it became too difficult to wrench myself away, I pushed open the door and stepped out into the corridor, just in time to see a familiar man in a cap disappearing up a nearby ladder.

"Damn!" I struck the side of the ship in frustration and fear.

"John, what is it?" Louisa came to the door and peered out at me in consternation.

"Nothing, my dear. Go back to your book. I must return to the deck, but I shall check in on you again soon."

I climbed as quickly up the ladder as my knee would allow and threaded my way through the crowds toward the bow of the boat. Both dinner sessions had ended, and hundreds of people crowded the deck and the lounge areas inside. Limping the circuit around the decks but unable to find my quarry, I settled into a deck chair to contemplate our future if we were to be found out. But the physical efforts of the day had taken their toll. I had just drifted off when a stern voice demanded, "Stand up and explain yourself, you swine."

I startled awake to find William Manning, his ruddy face contorted with rage, standing over my deck chair, his fists raised.

"Did you think you could abuse my sister's good nature and not pay the price?"

My mind whirled. Why was William here on the *Henry Clay*? He and my wife were last seen in Salem waving to us as we embarked on our trip to Saratoga Springs. That was two weeks ago. But then I recalled the many times I saw Mr. Cap following us, first on the train, then at the hotel, and today on the boat. The blood drained from my head. Of course. William had hired him to watch us, and now William had boarded the ship to defend Priscilla's honor.

"William, please sit and let us talk this through." He shook his head and gestured for me to rise and face him. The boat sluiced through the Hudson at a great clip, throwing off my balance, while another boat sped behind us, shooting sparks and soot into the air.

"What are your plans for your marriage?" He glared up at me, but at least he had dropped his fists.

"I don't know. I think Priscilla realizes that things have not been well with us, have not been for quite some time now." His eyes wavered a bit. This was not news to him.

"Louisa is your niece." He raised his fists again and took a swing. I ducked away and came up nearer the railing.

"Yes, but not by blood. I had no intention of wooing her. It was a gradual process of falling in love. Neither of us wanted to hurt anyone. We have been very careful to keep our secrets."

He grasped me by my lapels and pulled me down closer to his face. Neither of us was young anymore, and we were both out of breath. I fumbled for my stick, hoping it would give me an advantage, but then realized I had left it in Louisa's cabin. I played for time. "How did you find us? We made these reservations only a day ago."

"I know all your dirty little secrets. My man kept me apprised of your disgusting habits while I hid away in the opposite hotel. You will no longer be allowed to see my nieces or nephew. I will erase your name from our family and ruin you financially."

He pinned me with a bloodthirsty gaze, but then inexplicably, his eyes left mine to stare at something in the distance and then widened as if at some new foe. From behind me came a cry:

"The boat is on fire!"

I broke from William's grip and twisted to see a governess clutching the baby in her care, pointing towards mid-ship. Her employer and family all turned to stare at the flames shooting up from the engine room.

The unexpected tang of burning wood permeated the air, mingling with the sounds of women's screams and men's angry shouts. At mid-ship, a column of smoke billowed up from below, and the already hot July day became hellish. As I had feared, the fuel had overheated the boiler and engulfed the engine room, and now the deck and wheel, in flames.

A crewman materialized through a haze of smoke.

"Go aft!" he shouted as he sprinted past us toward the stern. But he turned back, coughing and spitting, to rush past us toward the bow. I could not conceive of why we should run to the aft of the steamboat through a bank of flames and instead clung to the railing to try and find my bearings. The governess attempted to pass me, but her hoop skirt hampered her, and I was reminded of Louisa. She and the child were in danger if she were still in her cabin.

"We must find Louisa!" I shouted to William. He nodded, and together we headed into the inferno towards the stern of the ship and her cabin, below deck. The heat intensified. My eyes ran with tears, and my throat closed against the ash and embers. Holding my handkerchief to my face failed to filter out the soot and ash. A cinder landed on my lapel and flared. I brushed it off with my hand and felt the sting of a blister rising.

Panicked passengers, screaming for safety boats, crowded the deck while officious crew members demanded that all should move to the stern of the boat, but my only concern was to find Louisa and bring her to the bow section where I felt sure we would be safe.

As we moved down the smoky deck toward the stairway, I heard my name float over the wind. In the distance, beyond the billowing smoke, Louisa had made her way up from her cabin to the railing. Although wary of the fire and fumes, she bravely stepped towards me on the deck along the rail. I held out my arms and called encouragement but was horrified to see a capped figure emerge from the haze.

She noticed him too, and her eyes widened. "You!" She pointed an accusatory finger at him and then turned and stepped more quickly toward me. He reached out to grasp her arm, and they struggled as he attempted to drag her back toward himself.

"No!" I tried to plow through the mob of passengers to reach her. William, too, moved quickly, but his intentions were different. He grabbed me by my coat collar and dragged me away from his niece and his accomplice. I fought back as hard as my sixty-nine years would allow and felt his energy flag momentarily.

But, "You will not escape." With a menacing smile, he took deliberate aim and kicked me savagely in my weak knee. I sank to the deck in agony, my head spinning, my vision shot with stars.

Through my misery, I saw Mr. Cap pull Louisa backward, but she struggled away from him and moved forward along the railing toward William and me, ignoring the smoke blackening her clothes and skin. "Uncle William, stop! It is not his fault!" She held her arms out in supplication and seemed unaware that Mr. Cap crept along behind her, hand over hand.

But even as they gained a few yards, the boat gave a horrendous quake as the bow hit the shore. William was thrown backward into the wall and fell to the deck. But Louisa, her arms outstretched, stood too precariously near the railing. Mr. Cap flung out his arm and pushed her toward the open water, and Louisa fell backward over the railing and into the chill of the Hudson.

William shouted, "No!" and reached toward the railing to try to catch her. I lumbered to my feet and lurched for Mr. Cap, but he ran to the bow of the boat. I gave up my pursuit and turned to the railing, shouting encouragements to Louisa as she mustered all her considerable swimming skills to hold her head above water. She made a little progress toward shore, but another woman flailing nearby flung herself onto Louisa in a mistaken attempt at salvage. Louisa gasped as the woman's arms encircled her shoulders and kicked to tread water, but she could not support them both, and the two women, their skirts encumbering their legs, sank together into the depths of the river. William gave a cry and dove into the water after them.

The river was teeming with other passengers who had jumped overboard to escape the fire that engulfed the ship's midsection. One woman with her baby clasped to her bosom dropped over the side just as flames reached out from the stairwell to light her skirt afire. A nurse picked up her young charge and straddled the railing before sliding over the side. Men and women ran this way and that, some with clothes aflame, screaming in panic. The stern of the boat was burning, and the only way to escape was to leap into the water.

Tears and soot caked my face. The heat from the fire was intense, but I was compelled to watch as William repeatedly surfaced and dove. His childhood experiences swimming in Salem and Maine made him fearless in the water, and his anger at me was forgotten in his desperate search for his beloved niece.

A crewman clasped my arm and tried to draw me toward the bow of the boat, but my injured knee buckled, and I argued that I was loath to leave the place I had last seen Louisa.

"You can save her from the shore, man! You can't help her if you burn to death on the ship," he shouted and convinced me to fling my arm around his shoulder and join the ranks of passengers hurrying to the edge of the boat to jump off safely into the sand. It seemed a cruel irony that such an easy egress would be possible for some when those on the aft and midsection of the ship had met such horrific ends.

We heard the screams and shouts of those souls still struggling in the water thirty feet from shore. William swam through the waves and crawled onto the sand, exhausted. I found a piece of driftwood and used it as a crutch to limp back and forth on the shore, shouting Louisa's name out into the wind until my voice gave out. A sodden female survivor shook my arm and pointed at the stern of the ship, where a tiny toddler stood near the railing, obviously searching for his mother. He screamed for her as flames engulfed his tiny frame. The woman let go of my arm and fell to her knees, keening.

A bystander slung a blanket about my shoulders and entreated me to sit and take a sip of brandy, but I could not stay still. As bodies washed toward shore, William and I waded into the water and guided the souls in, peering at each face, at the clothing and jewelry, hoping and not hoping that each one was Louisa. If she did not appear, she could still be alive out there, clinging to a chair, a plank, able to come back to us. We, along with other survivors and bystanders, stayed at this grim duty for hours. One of the women, out of great kindness, volunteered to position the female bodies in peaceful repose as if asleep on the sand to give their family members some comfort.

As the light faded, William stood staring out into the water. "I will send a wire to your wife to say that you are safe but that Louisa did not survive." His voice caught, and I understood that he blamed himself for his accomplice's deed. He shook his head and turned toward town. I could not grasp his guilt while I so profoundly grieved. Louisa and our child were gone, and my life would never be the same.

A sympathetic fisherman allowed survivors to camp on his property, and I spent the night on the floor of his porch. When I awakened from a violent nightmare of Louisa burning like that poor toddler, I was almost grateful that she did not die in the flames. But drowning was a lonely and painful death. My heart contracted in grief for her and for our child.

I struggled to my feet in the early morning light and joined a group of survivors being interviewed by the local constabulary regarding clothing and jewelry worn by the dead so that they might make identifications. "Time in the water will obscure your loved ones' features, and the coroner will have a better chance of making the correct identifications with your information," explained one portly officer.

"Maria Louisa Hawthorne was wearing a silver and garnet brooch engraved with the name Rachel Forrester, and her pocket held a handkerchief embroidered with an H, for Hawthorne," I informed one of the jurors standing on the sand taking testimonies from the survivors about their missing loved ones.

"There will be an inquest, and the evidence we collect will be used to try the villains who decided to race with hundreds of innocent souls aboard," he assured me.

It was time to return to Salem. "You should leave on the next coach," William said. "Let the constables do their work. With your injuries, you would only be in their way. I will wait here to identify the body and escort it back to Salem. Go home to your wife. But stay away from Nath and Sophia. I will send the news to them as well."

"What of the villain in the cap?" I resisted the urge to strike my disloyal brother-in-law and instead seized his arm to confront him directly.

William refused to meet my eyes. "His orders from me were to follow you and report your doings. I would never have wished Louisa harm." He glared up at me then, his eyes glistening, but his tone roughened to the growl of the docks. "When I find Horace Lovelace, he will be made to pay for his part in her death, of that, you may rest assured."

The stagecoaches loomed onto the boardwalk, the horses' hooves drumming a dirge on the planks. We survivors had no luggage. Our clothes were still wet, our spirits bedraggled. Some wept, some slept in fits and starts. I could not sleep. Louisa's last moments of life played over again in my mind, and I tortured myself with imagined rescues. If only I had confronted Mr. Lovelace earlier, or if I had but stayed with her in her cabin. I tried to soothe myself with memories of the good times, the sweetness of her head resting on my shoulder; her lilting voice reading to me from the latest novel, her wry humor; her graceful waltzing at the Columbian Hotel. But I knew I would never forgive myself.

Mr. Lovelace's actions continued to haunt me throughout my journey. If William had not directed this villain to murder Louisa, then why would the man have taken it upon himself to do so? Someone else must be at the bottom of this evil deed. A cold hand squeezed my heart as I contemplated who might have wished Louisa and our unborn child dead. Only Priscilla had the motive, the means, and the opportunity.

After an arduous journey, most of which I am grateful to say I do not recall, we arrived in Salem in the early evening. My injured knee ached as I struggled out of the coach and onto the street. The news of the *Henry Clay* disaster had reached the city, and people crowded about the coach, shouting questions. My name was not on the list of survivors, so I was greeted with muted cheers when I was recognized.

Salem officials had been instructed to interview any survivors, and thus I was delayed in my return home. As I fitted my key into the lock, it turned from within, and I stood face to face with my wife. She looked me up and down, made a noise of disgust, turned, and led me into the bathing chamber where she systematically stripped me of my coat, waistcoat, shirt, and suspenders.

"Remove your pants and undergarments and give them to the maid." No kiss. No embrace. She rang the servant bell while I complied with her instructions and then wrapped myself in the dressing gown she offered. Bridget appeared and broke into a fit of tears and smiles. At least someone in this household was pleased to see me alive. She gathered up the rumpled, damp clothing and retreated to the laundry room.

My wife added a log to the fire. "Come. Warm yourself." She sat and took up her basket of knitting. I lowered myself onto the winged chair opposite her and closed my eyes. If we were going to confront one another, I must gather my strength.

Her tone when at last she spoke was as frigid as the waters of the Hudson. "William has wired his observations. You know, of course, that we may never speak to the rest of the family of your transgressions. Louisa's reputation must remain publicly unsullied. You and I will go on as before." She pulled at a strand of wool caught in its ball. "William's business ventures have not been successful of late. You shall make him solvent." Our eyes met at that last comment, and I knew that I faced a lifetime of payments to William.

I passed a cold hand over my face to calm my nerves. "Priscilla, please understand that Louisa and I did not wish to hurt you. We tried very hard to keep our relationship secret. This opportunity arose, and we seized upon it, not to wound you, but to honor our feelings."

She uncoiled from her chair and stood above me, a python eying its prey.

"I will never forgive you. My niece is dead, as is my marriage. Your guilt is beyond comprehension." Her voice rasped with righteous anger.

This was too much. I stood as well, fixed her cold emerald eyes with my own hot amber, and confronted her with the rage that I had suppressed for far too long.

"You speak of guilt. But I would ask you about the villain who followed Louisa and myself around Saratoga this past fortnight and whom I witnessed shove your niece into the Hudson River. And do not try to foist the blame upon your brother. William has disavowed any knowledge of such a murderous plan. He will find the individual responsible and absolve himself. You will be discovered, and the family informed of your brutality."

"You have no proof." Her face was white, but her voice was steady. She knew she was correct. "It is only William's word against mine. If William were to use violent tactics to wring a confession from some benighted sailor, it would never hold up in court. And if you insisted on a public accusation, you can be sure that I would reveal your disgusting relationship with your niece, and your reputation would be instantly ruined." She smirked at my guilty expression.

"Now." She turned toward the stairs, her head held high. "I must go and prepare for Louisa's funeral. It is my responsibility, as the most pious, to plan the service. I am sure that Nath and Ebe will be of no use."

Her black skirts hissed across the wooden floor. I sank into my chair, cradled my head in my hands, and wept bitter tears, grieving for Mary Wood, John Stephens, Louisa, and our unborn child long into the night.

Priscilla Manning Dike
4 Andover Street
Salem, Massachusetts

September 17, 1852

My Dear Thomas,

It is done. We have succeeded. And no one is the wiser. William owns his greed's transgressions. John concedes his lust and guilt. But our sins must forever remain covert.

You were clever to go on retreat. I missed your firm hand. But the revelation of our complicity would be our undoing. Besides, planning funerals has become, for me, second nature.

Summer requires a quick burial. A waterlogged corpse makes it doubly so. Louisa would be laid to rest alongside her mother. An errand boy delivered my orders that a fresh grave be dug at once.

Andover Street seemed the most appropriate venue for the reception. Necessary refreshments were baked. Hannah dripped tears into the biscuit dough. A blubbering Bridget set the table with my best linen and china.

William escorted on the train the pine box holding the bloated, decomposing body. Ebe washed and dressed it. John kept vigil in the parlor where the casket reposed. Candles and incense could not mask the odor of decay. Yet Bridget could not persuade him to stand down until the pallbearers lifted the coffin into the wagon for its final journey.

There was no time for mourners' lengthy stage rides or train trips. Errand boys delivered black-edged death notices only to family members in Salem. Nath and Sophia, in Concord, could not be contacted in time. Thus, a paltry crowd of local cousins dotted the church pews.

Ebe reluctantly shared the front row with Robert, William, John, and me. She glared at each of us in turn before slumping to the end of the pew. If she thought anything suspicious about her sister's death, she did not voice it. But her attitude remained disdainful throughout the service.

Family members came to the pulpit to say a few words. Several cousins spoke of kindnesses paid, support offered, illnesses healed. It was all I could do not to vomit in the aisle.

The expectation that John would speak was palpable. He was the last to see her alive. Yet I feared that if he stood at the pulpit, he would tell the truth as far as he knew it. Their affair. His suspicions about her killer. He would spill it all, reputation be damned. This would be unacceptable.

Rebecca Forrester finished some maudlin story about Louisa nursing her through influenza. Before John could rise, I took the pulpit.

"We must hear from Ebe, who knew Louisa best. And then you are all invited to Andover Street for further reminiscing."

Ebe slunk to the pulpit. That a self-described hermitress would stand before the congregation was testimony to her grief. She looked directly at John and spoke the truth through coded words. "Louisa searched for the love of a father she never had. Her death is a double tragedy. If there is a god, she will be reunited with those loves in Heaven. And the parties responsible for this debacle will be forced to pay."

I waited for a reaction. But there was no questioning murmur from the crowd, only the quiet sniffs of mournful friends. The sinner's path to hell had been subtly paved.

John stayed at the gravesite till the hole was filled. I hosted the mourners on Andover Street. When at last he came back to the house, we kept clear of one another. Our lives would revert to the thrust and parry of recent years. But his outside support, unlike mine, had vanished forever.

There is no proof that Louisa's death was anything but a tragic accident. The *Henry Clay* hearings have focused only on the culpability of the owner and his crew. Public outrage at the disregard for safety in pursuit of a racing victory is high. The irony that many drowned while others were rescued but a few feet away has captured the public's attention. Murder charges against the captain are a distinct possibility. Unless a witness comes forward, the truth of the situation will never be known.

Please visit Andover Street when you are returned. Your potent presence is sorely missed.

Yours in Christ.

PMD

Margaretta and I were two of the cousins who did not receive the black-edged notice of Louze's death in time to attend the funeral. When we did learn of the accident through the Steubenville newspapers, I lapsed into a three-day spell that neither Margaretta's ministrations nor the local tavern's libations could alleviate. I grieved for my cousin. I worried about my father's health after such an ordeal. And while grateful that he had survived, I was angry that once again, he had put a woman in jeopardy and then failed to save her even while he survived. Finally, I felt guilty for making my cowardly escape to Ohio and leaving Louze to her fate in Salem.

I sent my father, through Nath so that my stepmother would be unaware, a letter of condolence and an invitation to visit us in Steubenville if ever he felt the need to leave Salem and the viper's nest in which he lived. Although he wrote back to accept, he never came. Perhaps his conscience would not allow him. Or he deduced correctly that I had not truly forgiven him.

We continued a desultory flow of correspondence, with mutual promises to visit, but we never followed through. Margaretta's mother's illness prevented me from attending Nath's funeral, and when my beloved Uncle Nathaniel died in 1867, and I ascended to ownership of the Emporium, my father did not attend the funeral or give me his merchandiser's blessing but sent his condolences and an excuse about failing health. He died in 1871 without meeting Margaretta or seeing our home. His post mortem treatise became our final communion.

Now, after a week of sleepless nights reviewing the horrors of my cousin's death and discovering my stepmother's extreme cruelty, I sat again in Dr. Voight's Pittsburgh office while he scratched a new date on a fresh sheet of paper and I squirmed under his microscope.

He observed my quickened breathing, pallor, and hunched posture, recorded his findings, and then said, "I see that you are under duress.

But if you feel able, let us return to the evening of your public spell. Did anything else, apart from the mention of your domestic tragedy, occur at your cousin's celebration that might have added to your anxiety?"

I closed my eyes against the vision of Louze's brooch on Virginia's gown, but I knew I must eventually confess, and so I admitted, "Virginia was wearing a pin which reminded me of someone from my childhood."

"I see. This is good. We have not yet explored your young life. Tell me about your family." He kept his eyes on his paper as he recorded my answer.

"The Dikes immigrated from Ireland to Massachusetts in the 1600s. My uncle moved to Steubenville to open a retail business. I joined him and became a partner, and then, after his death, the owner of the Emporium." I recited all this by rote as if it were about someone else.

"Indeed." Dr. Voight paused as if expecting more. When I remained silent, he prodded, "But your youth was spent where?"

"In Salem, Massachusetts." My voice sounded strained, my hands clutched the armrests of my chair, and my breath quickened.

Dr. Voight steepled his fingers and narrowed his eyes. "Mr. Dike, I notice a reluctance on your part to speak of your childhood. When asked about your family, you avoid mentioning your mother or your father or any siblings, and your body tenses."

I sat discovered, mute at both the knowledge that I did not want to speak of my parents or my sister and at the physical reactions that their specters engendered. In the interest of conquering my feelings and eventually healing, I attempted to obey the doctor and murmured, "My mother died when I was a child. I lived with my sister and my father, and his new wife. Then my sister died, and I came to Steubenville." I was aware of the tremor in my voice. A bead of sweat trickled down my back, and my hands again clenched the chair arms.

Dr. Voight rose and came to stand next to me. His cool fingers found my pulse, which he counted with his pocket watch. When about a minute had elapsed, he returned to his desk, folded his hands on its top, and spoke calmly as if gentling a nervous pup. "Mr. Dike, your anxiety is thwarting our work. Therefore, I would like to try a different technique while we explore your early childhood. A notable French physician has had great success with an ancient method for the management of pain, both physical and emotional."

I must have looked skeptical as he sat back again and steepled his fingers. "It is entirely harmless, I assure you. It is simply a way to foster more complete relaxation so that the mind and heart may make connections that both would otherwise avoid. Have you heard of hypnotherapy?"

"I have read reports of hypnotists in carnival shows forcing women to quack like ducks and reveal private parts of their anatomy," I said, unconvinced.

"Those men are charlatans." For the first time in our sessions, Dr. Voight raised his voice, but he took a breath and continued more calmly. "Hypnosis cannot make one do anything that one would not ordinarily do. But it can open the subconscious to reveal memories and emotions that have been suppressed for protection."

I could feel my pulse rising again and my hands clenching of their own accord. The doctor observed this, too, and said, "Mr. Dike, your body seeks to protect you. I believe that is the reason for your spells. But I think that you would not be here if you did not wish to conquer your fears. I cannot promise you that we can make you entirely well, but the technique I am offering has the highest chance of success. Will you risk it?"

Would I? I met the doctor's unwavering gaze and thought of my sister, and Louze, and all our unborn children, and the miserable guilt that had plagued me since my youth. If I threw my desperate caution to the wind and relinquished myself to this powerful technique, it might result in a new life for myself and my loved ones. I took a deep breath and deliberately relaxed my hands. "I will."

"Wunderbar." He pulled forward from the side of the fireplace a small divan and gestured toward it expansively. "Please, Mr. Dike, make yourself comfortable."

I felt ridiculous lying on a couch in a doctor's office, especially at this time of day, but still, I complied. He draped a jacquard shawl across my legs, threw another log on the fire, although the day was warm, drew the drapes, and lit a single candle on his desk. Then he pulled his watch from his vest pocket and sat in the chair across from the couch, the watch dangling from his fingers.

"Mr. Dike, please keep your eyes on the watch." It hung in front of me, but at a steep upward angle, so that my eyes were forced up and in. "Focus, Mr. Dike." I squinted at the watch, its spinning gold back glittering in the candlelight. "Listen to my voice, Mr. Dike," murmured Dr. Voight. "Keep your eyes on the watch. You will notice that you are feeling drowsy, but do not close your eyes. You will only close them when I tell you to do so." Indeed, I felt drowsy, but I complied, gazing unwaveringly at the watch. He continued, "I will now count to three. When I say three, you must close your eyes, and you will not open them again unless you raise your left hand and count to three. Are you ready? One, two, three."

The room went dark. I had entered a void, but it was not the frightening dark depths of a spell, more like a soft gray cloud in a vast horizon, pillowing my body and my mind. I relaxed into the sensations until a distant voice coaxed me back.

"Mr. Dike, can you hear me?" I think I nodded. My body felt disconnected, as though my head were floating untethered in those gray clouds.

"I am going to ask you some questions. You are perfectly safe. But if you become frightened, remember that all you need to do is to raise your left hand and count to three. Do you understand?"

Again, I believe I nodded.

"Good. Now. Let us go back in time to some of your earliest memories." There was a pause, and the disconnect deepened as I breathed into the void.

"John Stephens, how old are you?" The voice floated from somewhere behind me, and I somehow felt compelled to answer.

"Three." My voice was a child's mournful squeak, yet oddly, I was not frightened and relaxed into the sensation.

"Are your mother and father and sister with you?"

"No. Mama coughed, and now she is gone, and Papa is unwell."

"How is he unwell?" The voice sounded vaguely sing-song, and I answered in a similar fashion.

"He is sad because Mama is not here. So, we live with Grampa and Gramma." The subject matter was distressing, but somehow, I did not wish to escape this velvet interrogation.

"I see." There was a pause. "Let us move forward in your memories." There was a pause. "How old are you now?"

"Eight." My voice had deepened to a tenor.

"Are you still in your grandparents' home?" The voice soothed, like soft rain, enveloping me in gray softness.

"No, Papa, Mary Wood, and I live in our own home in Salem. But we play with our Hathorne cousins at their house."

"Do you like your cousins?"

"Ebe is mean. Louze is sweet. Nath is my best friend." I felt a gentle longing, but it was not objectionable. I sighed.

"Tell me what you are feeling, John Stephens.," said the voice. "Do you miss your cousins?"

"Yes. But they live with . . ." A shiver ran through me, and I clutched the shawl to my throat.

"With whom do they live, John Stephens?"

For the first time, I felt anxious. My hands clenched into tight fists above my chest.

The voice said, "You are safe here, John Stephens. Whomever you are remembering cannot hurt you now."

"Yes, she can." My mind and body fought towards consciousness, too terrorized to continue this game. My left hand twitched, but the voice gentled me through it.

"Breathe, John Stephens." I took a deep breath, and my body relaxed.

"Good. Now then. You can confront her here. Tell me whom you fear."

I whispered, "Their aunt."

"Is she not kind?" The voice stayed neutral, despite the frightened tone in mine.

"No." The tears that had been threatening now flowed freely down my wrinkled cheeks, though I could have sworn that I was a boy. The voice allowed a bit of time to elapse before continuing.

"Let us move forward. How old are you now?" The voice hovered in the air behind me. I did not dare to follow it into the darkness to answer. But I did.

"Thirteen." My voice broke as if I were a youth again.

"Are you at home?"

"No, I am at a party."

"Are your Papa and sister with you?"

"Yes." My voice turned sullen. "But so is the aunt. Papa has married her, and now I must call her my stepmother."

"Does she still frighten you?"

"Yes." My voice yodeled on this, and I cleared my throat just as I did as a youth.

"Who else is at the party?"

"My Hathorne cousins. Louze is wearing a pretty dress and a pin, and I want to dance with her. But she wishes only to dance with Papa, and his wife is angry."

My legs kicked at the shawl, and my fists clenched the couch cushions.

The voice waited until I had settled before continuing.

"John Stephens, breathe. How old are you now?" The silken voice pulled me toward a dangerous place. I did not want to follow, but I relented.

"Thirteen."

"Are you still at the party?"

"No, I am in our house with Mary Wood and my stepmother." My hands clenched the sofa cushions.

"Are you safe?" The voice stayed perfectly steady despite the tension in my own.

"No."

"Why?"

"My stepmother is not kind." My thirteen-year-old voice sounded both scared and angry.

"How so?" The voice was soft but unrelenting.

"She punishes us. For nothing. Mary Wood coughs and coughs. I feel guilty for leaving her at home while I go to school." Anger predominated now, and the couch cushions were damp.

"Tell me more."

"It is a Saturday in December, but it is warm. I try to give Mary Wood her scarf, but my stepmother pushes us out the door." The anger reverted to sorrow and guilt. "Mary Wood is dead, and it is all my fault."

"How is it your fault?"

"She is dead from the warm wind because I wanted to escape." My throat tightened so that I could barely speak.

"Escape from what?"

From the depths of my guilt, I whispered the dreaded name. "Priscilla." My voice rose with each self-recrimination. "I could not keep Mary Wood safe. I could not keep Mama safe. And I could not keep Louze safe." Tears flowed, and I had no will to stop them.

From the void, the voice murmured, "John Stephens, you were a child. It was not your responsibility to keep your sister safe. Or your mother. Or your cousin. None of your family's tragedies were your fault. Your father did not keep you safe. It is your father whom you must forgive."

Through the gray cloud, a thunderstorm erupted as memories flashed.

Mama holding me close, her hair smelling like sunshine.

Papa lying in bed, weeping.

Gramma comforting me in her plump, welcoming arms.

Mary Wood holding my hand.

Louze dancing with Papa.

Mary Wood coughing.

Mary Wood lying in her coffin.

Louze drifting in the Hudson.

And Priscilla, a blood-stained belt dangling from one hand and a dripping handkerchief in the other.

My left hand rose of its own accord, and I counted, "One, two, three."

I bolted upright on the couch, unable to breathe, sweat pouring down my back, flashes of light stabbing my eyes. The doctor held a glass of brandy to my lips and murmured, "Just a sip, to bring you back to the present." His cool, dry hand found my wrist and counted my pulse until we were both assured that it had slowed.

Doctor Voight returned to his desk. He allowed several minutes to elapse while I dried my eyes and blew my nose before he said, "Mr. Dike, I have made a diagnosis. I believe that you suffer from vascular headaches, which are often one-sided and can be triggered by sensations or smells and exacerbated by anxiety. You worked very hard today to uncover the childhood roots of that anxiety. Now I wish you to rest and ruminate on those findings. You may find that you recognize more provocations as you reconsider your life. Recognition is the first step to eradication."

I nodded, too overwhelmed to speak but optimistic for the first time in years that I might finally find a cure.

He smiled slightly at my grateful expression and said as he wrote out a card, "I shall see you in a month when you have more fully explored your emotions. In the meantime, if you find yourself in the beginnings of another spell, use the post-hypnotic suggestion that worked so well today. When you feel your anxiety rise and your fists form, breathe, unclench and raise your left hand, and count to three. You may be able to stop the headache. We shall discuss your experiences next time, and I can prescribe medication then if the post-hypnotic suggestion proves insufficient."

I did not remember the train ride home. When I hobbled in the front door, Margaretta took one look at me, tucked me into bed, and ordered a cold compress. "Did he help?" she asked, her forehead creased even more than usual with worry.

"I am not sure," was all I could answer.

"Well, you are safe now." She kissed me on the cheek and held my hand until I fell asleep.

My dreams were peaceful, and at dawn, I awoke feeling more refreshed than I had since the documents arrived. As the weeks progressed, I found myself gradually forgiving both my father's weaknesses and my own childish foibles. With Margaretta's help, I eased myself again into reading the rest of the collection, this time with an explicit purpose, aided by a clear conscience. And when I felt my fists forming, I breathed deeply, raised my left hand, and counted to three. Most of the time, I was able to stave off the spells, and I hoped that I might, with some dogged determination, yet solve the mystery of my cousin's inheritance.

John Dike
4 Andover Street
Salem, Massachusetts

(October 10, 1871)

In 1860, after the Hawthorne family's return to the Wayside from Europe, I received concerning letters from Nath and Sophia regarding their daughter Una's illness contracted when they traveled abroad in service to President Pierce.

According to Nath, *"*Una has taken what seems to be the Roman fever by sitting down to sketch in the Coliseum, and now suffers from fits of exceeding discomfort, occasional comatoseness, and even delirium."*

When they returned to Concord, Sophia reported:

*"*No one shared my nursing because Una wanted my touch and voice. For days, she only opened her eyes long enough to see if I were there. For thirty days and nights, I did not go to bed; or sleep, except in the morning in a chair, while Miss Shepard watched for an hour or so."*

A mutual friend wrote, *"*She exhibited one of the most fearful attacks of dementia ever suffered from a condition of fury dangerous to everybody and everything about her."*

Thus, I traveled to Concord to visit Nath and his family and to assist in Una's care. I felt an almost grandfatherly connection with the children. Perhaps it was because I had assisted in Una's birth. Perhaps it was because I had lost my darling daughter and my unborn child, and my childless son lived so far away. No matter. I knew Nath and Sophia needed help, and I gave it with all my heartfelt sympathy.

～～～

"Mr. Dike, I am so happy to see you!" Nine-year-old Rose threw her arms around my waist and hugged me hard. "We have missed you." She took my big hand in her tiny one and half coaxed, half dragged me into the parlor of the Wayside. Nath and Sophia rose to greet me, and we embraced.

"You look exhausted, both of you. Have you slept? And how is Una?" Nath wiped his face with his handkerchief, Sophia dropped back into her chair, and they both shook their heads.

Nath said, "At the moment, she is sleeping, and the doctors tell us we must make sure she has as much rest as possible. But her fever persists. Last night she tossed and turned so much that we feared for her sanity. Today she hardly recognizes us. She is in a trance half the time. I wish we had stayed here in happy Concord instead of going to cursed Italy."

His hoarse voice trailed off. I put a reassuring hand on his thin shoulder and noted the sharp bones jutting through the cloth of his coat. He was not the hale man I knew before he ventured to the continent.

"I can watch over her. I have experience with sick children, as you know. You should both go and rest. Or, Nath, perhaps you could take a walk. It will do you good."

Rose stood near me. "I can help Mr. Dike." Her stoic voice seemed surprisingly mature for one so young. Her dark hair was drawn back in a serviceable bun, and she stood straight and strong as she spoke. "I am not afraid of illness. Father, you and Mother, stay here. Come, Mr. Dike, I will show you to her room." She again took my hand in hers, and we climbed the steps to the second floor.

The familiar sick room smells permeated the landing, transporting me back in time to Mary Wood's death. I would not wish that pain on any parent. I heard Nath and Sophia in the parlor making plans for their day now that they had some support, and I felt gratified that my presence would be a help to them.

Rose motioned me to be quiet and then opened Una's door. The curtains were drawn, but Una's eyes gleamed in the dim light. Her auburn hair spread disheveled on the pillow. She raised one hand in greeting, then dropped it as if its weight were too heavy a burden.

"Mr. Dike. Thank you for coming to see me. You know I may not last the day." She said it matter-of-factly as if she had already accepted her fate, so remarkably mature for a girl of only sixteen. But Una had always been fascinated by death; Louisa had reported to me her odd behavior at Betsey's sickbed.

"I want to give you something. Please go to the bureau and open the top drawer," Una said. I obeyed and awaited further instructions. "Do you see a handkerchief folded into a bundle? Please unwrap it."

I wept when the content of the monogrammed handkerchief was revealed. Inside lay a smoke-tarnished silver and garnet bar brooch, the very one that Louisa wore on our final day together. My knees buckled, and I dropped into the chair in the corner. Rose, like a good little nurse, came to my aid, but I patted her arm to reassure her. "I am fine, dear. This pin just reminded me of a very special day." I caught Una's eye sparkling in the gloom.

Una continued, "Aunt Louisa used to speak of you often when we went on walks in the woods. She always said that you were a kind gentleman. And Mama and Papa told me that you and Aunt Louisa were special friends. After her funeral, I asked Papa for the pin and handkerchief to remember her by, but I think Aunt Louisa might want you to have them, now that I am dying. Please take them and remember us both."

Tears splashed down upon my hand, wetting the pin. I blotted my eyes with my own handkerchief and wiped the brooch dry.

"Will you pin it to my lapel, please?" Rose complied and then took a step back to admire her handiwork.

"It looks very nice on your coat, Mr. Dike. I am sorry that it makes you sad, though."

"Thank you," I murmured to Una, but she had closed her eyes. Her forehead felt warm to the back of my hand. I motioned to Rose to go downstairs and then drew up a chair and sat by Una's bedside until I was sure she rested with ease.

I sought out Sophia to give my report regarding Una's fever and spent time with Rose until her older brother Julian came home from school, and I could aid Sophia at her vigil. I returned to Salem and the business only when I was assured that Nath and Sophia had friends and neighbors who could assist with Una's care.

As the weeks dragged on, Una continued her decline. Dr. Bartlett diagnosed it as malaria-induced dementia and dosed her daily with homeopathy, but her parents were frantic to find a cure. Electric shock therapy in a clinic in Boston seemed effective, but only for short bits of time, and then the frenetic episodes would start again. Sophia, never a strong person, was skeletal from worry. Nath's health also deteriorated. When I visited the Wayside periodically, I watched him struggle up the path to the larch woods he used to walk with ease. Rose and Julian seemed subdued, too, as though they knew the house were on a death watch.

This focus on mortality reminded me that I must draw up a will so that all my holdings would go to Priscilla and John Stephens should my health take a turn for the worst. I traveled by train into Boston to our lawyer's well-appointed offices on West Street. A clerk took notes of our conversation while his employer pontificated.

"Often," Mr. Hillard explained, "the wife inherits everything. However, you may bequeath funds to your servants and other associates, as well as set up a trust for your son and daughter-in-law. Do they have any issue?"

"No, I am sorry to say. But they have cousins with whom they are very close. I believe, in the event of John Stephens' and Margaretta's deaths, that these cousins are to be the beneficiaries. Their names are Mr. and Mrs. Thomas S. Blair. Her first name is Virginia, nee Dike. At their deaths, their surviving son George Dike Blair would be the sole remaining heir."

"Excellent. Are there any possessions you wish to leave to anyone in particular?" I thought of my ships, my house, my books. There were only two items that I would prefer Priscilla not to inherit or sell.

"I bequeath a handkerchief embroidered with an H and a small silver bar pin with a garnet set in the center to my son John Stephens. He is to keep them in his immediate family and not sell or destroy them. In the event of his death, and that of his wife, they are to go to Virginia and her husband and then on to George."

"Is there to be any paperwork attached to the objects, Sir? Insurance for the jewelry?" asked the clerk. I thought back to that terrible day in 1852. The pin and handkerchief were precious to me, but they had historical significance as well. There must have been some documentation regarding the identification of the bodies after the disaster.

"I would be grateful if you would do some research. You might contact the Collyer Shipping Company and have them send you copies of the listings of properties of the dead. They would be under the name Maria Louisa Hawthorne. The pin and handkerchief were items used to identify her body after the *Henry Clay* incident. I wish the paperwork to accompany the pin and handkerchief as documentation of the legacy."

Mr. Hillard looked a bit surprised by my explanation, but his clerk nodded and jotted down a few more notes. Mr. Hillard added, "The next time we meet, you will sign the will and take a copy for your records. Thank you for coming in. Safe journeys." He shook my hand goodbye, and I returned to Salem with the assurance that my will and legacy were secure and that Louisa's possessions would be curated for posterity.

(October 15, 1871)

Unfortunately, I must record another devastating death in the Hawthorne family. My dear nephew Nath, who for years had suffered with an undiagnosed gastric illness, died May 19th, 1864, in his sleep, while traveling in New Hampshire with his good friend Franklin Pierce. Sophia was too fragile to plan the service, and so the arrangements fell to her children and friends.

Nath's funeral became the event of Concord's spring season and a day of bereavement for all who loved literature. Admirers, family, and friends filled the pews in the white church on the green, and Nath's favorite flowers, apple blossoms and lily of the valley, perfumed the chapel. Aromatic orchards would forever remind me of that mournful day.

"Thank you for helping us plan the service, Mr. Dike," whispered twenty-year-old Una. By some miracle, she had not succumbed to the Italian malaria and its aftereffects and had grown into a lovely young woman, with the Manning's distinctive auburn hair. Her eccentric personality, however, remained unchanged.

She and I were seated in the front row of the church, waiting for the pallbearers to escort the casket down the aisle. Sophia sat slumped further down the pew next to her other children. Rose, at thirteen even more the confident nurse, held her mother's hand. Eighteen-year-old Julian, who left final exams at Harvard College for this family emergency, stroked his sparse mustache to keep from weeping. General Pierce, in uniform, sat at attention on the aisle. I leaned forward to check on Sophia. She had been almost catatonic since Nath's death, and I worried for her state of mind.

Sophia seemed stable for the time being, so I leaned back and said to Una, "I am here in support of your family and to make sure your mother survives the ordeal. Having experienced too many funerals of loved ones, I understand how difficult they can be." Of course, I was thinking of Louisa's when I said this, but Una was very young at the time, and I did not expect her to understand.

But she did. "I was thinking of Aunt Louisa just the other day when I walked to Walden Pond," Una said to me with a contemplative gaze that I could not quite interpret.

Ebe sat with Louisa May Alcott and her family several rows behind us. Louisa May had kindly sent Sophia a bunch of violets picked from the Old Manse in Nath's honor. I turned to the Alcotts' pew and nodded my gratitude to Louisa May, who looked healthier than the last time I had seen her, despite the ravages of typhoid she had contracted while nursing soldiers in the war.

I attempted to catch Ebe's attention. She glared at me as usual but then dropped her gaze and dabbed at her eyes with a handkerchief. She had insisted on sequestering herself away from Nath's family, as she and Sophia had never liked each other, and the children found her cold and unloving. But the death of her dear younger brother, and final sibling, must be excruciating, and I hoped that the gregarious Alcott family would help her manage her grief.

The bells tolled, and the chapel door opened. Down the aisle came the coffin. In proof of Nath's literary worth, every living intellectual and social dignitary of his generation paced by its side, including Mr. Emerson, Mr. Longfellow, Mr. Holmes, Mr. Alcott, Mr. Agassiz, Judge Hoar, and Mr. Whipple. As they neared the pulpit, Sophia gave a little whimper, and Rose squeezed her hand while Julian put his arm about her shoulders. Una reached over to hold her mother's other hand, and I closed my eyes and focused my thoughts on giving her strength. The coffin came to rest in the front of the hall, and Julian rose to place a manuscript of an unfinished last romance, along with two wreaths of tea roses and orange blossoms, on the burnished top.

The service was lengthy and Calvinistic. Nath would have hated it. James Freeman Clarke, who had also officiated at the Hawthorne's wedding, presided. After friends and colleagues extolled talents too soon extinguished and stories and romances outlasting their creator, the bells chimed again to send the soul on its way. The congregation, some in Union blue, most in the somber colors of grief, exited the church and walked in procession behind the hearse carrying the casket to Sleepy Hollow Cemetery.

Birds sang, springtime blossoms scented the air, but again I endured the burial of a loved one: the thud of the dirt hitting the coffin, the whimpers of the mourners, the prayers at the graveside. I wept for the loss of my supremely talented nephew taken too soon, with many more years of transcendent writings never to be published.

General Pierce led mourners to an impromptu reception at the nearby Old Manse and asked Rose to escort Sophia back to the Wayside and to bed. Friends would host the bereaved and let the children and widow have a little privacy at home.

Later, as I returned to the Wayside, I remembered the letter Nath had sent detailing his struggles with the property.

I have been equally unsuccessful in my architectural projects; and have transformed a simple and small old farm-house sold to me by Bronson Alcott into the absurdist anomaly you ever saw; but I really was not so much to blame here as the village-carpenter, who took the matter into his own hands, and produced an unimaginable sort of thing instead of what I asked for.

Indeed, the building was a hodgepodge of connective architecture. The writing tower he designed for himself was the crowning achievement. I thought it more practical than absurdist, but perhaps only because I recognized in it his attempt to recreate his Herbert Street's Owl's Nest.

While a tearful Sarah tidied up after a mournful family supper, I collapsed in Nath's chair in the parlor to read a bit before going to bed. Pigwiggin the Third leaped onto my lap. I sipped my glass of whiskey, stroked the cat, and thought about my nephew and friend. Did he think I took advantage of his sister? I twirled the amber liquid in the glass and pondered our later correspondence. He never confronted or accused me, but his books were full of sensual themes, possibly reflecting our extra-marital affair.

Ebe padded into the room and, with a feline grace, curled herself upon the settee. She carried a cup of tea and her knitting basket. The sharp tang of the camphor oil sachet emanating from the yarn reminded me unpleasantly of my wife. After taking an inordinate amount of time arranging her hooped skirt and mourning shawl, she removed the yarn from the top of the basket, squinted at the instruction pamphlet she had pulled from the bottom compartment, and knitted an entire row before paying me any mind.

"I was surprised that John Stephens and his Ohio flower did not grace us with their presence," she said, eyeing me for any signs of trouble regarding my missing son.

"Her mother is quite ill, and they could not leave her for such a long journey," I said, my voice a little defensive, as I, too, had wondered at John Stephens' absence at his best friend's funeral. "But they send their best wishes and promise to visit soon. The train makes traveling much easier these days."

"Then what is Aunt Priscilla's excuse?" she asked, peering at her work. "I was hoping to ask her for some advice on this project."

"Mrs. Dike was also unable to make the journey due to church obligations. She sends her condolences. Perhaps you could visit us in Salem and have a knitting tutorial."

Ebe chuckled sarcastically. "So that you can seduce me too? I think not, John. We are both too old."

I felt the blood rush to my face, but when I stood to take a dignified leave, she stopped me with both a raised knitting needle and a more sober voice. "I am teasing. I know that you and Louisa loved each other deeply. My only regret is that you could not keep her safe." She pointed the needle at my heart for emphasis.

My eyes welled at this attestation of our love, but I recovered my composure enough to defend myself in a quiet but firm tone. "I did all that I could to save her. And I miss her each and every day. However, I hardly think this a subject for such public discussion."

"Oh, not to worry. I believe your secret is safe here among your friends. And I would never say anything overt to Aunt Priscilla. She deserved your disloyalty after abusing your children."

I nodded, not surprised at Ebe's breadth of knowledge and grateful for her barbed solicitude, but before we could continue, Una, Julian, and Rose joined us to engage in conversation about wills and documents and whether Sophia and the children would stay at the Wayside or move to Europe as Sophia insisted that she must.

"I will certainly support you in whatever decision you make," I said, "but for now, I think we must all go to bed. We have been up since dawn, and your mother will need us tomorrow to help her make her plans. I shall see you in the morning."

Una caught up with me in the hall. "Mr. Dike," she whispered, "I wish to discuss something with you. Please follow me to the study." She seemed so secretive that I tiptoed up the stairs behind her and eased the door to Nath's tower room closed with a stealthy hand.

"I found this recently in one of Papa's old journals. I tore it out because I did not want anyone else to see it before I showed it to you." She held out a page with an uneven edge. The penmanship was certainly Nath's. I read it, first with interest, then with shame, and finally with dread.

August 13, 1852

My sister is dead.

We were in happy receipt of her letter from Saratoga Springs promising a visit to our Wayside home. But in her stead came a friend with tragic news. "Your sister Louisa has drowned in the Hudson River, in the Henry Clay Steamboat disaster!" My wife and children reached out to me for comfort, but in a desperate plea for privacy, I retreated to lament alone on my larch-wood path. That Louisa, so adept in the water, should succumb to Margaret's fate, seemed unfathomable. Of all modes of death, I think drowning is the ugliest.

To further add injury, Ebe's letter announcing the Salem services arrived too late at the Wayside, and so Louisa was laid to rest beside our mother, and I was none the wiser. I could not publicly grieve but must wait until circumstances allowed for me to mourn with our family in Salem.

My elderly yet stalwart uncle John, Louisa's ostensible charge and traveling companion, wept as he recounted to me her last moments on board the burning ship and his failed attempts at her rescue, yet his demeanor seemed circumspect, his eyes downcast. My aunt Priscilla gave him no wifely succor, and only with her sullen brother, William exchanged silent, stern communions the meanings of which I could not glean, and I rode back to the Wayside more suspicious than enlightened.

Sophia awakens from hellish nightmares in which Louisa drowns and burns in concurrent agonies. Una pins upon her breast Louisa's favorite broach, the engraving tarnished, the garnet singed. Julian begs for comfort, yet I cannot comply, but alone must trudge the larch-wood path, my melancholy at war with my suspicions.

Louisa is dead, yet there is a mystery here. Perhaps when the grieving has subsided, more of the plot shall be revealed. My uncles and aunt must be made to testify to the truth of my sister's demise and reparations made. But should they choose to maintain their silence, I vow to write an accusatory romance avenging Louisa's suspicious death and revealing to all the villainy coiled beneath.

"Do you know anything about the 'mystery' to which my father alludes?" Una's customary sarcastic lilt had taken on a confrontational tone, and with hardened eyes, she stared me down, demanding an explanation.

I shook my head, hoping that my dishonesty would not shine like a beacon from the steady gaze I locked upon hers. "I do not."

"And did Papa ask you to testify to anything?"

"No," I said, "I had already given him my account of the incident. Louisa stood aft by the railing, I nearer the bow. When the boat ran aground, she fell into the river, and I was helped by a sailor to jump onto the sand."

"What of William or Priscilla? Why should they be made to testify?"

"Perhaps your father detected some tension between Priscilla and myself. Both she and William suspected the truth about my relationship with your aunt Louisa." I shifted the subject away from the dangerous specter of Mr. Lovelace. "But do you think Nath wrote a romance about Louisa's death, as his last line suggests? Was that perhaps the subject of the document that was placed upon the coffin today?"

"No, that was the first chapter of another of his tales about finding immortality. His failing health dictated his interests in the end."

"And you have not found any manuscripts hidden in your home? I ask this with some personal concern, for if Nath wrote of our love affair, it could mean public ruin for me."

"I understand. But Julian and I have searched this absurd house from top to bottom, especially here in Papa's tower, for any undiscovered pages. We wouldn't want future owners to stumble upon a new work that should belong to our Mama. Or," she dropped her gaze momentarily, "that might harm a friend."

"Has your mother seen this notebook page?" I wondered if Sophia were cognizant of Nath's suspicions regarding Louisa's death.

"I honestly do not know. My father always shared his writings with her. But when Aunt Louisa died, Papa focused on the Pierce biography to distract himself, and this page and the promised romance were probably forgotten in that effort."

"So, what do *you* think the 'mystery' might be?" I kept my face as neutral as possible, while scanning hers for indications of further suspicions.

She shrugged, apparently appeased. "Perhaps, as you say, it was merely domestic tensions. Or it had something to do with the steamboat company's responsibilities already exposed in various legal channels. But." She put an apologetic hand on my arm, "I had to ask. Aunt Louisa deserves to rest in peace."

"I agree. And I appreciate your efforts to discover the truth. Now I think it is time that we said good-night. Tomorrow will be a difficult day for all. May I keep this?" I tucked the notebook page into my jacket pocket at her acquiescence and followed her down the tower stairs.

My chamber was in the east wing of the house. I did a cursory search of the rooms and found no secret manuscripts, only dust balls, and mouse droppings. If a new Hawthorne romance detailing my sins were discovered in my lifetime, I would have to accept the consequences. But more important was the notebook page with Nath's veiled description of the 'villainy coiled beneath', insinuating Priscilla's guilt. I resolved to include it in the documents and artifacts comprising John Stephens' inheritance.

✑✑✑

Circumstances dictated that I would be the sole representative of the Manning and Dike families at my nephew's funeral. John Stephens and Margaretta could not make the journey. Priscilla did not wish to travel with me. Robert had died nearly twenty years before. Only one other family member remained, and he would not have attended anyway, from a sense of trespass and because he was ill.

✑✑✑

"John, William has not been well. His cough has deepened, and the doctor fears the worst. I must go to the church and pray for his soul. Can you look in on him for me, please?"

Priscilla stood by the door, adjusting her gray bonnet in the mirror. Her brother lay dying, but she hadn't the heart to sit by his side to comfort him. She preferred the company of her reverend.

"Of course, my dear. I shall go immediately to see him." My businesses had prospered in these last few years, and I supported William monetarily, as I had promised my wife. But I held no favor in him, not since that fateful day on the Hudson. However, he was family. I knew my responsibilities.

William was dying. His gray face, putrid breath, gasping cough, and blood-tinged handkerchief told me this as surely as the doctor's strained expression. William reached for my hand and gestured for the doctor to give us privacy. I bent my ear to his mouth.

"I am sorry," he gasped. "Please forgive me. I did not mean to hurt anyone."

I took out my handkerchief and blotted the tears from his eyes. "Louisa knew that. If anyone is to blame, it is I, for choosing the boat." A tear slid down my own cheek. After all these years, the guilt still stung.

"No, you do not understand. Please. Go to my desk." I looked him in the eye to make sure he was of sound mind, then walked to the crescent, claw-footed desk in the corner.

"Take out the drawer on the right," he directed. I pulled it out. "No, take it all the way out."

I complied, setting the drawer on the floor. "Reach your arm in as far as it will go," whispered William. I followed his orders, feeling around in the void of the desk with my fingers. Something brushed my thumb. I grasped hold of a slip of paper and pulled it out.

"Read it," he gasped. I opened the folded sheet of stationery. The letterhead was missing, and it was signed only with initials, but I recognized my wife's penmanship.

In reading it, the suspicions that had plagued me these twelve long years were at last proven. We were indeed being followed on the train, in the hotel, on the boat, but not solely at William's direction. Mr. Lovelace was on the *Henry Clay* to do my own wife's murderous bidding. The blame for Louisa's death rested squarely on Priscilla's shoulders.

I sat at William's side and shook his shoulder to rouse him. "How did you come by this?"

He shrugged beneath my hand. "I have friends on the docks who know how to encourage cooperation. After he relinquished the letter, I let them do with him what they pleased. His body was never recovered."

The blood rushed in my ears, and my heart pounded. I leaned over the edge of the bed and put my head between my knees. William laid his hand on my shoulder. We stayed in that pose of guilt and repentance until I noticed that the hand on my shoulder had grown cold. I raised my head and looked at my brother-in-law. His half-opened eyes glistened, unseeing in the flickering candlelight. I reached out a gentle hand to close them, then sat back to reread the incriminating directive.

It proved that Priscilla was complicit in Louisa's and our unborn child's death. I now had two choices, one heroic but reckless, the other cowardly but prudent. I could make public my wife's guilt and suffer the consequences of a trial, her revelation of my affair with Louisa, familial pain as Ebe, John Stephens, Sophia, and the Hawthorne children testified under duress, and my probable business ruination. Or, I could continue as before, treading carefully around the snake in the grass while supporting my extended family and friends, building my business, and seizing the opportunity of a post mortem confession to reveal the truth. I chose the latter.

I folded the directive into my breast pocket, opened the door, and informed the doctor of William's death. On my way home, I resolved to say nothing to Priscilla of William's confession but to remand her directive to my safe, along with the pin, the handkerchief, and Nath's notebook page. I delivered a package containing those articles to the Hillard law office the next day, with the stipulation that the contents, along with my will, should go to John Stephens when I passed, just as we had discussed.

John Stephens, my health has declined significantly, and I shall be unable to continue writing this treatise, but I wish to convey to you my sincerest apologies for my failure to protect you from familial villainy, from which you suffered, and Mary Wood paid the ultimate price. I bequeath to you this document and these artifacts so that you might better understand my decisions concerning my marriage, our lives, your stepmother's guilt, and my subsequent actions. Do with them what you will.

I remain your loving Papa,

John Dike

John Dike
4 Andover Street
Salem, Massachusetts

October 20, 1871

George Hillard, Esquire
14 West Street
Boston, Massachusetts

Mr. Hillard,

    As I write this, I can feel my time running short. Mrs. Dike has ordered continuous nursing care, and I am certain that you can see by my penmanship the weakness in my hand. When Miss O'Malley delivers this document, I beg you to assure that only my son or his descendants shall inherit it, along with my will and the personal articles. Thank you for all your assistance.

    Sincerely,

    John Dike

Priscilla Manning Dike
4 Andover Street
Salem, Massachusetts

November 10, 1871

My Dear Thomas:

Your absence was sorely noted at John's funeral. Instead, your wife Eleanor paid me your condolences. She and Ebe visited before the service. Ebe asked her about your welfare. They seemed to have much to talk about, as cousins often do. I trust that you have not given your wife any cause for suspicion.

Once again, we must not display our collusion. I look forward to your happy return now that my husband is safely in his grave. Analyses of his funeral and the reading of his will are below for your perusal.

And soon, I will have need to lean upon you even further. My health has taken a turn for the worse. Dr. Peabody has promised me very little time to put my affairs in order. You have always had my undying affection. I have hoped that the feeling is reciprocal. Over the years, I have given gifts to the church and to you as earthly symbols of my devotion. Please now accept this emerald ring as the current token of my gratitude. I trust that it will give the church more satisfaction than it has ever given me.

⌒⌒⌒

"What lovely flowers," Margaret Felt effused. She greeted me with a proffered hand as we gathered in the church foyer before John's funeral. When I refused to take it, she dropped the hand but still would not let me pass. She insisted on preserving the myth of my husband's sainthood. "Mr. Dike so often inquired, in a kind manner, after the children and me. His feelings were very tender. He would have been so humbled by all this attention." Satisfied that she had said her piece, Mrs. Felt sailed by me, a schooner in black serge. She moved to embrace my recalcitrant niece. Ebe shuddered and backed away to stand with Louisa May Alcott.

Although thirty years apart in age, Ebe and Louisa May became close friends after Louze's death. Perhaps Ebe felt a need to replace her sister. At any rate, Louisa May's success as a writer—her book for brats, *Little Women*, and her scandalous adult novels were inexplicably popular—seemed to have piqued Ebe's interest. The two spinster authors and quasi-philosophers apparently found much in common.

The Dike, Hawthorne, and Manning families were not nearly as well-represented at the service as were John's friends and business associates. Sophia's children were in Europe mourning their newly deceased mother. My brothers and sisters had all passed. John's brother Nathaniel had predeceased him by several years. But John's son John Stephens and his wife Margaretta traveled from Steubenville to pay their respects.

"Mrs. Dike, thank you again for inviting us to stay in your home. John Stephens has always spoken of it with great affection." My plump, fashionable stepdaughter-in-law Margaretta smiled at me with dubious sincerity.

Ebe gave a rude little snort. She retreated, arm in arm with Louisa May, to the back of the church. She refused to sit in the front pew with the family. Ebe did not suffer fools gladly. Margaretta, with her stylish clothes and ingratiating manners, put neither of us at ease. Still, I was content to see my stepson John Stephens, despite our difficult early relationship. He had put on weight, affected a little silver mustache, and looked quite the successful merchant. How interesting that he and Margaretta had never produced any children. But they seemed affectionate with one another. I supposed their barren condition was not due to the same reason that John and I had remained childless.

Margaretta's simpering expression changed to concern. "But tell me, are you entirely well? You look rather," she paused to find an inoffensive phrase, "pale."

"I am orchestrating my husband's funeral. How should I look?" Her plump face pinked at my aggrieved tone. I would not reveal to John Stephens' little tart my private health concerns. I turned my back on her and sought out the organist to play the prelude.

Mourners from all walks of life filled the church. Business associates shared pews with sea folk, merchants, Irish servants, and women of questionable character. Some of them I would not have in the house. But John made time to see them in his shop or on the docks.

John Stephens delivered a heartfelt eulogy. He spoke with eloquence of John's great heart and loving nature.

"My father was a friend to all," he began and then told a maudlin story about Captain and Mrs. Felt. By the time he revealed the sentimental conclusion, there were many moist eyes in the congregation. But I shed no tears. I knew the truth about my husband and his philandering. No sweet story would wipe the slate clean in the eyes of God or in mine.

In the cemetery, we sang one last hymn. Then it was time for each of us to shovel a spade of earth into the grave. I closed my eyes and imagined John and Louisa in each other's arms in Paradise. Anger gave me strength. The result was a hard-flung cascade of dirt onto the coffin lid. I smirked at the hollow sound. It was at that moment that one became fully aware of the finality of death. John Stephens mistook my grimace for mourning and crossed to stand next to me. He touched my elbow. It was all I could do not to shake him off. He sensed my discomfort and rejoined his wife.

For several minutes, Bridget stood silently at the grave. Then, shoulders hunched, she walked back to ready the house for the reception. John Stephens, Margaretta, and Ebe waited for me at the carriage. It was not sorrow that kept me kneeling. It was the dread of putting on a show for the gathered mourners. I bowed my head one last time to thank God for allowing me to spend my last days on earth without my disloyal husband. Then it was time to rejoin my family to continue my ruse as the grieving widow.

But I had not wagered on the struggle to stand. My devilish weakness surprised me at the most inopportune times.

John Stephens and Margaretta rushed to my sides and pulled me to my feet.

"Mrs. Dike, are you quite well?" Margaretta's overwrought clucking echoed in the quiet of the cemetery.

"It is but my grief overtaking me. Nothing more." I mustered the strength to walk back with them to the carriage. I would not give them ammunition for gossip.

Four of us traveled the next day to the lawyer's office in Boston. Ebe insisted on coming. "You might need my support," she said, noting my slowed gait. More likely prurient curiosity compelled her. John Stephens and Margaretta were solicitous as well. But their pretty manners probably hid a concern that I might contest the will to ensure that their inheritance would not be as generous as they hoped.

We gathered with the lawyer and his staff in the West Street office and awaited our fates.

Mr. Hillard, his manner as stiff as his starched collar, addressed us. "Mrs. Dike, Mr. Dike left to you the bulk of the estate. He established a trust for John Stephens and his wife, Margaretta. The rest shall be distributed to servants and business associates."

I was content with this arrangement and moved to stand. Mr. Hillard motioned for me to stay seated. "There is one more item, a matter of some personal articles which Mr. Dike specifically bequeathed to John Stephens, who is his only surviving issue." He handed a large, gray paper envelope to John Stephens. "The instructions are specific. My staff has copied the pertinent page of the will. You will find it enclosed therein."

John Stephens nodded and gave Margaretta a private glance. Neither of them looked at me. My face flushed in shame and anger. Even in death, John had the ability to embarrass me. Ebe, ever the nearsighted observer, squinted from one face to the next, gauging our reactions.

John Stephens stood, unwound the string from the button on the top of the envelope, and spread the contents out on the desk. We all gathered to stare at the various pieces of this unexpected puzzle.

The pin and handkerchief, I recalled, belonged to Louisa. I wondered about their significance. John Stephens stroked the pin gently as if it were a magic lamp and Louisa the genie. But she would not be so easily conjured.

The sheet of notebook paper in Nath's penmanship was a surprise. Perhaps he had bequeathed his cousins some gloomy romance. Ebe brought this page close to her weakened eyes to peruse. Her brother had always been her obsession.

And then gooseflesh prickled my arms. I recognized an incriminating piece of evidence. I read it even as I remembered it. It was forever branded in my brain:

July 1, 1852

Mr. Lovelace,

Mr. Dike's itinerary is as follows: He and Miss Hawthorne will board a train from Salem to Boston on the fifteenth day of this month, and there change for the train to Schenectady and on to Saratoga Springs. They will be boarding at the Columbian Hotel and will start their return journey by train on July 30.

Mr. Manning will arrange your accommodations. Report to him your findings, but do not reveal to him our agreement.

As we have discussed, an accident or some other calamity resulting in the death of mother and child will earn you significant sums. Wire me as soon as you have completed your task, and payment will be arranged. But be advised: No one must know of our relationship or the true nature of your mission, or this contract will be null. I trust you will be discreet.

PMD

I had been careful to use a second sheet of stationery without the letterhead, and I had merely printed my initials at the bottom. But my family would certainly recognize my writing. I made a move to snatch the paper. Ebe blocked my way to the desk. She thrust aside my outstretched hand and picked up the directive. She held it close to her weak eyes to read. She glared at me when she had finished and handed the page to John Stephens. He read it with an obvious dawning realization. Then, with a meaningful stare, he passed it to Margaretta.

This would not be my judgment day. I again snaked a hand out to seize the page. Margaretta held it fast, but I succeeded in tearing along the fold the bottom half bearing my damning directive and my initials. I held it aloft, met Ebe's eyes, shredded the paper, and stuffed the pieces into my reticule.

I escaped the room, but Mr. Hillard caught me as I tried to retreat down the hall. His grasp bruised my arm as he turned me round to face him.

"Your husband protected you by suppressing evidence. Do not insult his good graces by trying to destroy the inheritance he bequeathed to his family. Your fate rests with them." His grip barely loosened as he escorted me back into the room to face my judge, jury, and executioners.

John Stephens addressed me in a voice both cold and strident. This was not the shy boy once under my command. This was a man intent on revenge. "The child you paid Mr. Loveless to murder would have been my sibling. And Louisa was my beloved cousin. And your own niece. You really are a monster without conscience." Margaretta tugged at his arm in a futile attempt at control.

"I was nowhere near that boat," I said, my voice as calm as I could manage. I patted my reticule and then pointed to the half-page still in Margaretta's grasp. "And now all you have is circumstantial evidence. If you must blame someone for Louisa's death, I suggest John for putting them in harm's way."

Mr. Hillard insinuated himself between John Stephens and myself. His tone was cold, and his manner authoritative. He would not be deterred by a family squabble. "There is an addendum to the legacy that Mr. Dike bequeathed to his son." He gathered the artifacts and loose pages, stuffed them back into the envelope, and handed it to John Stephens along with a folded sheaf of documents, sealed with wax. "This was delivered to me very recently by a trusted source. I suggest you read it elsewhere."

With a wrathful eye fixed upon me, John Stephens tucked the documents and envelope into his inner coat pockets and patted them to indicate their security. He turned his back and held out his hand to his wife to stand by him. She complied. Ebe stayed silent, taking no sides.

I wound my way past them all and out of the room, my head held as high as my flagging energies allowed. I refused to be a party to this trial by assumption.

Ebe and I said our farewells to John Stephens and Margaretta at the train station. John Stephens at first ignored me, but Margaretta's manners would not be so easily dismissed. "Thank you, Mrs. Dike, for your hospitality. I am sure Mr. Dike would have appreciated the service."

"But know that the items left to us will be kept safe." John Stephens stated this promise with a modicum of threat. Ebe and I waited on the platform as the train steamed off, and then boarded our train for Salem. It was a silent ride.

That evening, Ebe joined me in the parlor. Her skirts rustled as she perched upon the sofa with her knitting basket in her lap. She pulled up the bottom of the basket to retrieve an instruction pamphlet. The familiar odor of camphor did not have upon me its usual soothing effect. She put the basket on the floor and squinted at the instructions as she counted her stitches.

"What do you suppose really happened on that ship, Aunt Priscilla?" She kept her eyes fixed upon her knitting.

"I am sure I do not know." My tone was as casual as I could muster under such duress. "Your uncle and sister were taking the waters in Saratoga Springs and made an unfortunate choice of travel home." I paused to contain myself but could not suppress the sarcasm in my voice. "Perhaps God was punishing them for some indiscretion."

"As he is punishing you?" Ebe peered at me over her knitting. "Tell me, why are you so pale? You move as if something pains you. Have you consulted a doctor?"

"I do not see that it is any of your business." She raised an eyebrow in silent interrogation. She would find out another way. Bridget, perhaps. I gave in.

"However, if you must know, the diagnosis is a tumor in my womb. Apparently, my childless fate has had other repercussions."

A nasty little smile played on Ebe's lips before she could control herself. "How appropriate that your sin should manifest itself as a disease of your very femininity."

This was too much. "My sin is nothing compared to your sister's and your uncle's."

"Their only sin was love." Ebe's eyes glittered with anger and grief. "She told me all about their romance, but the diary entries I discovered in her armoire detailed the underlying dangers. Yours was the sin of jealousy. And today, we read of murder. Had Mr. Lovelace not been on the boat at your direction, Louisa and her child might still be alive."

My voice rose in indignation. "How dare you defend them? I am the wronged wife. God will give me my just rewards in heaven. I am sure John and Louisa are enjoying each other's company in Hell."

Ebe's voice dropped almost to a whisper. "You are a cold, cruel woman. John served you for nearly fifty-four years. He provided for you, attended to you, even lied for you. He would have loved you if you had given him half a chance. But you drove him into her arms. Louisa and John had the sort of romance of which poets dream. If there is a god, surely he would not punish them for their feelings."

I unwound slowly from my seat and reared, a wounded cobra ready to strike. Ebe sprang from her perch. We confronted each other, two formidable women, each with an agenda to uphold. I, being the taller, had the advantage. I glared down upon my prey, leaning in for full effect. "If you feel so strongly, perhaps you should write an article accusing me of murder," I said, venom dripping. "I am certain there would be many people who would like to see me put in my place."

"Perhaps I will," she said through bared teeth. "I am very curious to know what the documents John Stephens inherited might divulge, and if they verify the information we read today, I may be inspired to take up the pen my brother so tragically dropped." And with a swirl of skirts, she stalked from the parlor, knitting basket in hand.

I retired to bed. With the aid of laudanum, I enjoyed the peaceful slumber of the righteous. When I arose in the morning, Bridget informed me that Miss Manning had departed on the stage to Beverly.

I wondered if Ebe would make good on her promise. But I would simply deny everything. And if there were a danger of my being exposed, I would point to the treatise and the diaries, divulging my husband's and niece's indiscretions, and proffer myself as the wronged wife. Society would take my side. And John's and Louisa's reputations would be forever ruined.

God knew I was in the right to punish my husband for his sins, as God must have punished my evil uncle so many years ago. I had nothing to fear when I stood for judgment before St. Peter. And I was quite certain that I would not be greeted by my philandering husband or his pregnant whore when I, at last, entered those Pearly Gates.

Yours in Christ,

PMD

Priscilla Manning Dike
4 Andover Street
Salem, Massachusetts

Saturday. Noon.

Dearest Thomas,
My body has betrayed me yet again.
From whence a baby might have birthed spurts naught but crimson
    scum.
Incense cannot mask the stench.
Poppy cannot dull the pain.
With each spasm, I writhe impaled upon a pike.
My screams are noted only by a nurse.
The family's vile defection was predicted.
Bridget's base betrayal was presumed.
Salem's abject apathy was expected.
But your disdain may rival just the cancer in its doom.
Please.
I beg you.
Send a missive that I might dote upon your call.
Each labored gasp brings more infernal torment.
But I shall strive to cling
To this hellish world
Until last rites
Are laid upon
My brow.
That I might reap
My just deserts
At last.
Please. For God's sake. Be quick.
Your
Priscilla

"All rise for the honorable Judge Braddock." The pompous court officer wallowed in his role in this sensational drama, rolling his 'r's and clasping his hands above his uniformed paunch. It was probably his largest audience yet, as such infamous cases did not often arise in the Pittsburgh Municipal Court. Members of the press, the jury panelists in their box, and a full gallery of curious onlookers stood in attendance, waiting for the black-robed judge to climb up to the bench, take his seat, and preside over a historic hearing.

Virginia sat in the front of the gallery behind the counsel table to observe Tom's performance in his most consequential trial to date, but as Margaretta's health had taken a downward turn in recent months, she and I sat further back in case she needed to leave unexpectedly. She had a future appointment with one of the doctors in Virginia's sphere but was unwilling to take focus away from the hearing. As worried as I was about her worsening condition, I was also grateful that she was well enough to witness the culmination of our efforts, and I did my best to make my frail wife as comfortable as possible during the lengthy proceedings.

Unfortunately, no one else from my generation of Dike and Hawthorne families was still alive to witness the resolution of our domestic tragedy, but a myriad of Nath's readership had ventured out in the summer humidity to lend their favorite author's family much worshipful support.

These young women, fanning themselves with their dogeared copies of *The Scarlet Letter*, craned their necks to fix their doe eyes on their hero, Mr. Blair. I could feel my shirt wilting under the gray worsted of my suit as I tried to cool Margaretta with her little pleated fan. A fug of wet wool, perfume, and perspiration hung over the courtroom, and I felt some affinity for the judge's probable discomfort in his limp black robe.

"You may be seated," intoned the officer, and the overheated gallery settled restlessly under the watchful eyes of the gargoyles decorating the columns in the gothic courtroom and the oil portraits of past presidents and judges hanging along the dark wood-paneled walls.

"May it please the court, I would like to restate my appeal." Tom, on the other hand, looked crisp and professional in a black morning coat and bow tie, his receding mane of salt and pepper hair combed neatly back, and his spectacles perched forward on his Roman nose. "Although thirty-two years have passed since the *Henry Clay* steamboat disaster, fresh evidence discovered last year in an unexpected inheritance suggests a change of one cause of death from accidental to murder, an important development no matter how late in coming.

"Therefore, I refer your Honor to a letter from Mrs. John Dike to the Reverend Thomas Carlisle, dated November 11th, 1871, in which Mrs. Dike quotes her own directive to an accomplice." Tom read the pertinent passages aloud to the spellbound court from a copy penned by his law clerk.

A murmur ran through the crowd of acolytes as the Hawthorne name was invoked, and several reporters scratched hasty notes for their evening editions. The judge and grand jury members, having heard this testimony before, remained silent.

"Quiet in the courtroom," demanded the overbearing officer, still enjoying his time in the limelight.

"May I continue, your Honor?" asked Tom. The judge nodded, and Tom said, "In the same letter, Mrs. Dike states,

This would not be my judgment day. I again snaked a hand out to seize the page. Margaretta held it fast, but I succeeded in tearing along the fold the bottom half bearing my damning directive and my initials. I held it aloft, met Ebe's eyes, shredded the paper, and stuffed the pieces into my reticule.

Tom removed his glasses and paced before the judge's bench. "Your Honor, the pieces of the bottom half of the directive to Mr. Lovelace were never recovered. However, following the discovery of Mrs. Dike's letter, I submitted to the grand jury the existing half-page of the directive, which had been preserved by Mrs. Dike's stepson, as well as the

letter quoting it in its entirety. The similarities in penmanship and the
letterhead prove that Mrs. Dike was the author of this directive. I also
submitted a first-person witness account by Mr. John Dike, describing
Mr. Lovelace pushing Miss Hawthorne overboard, as well as describing
Mr. William Manning's confession regarding the hiring and subsequent
fate of Mr. Lovelace."

Tom stopped and faced the court. "There should be no question that
Mrs. Dike commanded Mr. Lovelace to kill Miss Hawthorne and her unborn child." He set his spectacles back on his nose and padded back to his
table while reporters, onlookers, and the jury murmured their agreement.

The magistrate pounded his gavel and informed the court, "The *Henry
Clay* steamboat disaster was a federal case. Mr. Blair's evidence was given
to general counsel, and a grand jury convened. They deemed the evidence
worthy to indict the perpetrator, deceased, *in absentia*. The matter would
have ended quietly with an amendment to the inquiry, but the victim's
noteworthy family sparked more public interest than might otherwise be
expected, and so this hearing, in Mr. Blair's jurisdiction, was convened."

The murmurs grew louder to echo his explanation. The Hawthorne
name was still significant due to Nath's continued popularity, and his disciples made their support for the convictions of his sister's killers audible.

"Quiet in the courtroom," again reprimanded the officer.

"Let it be known that Priscilla Manning Dike's conspirator, Horace
Lovelace, was found guilty of the murder of Maria Louisa Hawthorne,"
declared the judge and then pounded his gavel without much effect as the
audience cheered over the repeated berating of the now perspiring officer.

Virginia, with Margaretta and myself limping behind, followed a
triumphant Tom as he wove through the throng of well-wishers to the
sunny courthouse stairs, where we were met by a gaggle of reporters,
papers, and pens poised for the scoop of the day. Tom took a stance on
the top step and nodded at one fox-faced journalist, who tipped his hat
in thanks before asking his question.

"Mr. Blair, Nick Jones from the New York Times. Miss Hawthorne's
fate is certainly a sad one, but the disaster occurred thirty-three years ago,
and the amendment had already been ruled privately. Why make such a
public spectacle?"

Tom shook his head. "It's never too late to reveal the truth. Miss Hawthorne's family and friends want the world to hear the verdict about what really transpired on the Hudson in 1852. To that end, I would like to read a telegram." He pulled a yellow slip of paper from his pocket and read aloud, "Congratulations. Stop. The Hawthorne family may now rest in peace. Stop. Signed," he paused so that all might hear clearly the signatory, "Miss Louisa May Alcott."

Many hands shot up in the air, but Tom pointed to a portly man in the front.

"Bill Paisley, Pittsburg Gazette. Miss Alcott speaks for the Hawthorne family, but what about the unborn child? Was Mr. Dike the father?" The reporter narrowed his eyes at me through a plume of smoke fuming from the cigarette clenched in his jaw, and I bristled.

"That's all for now. Thanks, boys, we'll see you again soon." Tom steered the four of us down the marble steps, away from Nath's devotees, the reporters, and questions that might become too personal for comfort, and sheltered us in the shade of the staircase before we braved the hansom cab ride to the train station in the June warmth.

"Thank you, Tom, for taking this project on. You have no idea how much lighter my shoulders feel today." I pumped Tom's hand with a bit too much enthusiasm, exhilarated as I was from the events in the courtroom and the attention from the reporters.

He answered with his usual desiccated delivery, "Don't assume that I did it solely for you. The press will be in my office every day now until all their questions are answered. The publicity will be huge because of the Hawthornes and Miss Alcott, and my usual client fees will double."

He unbuttoned his coat and loosened his tie, both in deference to the June warmth and his excitement as he made his next point. "But I didn't read the entire telegram to the press." He drew the yellow slip from his pocket and read the final line: "'Letter to follow. Stop.' Have you received a letter from Miss Alcott?"

I shook my head, surprised and confused, and turned to Margaretta, who shrugged her thin shoulders and murmured weakly, "We have been away for several days. Perhaps it is in the post at home?"

"Keep me apprised. A letter from Miss Alcott would add even more interest to an already historic case."

"Then you and Virginia must come to Steubenville," said Margaretta more forcefully, a frail hen trying one last time to gather her brood. "We at least owe you dinner if not a weekend away. Perhaps we will have received Miss Alcott's letter by then."

"Only if you feel up to it," said Virginia, gently hugging her aunt's diminished waist. Tom handed the ladies into the cab, and the four of us bade our goodbyes at the train platform. I watched over my beloved wife as she slept through the short journey home, dark circles shadowing her eyes, her breathing shallow and strained. Houseguests might prove to be too much, but something told me that the culmination of the Hawthorne saga was at hand, and my loyal wife would desperately want to witness its end.

Louisa May Alcott
48 Hanover Street
Boston, Massachusetts

Mr. John Stephens Dike
100 Market Street
Steubenville, Ohio

June 11, 1885

Dear Mr. Dike,

It is with great interest that I have followed in the Boston papers the lengthy efforts to bring your cousin Louze's killers to justice. Louze was very kind to me in some of my darkest times, and I am sorrowful that, due to my ill health, I was unable to attend the final hearing. But I am grateful that she had the noble Mr. Blair to reveal the truth beneath her death.

And please also accept my deepest sympathies upon the more recent loss of your other Hawthorne cousin. Ebe and I grew to be very close after Louze's passing. Perhaps I supplanted Louze's sisterly sympathies, or we simply enjoyed each other's strange humor, but Ebe and I shared an extraordinary friendship, and I miss her more than I can say.

According to the papers you inherited from Ebe familial documents with which you and Mr. Blair proved the truth of Louze's tragic death. Of course, you recognized the treatise written by your father, Mr. John Dike, but also included were documents formerly unknown to you, such as diary entries from Louze and letters from your stepmother.

Although you now know that Ebe found Louze's diary entries hidden in her old armoire and kept them safe until they might prove useful, the letters from Mrs. Dike to her reverend had been discovered by his jealous wife Eleanor and given to Ebe in a fit of pique, and Ebe also secreted those away.

Ebe wished to use the documents as ammunition against your stepmother, but she had not the legal expertise of your Mr. Blair, nor did she wish to bring notoriety upon herself or other innocent witnesses, including yourself. Instead, she wove together the various documents to form a disjointed narrative from which she planned to construct, with my help, a sort of literary revenge.

To that end, she and I toiled in my Boston rooms to parse three people's rambling personal entries into a cogent third-person novel, intent on proving one transgressor's guilt. We had honed it to what we thought would be a bestselling thriller, but we were forced to postpone publication because of the threat of a lawsuit. Although we changed the names of all the characters so that only those individuals close to the scandal would recognize themselves or their families, the Tabernacle church had very deep pockets, and Roberts Brothers Publishers could not undertake the threat of litigation.

As the publication of that manuscript was delayed, my other projects took precedence, and Ebe's novel languished alone with her in Beverly. It was always my intention to make my way to her home to edit our final draft, but as Ebe's health deteriorated, her eccentricities increased, and she insisted on secluding herself.

After her funeral, I queried your cousins, the Elliots, and although they searched Ebe's room, they were unable to discover the manuscript. My fear is that she may have secreted them away in an unknown vault or safe deposit box to protect her family should the meaning of our work be misconstrued, and she be unable to defend it.

Beneath her prickly demeanor and caustic wit beat a loyal and affectionate heart. Her writing skills rivaled those of her brother's, and I mourn not only the loss of my dear friend but also a provocative piece of literature. If you have discovered the manuscript in your inheritance, I beg you to return it to me. As all the secrets have been so publicly revealed, the publisher will be unlikely to protest. Indeed, the notoriety might boost sales, and Ebe would finally receive the recognition she deserves.

Very Truly Yours,
Louisa May Alcott

"Obviously, you did not find a priceless Alcott manuscript among the documents in your inheritance. All that fictionalized romance and murder mystery lost to the ages. What a pity." Tom tossed the letter onto the coffee table and took a disappointed sip of brandy. Cook, with Margaretta directing from her nest of blankets on the couch, had outdone herself with a delicious dinner of choice meats and produce from the Emporium, and we had just ended the meal clustered in the parlor around Margaretta, with brandy for the men, chocolate cake for the ladies, and the documents and Miss Alcott's letter for entertainment.

No fire burned in the grate on this warm evening, but candles added mood lighting to the gas sconces. After reading about my relatives' more rustic experiences sixty years ago, I was grateful for the many new amenities that the latter part of the 19th century had wrought. Soon Steubenville would be on the telephone line, and a gathering like tonight's might be moot.

"The documents proved Priscilla's guilt, and for that, we should all be grateful," tutted Margaretta softly, as Virginia served her aunt a tiny slice of cake in deference to her diminished appetite and then a generous portion for herself. "But if we found the manuscript, perhaps we could persuade Miss Alcott to give some of the money to the Steubenville Female Seminary. I have read that she is quite charitable, and a school for girls might appeal to her."

"John Stephens, did you know about your father and Louze's love affair?" asked Virginia, savoring a bite of the silken cake while her attention returned to the more romantic aspects of the documents.

"Yes. I was jealous at first, but then I approved. I hated Priscilla, and I wanted my father to be happy. Louze made him so." I smiled sadly, remembering that day in Newburyport when I finally accepted their mutual attraction.

Virginia touched the white satin bodice of her gown where she had pinned Louze's bar brooch, this time with my blessing. "I feel as though Louze is with us tonight. Nath and Ebe as well. They are all grateful to you and Tom for revealing the truth."

"Didn't you say that Nath vowed to write a book about Louze's death?" Tom stretched out in his wing chair and tipped his snifter toward the documents.

"He inferred in a notebook page that he would write a romance avenging his sister," I said, rifling through the documents and finally flourishing the page, "but his children searched the Wayside, and the manuscript was never found. That is why Ebe vowed to write a book herself. Or, at least, that is what Priscilla quoted in her penultimate letter."

"May I see those last pages?" asked Virginia, reluctantly putting down her fork as I handed her the pertinent stack. She took her spectacles from her handbag and read aloud, "Priscilla says to Ebe, 'If you feel so strongly, perhaps you should write an article accusing me of murder. And then Ebe replies, Perhaps I will . . . I may be inspired to take up the pen my brother so tragically dropped. And with a swirl of skirts, she stalked from the parlor, her knitting basket trailing the scent of camphor in its wake.'" Virginia peered at me over the half-moon of her spectacles. "Didn't you inherit Ebe's belongings along with the documents?"

Margaretta's gaunt face lit up. "Yes! Tom, you were here. Remember the crates, and the horrible camphor odor, and John Stephens' spell? Ebe's possessions are still up in the attic."

All eyes turned to me. Would I be able to search the furniture without having a spell? I was not at all sure myself, but I stood, a grizzled working-dog corralling his herd. "Let us all go to the attic and see what we might find. If Ebe is truly here, perhaps she will guide us."

Tom removed his jacket and rolled up his sleeves, Virginia stowed the letter and her spectacles in her handbag in case they were further needed, and stood with her husband, brandy and cake forgotten, at the ready for whatever was required.

The gaslights had not been extended to the attic, and so Tom and Virginia lit two storm lanterns to light the way. I helped Margaretta climb one unsteady step at a time, and our slowly ascending shadows danced across family oil portraits hanging on the staircase walls, the ancestors seemingly nodding their approval of this misadventure.

The hot, overcrowded attic burst with discarded trunks and wardrobes, but it was quite easy for me to pick out Ebe's orphaned furniture from our household's clutter. Hannah's dented caldron loomed in one corner; Louisa's armoire, with a smashed-in panel, leaned in another. Several broken wooden chairs had been upended on the top of a scrubbed oak table, and in the far corner, the crescent, claw-footed desk crouched, still emanating that fearsome stench.

I stowed Margaretta in a faded armchair, and Virginia and Tom set the lanterns in the center of the table, illuminating dust balls and footprints on the floor, but no mouse droppings.

"Phew. At least that camphor kept the mice and moths away," said Virginia, fanning her nose with her hand. "Priscilla mentioned that Ebe used it, so perhaps we should search the desk since that is where the smell is coming from."

Tom waved at me to stay away and then grunted in surprise at the weight of the desk as he pulled it from the wall and pushed it into the middle of the room, stopping to wipe his face with his sleeve before gesturing to the rest of us to approach.

"This might be the same desk in which William Manning hid the directive to Mr. Lovelace. Maybe it was the family's hiding place?" suggested Margaretta, her voice stronger with the excitement of the hunt. She looked at me to check her history of the piece. When I nodded, she said, "Do as William told John Dike to do and remove the drawers."

Virginia, unmindful of her white gown, knelt in front of the desk and took out all the drawers, checking the insides before setting them aside and squatting back on her heels for further instructions.

"The smell is stronger," I warned, holding my left hand up over my nose and counting to three under my breath, hoping to stifle an oncoming spell.

"Indeed. Let's see what's inside." Tom crouched next to Virginia and reached his arm all the way in to the back of the desk from the right bottom drawer hole. He leaned in and said, "I feel something! But it's stuck." He rocked back and forth, his arm swallowed up by the drawer maw, and then fell back, a piece of wicker clutched in his hand. "It's a basket, but it's held firm by the sides of the desk. I need someone to push on it from the other end."

I crouched on the other side, held my breath against the stench, reached my arm in the opposite drawer hole, and pushed toward Tom what seemed to be a woven object. With a squeal, the object gave way and slid along the desk bottom toward Tom, who pulled it out and with a triumphant fanfare, held up a worn wicker basket, two black yarn balls with needles piercing their sides balanced on top.

I leaned back, gagging at the smell, and Margaretta reached a skeletal arm out to me, her face drawn with worry, but I shook my head at her concern. "I am fine. Dr. Voight's techniques have kept me safe. We must discover what is in that knitting basket." We turned our attention to Tom and Virginia, who had pulled the yarn out of the basket and were examining its interior.

"There's nothing in there but some old yarn." Tom's dust-covered shoulders sagged in disappointment. He pulled one of the chairs off the table, set the basket in its place, and sat, mopping his face again and catching his breath.

"Perhaps there are more clues in the letter," suggested Virginia. She took her time perusing the document while we all waited, our patience growing short. Finally, in a jubilant voice, she read, 'Ebe pulled up the bottom of the basket to retrieve an instruction pamphlet.'"

I roused myself from the floor and held the lantern over the basket while Tom took a closer look. He fished a penknife from his pocket and carefully worked the tip around the edge of the false bottom of the basket. The bottom gave way, and all four of us took a breath and peered in.

A large, gray envelope nestled in the base of the basket. With an excited bark of laughter, I pulled it out and opened the flap to reveal a thick manuscript, and I read aloud to my dear friends and family the title page: *The Hawthorne Inheritance*, by Louisa May Alcott and Elizabeth Hawthorne.

A new Louisa May Alcott novel was a best seller before it hit the presses, and *The Hawthorne Inheritance*, with all the earlier publicity surrounding the hearing, was even more in demand. By the time it was displayed in the Steubenville bookstores, eager Alcott fans were already lined up on the pavement, ready to lose themselves in a torrid tale of illicit romance and murder.

I was aware of none of this, however. I sat, desolate, at my beloved's bedside, guarding her as she had always brooded over me. The wasting disease, most likely cancer of the intestine, advanced quickly, and despite the efforts of several doctors in Virginia's sphere, Margaretta continued her swift decline. With the blessings of laudanum, we kept her comfortable. Virginia and Tom joined me at the vigil when they could, but only I was present at the end of August when she took her last breath and closed her kind blue eyes forever.

Many Emporium employees, past and present, attended the funeral, as did a good number of the students, staff, and volunteers from the Steubenville Female Seminary. Their headmaster thanked Margaretta publicly for encouraging Miss Alcott's very generous donation to the school. Virginia gave a stirring eulogy praising Margaretta for her philanthropic works, and Tom and his son George represented the family as pallbearers. We laid her to rest beside her sister Anna and my Uncle Nathaniel. George and Tom had to lift me to my feet after the internment, as I would have faithfully knelt at her graveside forever.

The Blairs insisted that I stay with them in Pittsburgh. I sat listlessly at their table, half-listening to tales from Tom and George about the steel business and Virginia's stories of medical miracles. But it was a Newfoundland pup named Major, brought home by Tom one evening, who finally lifted me out of my depression. Major followed me from Pittsburgh to Steubenville when my instinct to work resurfaced and the siren song of the Christmas season drew me back to the Emporium.

I delighted in doing whatever the manager directed, and my old knees would allow, be it helping customers, stocking shelves, or driving the younger employees mad over my ineptitude with the telephone, which had changed the retail landscape enormously, diminishing foot traffic but enhancing customer service and inventory control. Now ordering a partridge in a pear tree, or even ten lords a-leaping, would be just a phone call away. It was a difficult but worthwhile challenge. As I told Jimmie Ross, recently named stock clerk in charge of grain shipments, sometimes even an old dog can learn new tricks.

AUTHOR'S NOTE

The Hawthorne Inheritance is a work of fiction based on historical events.

Research into John and Louisa began several years ago when I discovered in my late father's effects various ancestry documents and articles pertaining to the *Henry Clay* steamship disaster. My father was not the romantic sort. Where he saw dry history concerning the differing fates of two family members, I saw a possible love story requiring exploration.

Through more familial research, I learned of my great-great-great-grandfather Nathaniel Dike; his daughter Virginia, married to Thomas S. Blair, and thus my great-great-grandparents; my great-great-great-granduncle John Dike; his son and my cousin six times removed, John Stephens Dike; and finally, John Dike's marriage to Nathaniel Hawthorne's aunt, Priscilla Manning.

Consequently, through Hawthorne biographies, letters, and literary criticism, as well as several of Hawthorne's novels and stories, I learned more cogent details about the Manning, Hawthorne, and Dike families. The Dike/Blair connection to the Hawthornes through John Dike's marriage to Priscilla Manning became the inspiration for the triangular thesis of this book.

John Dike was reported by historians and in family letters to be of a conscientious character. His kindly and generous nature, love of children and animals, romantic bent, and ability to rise from the ashes of business ruin were admirable. However, his bout of melancholia after his first wife's death and his emotional reactions to his daughter's death and his son's defection evidenced a softer side. Therefore, he seemed a worthy romantic hero and sympathetic narrator of his family's tragic loss and redemption.

Louisa was described by Hawthorne historians as the most "normal" person in the Hawthorne family. Unlike Ebe, a writer and self-professed hermitress, or Nathaniel, a complicated character and famous author of gothic tales, Louisa kept house for her mother, nursed various cousins through illnesses, and entertained the neighborhood with games of

Whist while pining for the father she never knew. Her letters, full of humorous descriptions of family foibles and wardrobe malfunctions, revealed a woman of wit, intellect, and empathy. That she remained a spinster seemed a surprise.

Priscilla, on the other hand, was cited in her family's letters as hyper-religious, strict, and cold. Sophia described Priscilla as sitting like a stone statue at her sister's deathbed. Priscilla and John had no children, though John had two from his previous marriage. Her barren state could have had biological reasons, but other Manning siblings bore children. And of all her family, she was the most likely to be offended by any perceived sinfulness. However, any illegal activities described in this book are purely fictitious.

Finally, John Stephens Dike was the force that bound together the Hawthornes and the Dikes. According to letters from both young men, he was Nath's best friend and allowed his cousin a peek into the Dike family household. When John Stephens finally escaped Salem and fled to Steubenville, he never looked back, despite his father's and Nath's plaintive letters pleading for his return.

All the chapters are written as monologues because I wanted my relatives to have a chance to speak for themselves. Many of their words, and of those around them, are direct quotes from letters. John Stephens, John, and Priscilla, all reminisce, but Louisa writes in the first person present because her voice is extinguished tragically early.

Here are the historical facts which informed many of the chapters: The pre-1800 Dike family history (albeit somewhat truncated), was as recounted; in 1809, John Dike, Junior's wife Mercy died, and John suffered a bout of melancholia, lost his business, and lived with his two children at his parents' house for several years; he dropped 'junior' from his name after he left his parents' house; he partnered with the Mannings in business in 1815; he married Priscilla in 1817; she remained childless; John's children befriended the Hawthorne siblings; Nathaniel and his siblings grew up and stayed in their family's house well into adulthood; their father died at sea three months after Louisa was born; Priscilla killed two snakes in Maine; Nathaniel and Louisa attended dance lessons at Mr. Turner's school in 1820 where Nathaniel was applauded for his grace and ability, despite a mysterious limp in earlier childhood; Mary Wood Dike died at age fifteen; Captain Jonathan Felt's wife Margaret wrote several letters praising John Dike's sympathetic nature; Louisa lived with the Dikes off and on from that time; Louisa and Elizbeth never married; John Stephens Dike moved to Steubenville, Ohio to join his uncle Nathaniel in business and married his aunt's sister Margaretta Woods in 1831; They remained childless; The Steubenville Female Seminary was a well-respected school for girls from 1829 to 1898; in 1830 Anna Woods Dike and Margaretta Woods Dike both signed the Ladies of Steubenville petition imploring President Jackson to allow the Native Americans to stay on their land; John's businesses failed several times, but he died a fairly wealthy man; John had a religious conversion in 1831; Sophia wrote in a letter of the three Hawthorne siblings being 'swallowed up like spirits in their cloaks' at a Hurley-Burley (yes, Susan really did call them that); Louisa shared a dinner with her brother and sister-in-law and Margaret Fuller in Concord at the Old Manse in 1842; Una Hawthorne was born at the Old Manse in 1844; Virginia Dike married Thomas S. Blair, a Harvard educated inventor, in 1847; Louisa May Alcott and her family lived in poverty in Boston in 1850; Saratoga Springs was a popular resort town in the 1850's with a famous Promenade and curative waters; Louisa and John stayed at the Columbian Hotel in Saratoga Springs and instead of taking the stage, made an unfortunate last minute choice of transport home in 1852; The *Henry Clay* disaster unfolded much as described, including the horrible fate of the toddler; in the federal inquest, witnesses testified that Maria Louisa Hawthorne read *Pilgrim's Progress* in her cabin, was visited by her uncle John Dike before the boat caught fire, and then jumped overboard as the boat burned, while John Dike waited to disembark after the boat rammed the shore; despite the inquest, all officers and the owner were exonerated, although racing on the Hudson was subsequently prohibited; a pin marked with the name Rachel Forrester and a monogramed handkerchief were used to identify Maria Louisa Hawthorne's body, and were later given to Una Hawthorne by her father; Una contracted malaria in Rome and suffered treatments including electric shock therapy, which enhanced her already eccentric personality; Rose Hawthorne became a nun and founded the Dominican

Sisters of Hawthorne for cancer care; Julian Hawthorne became a writer, and was jailed briefly for mail fraud; much of Nathaniel's funeral in 1864 was as described; Elizabeth Hawthorne wrote and published numerous articles and book reviews over her lifetime; Louisa May Alcott wrote popular fiction for children and adults from 1868 to her death in 1888: Priscilla Manning Dike died in 1873; psychotherapy and hypnotherapy were new medical techniques forged in Europe but accepted in America by 1884; Telephone lines had been installed from New York to Boston and other cities by 1885; Margaretta Dike died in August of 1885; John Stephens Dike died in 1891; and several cats named Beelzebub roamed the Old Manse and the Wayside.

Historical fiction: Some family members have been combined or gone unmentioned for the sake of simplicity; some dates have been changed; there is no record of John and Louisa attending Una Hawthorne's birth, although Dr. Bartlett's comment about the baby's looks is quoted almost verbatim from one of Sophia's letters; there are no mentions of an impromptu performance by Louisa May Alcott and her sisters in the Old Manse parlor, although Louisa May Alcott wrote that her family was friendly with the Hawthornes; Louisa's unexpected pregnancy was not recorded or discussed in any Hawthorne family letters; The *Henry Clay* jurors' reports did not describe in detail Louisa's plunge into the Hudson, nor was a Horace Lovelace ever found guilty of the murder of Maria Louisa Hawthorne; Thomas S. Blair attended Harvard and worked in the steel industry, inventing "Blair's direct process" for making iron; and a will, notebook page, damning directive, and an unpublished manuscript by two outstanding nineteenth-century women writers, have yet to be discovered.

As far as Hawthorne's biographers are concerned, John Dike was simply a kindly member of the Hawthorne family who made an unfortunate choice of transportation home while traveling with a beloved niece. But I contend that John and Louisa actually enjoyed a happy and fulfilling love affair and that through the lens of the *Henry Clay* disaster, their relationship could finally revealed.

For more information, please visit my website,

https://www.the-hawthorne-inheritance.com/

BIBLIOGRAPHY

Abel, Darrel. *The Moral Picturesque*. West Lafayette, IN: Purdue University Press, 1988.

Alcott, Louisa May. "Behind A Mask or, A Woman's Power." *The Flag of Our Union*, 1866.

————. *Louisa May Alcott, Her Life, Letters, and Journals*, edited by Ednah D. Cheney. Boston: Roberts Brothers, 2011.

Beal, Rebecca J. *Jacob Eichholtz 1776–1842: Portrait Painter of Pennsylvania*, Philadelphia: The Historical Society of Pennsylvania, 1969.

Bradley, Hugh. *Such Was Saratoga*. Garden City, NY: Doubleday, Doran and Company, Inc., 1940.

Cheever, Susan. *Louisa May Alcott, A Personal Biography*. New York: Simon & Schuster, 2010.

Gaeddert, Louann. *A New England Love Story*. New York: Dial Press, 1980.

Hansen, Kris A. *Death Passage on the Hudson*. New York: Purple Mountain Press, 2004.

Hawthorne, Julian. *Hawthorne and His Circle*. New York: Harper and Brothers, 1903.

Hawthorne, Nathaniel. *Hawthorne's Lost Notebook, 1835–1841: Facsimile from the Pierpont Morgan Library*, transcribed by Barbara S. Mouffe. University Park, PA: Penn State University, 1978.

————. *Hawthorne's Notebook, 1835–1841*. University Park, PA: Penn State University Press, 1978.

————. *Mosses from an Old Manse*. New York: G. P. Putnam's Sons, 1846.

————. *The Blithedale Romance*, Boston: Ticknor and Fields, 1852.

————. *The Letters, 1813–1843*. Columbus: Ohio State University Press, 1984.

Herbert, T. Walter. *Dearest Beloved; the Hawthornes and the Making of the Middle-Class Family*. Berkeley: University of California Press, 1993.

Marshall, Megan. *The Peabody Sisters: Three Women Who Ignited American Romanticism*. Boston: Houghton Mifflin Harcourt Publishing Company, 2006.

McFarland, Philip. *Hawthorne in Concord.* New York: Grove Press, 2004.

Mellow, James R. *Nathaniel Hawthorne In His Times.* Boston: Houghton Mifflin Harcourt Publishing Company, 1980.

Miller, Edwin Haviland. *Salem Is My Dwelling Place.* Iowa City: University of Iowa Press, 1991.

Miller, M. A., *Meet the Blair Family.* Hollidaysburg, PA: The Blair County Historical Society, 1946.

Mitchell, Thomas R. *Hawthorne's Fuller Mystery.* Amherst: University of Massachusetts Press, 1998.

Moore, Margaret B. *The Salem World of Nathaniel Hawthorne.* Columbia, MO: University of Missouri Press, 1998.

Roman, John, illustrator. *Concord in the Days of Thoreau.* Poster, 1845.

Saxton, Martha. *Louisa May Alcott, A Modern Biography.* Boston: Houghton Mifflin Harcourt Publishing Company, 1977.

Tressel Alson, Carlee. *Rolling On: Two Hundred Years of Blair Iron and Steel.* Parafine Press, 2021.

Young, Philip. *Hawthorne's Secret: An Untold Tale.* Boston: David R. Godine, 1984.

ABOUT THE AUTHOR

KATE DIKE BLAIR grew up in The Vermont Book Shop in Middlebury, Vermont. She fondly remembers at the age of four, hiding under the best-sellers table and guessing customers' identities by their shoes, at twelve, spending Sunday mornings reading *Little Women* while her father and genial proprietor Dike Blair processed special orders (no Internet!), and lunching with Robert Frost. After ten years treading the boards of local community theaters, she earned her Diploma in Theater Arts from the Wykeham Rise School for Girls in 1971.

She graduated from Boston University with a Bachelor of Arts in English Literature in 1975 and clerked in Boston book shops before earning her Certificate of Medical Assisting in 1979. Specializing in occupational health, she created with two partners the company Health Research Associates, and taught NIOSH Approved Spirometry to hundreds of health professionals at BU and Harvard.

In 1987, she helped launch *Ponderings*, a newsletter for the Friends of White Pond, a local lake association. In 2004, she joined the actors' union SAG-AFTRA. When her father died in 2009, she discovered in his effects his research regarding their Hawthorne and Dike ancestors and the *Henry Clay* steamship disaster. While her father focused on straightforward history, she envisioned a complicated love story, and her quest for cousin Louisa Hawthorne's true fate began.

Kate now juggles writing books, plays and newsletters, medical consulting, and performing on stages and screens large and small. She resides with her family in Concord, Massachusetts.

Made in the USA
Coppell, TX
13 December 2021

68451570R00152